A BRANCH OF
SILVER
A BRANCH OF
GOLD

ANNE ELISABETH STENGL

ROOGLEWOOD PRESS

Raleigh, NC

© 2016 by Anne Elisabeth Stengl

Published by Rooglewood Press

www.RooglewoodPress.com

Printed in the United States of America

ISBN-13: 978-1-942379-11-9

This is a work of fiction. Names, characters, incidents, and dialogues are products of the author's imagination and are not to be construed as real. Any resemblance to actual events or persons, living or dead, is entirely coincidental.

Cover art and book design by A.E. de Silva
Stock Image: iardacil-stock

This story is for Mummy.

But really all of them are for Mummy,

whether or not the dedication officially says so.

Because not a single one of my stories

would be the best it could be without her.

BEFORE THERE CAN BE A BEGINNING, THERE MUST FIRST BE AN END. *Otherwise, what is there to begin?*

This truth I have learned in pain. This truth I have learned in suffering. This truth I have learned in gladness, for O! What sweet relief it is to my spirit! Though I am bound, I know that my binding will last only until the end. And then . . . and then . . .

But in the meanwhile, what a long ending it seems to me.

See now the worlds beyond my lonely window. Great worlds in which I once walked. Lovely worlds in which I will never walk again. See now the Between which separates those worlds, both the Near and the Far. The Far is always much nearer than mortals suppose. And, likewise, the Near much farther than Faerie-kind will admit. But as I sit here in my window, I feel it all so close to me. I gaze out through the slit in the stone wall, and I see the mortals rising to greet the new day. I turn where I sit and see the tall trees surrounding me on all sides, and moonlight bathes the forest floor at my feet.

Near and Far. Night and Day.

And in Between, the Wood stands tall.

There are figures moving through the Between. I see a shadow stalking. I see a wind spirit blowing. I see a curse shimmering, opening wide the gates.

And so Faerie-kind will once more cross over the boundaries to prey upon the mortal world. So it must be.

So it must end.

ONE

THE WORDS WOULD NOT STAY PUT. HE HAD JUST WRITTEN THEM, SO he knew exactly what they should say. But they wouldn't say it. At least, not in a way he could understand. They swam in weird undulations across the page, incomprehensible as a child's scribblings. The more he studied them, the stupider he felt.

Master Benedict Cœur, son and heir of the Marquis of Canneberges, sat at his desk, his head in his hands, and felt profoundly sorry for himself. His eyes blurred with fatigue, and he should probably go back to bed. But this thought made him shudder. He'd spent all night in that bed, staring up at his canopy, unable to sleep save in stolen snatches. The moment the sky began to lighten, he'd crawled out from under the counterpane, lit a candle, and pulled out his documents. Anything to fill his mind, anything to block out the crowd of thoughts that had kept him company through the long hours of darkness.

Only now . . .

He groaned and closed his eyes, his head still propped and bent. Cold morning air blew through his open window, and he wished he dared shut the glass and stoke up his fire. But Doctor Dupont would be furious at such blatant disregard of his apothecarial commands. And Benedict lacked sufficient energy to face the good doctor's fury this morning.

If only he dared steal a horse. Probably a foolish notion, but he rather liked it anyway. Technically it wouldn't be *stealing,* since he was heir to his father's estate and, therefore, practically owned all the horses and the stables and . . . well, everything. Legally, of course, it all belonged to his father. The marquis wasn't home, however, so who would gainsay his heir? But Doctor Dupont was officially in charge during Monsieur the Marquis's absence, and Doctor Dupont had strictly ordered the stable hands to allow Benedict nowhere near a horse.

But the stable hands weren't the brightest lights in the county. And it would be an adventure, just the sort of adventure Benedict would have pursued only a year ago: Steal a horse right out from under the grooms' noses, then up in the saddle, away across the fields, and dragons eat all scholarly pursuits!

Victor would have told him to do it. Benedict could almost hear his best mate urging him even now: "*You've got all your life to worry about memorizing Corrilondian conjugations and declensions. But today will be*

over before you know it!"

"Today will be over before you know it," the young scholar whispered. How true those words had become to him these last long months. He shook his head, shook away the memory of that voice, and tried once more to concentrate on the difficult lines of Corrilondian verbs and nouns. Learning a foreign language was difficult enough without the words swimming around on the page like so many—

BANG.

Benedict startled upright in his chair and sat like a hare frozen at the sound of a hunter's bolt whizzing past.

BANG.

BANG. BANG.

BANGBANGBANG*BANG.*

Had a hurricane entered the house somehow? Right over his head, in the Great Hall above?

Eyes wide, mouth gaping, Benedict stared up at his ceiling as though he could somehow see through it and discover the cause of the uproar.

Another great *BANG,* and something roared down his chimney and burst into his room. Something invisible, something strong. Something most certainly *alive.*

It blew out the fire, then roared across the chamber to his bed and tossed the blankets awry, whirled around the four bedposts, and made the canopy and curtains balloon like sails on the high seas. It tore around the periphery of the room, knocking books and ledgers from their places, then caught up all the work upon Benedict's desk and spun it into a swirling white storm.

Benedict shouted but couldn't hear his own voice over the howl of the wind and what he recognized suddenly as high, wild, insane laughter. Never in his life had he heard a voice utter such inhuman sounds. He flung up his arms to protect himself from papercuts and flying penknives.

Then, as though seeing it suddenly, the wind—given something close to a physical form by virtue of all the papers clutched in its invisible arms—darted for the open window and flung the casement wide open to crash against the outer wall. The laugh trailed away across the moat and into the morning-lit fields beyond Centrecœur House.

Benedict stood in the middle of his chamber and stared at the destruction around him, at all his hard work strewn, scattered, or stolen.

"Dragon's eyeteeth," he cursed.

Then, catching up his hat and cloak, forgetting his fatigue, he rushed from the room. If ever there was a time to steal a horse and give chase, that time was now.

SOMEWHERE OUT THERE IS SOMEONE WHO CAN HEAR ME. I KNOW *this must be true. I sensed it hours ago, before the sun crested the horizon. I felt it at the turning of Yesterday into Today, at that dark and most magical moment of Midnight. Yesterday she could not hear me. But today . . . today I believe she can.*

So I sit at my window and watch the sun spill across the fields, forests, and bogs of this mortal land where once I walked. And I send forth my heart, crying out to her.

This time. Maybe this time.

I do not wonder whether or not she'll hear me. I wonder whether or not she'll answer.

TWO

ON THE MORNING OF HER FOURTEENTH BIRTHDAY, JUST AS THE SUN
rose and Rufus the Red, the family rooster, raised his voice in raucous
welcome of the new day, Heloise opened her eyes, stared at the thatching
just overhead, and thought: *Mirror.*

It wasn't really a thought. At least, it wasn't like any thought she
had experienced before. It was more like an impression. Or a suggestion.
Lying there in the pile of straw that was her bed, wrapped tightly in a
woolen blanket, she whispered softly, so as to make no sound but so that
her breath formed little curls in the air above her lips, "What mirror?"

A foolish question. There was only one mirror. Oh, she knew as a
distant sort of truth that other mirrors existed. She knew this just as she
knew there was a world beyond Monsieur de Cœur's estate of
Canneberges. It may be true, but she never expected to see it, so it didn't

particularly matter. The same held true when it came to mirrors. As far as her immediate world was concerned, the only mirror that mattered was her mother's small glass.

Mirror.

There it was again. That word tugging at the ear of her consciousness. Heloise's frown deepened.

Her name was Heloise Flaxman, though when she was younger she'd thought it ought to be Flaxgirl, which would make more sense. A few years ago she'd asked her older sister, Evette, about the incongruity of her name. Evette had told her that "Flaxman" let everyone know Heloise was the daughter of one of the many flax farmers on the estate. The name gave her a place. It gave her standing.

Heloise, only nine years old at the time, had gone about her daily tasks, her brow knitted in serious contemplation of this new knowledge. Later that same afternoon, while she and Evette fed Gutrund the pig, she'd asked, "Since Meme is a spinner, can't I be Heloise Spinnerwoman? Then everyone would know I'm the daughter of a spinner. And spinning is more interesting than farming."

"No," said Evette. "That's not how things are done."

Thus ended their discussion. When it came to questions of "how things are done," Evette could not be convinced to think creatively. So Heloise had resigned herself to being Heloise Flaxman for the foreseeable future.

This morning, however, when she awoke as always to the passionate crowing of Rufus the Red, she didn't feel quite like a Heloise Flaxman anymore. She felt changed. Not older, necessarily, but . . . bigger. As though there were more of her than there had been the night before.

Sitting up and unwrapping herself from the tangle of her blanket, she cast a quick glance to the nearby pile of straw where her sister slept. But of course Evette had already risen, dressed, and had climbed down from the loft to the kitchen below, where she helped Meme get breakfast for Papa and the boys. Evette was never one to sleep late. It's not how things were done.

Down in the main room Heloise heard the scuffle and shouts of her brothers Claude, Clement, Clotaire, and Clovis engaged in their morning brawl, accompanied by the high-pitched squeals of baby Clive goading them on. Underscoring all other noises murmured the patient voice of Evette in her accustomed role of peacekeeper. Heloise woke to this chorus every morning, but today these familiar sounds seemed strangely distant.

Mirror.

The word was in her head still. She climbed out of the straw and crawled across the loft floor to a carved cedar box tucked away in the corner. Heloise's grandfather had made that box for her mother when her mother was a child. Its contents were as familiar to Heloise as her own two hands. She lifted the lid, breathed in the scent of cedar, and looked down at folds of creamy linen: Meme's wedding gown.

Heloise had no interest in this whatsoever. Meme often spoke of how Evette would soon wear it in her own wedding; Evette was at an age when their mother could scarcely look at her without speaking of weddings and babies, as though Evette were already betrothed and settled. Lately she'd taken to saying on a near-daily basis, "We'll have a wedding in the family before this spring is done; you mark my words!" To which Evette always smiled and made no reply.

Weddings and Evette—they went together like dye and mordant in Heloise's mind. She never pictured herself in the bride role. After all, she was *not* Evette.

Wrapped up inside the gown, tucked away for safekeeping, was the little black-framed mirror, the prized treasure of the Flaxman household. This Heloise unwrapped from the gown with great care, leaving the mounds of linen to lie unheeded in her lap. Gently she lifted the mirror, angling it so that she could not see her face. She wasn't afraid, exactly. Maybe a mite anxious. But not afraid. Certainly not.

Mirror, said the thought in her head.

"Yes. Yes, I know," Heloise whispered. By now she thought she knew why the thought was there: Today was her birthday. On every birthday Heloise could remember she'd awakened wondering if she was any different than she'd been the night before, but one furtive glance in the spotted glass always showed her to be the same as ever. Maybe a little taller than she'd been a year ago. Perhaps with a few more freckles. But still very much herself.

Not this morning. This morning she knew that she was still herself . . . but something more besides.

Heloise heard Papa say goodbye to Meme, and then he and Claude and Clement, the two oldest brothers, set out for the flax fields. She heard Meme tell Evette that the south-end dye house had sent a request for more oak bark and could she please inform her sister as soon as she saw fit to rise? Then, not waiting to see her younger daughter or wish her a fortunate birthday, Meme gathered up baby Clive and left the cottage. Out to the spinning shed, where she would spend the rest of the day. At any moment Evette would call up the ladder, asking in her sweetest, most patient voice whether or not Heloise planned to join them that morning.

If she was going to look at herself, it had better be quick.

And really, what was there to worry about? A strange *feeling?* What did that even mean? Nothing and nonsense, certainly.

Heloise flicked the mirror upright.

The glass was warped along the top, making the viewer's forehead look much fatter than it was. But it still gave a much better reflection than Gutrund the pig's water trough, which was the only other place Heloise had ever seen her own face. No other farmer's cottage in all Canneberges boasted a mirror, at least not as far as Heloise knew. It made her wonder if her batty old grandmother's wild claims that they came from "noble stock, way back when" might hold some kernel of truth, if this mirror might be the last heirloom of a highborn heritage.

Heloise gazed at her reflection. No new freckles. Well, that was something. She had not yet braided her hair for the day, and it stood out around her head in an enormous halo of fuzzy curls, giving her a wild, fey aspect which she rather liked. Her brows bunched in a tense knot, which was not unusual for Heloise, who tended to look upon the world through pensive eyes.

But was she changed?

"Heloise! Will you be joining us this morning?" Evette called from below, exactly as predicted.

"Yes, coming!" Heloise shouted back. Still she did not move. Her hands clutched the polished frame of the mirror, drawing it closer to her face until her breath fogged the glass. That was no use. Frowning harder, she caught the hem of her sleeve in her fingers and rubbed away the fog. And there was her face again, looking up at her through the spots and speckles. Something was different. She knew it.

Mirror.

"Heloise, there'll be no pottage left if you don't hurry your feet."

"Coming! Coming!" Heloise tossed the words over her shoulder and slowly lowered the glass into the pile of wedding gown, then began to fold up the soft fabric. Her hands froze. Her frown deeper than ever, she leaned down close to the glass, pulling back the linen once more.

Slowly, with extreme deliberation, as though determined that she wouldn't miss it . . . her reflection winked at her.

"I saved some for you," Evette said, holding up a bowl of salvaged pottage. "It's gone cold, but you'd better eat it anyway."

Heloise, her hair still wild about her face, jumped the last three rungs of the ladder and landed with a thud in the floor rushes. Ignoring Evette's exclamations that now she'd have to sweep the rushes flat again, Heloise took the proffered bowl and squeezed onto the hearth bench between brothers Clotaire and Clovis who, having called a truce, were finishing their own breakfasts. She rolled a piece of stale flatbread into a spoon and shoveled a glob of pottage into her mouth. It was clotted and cold. She swallowed without noticing.

She was too busy thinking: *I must be going mad.*

Before her eyes swam the image of her own face, fat forehead and all, gazing up at her from the mirror glass. She took another bite and a third, chewing the bread slowly and saying nothing even when Clovis pinched her arm and Clotaire tugged at a curl.

Oblivious to her sister's uncharacteristically taciturn mood, Evette bustled. She often bustled, for it was the right, farm-maidenly thing to do, and she always did the right thing. Evette bustled while Heloise galumphed; so it was no wonder that half the boys on Canneberges estate were bringing Evette clusters of posies tied up with string while Heloise had yet to receive even one wilted blossom from a single daring admirer. Evette was the perfect example of everything a young man looked for in a future farm-wife. Heloise was just . . . Heloise.

Evette fetched the broom and smoothed out the ruffled floor rushes

—which she had only just finished smoothing in the wake of her brothers' morning fracas. But that was Evette for you: The more fruitless the task, the more sweetly she pursued it.

"Meme let you sleep long since it's your birthday, Heloise," she said, touching Clovis's bare feet with the broom bristles. He obliged by lifting them, and she swept beneath. "But she asked me to tell you that the south-end dye house sent a request for more—"

"I heard!" Heloise snapped even as she pushed more pottage into her mouth.

Evette paused, broom upraised mid-swish. Her eyes took on that expression of, not anger, not irritation . . . but compelling *disappointment.*

There was never any satisfaction to be had in snapping at Evette.

"There's no call to be short," she said in her kindest, most long-suffering voice, the voice usually reserved for the rowdiest of the five brothers. "You are a young woman now, Heloise, not a child. It's time you started behaving with some decorum."

Clotaire and Clovis glanced up at Heloise's face. They saw the dark clouds gathering. As one, they hunched over their bowls, battening down against a storm.

Evette, unmindful, resumed her sweeping. "And you know, you really must learn to tame that hair of yours. It's not seemly to leave it loose like that. You look like a dandelion about to burst. And long braids are unbecoming on a girl of fourteen. I started pinning up my braids on my twelfth birthday. You don't want to look like a child, do you?"

Really, it wasn't the things she said. It was *the way she said them*.

No, honestly, it wasn't even the way she said them. It was *the way Heloise knew she meant them*. Always just shy of truly belittling, but in a tone so well-meaning that, no matter what, Evette would come across as the sweet, kind, endearing sister and Heloise as the unpardonable beast for not appreciating her. Sometimes it was just too much to be borne.

Heloise dug her fold of bread into her pottage. She tested the balance.

The next moment, Evette screamed, dropped her broom, and put both hands up to her face from which a great glob of pottage dripped.

To a chorus of yells and laughter from her brothers—and an immediate outbreak of pottage-flinging that would keep Evette busy cleaning up for ages—Heloise dropped her bowl, leapt to her feet, grabbed her basket, snatched her peeling knife down from its hook, and fled out into the cottage yard. Even as Evette called futile protests after her, she vaulted over the gate and darted on beyond to the flax fields above the bogs.

OTHERS HAVE HEARD ME IN THE PAST. MANY OTHERS, MOST LONG *dead. I think of them often as I sit in my window. I think of them as I never used to think of mortals when I lived in these worlds. They are each dear to me in their way, and I am sorry for what became of them. Such brave young hearts attempting the impossible!*

The impossible to which I call them.

But what choice have I? Or they, for that matter?

Sometimes I wonder if it would be kinder to never call to them at all. To let them mourn. To let them forget . . .

THREE

GRANDMEM FLAXMAN WAS AN OLD, OLD WOMAN WHO LIVED according to old, old ways. This meant that she rose several hours before dawn every morning, even though it was many years since there'd been any need for her to do so. She had long since moved herself and her belongings out of her dead husband's cottage—making way for her son, Cerf, his wife, and their ever-growing brood—and into a humble, shack-like dwelling up above the south-end bogs. She didn't even keep a goat anymore. Cerf always made certain she had food and milk enough brought to her every few days by one of her grandsons or by young Heloise.

So Grandmem had settled into an existence of . . . well, much though she hated to admit it, of uselessness.

But then, she thought, *you've been useless all your life. Especially when it counted most.*

Nevertheless, she always rose before dawn and sat, as she did this particular morning, watching the sunrise from her doorstep. It was a passable sunrise as far as sunrises went. A clear sky, a pale sheen of color fanning rosy-pink and then warm gold across all the world to wash away the frost that gathered here on the verge of spring. A thin film of ice on the edges of the cranberry bogs sparkled then melted away into nothing, like a Faerie's jewel when glimpsed by mortal eyes. Painters sitting where Grandmem now sat would be inspired to mix new pigments; poets would feel the need to sharpen their penknives and pare their goose quills down to delicate points. Oh yes, it was a very nice sunrise, truly.

"It don't compare though, do it, Cateline?" Grandmem muttered. In one hand she held a carrot, which she gummed occasionally, too tired just now to fetch her grinding stone and mash it into edible mush. She took it from her mouth and heaved a great sigh. "It don't compare to the sights you're seeing. But I think you'd be happy to trade. I know I would if I was you."

It had become so much more difficult in the last few years to drive away these melancholy thoughts, accompanied as they always were by lashings of self-reproach.

The sun continued to rise. Dawn lengthened into morning. And still Grandmem could not bring herself to get up from her doorstep and hobble inside. So she watched the morning, watched the flocks of songbirds singing their many choruses (which, she knew in her unromantic soul, were really nothing more than territorial battle cries but no less lovely for that), and continued to mutter to herself as she often did these days. "Are you eating finer things than last year's carrots, Cateline? Or do you even need food where you are?"

Then she saw a shadow that should not be there.

Long and low, it passed along the edge of the nearest cranberry bog. It had no source to cast it—at least, none that Grandmem could see. But Grandmem knew she did not have to see something for it to be there. She knew this better than anyone.

She slid the carrot back into her mouth, rolled it around thoughtfully, and watched the shadow lurk its way along. It was the lurkingest shadow that ever existed. "So," she said around the carrot. "He's back. He's come for *her* now."

Then she frowned, the many wrinkles of her face piling into a single point between her hairless brows. Thoughts came much more slowly than they once had. But they could be sorted through and arranged in coherent order if she was careful about them. The shadow . . . the melting ice . . . the vanishing frost . . .

Cateline . . .

"I wonder," Grandmem said even as the shadow slipped away up the hill and vanished into the still-deeper shadows of the Oakwood, the largest plot of forest on the estate grounds. She removed the carrot again and spun it slowly between her quivering fingers. "I wonder if young Heloise has met herself yet?"

So saying, she got to her feet. This in itself took some doing, but she was fired with a determination unlike anything she had felt in years. She dropped the munched-on carrot in the dust and, clutching her rough-spun shawl about her shoulders, set off toward the little track that wound its way over the flax fields and on to Cerf's cottage.

Before she'd taken more than a few tottering steps toward the path, she saw her granddaughter, Heloise, fly past in such a rush that one half expected to glimpse the Black Dogs themselves snapping at her heels. Heloise hadn't even seen her old grandmother. On she sprang like a barefoot rabbit over the fields, around the bogs, and up the same way the lurking shadow had gone.

"Hmmmm," said Grandmem.

She dismissed the ridiculous notion of following after the girl, of giving her some warning. What was the use? Besides, she'd never catch her. No, best continue to the cottage. Wait for her there. She'd be back, after all.

It wasn't quite time. Soon, but not yet.

Tightening her grip on her shawl, Grandmem continued on her way. Moments later a breeze blew past, trailing bits of paper in its wake. Grandmem's ears were not as sharp as they'd once been, but she distinctly heard a mad little laugh. She watched the paper trail until it too vanished up into the forest.

"Hmmmm," Grandmem said.

Disembodied laughs are enough to disrupt the balance of most minds.

Not hers. Her old memory was too stuffed with strange sights, sounds, smells, and sensations to have room for disruption. She continued on her way.

The beat of a horse's hooves approached. Grandmem peered ahead, squinting against the morning sun. A tall horse—an elegant horse. That could only mean gentry. With a muttered curse, Grandmem tottered off the path and nearly fell into a ditch. She was only an old serf-woman, hardly worth the four walls of the shack in which she lived. She couldn't share even a humble farm path with a great lord or lady. It wouldn't be decent.

She kept her head bowed, wondering if her knees still had it in them to curtsy. The horseman drew near and cast a long shadow across her.

"My good old mother," said a voice that, despite its trembling excitement, remained completely steeped in courtly courtesy. "Tell me, have you seen . . ."

The voice trailed off. Grandmem, who disliked being called "my good old mother" even by her own son, glared up at the horseman. He boasted a head of straw-colored hair all tumbled about in fashionable curls. His face was young and too oddly angular to be considered quite handsome, though he was eye-catching in his way.

Most noteworthy was the manner in which he sat there on his tall horse, frowning, his mouth still open.

Grandmem recognized him at once: the Honorable Benedict de Cœur of Canneberges, only son of the Marquis and Marquise de Canneberges. Come home from university for the winter due to illness, if she recalled the farmer gossips correctly. She regarded the young fellow through one eye, the other squinted shut. She had been around long enough to learn a thing or two about reading faces and expressions. And she could see that, young lordling though he was, Benedict was deeply embarrassed.

"Um," he said, trying to find words that would not come.

"If you're wondering," said Grandmem, "if I saw an invisible breeze blow by, carrying paper-bits behind it, I did. I did, yes. Not two minutes ago. And it was laughing, yes, like a very fiend."

"You did?" The young scholar brightened considerably. Which is to say, his pale face flushed an impressive crimson. "Which way did it go?"

"Up yonder, toward the Oakwood," said Grandmem, indicating with a nod of her head. "You'll be knowing, being the great big lord-man you are, that it is bad luck to chase after laughing breezes?"

But Benedict had no time for luck, be it good or bad. He fumbled in his pocket for a coin, found none, and blushed again with still greater embarrassment. Grandmem could have rolled her eyes, but no one would have seen them behind all her wrinkles, so she didn't bother.

"Away with you now," she said, as though she were the lady and he the serf dismissed at her word. "Away, and may you find a luck to your liking."

The young lord tipped his hat and urged his tall horse onward up the trail after the wind and, though he did not know it, after Heloise as well.

32

Grandmem watched him go. Then she said, "Hmmm."

And continued on her way.

It is amazing what a good rage and a good run can do to return a sense of order and reasonableness to a mind disturbed. By the time Heloise, panting and gasping at the painful stitch in her side, reached the outermost fringes of the Oakwood, she had nearly convinced herself that what she had thought she'd seen in the mirror was nothing at all. Purely dreamed up. Imagined. Fancied. Nonsense, really.

Besides, even if by some strange twist of madness she truly had seen her reflection wink while she herself was wide-eyed and staring—which, *pfffsh*, was ridiculous—did it really matter? Evette was still the most obnoxious and bothersome person ever to walk the fields of Canneberges; and it was surely far more worthwhile to spend a morning contemplating the various grievances inflicted by a perfect sister than worrying about reflections, winking or otherwise.

So Heloise paused a moment just within the shadows of the forest, bent over with her hands (one clutching the long handle of her peeling knife) on her knees, waiting until the stitch in her side eased. Despite the pain, she couldn't repress the smile tugging at the corners of her mouth even as her brow continued to frown. The sight of Evette with pottage on her face, her jaw dropped, her eyes tightly squeezed shut, her scream filling the cottage—that was a memory to treasure indeed! It was a rare day that saw Evette even remotely discomfited.

Heloise's smile soon vanished, however, as she straightened up and entered the Oakwood. The first faint notes of what would soon swell into a full chorus of shame already played in the back of her mind. After all, Evette hadn't done anything so terribly wrong. She was just . . . perfect, sweet, well-meaning, and kind-hearted. She was just herself.

"And you, Heloise, are a beast," Heloise muttered. By now her frown was quite severe and, though she did not know it, she looked like a wrinkle-free reflection of her stern-faced grandmother in that moment.

As she proceeded into the forest, she caught her wild hair in both hands, parted it down the middle, and tied it in braids. It was so thick that each braid was fatter than her own wrist. Considering Evette's kindly suggestions over breakfast, she almost wound them up on top of her head like a young woman should. But no. She may be a beast; but she was her own beast, and let no one try to tell her otherwise! She had no hairpins on her anyway.

With this decision firmly in mind, she chose the left-hand trail into deeper Oakwood and set off at a leisurely stride, her basket bouncing on her hip. Oakwood was not so called because it was made up entirely of oaks, nor indeed were oaks the most prominent tree to be found there. But they were the most *important* tree, and few people ventured into the wood above the south-end except to gather oak bark. The prosperity of

Canneberges depended on oak bark, which could be boiled down for its strong tannins, the best and least-smelly fixative known for dying cloth. Canneberges estate was famous throughout the kingdom—and kingdoms beyond—for its bolts of rich red linen.

Heloise, as one of the primary bark-gatherers of the south-end, was an essential part of that fame.

"Heloise Oakwoman," she whispered to herself as she approached the first tall oak in her path. Oakwoman would be an excellent name for her, a name with standing completely distinct from her father's. But it was unlikely at best, and she knew it. No one was called Oakwoman. It wasn't how things were done.

Heloise dropped her basket among the roots, tucked her long skirts into her belt, and, knife gripped between her teeth, climbed into the lower branches of the oak. As she went she growled a different name around the knife: "Heloise Pigman."

Because, truth be told, that name was much more likely. In another few years—very few now, though she rarely allowed herself to think about it—she, like Evette, would be pushed, prodded, and eventually matched up with some farmer or dyer or pig-keeper lad. Then she would take on his name. His standing.

"Wouldn't you just *hate* to be a Pigman?" Heloise had asked her sister not many weeks ago while the two of them, bundled warmly against the last of the winter snows, made their way across the yard to feed Gutrund the sow.

Evette, reaching into the pen to scratch Gutrund behind the ear just where she liked it, had smiled sweetly. "Pigs are important," she'd said. "And the pig-keepers up at the Great House are respectable men of good standing."

Heloise made a face. "Respectable or not, they stink worse than Gutrund here. Whenever Gy Pigman comes calling, it's all I can do not to pinch my nose before he's stepped over the threshold!"

Evette, still smiling, dropped her eyes demurely. Gy Pigman was one of her many and most ardent suitors. "You know, Heloise," she said then, "we don't have the right to be as choosy as all that."

Heloise had frowned at this statement. Hers was a temperament prone to scowls, and the oncoming advent of adulthood combined with her sister's never-ending practicality only dampened the little good humor with which nature had deemed fit to grace her. "Then *you* marry Gy if you must," she'd declared, dumping the table scraps and root vegetables so quickly that they slopped over the edge of Gutrund's trough. "*You* marry him, because if you don't, he might come calling on me next. And *I* wouldn't have him for all Madame de Cœur's silks and jewels!"

"Oh, Heloise," said Evette, "I wouldn't worry. I doubt very much Gy will ever want to come calling on you."

Anyone else delivering such a line would have deserved—and likely received—a smack in the face. Not Evette. She spoke it with the utmost sincerity, truly intending to comfort her sister.

It was unbearable.

So Heloise had whirled about, empty slop-bucket swinging, and stomped back to the cottage. Evette, her smile never wavering, had followed in silence behind. After all, if you were a respectable young woman, you must marry a respectable young man, take his name, assume his standing, and raise his children. It was how things were done. Especially by the daughters of flax farmers.

These thoughts and memories crowded in stormy lines between Heloise's brows even as she perched on the lowest branches of the obliging oak. But she couldn't bear to consider them long, so she shook her head and concentrated instead on the task before her.

One searching hand ran over the trunk, seeking old scars. There were a few, but not many; Heloise was always careful not to take too much bark from any one tree. She climbed higher to a place where the tree had not yet been cut. There, her legs wrapped tightly about a thick branch, she set to work peeling long strips of bark. This was the best time of year for harvesting oak bark, just as the sap began to rise. Using the technique her father had taught her, she gently stripped away long peels, which she dropped to lie in curls among the roots below, waiting to be gathered. She worked efficiently, ignoring the numbness in her fingers and toes, glad for a task to occupy her hands. Usually she brought along Clovis or Clotaire to gather for her, but she was just as happy to be alone today.

"Heloise Pigman," she muttered as she worked. "*That's* a person I never want to meet." She wouldn't either. Not if she could help it.

Yet this repulsive version of herself danced before her vision like the phantom of a future destiny. Determined to drive it away, Heloise started to hum.

It was an odd little tune she hummed. Indeed, it might be a stretch to call it a tune, at least by mortal standards. With all of the charming folksongs common to that region, Heloise could have entertained herself with quite a lovely personal concert. But she never thought to hum any of those songs. Only one tune could possibly be hummed at this time of year by the people of Canneberges . . .

Now, when the snows were melted away . . .

Now, when the sap began to rise . . .

Now, when in three days' time the sun would set upon the last day of winter and rise upon the first of spring, only one song echoed in the heart of any man, woman, or child of Canneberges. The old, old song. The sacred song.

Heloise hummed Le Sacre.

But it was not a song meant for humming. It began simply enough, but as it progressed, it changed. And as it changed, it grew. Heloise could hear it in her head even as she'd heard it every year since before she could remember—the soulful moan of a shawm like the sound of a tree's old spirit come to life, and the higher sighing of pipes offset by beating tabors. Then, rolling in like thunder from the sea, the much deeper boom of the copper timpani, a sound she could never hope to produce in her small throat.

Once all of these joined together and built to a crisis point, suddenly they ceased, and the solo voice of a young maid rose up in the darkness. She sang alone at first, but soon other voices joined hers and swelled into a great ensemble of sound, voices singing in a language unknown to anyone in Canneberges yet as much a part of their lives and culture as the flax and the cranberries they sowed and harvested each year.

Heloise hummed the opening melody. In place of the tabors and timpani, she tapped out rhythms on the oak branch and trunk. Then, after a breathless moment of silence, she opened her mouth and sang the strange, strange words:

"Cianenso

Nive nur norum.

Nive noar—garph, gug! Blegh!*"

So her singing ended in a fit of coughing as the melody soared out of her range. She grimaced, adjusted her grip on her peeling knife, and began the song again an octave lower. Nevertheless, when she came to the high-soaring third line she coughed again, unable to get the incomprehensible words out.

Oh well. She was only fourteen. She had four years to practice before she would be obliged to sing Le Sacre in public and dance with the maidens of the estate. Heloise began to sing again, sighing out the first word, *"Cianensooooo."* It always amazed her how much passion she could put into her voice when no one was listening.

At least, no one so far as she knew.

Across from the oak tree in which Heloise worked stood a dark, heavily shrouded pine. This was a solemn tree with no musicality in its limbs, yet at the sound of Heloise's halting voice a sudden interest seemed to rise up from the shadows beneath it. Branches moved ever so slightly.

And something secret gazed out.

After humming the first haunting notes faster the third time around—like a horse speeding up before it leaped the fence—Heloise opened her mouth and tried the strange words again. "*Cianenso!*" she belted out.

Within the shadows of the pine, a voice echoed hers: "*Cianenso.*"

This voice was so profoundly deep that Heloise could not hear its singing over her own vocalizations. But when she came to that tricky third line and once more broke off in coughing, the second voice continued without her:

"*Nive noar-ciu, lysa-ciu.*
Nivee mher
Nivien nur jurar
Nou iran-an!"

Heloise, one hand clutching her knife, the other gently guiding the newest strip of peeled bark, froze. Her eyes rounded, staring at the trunk before her. In that moment she was aware of every curl of bark, every splotch of lichen, every rough contour. Everything struck her sight with such heightened awareness of being that she would have been overwhelmed . . .

. . . except that every other sense of her body suddenly fixated on the sound behind her.

The voice sang on, as strange as the words being sung. So strange, so deep, so wild, and so dangerous that it seemed to somehow *belong* with the words, as though each were a part of the others: words and voice and melody.

But worst of all . . . or best . . . or most dreadful . . . Heloise suddenly understood what was being sung. For the words, though they remained the same upon her ear, plunged down inside her head and twisted, taking on new shapes, new sounds, new colors, taking on form and substance that she could suddenly comprehend. She heard the voice in the shadows behind her singing:

> *"Night so hopeless and so pure.*
> *Evening comes to promise*
> *All my children*
> *Of a deeper night."*

The voice faded away slowly, like the gentle fading of darkness into dawn. Then all was still.

If I think about it too long, I won't ever move again, Heloise thought. Next she thought: *You're already thinking too much. Stop it at once.*

Then she thought: *You're still doing it.*

With a wrench of her spirit far more abrupt than any movement of her limbs or muscles, she turned around. The branch she sat on swayed, its bare twigs scraping against one another. She stared at the fir tree behind her. The sound had come from that tree. But who had sung? The tree? No. She'd never heard a tree speak, much less sing, though she'd listened often enough just in case. And even if, by some chance, trees *did* sing, she was quite certain no tree ever sounded that dark. That feral.

That bloodthirsty.

Stop it, she told herself. *Stop thinking. Do something!*

Few options came to mind, however. She could either stay where she was in the tree, hoping whatever had sung those words—whatever had painted those sensations in her brain—couldn't climb trees, or . . .

Evette would never have done what Heloise did next. Evette would have stayed put and possibly tried to cajole the secret lurker out of hiding with the force of her own persuasive sweetness. She would then have reasoned with it until, unable to bear one more word of reasonableness, it either ate her or ran away forever.

But Heloise was not Evette.

She turned her knife blade-down and dropped it carefully between the branches. The blade plunged into a mossy patch between roots, the handle vibrating gently on impact. Scarcely taking her eyes from the fir tree, Heloise swung herself down, branch by branch. Her braids caught on bits of twig, but she pulled them free and kept descending. Before dropping to the ground from the last branch she may have hesitated, wiped nervous sweat from her lip, and stared extra hard at the shadows under that tree. But she would never have admitted this to a soul.

After landing in a crouch on the hard forest floor, Heloise paused only long enough to draw a breath before snatching up her knife. Slowly she rose and stepped carefully toward the fir tree, which grew from the bottom of a ditch on the far side of the path, its lowest needle-veiled branches brushing the earth to create a perfect, cave-like hiding place.

Heloise, her body sideways to make the smallest target possible, her knife upraised and poised to plunge, drew near. As she approached, her movements slowed as though she pressed against some invisible force. But she didn't stop. One cold step at a time, she progressed.

Something was under there. Something . . . She could hear it breathing. Something big.

Something too big to fit in that small space.

Something impossible.

She tried to swallow, but her mouth and throat were too dry. Her eyes narrowed beneath her frowning brow, as though she could somehow force them to see the un-seeable.

If you run away, it will pounce on you from behind, she thought. *So it's a good thing you're not thinking about running away. Absolutely.*

She no longer breathed. Her lungs were too tight to allow for breath. But *it* was still breathing. Deep, deep breaths.

"Who—who is there?" Heloise said.

Even as the words left her mouth, a sudden gust of wind caught them up, whirled to the top of a tall tree, and plunged back down to the forest floor. Heloise, her braids and skirts billowing in that wind, glanced after it. Realizing her mistake at once, she forced herself to look back at the fir tree. Its branches shivered as though something had just rushed out from under it. But nothing could be seen, no shadow, no form.

The heavy presence she had sensed only moments ago was gone.

The wind, meanwhile, was very present, and it burst out laughing, an insane, high laugh. Heloise, furious, brandished her knife, but what could a knife do against a wind? As it gusted in her face, tugging at her braids again, she slashed, but to no avail. The wind only laughed harder.

Little bits of paper whirled around Heloise like a small tornado. Tiny papercuts nicked her hands and cheeks. Grinding her teeth, she threw up her arms to protect her eyes.

The wind laughed so loudly that Heloise didn't hear the sound of approaching hooves. So when young Master Benedict de Cœur rounded a turn in the path, his horse shied, and he shouted, and Heloise's story almost came to a swift and crushing end.

But just at the last, the horse was able to pivot, and Heloise herself, despite the force of the wind, fell down the slope and landed in the fir tree's branches. Benedict, less fortunate in his landing site, sprawled on the path and stared up at bare twigs whirling against the sky as his vision spun. His horse galloped on down the path and disappeared into the trees.

"Iubdan's beard," Benedict cursed. Then he coughed, propped himself up on one elbow, and turned to scowl at the wild-haired maid in the ditch. "Iubdan's crown and beard, girl, what do you think you're doing?" he snarled.

And then he blushed.

FOUR

THE FAMILY OF CŒUR, LONG TIME MASTERS OF CANNEBERGES AND other great estates across the kingdom, were red-bearded, red-blooded, red-tempered men. As red as the cranberries in the bogs; as red as the dyes with which the dyers stained their reams of fine flax thread. Their great ancestor Rufus the Red (for whom the Flaxman family's rooster was named) was a man of such bloody history that all painted depictions of him were done entirely in shades of crimson and scarlet, and the only carvings were rendered in redwood.

Such was Benedict's heritage. But he doubted very much that Rufus the Red (his ancestor, not the rooster) had suffered under such a curse of blushes as he battled every day.

For Benedict's red blood, much to his chagrin, was severely checked by the delicate, refined blue blood of his mother's family, the Bellamys: a quiet, thoughtful assortment of aristocrats whose hereditary taste inclined far more toward poetry, introspection, and good-breeding than ruthlessness.

Thus Benedict, though he boasted a temper as potent as any among the descendants of the famous Rufus, also boasted a quick-rising shame that countered all expressions of fury with immediate expressions of abject apology. Thus in his father's eyes he was a wet puppy; in his mother's, a hot-headed hound. He could never win.

"I mean to say," he said, still propped on his elbow and watching the peasant girl disentangle herself from the branches of a fir tree, "I do apologize. I shouldn't have sworn at you like that."

"You're dragon-eaten right!" Heloise snapped, her head emerging from the ditch. Her braids had mostly come undone, and wild curls stood up around her head, giving her the appearance of some strange forest spirit of wicked intent rising up out of the soil itself. Her eyes flashed with what Benedict took to be rage but was more surprise than anything.

His blush deepened. He had never heard a girl use such a curse. Cursing by the Dragon was something only the most daring of the older boys at university ever tried, and then only behind the headmaster's back.

But peasant girls weren't like *normal* girls. They were uneducated so possessed no breadth of understanding. One couldn't expect too much from them, now could one?

Still blushing but assuming an expression of noble condescension and forbearance, Benedict picked himself up, brushed himself off, and strode to the ditch. There he bent, one hand on his knee, the other extended to Heloise.

She stared at it. He might have been offering her a spider, so great was the disgust curling her lip. "What do you want?" she demanded.

"Um. I'd like to help you up?" Benedict said. It was more a question than a statement, as though he wasn't certain this was the right response to give.

Heloise continued to stare. Then she shrugged, kicked a bare foot free of her tangled skirts, and pulled herself upright. "I don't need help," she said, then took a step and almost slipped back down the incline. Out of pure necessity her flailing hand caught his, and she found herself held in a firm grasp which drew her back up onto the path.

It was then that Heloise caught sight of Benedict's hat lying in the middle of the road and she knew whose hand she held and at whom she had just so roundly cursed. Now it was her turn to blush.

Heloise had never before seen Master Benedict close up. He had been away at university for several years now, only home for the occasional visit, and she could not recall having glimpsed him even once during those intervals. She knew the general idea of what he looked like, however: tall, fair, and thin, like his mother. All the farm girls of Canneberges claimed that he was handsome, though now that she saw him up close, Heloise thought his features rather more odd than attractive. In fact, she thought he looked a bit like Rufus the Red (the rooster, not the ancestor).

But everyone on Canneberges estate knew that the marquis's son wore a bright blue cap set with trailing peacock feathers. There wasn't a hat like it to be seen anywhere else on the estate and not a finer one to be had in all the kingdom. Or so the dyer boys claimed, with no little envy. After all, who wouldn't want a hat adorned with peacock feathers?

And this was the hat Heloise now saw with one feather bent and broken at a terrible angle.

"Oh, sweet Lights Above," Heloise whispered. She shook her hand free of Benedict's grasp and tried to curtsy so hard she almost sat down. "Master Benedict! Sir! I—"

I wish I had pinned up my braids like Evette suggested.

The thought flashed through her brain, and it was enough to make her want to gag. Dragons blast it! Why was Evette *always* right?

Benedict waited a polite interval to see if the peasant girl would finish her excuses or explanations. But she had apparently lost all power of speech. "Well," he said at last, "no harm done." He turned to fetch his hat and immediately spotted the inaccuracy of that statement. "Oh." He picked up the hat, and the broken feather dangled forlornly before falling, leaving behind a sorry stub. The bright eye of the peacock feather gleamed in the dust of the path. "My man will have something to say about this," Benedict muttered, more to himself than to Heloise. He sighed and placed the hat on his head.

The next moment a great wind gusted, and the hat was off his head and caught in Heloise's hands.

She stared at it.

Benedict stared at it.

"Um," said Heloise.

"Um," said Benedict. He put out his hand. "May I have my hat back, please?"

Bobbing another curtsy, Heloise all but threw the hat at him. He accepted it with more grace and carefully set it at a jaunty angle over his hair. No sooner had his hands let go of the brim, however, when—

Heloise gasped as the hat hit her in the face. She caught it and dragged it down, her eyes round and staring into the equally startled gaze of Master Benedict.

"Excuse me, little girl," said he, "but would you kindly not . . ."

At least he had the good grace to stop talking. Heloise would grant him that, even if she couldn't find it in her heart to forgive him for calling her "little girl." (He wasn't that much older than she was! Perhaps closer to Evette's age than hers, but still!) She narrowed her eyes and watched him as he calculated whether or not there had been enough time for her to leap that distance, snatch the hat, leap back again, and slap it across her own face.

"Nope," she said, tossing the hat back to him. "It wasn't me."

Benedict flushed a brighter crimson than ever, if that were possible. "Then how—"

He didn't finish. Before he could, the wind caught the hat again and returned it to Heloise's hands. It giggled. And a strange, mad giggle it was, high-pitched and otherworldly. No human throat could make a sound like that.

Nevertheless, Benedict's brow lowered in a scowl which he focused on Heloise. She scowled back, determined he wouldn't begin to imagine that *she* had made such a twittering noise. "Here," she said, stepping closer and holding out the hat. "Take it."

Benedict, unused to being ordered about by girls, looked as though he would put up a fight. Heloise braced herself for verbal battle. But Benedict was not entirely made up of red Cœur blood. Bellamy rationality ruled at least half of his brain. So, without argument, he did as he was told and took hold of the brim of his hat. Heloise held on as well, and they clutched it suspended between them.

The breeze watched without eyes, tittering softly, poised to leap. Heloise glanced sideways at the sound, then focused her gaze on Benedict's red face. "When I let go," she whispered, "run."

Benedict leaned in to catch her words. "What about my horse?" he said, as though asking permission for something.

Heloise made a face at him. "Run after the horse then," she said. "I don't care. Just run—not yet! When I say."

Benedict's pale eyes scanned the air over her head and to either side. He dropped his voice still lower, so that she had to read his words on his lips. "Do you know what this is?"

"No. Why would I? Get ready."

Benedict shook his head. "I can't abandon you with . . . whatever it is. It wouldn't be . . . I mean, I mean it wouldn't be gentlemanly. Leaving a little girl alone in the forest and all. It wouldn't . . . I mean, king and honor and country and all that."

Heloise wrinkled her nose at him. But she could see that, despite his babble, he was in earnest, so she said, "If you stay here, we'll spend the rest of the day trading your hat back and forth. Maybe *you* have time to waste in an endless game of catch, but *I* have work to do. Now get ready."

"Um," said Benedict, working his way up to another protest.

Heloise didn't give him the chance. "Run!"

She felt the startled thrill run up his arms at the suddenness of her shout. Then, grasping the hat with both hands, he turned and fled down the path the same direction his horse had gone. His blue cloak flapped behind him, but he made good speed, she had to admit. Indeed, he might have given any of the farm boys on Canneberges estate some competition at the summer games if his dignity permitted him to join them. But then—and Heloise folded her arms across her skinny chest at this thought—fear can be quite an inspiration, and who knew how he would run under more normal circumstances?

The wind in the boughs of the oak tree overhead laughed hysterically at the sight then plunged down and swished off after Benedict like a dog snapping at his heels. Just as Benedict rounded the bend and disappeared out of sight into the trees, however, the wind stopped, whirled up, and came tripping lightly back to Heloise.

She could see it coming. Or rather, she could see the signs of its coming as leaves and pine straw on the path blew wildly off to either side and away, and little shreds of paper bounced along in its wake. Some small part of her brain told her that she should be afraid. But at the moment she felt more curious than anything.

This breeze giggled to itself, a most unnatural sound considering it had no throat or mouth with which to giggle. Heloise stood with her arms folded and waited as it approached. It swooped down, picked up the broken end of the peacock feather and twirled it about as though between two fingers before presenting it to Heloise.

She eyed it, one eyebrow upraised. "What? You expect me to take it? Like a gift?"

The breeze giggled again and went on twirling so that the iridescent eye of the feather gleamed and winked.

"You embarrassed me, you know," said Heloise, refusing to take the proffered item even when it was tickled under her nose. She swiped a hand and sent the feather tossing to the ground. "You embarrassed me in front of Master Benedict. The marquis's own son!" She snorted, and a smile wanted to tug at her mouth, so she scowled more fiercely. "Evette would have died if it was her."

"Died?" said the breeze, and then burst into a still more manic, "*Heeeeeeeeee heeheehee!* Died! Died! Would have died!"

So, Heloise thought. *So. It talks. It's alive.*

She felt all the blood in her face rush down her neck and away, leaving her ghostly pale and light-headed. But she was able to hold onto enough self-awareness to remind herself that breezes weren't really that scary, and ultimately wouldn't one prefer a breeze that talked rather than one that only laughed? After all, if it talked, surely it could reason.

Had her feet not been firmly rooted, she might have been tempted to run. "What's so funny?" she demanded. "Do stop laughing, at once. What is so funny about anyone dying?"

The breeze seemed to draw a long breath, which was odd considering it was made up of almost nothing but breath. Then, eager like a puppy, it wound its way along the ground to Heloise's feet. She felt puffs like fingers touching her toes and pulling at the hem of her skirts. Once more she almost ran. But she stood her ground.

"Mortal, mortal, mortal you are," said the wind. "Mortal you live and mortal you die. Oh, it is a strange and wondrous thing! Have you seen it? Have you seen this death?"

And there it came, flashing across Heloise's memory.

The image that returned to her every year on a certain cold night in the depths of winter, every year in that sleepless darkness.

The image of her mother standing over the open hole in the ground. Her mother, who couldn't hear her calling: *"Meme! Meme! Don't!"*

An image of hunching. Of shadows. Of grey skies overhead.

An image that was less about the sight than the sound: the weeping of a broken heart.

But this wasn't night. This wasn't winter. This was morning, morning on the edge of spring. The morning of her birthday. She wouldn't think winter thoughts now.

Heloise yanked her skirts out of the wind's grasp. "I live on a farm," she snapped. "We see death all the time. It's nothing special. Everyone dies. It happens. It just happens."

Even to the gentlest of souls . . .

"Ahhhhh!" sighed the wind, and its sigh was almost a moan. "So strange is your mortal world! So strange and so beautiful! Ahhhhh, the mystery of it all!"

"I'm guessing then that you're not a ghost," Heloise said. "If you were a ghost, you'd know about death."

"What is a ghost?" asked the wind.

But Heloise did not care to answer that. She cared about what was, not what wasn't. "So if you're not a ghost," she said, "what are you? An evil spirit?"

At this the wind laughed again, and it certainly didn't sound like something evil. Weird, yes; grotesque even. But not evil. The truth was, out here in the Oakwood, it wasn't as entirely out of place as it would be elsewhere. Heloise had always suspected that the wood was on the verge of speaking to her. Of laughing, of whispering secrets.

"All right, not an evil spirit," Heloise acknowledged even as the wind whirled around her, catching playfully at her braids. "So show yourself. Show me what you are."

The laughter stopped. Heloise felt a strong sense that the wind was trying to think and finding it rather difficult.

Then suddenly it darted away, dashed across the ground, and gathered up bits of leaves, pine needles, and, most of all, the torn pages it had stolen from Master Benedict's study. With these clutched in its airy arms, it leapt high into the air before Heloise and . . . and *fluttered*. That really was the only word Heloise could think to describe what she saw. The invisible being before her fluttered all the different bits it had gathered and formed a sort of outline, a sort of shape. At first it wasn't distinct enough for her to discern any specifics. But slowly the paper bits and leaves came together and created a shape, a shape just about recognizable. Leaves and papers formed a face . . . acorns and pine straw made eyes, eyebrows, even lashes . . . grasses, ferns, and bits of underbrush made skirts, limbs, and wild, curly hair . . .

"No!" Heloise cried, irritated now. "No, no, no! That's *me*. You can't be *me*. I want to see what *you* are."

At this, the wind heaved a sigh and dropped everything but the paper shreds. These it held in a bundle, as though it pressed them close to its invisible breast. "I don't understand," it said. "I don't know what you mean by *see* me. I am me, and I am here, and this is all of me. I am a sylph, a sylph I am, and this is all a sylph may be."

"A sylph!" Heloise breathed the word, and her heart leapt with equal parts delight and surprise. She had heard tales of sylphs before, many times over. There were legends aplenty handed down and around Canneberges, many of them talking of wind spirits such as this. Beings that existed outside of time as men knew it, but which would sometimes venture into time to wreak havoc upon time-bound creatures. Not evil, but full of mischief. A sort of . . . a sort of . . .

"Faerie," Heloise said. "You're a Faerie."

"Yes! Yes!" said the sylph, so pleased that it rushed at her with its paper shreds, tickling her and pulling at her hair. "Oh, clever, sweet, beautiful, dying mortal!"

"Here now, stop that," Heloise protested, trying to brush the creature and its paper away. She'd never tried to brush aside a wind before, and her efforts were completely unsuccessful. But her curiosity was powerful enough to drown out even her irritation. "What are you doing here?" she asked. "Do you live in the Oakwood?"

"Where is that?" asked the sylph, curling away from her, an invisible ribbon of movement.

"The Oakwood? It's here. Where we are right now."

"Where is Now?"

Heloise, having never been faced with a question quite like this, felt her mind go blank. But the sylph persisted eagerly enough. "Is Now in the Near World?" it asked.

Never one to confess ignorance if she could possibly help it, Heloise nodded. "Yes," she said with much more confidence than she felt.

"Oh no!" The sylph uttered another of its weird, manic laughs. "Oh no, I do not live in the Near World of mortals! I do not live in Now or in Time. I live in the Between, the great, the wonderful Wood Between.

But I felt a curse, a wonderful curse worked by a powerful Faerie Queen. And with the curse came many gates, gates opening into your world. I have never seen the mortal world before. I have never seen death. So I came through, and I found you, and I found this mortal magic."

Heloise listened to this explanation, her brow knotting in a frown. Though she hated to admit it even to herself, she couldn't understand a word. Or rather, the words were fine, but the thoughts expressed were entirely beyond anything within her realm of comprehension.

Deciding to change tack to something more reasonable, she plucked one of the paper remnants from the sylph's collection and held it up to her face for inspection. "What's this?" she asked, studying the squiggling ink marks.

"I don't know! It is mortal. Is it not beautiful?" said the sylph.

It must be writing, Heloise decided. If it was a drawing or an etching, she might recognize it. As it was, it looked as though some sort of tiny worm had performed a wriggling ink dance across the page, resulting in an assortment of bumps and lines.

Yes. Definitely writing. No doubt about it. Probably words even. That's what people tended to write, or so she was told. Words. She frowned, hoping it was an intelligent sort of frown, and studied the slip, unaware that it was upside down.

"Ahhhhh," said the sylph, and the way it gusted implied sudden anxiety. It plucked at the paper tentatively, as though afraid of angering her. Then, working up its nerve, it snatched the scrap out of her fingers and stuffed it back into its bundle. "It's mine," it said.

"Did you write it?" Heloise asked.

"No," said the sylph. "Mortals did. It is a mortal magic. And it is mine now."

Heloise eyed the sylph. It is difficult to eye something that isn't visible, but Heloise managed. "Did you steal it?"

"No!" said the sylph. Then, more softly, "Yes." Then, "Maybe?"

"Stealing is wrong, you know," said Heloise. She hated herself the moment the words left her mouth. She sounded just like Evette.

But the sylph didn't seem to mind. In fact it laughed again, and twirled about, wafting the paper around it like a swirling cloak. "That is mortal talk! Such mortal talk!" It whooshed up and down, and something caught and held Heloise's face, like two gentle, breezy hands. "I love you, mortal," it said. "You are so funny!"

Heloise had often wondered what a declaration of love might be like. Evette got them all the time, of course, but Heloise hadn't expected to receive any of her own for . . . well, years yet. If ever! Certainly never from something she couldn't see. "Um," she said, stepping backward out of the sylph's grasp. "Thank you. I mean . . . well, what does it say?"

"What does what say?" asked the sylph, still chuckling to itself and rubbing the bits of paper together to make a quiet susurrus chorus.

"The writing. What does it say?"

Something without a face or form cannot look confused. But the sylph certainly gave off a sudden *sensation* of confusion. She could almost see—well, not *see*, but *feel*—the invisible being tilting its head to one side. "I do not know," it admitted. All the bits of paper shifted into a great, ragged fan, as though the creature were holding them up for inspection. "I do not know what it says. But the Dame will."

"What dame?"

"The Dame of the Haven. She was mortal like you once. She understands the ways of mortal magic. She'll read these to me when I take them to her. She'll read all the little words . . . all the little memories . . ."

Heloise had never heard of such a person. Few people in all Canneberges could read or write—the marquis, his son, and the bailiff. As far as she knew not even the marquise had the gift, and she was the most highly educated woman imaginable, at least as far as Heloise was concerned. But then, she supposed, the world probably did consist of a bit more than the breadth and boundaries of Canneberges. Besides, she'd never before encountered invisible wind-beings, singing shadows, and (though she still refused to acknowledge this as real) reflections with minds of their own. Indeed, the world was opening up to all sorts of interesting possibilities.

"Where does one find this dame and this haven?"

"She lives in the depths of the Wood," the sylph answered readily enough.

"The wood? You mean this wood? Oakwood?"

"No!" said the sylph. Then, "Yes." Then, "Maybe?"

"Well, which is it?" Heloise looked about them at the tall trees surrounding. Oakwood was safe and familiar to her. She had worked within its boundaries for years now as a bark-gatherer. If there was any dame hiding in any haven anywhere within that acreage, surely she would know about it. Or someone in Canneberges would.

"It is . . . difficult." The sylph drifted to and fro before Heloise, trailing paper bits. "It is . . . it is all Between. And this is all so Near. And everything else so Far. I don't know the mortal way of saying it."

It was only then that Heloise noticed something which should have been obvious to her at once. Later on she would try to excuse herself to herself (she found herself to be quite a desperate nag sometimes), saying she was so distracted by hearing a wind speak at all, was it really her fault she didn't notice what language it spoke?

She noticed now, however. As the sylph sighed out the words *Near*, *Far*, and *Between*, she realized that she wasn't hearing them in her own mother-tongue. At least not when they first struck her ear. What she heard was a wild, lilting language full of depths and heights and unusual spices. A language unlike anything she'd ever heard—

No. No that wasn't true. It was the language of Le Sacre.

Not the same words; not the words she'd grown up singing softly to herself as she worked, sounding out the odd assortment of vowels and consonants. But she knew it was the same. And it was the language she had, but a few minutes ago, heard sung in a voice of pure darkness; the words striking her ear even as these did, then changing shape in her head, forming themselves into comprehension.

Suddenly she felt cold. It was a chill morning of course, and her fingers and toes were bare and numb. But this was a cold that started in the center of her heart and worked its way out to the extremities, not the other way around. It was a cold she might almost call fear.

"Was that you?" she demanded, her voice sharp and sudden. "Was it you I heard singing?"

"I'm always singing," trilled the sylph. As though eager to prove this statement, it called out a loud "Falalala!" that sent even the old fir tree cringing to its roots.

"No," said Heloise, pressing her hands to her ears against that cheerful howling. "No, was that you I heard before Master Benedict came? Was that you singing Le Sacre?"

"Le Sacre?" The sylph tasted the words curiously. "What is that? Sing it for me."

Heloise blinked, surprised by this abrupt request. But she could see no reason to refuse. Besides, she needed practice performing for an audience, and what audience could be less intimidating than this invisible one?

The sylph waited. It twirled in place, humming to itself, as patient as an ageless thought, never once feeling the passing moments of silence, for sylphs do not experience the world in moments. It trailed the paper shreds to and fro and waited for Heloise to sing.

She cleared her throat. Then she opened her mouth and forced the words. They came most unwillingly, thin, staggering things, starved of all beauty. But she forced them out:

> "*Cianenso,*
>
> *Nive nur nor—*"

The sylph screamed.

I HEAR THE SONG. EVEN FROM THIS DISTANCE, WHICH ISN'T AS VAST *as one might suppose.*

I hear the song. It is in her heart even when it isn't on her tongue. She does not have to sing it. The song sings her.

And even now I wish I could scream like the sylph as the words of that song reach out to my ear. O! Lumé above! What have I done? What have I helped to do?

FIVE

MANY MOMENTS PASSED BEFORE HELOISE COULD BRING HER TREMBLING limbs to pick themselves back up and put her on her feet. For a while she'd wondered if she would ever be able to move again. A sylph's scream has that effect: It can turn a man of iron into a quivering jelly.

Heloise's ears rang, and the resounding echoes were so jarring in her head that her eyes seemed to pulse with the throb of them. But she got up and brushed off the fallen sticks and leaves that covered her like a blanket. Several trees had broken and dropped large branches around her, leaving a terrible mess on the path. It looked as though a small hurricane had blown through. She was fortunate none of those limbs had landed on her head.

The sylph was gone. Heloise would have liked to tell herself that it had never existed to begin with, but she wasn't so foolish as to try.

Instead she straightened her garments and went in search of her peeling knife and gathering basket. Her basket had been blown well across the path, caught in the branches of the fir tree in its ditch. Only for a moment did Heloise hesitate to slide down and collect it. But the sylph was gone, and so was the shadow she'd heard singing; she needn't be afraid.

But they would be back.

Mirror.

Heloise froze, her hand tightening its hold on the peeling knife. But no, that voice . . . that thought had come from inside her own head. It wasn't the sylph. And it wasn't the shadow. It was an internal voice, speaking her own language.

Mirror.

"Forget the mirror," she growled.

All her peelings of oak bark had been tossed far astray; she found only a few of the largest curls. Well, she had a task to complete and no one to interfere. Why should she go running home, bellowing about invisible beasties? Or for that matter, why should she rush to peer into her mother's dim little glass? No point in that, no point at all.

Hiking up her skirts, she continued down the path to the next oak tree, dropped her basket among its roots, and clambered up into the lower limbs. Perhaps she wasn't as careful this time about checking for old scars. Perhaps she wasn't as gentle with her knife. But she did her job as she was supposed to.

68

Hoofbeats sounded in the forest once again. Heloise, perched in the oak, turned and saw a blue hat and cloak appear through the sylvan shadows. Master Benedict had found his horse.

He rode at a brisk trot right under her tree, never once looking up, and continued to the place where she and he had spoken; there he dismounted. Heloise, up in her tree, watched him silently.

"Little girl?" he called. His voice was anxious and his eyes were very wide as he surveyed the damage to the forest all around. "Little girl, are you here? Dragons blast it! Dragons blast and eat it! I should never have left her."

Oh. Heloise smiled a small, rather silly smile. So he'd come back to rescue her. A little late, to be sure, but still . . .

She almost called out to him. But when he cupped his hands around his mouth and shouted for all the world to hear, "*Little girl?*" she decided not to. Heroic rescue notwithstanding, she didn't think he deserved an answer to that.

With another curse or two, Master Benedict climbed back on his horse and rode away. Heloise watched him go. Then she returned to her peeling. In the distance, she could still hear Master Benedict's voice calling out the occasional, "*Little girl!*"

And behind that, the sylph's scream echoed in her brain. Only now, several minutes afterwards, did it begin to take shape in her mind, forming words she could understand:

"*Night! Night! The Song of Night!*"

She would have to think about that. Later. For now, the south-end dye house still awaited her delivery.

There could be no smellier place in all the world than the south-end dye house. Except—said a tiny, reasonable part of Heloise's mind currently uninfluenced by the assault upon her nostrils—possibly the east-end, west-end, and north-end dye houses. They, in their various fetid corners of the estate, each as far removed from the central manor house as possible, were probably just as smelly. But Heloise had never traveled far enough across the sprawling acres of Canneberges to verify it. Besides, her pride rather liked the distinction of *her* dye house being the smelliest.

The big dyebath sat inside the stone-walled house itself, and from the appalling stench wafting through the door and window openings, Heloise guessed the dyers had an impressive batch in the works. Outside the dye house, many little fires burned, tended by a host of sweaty dyer-boys. Some scooped shovelfuls of wood ash; some boiled great caldrons of stale urine. A few prepped other fires beneath caldrons near piles of oak bark ready to be boiled down for the tannins. To these Heloise must add her offerings.

"Hullo, Heloise!" one dyer-boy called cheerily. His eye held a hopeful gleam, and she knew exactly what his next question would be.

"How's Evette? Is she with you today?"

"Mmmhmmmph," Heloise said, which was the best greeting she could muster while trying not to breathe. She dumped her basket of oak-bark curls onto the waiting pile. "Mmmph," she said with a quick bob and a hint of a smile.

But the dyer-boy wasn't paying attention. He looked over Heloise's head, an expression of pure joy lighting his sweat-streaked face. "Hullo, Evette!"

"Hullo, Edgard."

Hearing her sister's sweet voice, Heloise whirled about. Great Lumé's light, what was *she* doing here? With everything else already on her mind, the last thing Heloise wanted to deal with was Evette's kindhearted pretense that their scuffle of that morning never happened.

Had she *really* thrown pottage into her sister's eye?

No wonder Master Benedict called her a little girl . . .

Heloise felt her face heat up, and she couldn't meet her sister's smile. But Evette went on smiling anyway, drawing up alongside Heloise and chatting to the dyer-boy just as though he didn't stink worse than all the pig-keepers in all the kingdom rolled into one. He bore the beatific look of a man receiving angelic blessings from above. It was almost enough to transform him from the plain, smelly, red-faced young lump that he was. But not quite.

Heloise tried to sidle away.

"Oh, dearest," said Evette, deftly linking arms with her. Heloise hated when Evette called her "dearest," partly because Evette always said it with such genuine affection. "I have only to deliver these new skeins for Meme. She gave me permission to ask the dye master if they have finished skeins to carry up to the Great House. Wouldn't you like to come with me? For your birthday? I know Meme wouldn't mind."

Heloise's face burned brighter at these words. Sure, Meme wouldn't mind. Meme wouldn't *care*.

"I should head back," Heloise muttered, extricating her arm from Evette's. She ignored the hurt look in her sister's eye. "The boys at home . . . you know . . . they'll break something. Or each other."

"Grandmem's come calling, and she's watching Clotaire and Clovis," Evette persisted. "Do come, Heloise. I know you love to see the Great House."

This, Heloise could not deny. An opportunity to see Centrecœur, the massive center of all Canneberges estate (some of the wings of which were more than six centuries old) was not to be sneered at. It was a rare chance that saw Heloise on the road to Centrecœur, and she hated to pass it up now.

She didn't answer, but Evette, knowing her sister well, took her sullen lack of protest for acquiescence. "It was lovely to see you, Edgard," she said, curtsying prettily to the dyer-boy and no doubt sending him into raptures without end. "My best to your mother."

"Oh, Evette?" the dyer-boy called before they'd progressed even two steps toward the dye house. Heloise groaned. She could guess what was coming now as well. It was remarkable how predictable everything about Evette had recently become. "Evette," said the dyer-boy, "are you going to Le Sacre Night?"

What a stupid question. *Everyone* went to Le Sacre Night. That was the whole *point* of Le Sacre. Heloise rolled her eyes and huffed.

But Evette turned her sweetest smile on the poor, gasping lad. "Of course I am. With my family."

"Would—would you let me escort you this year?" the dyer-boy asked.

Heloise sensed the pricking of ears around the dye-yard. All the other boys of certain age looked up from their various tasks. If looks could kill, that yard would be full of murderers. But poor stinky Edgard didn't seem to notice. His heart, his life, his fate, hung upon Evette's next words.

"I'm sorry," said Evette, still smiling. "I'm going with my family. But thank you for asking. That was most kind."

He could not have answered, so Evette did not make him. She dipped another curtsy and, once more taking Heloise by the elbow, led her away to the dye house. Heloise cast a glance back over her shoulder, and even she felt a dart of pity for the crushed Edgard returning to his fire-tending.

"Poor Edgard," Evette murmured. "I wish he wouldn't ask. I feel wretched turning him down."

"Well, why do you talk to him at all then?" Heloise hissed, not wanting to be overheard by the other boys in the yard. "You only get his hopes up. You should try snubbing him sometime. For his own good."

Evette cast her sister a sideways glance. On anyone else, her expression would have seemed irritated or possibly superior; on Evette it was simply concerned. "Edgard is a polite, respectful young man. I couldn't be anything less than polite and respectful to him. Besides, Fleur Millerman has her heart set on his asking her, and I know Edgar will get around to it once he thinks about it properly."

Evette would never see, of course. Heloise sighed, watching as Evette called into the dye house and delivered Meme's newly spun flax thread. Evette would never see that Fleur, for all her virtues, had one glaring fault against her as far as the boys of Canneberges were concerned: She wasn't Evette.

It wasn't that Evette was the prettiest girl on the estate. Heloise could think this without malice, even as the two of them gathered reams of red-dyed thread to be delivered to the Great House. Evette wasn't particularly pretty at all, certainly no prettier than Heloise, not even as pretty as Fleur Millerman or Agnes Shearman or even Edwidge Flaxman (no relation—there were lots of Flaxmans in Canneberges).

But Evette was by far the kindest. The sturdiest. The warmest, the most sincere, the most . . . the most . . . Heloise stopped. Mental listings of her sister's virtues could go on forever.

No, there was no doubt about it. Beauty was not the chief asset sought after by the young men of Canneberges. They all wanted something more. They all wanted Evette.

Heloise glowered over these thoughts for several silent minutes as she and her sister tramped up the long road, away from the stinky dye-yard and on toward Centrecœur. But the day had turned into a fine one, and though the sun was high, the air was still cool and fresh. It lifted Heloise's spirits, enough even to make her forget for a time that she'd talked to a wind only a few hours ago and listened to a shadow sing. Those strange events seemed too bizarre to have been real. Real was happening right now, walking this road beside her sister. She could even forget that she'd thrown pottage at Evette that morning. Mostly.

"You know," said Heloise after a while, "you'll have to accept one of them."

"I'm sorry," said Evette, turning a puzzled glance upon her sister. "Accept one of what?"

"One of your doting swains," Heloise said. "You'll have to accept one of them. For Le Sacre. Someone has to escort you now. You're eighteen."

"Oh." Evette shifted the heavy basket from one arm to the other. "Well. I told Edgard I was going with my family."

"Yes, but you don't mean that!" Heloise shook her head, her wild curls bouncing. "No girl goes with her family on the night she sings and dances. You're eighteen. It would be so childish!"

"And this coming from you?"

This was the closest to sarcasm Heloise could recall hearing from

 75

Evette, ever. It stopped her in her tracks. Evette, however, did not stop, and Heloise was obliged to trot in order to catch up, her shock so great that she could think of nothing to say.

They continued in silence to the top of a certain hill. From this prospect they commanded a fine view of much of Canneberges, including the great stone structure of Centrecœur in the near distance.

It was a grand house indeed. So ancient and yet so modern at the same time. There were rooms in the house that, according to legend, were part of the original castle built by the original masters of this land. But it had been added onto and improved so often over the years that little of the old structure existed. All that remained of the castle battlements was a single tower, which rose up proudly above the rest of the house and, indeed, above all Canneberges.

Heloise caught her breath as she always did when Centrecœur came in view. Sunlight reflected off of little glass-paned windows. Real glass! There couldn't be more than a dozen houses in all the kingdom that boasted real glass windows! Surely not even the palace of the king himself could be so grand.

A wind caught at Heloise's hair and whipped through her skirts. She shuddered and couldn't help listening for a laughing voice. But there was nothing. It was a normal sort of wind, she supposed.

"Come along," said Evette, and they continued down the hill.

After a few moments, Evette spoke again. "I have something for you. For your birthday."

This was a surprise indeed. Heloise couldn't recall the last time she'd received a gift. She was fairly certain it hadn't happened since her fifth birthday. Since that one, no one bothered to celebrate. Indeed, rarely did anyone so much as acknowledge the day.

"Since you're fourteen now, I thought you might like something special," said Evette. She paused, hefted her basket onto one hip to free her opposite hand, and dug down into her apron's deep pocket. She pulled out a folded square of linen cloth and handed it to Heloise.

Heloise set down her own basket so that she might accept the gift. She spied at once the little red flowers embroidered around the hemmed edges of the linen: cranberry flowers, Evette's trademark. Most of the sewing done at the Flaxman cottage was of the mending, repairing nature, but Evette found time as she could to try more delicate stitchery. There was hardly a garment to be had in the Flaxman household that wasn't decorated with red cranberry flowers and berries and trailing vines all stitched in leftover dyed thread considered not fine enough to send up to the Great House.

Heloise unfolded the linen and discovered that she held a white day-cap. It was the sort of cap worn by young women of the estate, covering their hair. She would have to pin up her braids in order to wear it.

Briefly Heloise wondered if she should feel affronted. Pressured even. But despite herself, she felt only a sudden warm glow of gratitude. "Thank—thank you," she managed, stumbling over the words. "It's very pretty."

"Try it on," Evette suggested.

But Heloise shook her head. Her hair was too untidy, mostly escaped from the braids as it was. "I'll wear it for Le Sacre," she said. "I promise."

Satisfied, Evette continued down the path. Heloise slipped the cap into her own apron pocket, hefted her basket and followed after.

It really was a shame Evette would soon have to marry. Farm wives never found time for such dainty handwork. Evette would have to give it up entirely when it came time to have babies and manage a household of her own.

Besides, if she married a boy like Edgar, she'd never be able to keep pretty things like that clean.

I SEE HER COMING FROM MY WINDOW. I SEE HER AND HER SISTER *approaching the Great House. So sweet are they, so innocent! So unaware of that to which they even now draw near. They will learn soon enough, more's the pity!*

But not yet. Let not their gentle oblivion be spoiled too quickly. Le Sacre Night is nigh.

Would that I had the wings to fly from this high tower. Would that I had the legs to run, the arms to reach out and enfold them both, to protect them.

But I have none of these things. Not anymore. I have only my voice. And so I cry out to her, to the cursebreaker.

When she is far from me, she cannot hear me well. She draws nearer now. Perhaps I may say a little more. Perhaps she will understand.

SIX

"MISTRESS LEBLANC SAYS YOU MAY COME IN," SAID THE HOUSEMAID once she deigned to answer Evette's knock at the back scullery door. "But she says you"—with a significant nod at Heloise—"must stay out."

"Oh, come now, Alphonsine," Evette protested gently, "you know Heloise! You and I watched her together along with your own sisters not long ago. You know she will be no trouble. Or, well . . ."

Evette's honesty would one day be the death of her. Heloise glared at the housemaid, who had only a year ago been nothing more than a miller's daughter and no better than any Flaxman girl. But a certain amount of luck and cunning (not to mention a significant bounty of golden hair that caught the bailiff's eye), had landed her employment in the Great House. And Lights Above forbid she should remember the peasant girls who had been her playmates!

"Mistress Leblanc's orders," said Alphonsine, narrowing her eyes at Heloise. "You stay out."

Evette turned to Heloise, her face wrinkled with worry. To be permitted into Centrecœur at all, even just into the scullery, was a thrill unmatched in the experience of any farmer's daughter. Mistress Leblanc, the housekeeper of Centrecœur, did not readily let the "unwashed urchins" of the estate into her spotless domain. But Evette, known as a neat, clean sort of girl, was sometimes allowed to pass through the scullery and around to the weaver room where she might deliver the new skeins in person.

She hated to leave Heloise behind. There was nothing to be done, however. Heloise, if known at all, was certainly *not* known as clean, neat, or anything of that sort.

"Don't worry," Heloise said with a dismissive shrug, though inside she really wanted to give that snobby Alphonsine Millerman's nose a twist. "I'll be fine out here. Go on in as you like."

Evette looked for a moment as though she might protest. Not keen on an argument just then (particularly not one in which Evette was sure to come across as even more self-sacrificial than usual), Heloise dumped her basket in the housemaid's arms, turned on heel, and strode off through the kitchen garden. Before she'd gone more than a few paces, she heard the door shut behind her sister.

Only then did Heloise heave a sigh. Not that she'd expected to be allowed inside the Great House. Still, sometimes she couldn't help *almost*

wishing she was a bit more like Evette.

The kitchen gardens of Centrecœur were not particularly interesting. Big, certainly, and newly tilled in preparation for the coming spring planting. But not interesting. Once the castle moat had cut through here just under her feet, but it had long since been filled in on this side, though a sort of muddy trench rimmed three other sides of the house (just deep enough to be unpleasant to wade through, but not deep enough to keep out any but the most timorous marauders). This side of the house also boasted the stables, which made things convenient both for the stable boys mucking out stalls and for the gardeners seeking to better the soil.

In another few months, the garden would be thick with thriving green things fit for the tables of lords and ladies. Just now, however, at the end of winter, there wasn't much to see.

Look in the mirror.

Heloise, wandering lonely through the nearly empty beds, stopped in her tracks. There was her own voice again, deep inside her head. But she hadn't . . . Well, after all, why would she start thinking about mirrors just now?

Look in the mirror.

"There isn't any mirror. Not out here," Heloise muttered, staring down at her own dirty toes as if they were the most fascinating things she'd ever seen.

Look in the mirror.

There might be a mirror in the Great House. As rich as the Cœur family was, there were probably rooms full of mirrors! Heloise looked over her shoulder, back at the house. Of course, she wouldn't dare sneak inside. If Mistress Leblanc happened upon her, she'd be flayed alive for sure. But still . . .

Heloise stepped carefully out of the garden (neatly avoiding various pungent offerings from the stables) and approached the imposing side of the house. This eastern wing had been built in more warlike days as a defensive structure, and there were few windows to be had. One small slit offered the only opening, and Heloise knew even before she put her face up to it that she would never fit her shoulders through to slip inside. Nevertheless, she stood on tiptoe and peered into the gloom.

Her eyes took a moment to adjust. Once they did, she found herself gazing upon a bundle of leaves. Another glance, and she saw that it was a bundle of, of all things, nightshade. A whole, enormous bundle of dried nightshade. She could still see the dried purple blossoms, like so many withered corpses.

A rumbling hum alerted her, and Heloise ducked just as a tall, somber figure in a strange hat passed by inside the window. The humming went on, and Heloise thought that, were the voice even remotely melodic, it might have been humming a tune. Curious, she peered through the window again.

The somber figure in the pointed hat could have been a magician straight out of one of the old stories. But Heloise knew that couldn't be true. She watched as he wafted around the room, tall, almost skeletal, his face a solemn mask incongruous with the tune in his throat. He selected certain leaves from various dried bunches of herbs hung about the dark chamber and, even as Heloise watched, ground them to powder and mixed them in a dark tincture.

Then he reached for the very bunch of withered greens hanging just before Heloise's face, tore out a handful of crackly leaves, and added them to his mix.

He must be a doctor. The doctor who, so rumor had it, the marquis had sent to Canneberges just a few months ago. It must be he, for who but a doctor—trained in his own weird arts—would dare to handle nightshade?

"I say, is that *you*, little girl?"

A startled thrill ran up Heloise's spine, and she whirled about, nearly falling over in her haste. There before her, atop his tall horse, wearing the blue cape and the cap with damaged peacock plumes, was Master Benedict. He stared down at her, almost as startled as she was. "It is you!" he exclaimed and swung down from his horse to approach her. "You're the girl from the wood, and—"

"Hush!" Heloise whispered, indicating the window behind her with a toss of her head. Master Benedict's eyes darted to the window, confused for a moment, then suddenly filling with recognition. A shudder passed through him, as though he'd just thought of something nasty, with too many legs, crawling down his arm. He beckoned Heloise to step away from the window after him.

He was, after all, the lord's son. What else could she do? Casting a last uneasy glance behind her, Heloise did as she was bidden and approached Master Benedict and his horse. He started toward the stables, leading the horse on a loose rein. Since he seemed to expect Heloise to follow him, she fell into pace at his side.

"What are you doing here?" he demanded.

"Nothing," she said, defensive suddenly. Then, remembering that he was a marquis's son and she was a flax-farmer's daughter, she added an awkward walking-curtsy and murmured, "Master Benedict. You see, my mother's a spinner, and we brought up some skeins—"

"No, no, I mean—" Master Benedict cast a nervous glance about as though afraid of being overheard. But out here in the empty kitchen gardens, still a good many paces from the stable, there was no one about. "I mean, what about that . . . that *thing?* That voice we encountered? I rode back as soon as I caught my horse and I tried to find you and I saw the damage and I thought . . ."

His voice trailed off. Heloise, wondering if he was embarrassed again, gave him a sideways glance, expecting his face to be ripe with blushes. Instead, she saw that it had gone strangely pale. Master Benedict stood suddenly quite still, holding the reins of his horse's bridle, but limply. A single tug, and the horse would easily get free.

"Master Benedict?" Heloise said. "I, um. I'm quite all right, as you see. Not to worry at all. I don't think it was dangerous, whatever it was, and . . . and . . . Master Benedict?"

His eyes closed. He swayed where he stood. Though he was quite tall, Heloise had the sudden impression that she could knock him over with a single flick of her finger.

But the next moment he shook his head quickly, and his eyes opened and focused on her face. "I'm glad you're all right," he said. The color slowly returned to his cheeks, and he took a few breaths, blinking slowly. Heloise saw his grip tighten on his horse's reins. "Perhaps," he continued, "it's better not to speak of it. You're alive; I'm alive. No harm done."

Look in the mirror.

The thought appeared in her head with such suddenness, Heloise couldn't stop herself. Her mouth opened, and she was asking the question before she quite realized that she intended to. "Master Benedict, do you have a mirror?"

Benedict frowned and turned his head to the side, like a bird studying an interesting beetle. "A mirror? Yes, of course. Why do you ask?"

"Well, I—"

"Heloise!"

Benedict, Heloise, and the horse all turned their heads at the sound of that startled voice. All three saw Evette, the empty skein baskets in her arms, approaching with all haste across the empty garden. She, thinking her sister was bothering one of the busy grooms, called in her gentle but firm way, "Heloise dearest, do come away and let the poor man—Oh!"

Heloise saw Evette's eyes fix upon Master Benedict's cap. She too knew all about the fabled peacock feathers. Her gaze flicked from Benedict to Heloise and back again. "Oh! Good sir!" She dropped a quick curtsy, then, thinking better of it, dropped another, deeper one just to be safe.

It was possibly the first time in her life Heloise had seen her sister at a complete loss. She smiled wickedly and addressed herself to the marquis's son. "Master Benedict, meet Evette, my sister. Evette, meet the Honorable Master Benedict de Cœur."

Somewhere, sometime in the long history of the worlds, there was probably a moment in which someone had done something more brazen. But one would never have known it by the look on Evette's face.

Master Benedict, flushing royally, tipped his cap. "I'm sorry," he said, though neither he nor anyone else knew what he apologized for. "Well, good day. Good day, Miss Evette. Good day, erh, little girl."

With that, he tugged on his horse's reins and led it away to the stables, casting only one final nervous glance back.

"Heloise!" Evette exclaimed, dashing to her sister's side and dropping one of the empty skein baskets so that she could clutch Heloise's arm. "That was *the marquis's son!* Talking to *you!*"

"Oh yes," said Heloise, as though it really wasn't worth mentioning, though inside she was nearly drowning with pride. "He broke a feather in his cap. Did you notice? What a fool he looks, riding around like that with a broken feather."

"Oh, Heloise," said Evette, "I do hope you didn't *say* that to him!"

Heloise only smiled.

IN MY YOUTH I NEVER FELT THE PRESSURE OF TIME. I NEVER *understood what it was that mortals suffered, constrained as they are by moments, by years.*

But now I feel it. As I watch her walk away, across the fields, almost beyond the reach of my voice, I feel the crush of Time all around. And I wonder . . .

Is it worth it?

Is he worth it?

It is a question I have asked myself since the beginning of this endless ending. I can only pray the answer in my heart proves true.

I will continue to call to her. There is nothing else I can do until Le Sacre Night.

SEVEN

GRANDMEM SAT IN THE DOORWAY OF THE FLAXMAN COTTAGE, watching Rufus the Red strut about the chicken yard and listening to the clamor of her two young grandsons, who were attempting to make themselves taller by hanging each other upside-down by turns from the loft. Grandmem supposed there were more profitable ways they could spend their time, but she was too tired from her walk to come up with any.

Her daughter-in-law, Cerf's wife, was locked away in the spinning shed as though she hadn't a care or concern in the world besides the endless spinning of flax. But that was Berthe for you. She'd never been quite so strong in heart, limb, or mind as she needed to be. And since that day nine winters ago, well . . .

But Grandmem, other than a brief, growling judgment muttered between thin lips, had no time to concern herself with Berthe and her troubles; no more than she had time to bother with Clovis and Clotaire and their elongation attempts. She kept her eyes fixed on the path, watching for any sign of her youngest granddaughter.

Because today was the day. How well she remembered it! Today was the day, and Grandmem had to speak to Heloise. She must find out if it had come upon her yet.

"Good day, Mistress Flaxman," said a smelly young man who suddenly seemed to be standing in her sunlight, twisting a handful of limp wildflowers in his hands. "I—I hope you're well?"

Grandmem scowled up at the lad. If he wasn't Galehot Pigman's grandson, he wasn't anybody, she decided. Her scowl deepened. She'd never liked Galehot Pigman. He'd spent most of one summer, ages ago now, calling on her with wilted posies and struggling to comprehend the meaning of simple words. Like "no," for instance. Or "go away."

"Um," said the young Pigman, "is Evette around?"

Grandmem, lacking a carrot to gum, sucked on her one tooth instead. She eyed the young man until she could see she'd made him twice as nervous. Then she said, "Probably not."

There was a crash inside then a shout. A moment's silence. Then one of her grandsons whispered, *"Do you think she heard that?"* answered by his brother's hasty, *"Shhhhhhhh!"*

Grandmem leaned back against the doorpost, slowly stretching her stiff legs out before her. "You can wait inside if you like."

The young Pigman stared into the huddled silence beyond the cottage doorway. "I'll just, um . . ." And he scuttled away to wait by the cottage gate instead. Grandmem watched him go, her old eyes narrowed. For a Pigman, she decided, he was almost articulate. Too bad for him. He didn't know what was coming.

He never would know.

Grandmem listened to the clatter of something being scraped into a pile inside, followed by further sounds of some destructive sin being hidden. She watched Gy Pigman kick his heels as he sat on the gate, and saw when he was eventually joined, first by a second Pigman (Pigmen were easy to spot or, as it were, *smell* a mile away) and then by a dyer-boy (which were even easier to distinguish). Tensions swiftly heated among them as each tried to hide his own clutch of wildflowers from the other two. Grandmem half wondered if she'd have a nice little brawl to entertain her while she waited.

But before things reached an interesting crisis, Evette's neat white cap appeared on the horizon and, bobbing along beside it, the robin's-nest tangle of Heloise's curly head. The two came down the path, empty baskets swinging from their elbows, chatting the way sisters do, always just on the verge of either giggles or a spat.

Sisters. Never was such a bother as a sister. Never was such a bother or a love . . .

Both girls spotted the waiting youths at the same moment. Though she was too far away to hear it, Grandmem could see the irritable sigh as it left Heloise's body, slumping her shoulders. Evette, however, only smiled sweetly and curtsied to the lads. From that distance Grandmem couldn't tell if her smile was especially sweet for any one of them. She doubted it.

As Evette remained by the gate to visit, Heloise shouldered her way through the gathering and stomped across the cottage yard. Lights Above, what an ungainly thing she was! But then—and Grandmem smiled ruefully at the thought—had she herself been any different?

"Hullo, Grandmem," Heloise said, scarcely looking at her old grandmother even as she spoke the greeting. She peered over Grandmem's head into the cottage and saw Clovis and Clotaire sitting quietly in the pool of light coming through the back door and twisting rough flax into twine, as demure as two smut-faced angels. She wondered what they'd broken. They were only ever this quiet after working some destruction.

"Heloise," said Grandmem, reaching up and catching the girl by her wrist. "Heloise, sit with me a moment, will you?"

Heloise huffed another sigh. Her grandmother was a strange old lady and not the best conversationalist in the world. But she was her grandmother, and her grip was remarkably strong. So Heloise took a seat on the doorstep, setting her basket off to one side. From here they had a fine view of the three ardent suitors striving to impress Evette.

Heloise put her chin in her hand. "The swains are sighing," she muttered into her palm. "They all want to escort her to Le Sacre."

"Aye," said Grandmem. "They do that." She turned one eye upon the girl beside her, the other eye squinting against the sun. "But they'll forget her soon enough."

"Pffffph," said Heloise, a less than genteel sound.

"Mark me," Grandmem insisted. "They will. They'll forget all about her, as will everyone else. Just like they forgot about Cateline."

A chill swallowed up Heloise's grouchiness. She suddenly felt that the ragged person beside her was too close. She tried to slide away, but there wasn't much room on the doorstep, and her grandmother still had a hold on her wrist.

"They sighed for Cateline like that," Grandmem went on. "They came to woo her by the dozens, or so it seemed to me. I was jealous. Yes, I was. As jealous as you are now."

"I'm not jealous," Heloise growled.

"You are."

"I don't want stinky Pigmen bringing me handfuls of weeds!"

"Never said you did." And there was that one-eyed stare again. The one that was just a mite too keen for Heloise's comfort. The one that said, *We're too much alike, girl, for you to hide anything from me. I know your secrets inside and out. I know them better than you do.*

Heloise squirmed. It wasn't a nice thought, the thought that she and her crazy old grandmother were anything alike. Because . . .

Well, because Grandmem was crazy. Everblooming crazy, as the saying went.

"Cateline was much like your sister," Grandmem went on, still staring at Heloise, "save that she had a special smile for one young lad, Marcel Millerman by name. Sometimes I almost thought he might remember her, even though the rest forgot. I thought he might remember that smile. I'd watch Marcel now and then as the years went by. He'd get a look about him that made me wonder. But I never did ask him. I was afraid it might break his heart, which was already so full of unremembered sorrow."

"Grandmem," Heloise said, "I need to get to work. I have to fetch the water, and Gutrund needs—"

"There'll be no one else to remember your sister," Grandmem continued as though Heloise hadn't spoken a word. "They'll all forget her. Just as they forgot Cateline. You'll be alone with your memory."

Once more that dark chill rippled through her, strong enough that Heloise forgot her sulk, forgot her strange experiences of that morning, forgot even her mother sitting in the spinning shed, spinning away the day as though it could not end soon enough. She felt the tightness of her grandmother's fingers on her wrist, the intensity of that one old eye fixed upon her face.

But Grandmem was crazy. She always had been. Heloise's father had explained this to Heloise years ago, very carefully. Grandmem was crazy because she always talked about her sister, Cateline.

And Grandmem had never had a sister.

"It has to be you," Grandmem said, leaning in so that her carroty breath blasted in Heloise's face. "When the other one died, I knew then. I told myself, 'It's settled now. It'll be young Heloise.' But I always thought it would be you, even when *she* was alive. You were the stronger of the two. But that doesn't always mean—"

Suddenly Heloise found herself indeed much stronger than she'd been only a moment before. She stood up, wrenching herself free of her grandmother's fingers. She held herself together, very still, very controlled; it was marvelous to her just how controlled she was. If only they knew, they'd be so impressed. Everyone. Everyone would admire all this fine control with which she kept herself from slapping that old woman's ugly face.

She said, "They'll never forget Evette. They'll never forget Hélène. And they'll never remember Cateline, because there never was such a person."

With that she turned, took a few steps, realized she was not going anywhere, and turned again, this time toward the stream. She stopped again, realizing she didn't have a bucket. The bucket was in the cottage, on a peg beyond Grandmem.

She froze, her hands clenched into fists, not wanting to face her grandmother.

In an elaborate performance of crackles and groans, Grandmem stood up from the doorstep, drew herself as tall as she could, and tugged her shawl tight. "Heloise," she said, "I came to ask you one thing. I came to ask . . . have you met yourself yet?"

Heloise didn't answer. She couldn't. At the moment her ears were roaring with too much rage to comprehend the words.

"You have to meet yourself," said Grandmem. "You have to face yourself. Or you'll fail. Just like I did."

Heloise heard her grandmother's shuffling footsteps. Then she felt the claw-like hand on her shoulder.

"When they've forgotten," said Grandmem, her whiskery chin close to Heloise's ear, "come to me. I won't remember either. But I'll believe you when they don't. And I'll tell you what I can."

She let go. Heloise heard the same shuffling steps, this time moving away. The shuffling paused. Grandmem said, "Bring the mirror with you when you come."

Mirror.

With that, she left the cottage yard, shouldering between Evette's admirers on her way.

Papa and the older boys had already eaten and sat relaxing in front of the fire before Meme finally came in from the spinning shed, baby Clive asleep in his sling on her back. She glanced around the cottage, saw that Evette had already fed everyone and built up the kitchen fire to keep away the cold, and nodded her approval. She passed silently through the room to the lean-to where she and Papa slept and disappeared inside with the baby.

She didn't look at Heloise.

Heloise, involved in a game of stick-back with Clotaire and Clovis, pretended not to notice. She hadn't looked up when Meme entered the cottage door. She said not a word, but kept on smiling and even teasingly jabbed Clotaire, causing his stick tower to topple and both boys to roar at the unfairness.

But through it all, every sense of her body and being was fixed upon her mother. Her mother who never spoke to her on this particular day. On her birthday.

When Meme disappeared into the lean-to, Heloise dropped the smile from her face. Sitting back, she let the boys continue the game and pretended to watch. But she couldn't see what went on right before her eyes.

She heard Meme come back into the room after having bedded down baby Clive. She heard the swish of rough skirts as she drew a stool up alongside her husband's. She heard the clicking of bone needles as Meme began mending a tear Clement had put in his shirt while out in the fields that day.

She heard Meme say, "So, Evette, I saw young Gy Pigman leaving as I came up from the shed. A fine young lad is he. Will he be escorting you to Le Sacre?"

Heloise didn't wait to hear her sister's answer. She couldn't. She was out the door and in the dusk-filled yard before Evette had a chance to open her mouth.

Evette. Le Sacre. The fine young lads.

As if any of that mattered!

She stood a moment a few paces beyond the door, waiting in case someone called out to her, in case someone urged her to come back. She would ignore them, of course. She would storm away just as intended. But she would like them to call.

They didn't. No one noticed she was gone.

Heloise kicked the dirt with her bare toes and made her way to Gutrund's pen. She didn't have any real reason for choosing this direction. Her feet happened to take her that way, and she followed them without question. Gutrund grunted a friendly sort of grunt when Heloise leaned over the slats and rubbed the big sow behind her ear.

Still no one came after her. On her birthday.

On *their* birthday . . .

"Meme! Meme! Don't! Don't throw her away!"

A little girl screaming. Pulling at her father's arm. Pulling free and running across the field to the small hill where no one ever went. The small hill dotted with the upright wooden markers.

The small hill in which a fresh hole now yawned. Over which Meme stood and wept.

"Meme, don't throw away my sister!"

"Dragon's *teeth*." Heloise cursed so sharply that Gutrund startled, as much as a contented, well-fed pig can startle on a calm, clear evening. The sow backed away and went to lie down in her comfortable sludge on the opposite side of the pen. Heloise hardly noticed. She pounded the wood slat with her fist then leaned her forehead against it, risking splinters without care.

She wouldn't cry. She wasn't a crying sort of person.

Mirror.

Dragons blast it, was that a tear?

Sniffling loudly, Heloise swung herself up onto the top slat then over into the pen. She marched over to Gutrund, her feet squelching in the mud, and sat down beside her with another squelch. Leaning back against the big, warm, bristly body, she drew her knees up to her chest and sat there, trying not to think.

Mirror.

Trying not to remember.

Mirror.

And she whispered to herself, or possibly to the pig, or to no one at all: "It's my fault. I shouldn't have been so strong."

The wind sighed such a forlorn sigh, one could believe it was a mother's lament in the night. Heloise shuddered.

Mirror. Mirror.

Mirror!

Heloise wasn't crying anymore. She frowned at Gutrund's water trough just opposite her. Gutrund's water trough, which she had filled with fresh water from the stream but a few short hours ago.

She got up. Her rump was soaked with mud, and she couldn't begin to imagine the scolding she would get from Evette when she walked through the door. (Not from Meme. Meme wouldn't notice. Not today.) She ignored it, however, and approached the trough to grip the edge of it with both hands.

Above, the sky grew darker, filling with stars. The stars gleamed brightly, caught in the reflection of water there between her hands. It wasn't the best mirror in the world. But it was better than nothing.

Heloise leaned over.

It was too dark to see much more than an outline. A crazed silhouette of mane, a deep shadow under her brow where her eyes should be. A neck, shoulders, but no visible chin, not from that angle. Heloise gripped the trough tightly, the knuckles of both hands white.

But her reflection tilted its head. Then it lifted a hand and waved at her.

"Heloise!"

She didn't scream. She swallowed the scream with a gulp that nearly choked her. Looking up sharply, like a thief caught with his hand in the jewelry box, she saw Evette leaning over the pen slats, frowning.

"Heloise, your skirt! What are you doing out here?"

Heloise didn't answer. Her heart ramming so hard in her throat she feared it might burst through, she backed away from the trough, still saying nothing. What was she supposed to say? *I'm out here sulking because Gutrund doesn't hate me, and I think Meme does, and my reflection just waved at me.*

No. That wouldn't do. So she kept her mouth shut.

Evette sighed. It was the sort of sigh that said she knew what Heloise was thinking (which was often true, but this time definitely not—at least not completely), and she understood, sympathized even. She reached into the pen as though to take Heloise's hand.

Heloise wouldn't give it to her.

"Dearest," Evette said in that kind voice, the one that made Heloise want to spit, "she'll be better tomorrow. It's a hard day for her, you know that. But she'll be fine in the morning, she always is. You have to let her—"

"I don't have to do anything," Heloise snapped. "And I don't have to care, either!"

With that, she squished to the other side of the pen, side-stepped Gutrund, and vaulted over. Ignoring Evette's gentle protests, she returned to the cottage, slipped in through the back door, and scrambled up to the darkness of the loft where no one could see her or her muddy skirts.

She wiggled out of the soaking garments, pulled on her only spare shift, and slid beneath the rough woolen blanket on her pile of musty straw. Pulling the blanket over her head, she squeezed her eyes tight and wished, so desperately wished, that her birthday would be over.

No matter how tightly she squeezed, she still saw it. She saw the shadowy hand waving up at her from the water.

Mirror . . . .

The hours of night crept slowly by, full of mystery and equally full of sleep. All Canneberges bedded down against the cold and the darkness, waiting in silence for the distant dawn. But before the dawn could come, first there must be . . . Midnight.

Rufus the Red, roosting in his coop, sensed the Midnight first. His combed head came up, his bright eye flashed, and he bellowed a rooster's challenge so loud that it woke his entire harem, Gutrund in her pen, and all the Flaxman family in their beds.

"Something's wrong," said Papa, scrambling out from under his blankets. "A fox!"

"A fox! A fox!" The shout went up throughout the household as the boys threw back their covers and darted for the door, trouserless, long shirts flapping to their knees. Heloise and Evette, up in their loft, leapt from their straw beds and all but fell down the ladder.

"A fox! A fox!"

Like an army called to the battlefield, the Flaxmans poured into the yard. By then every hen had joined her cackling to Rufus's bellows. Gutrund grunted and squealed in her pen, and the goats screamed the most unearthly cries.

Heloise ran with Evette to Gutrund first. A fox couldn't make her squeal like that, surely! Nor could it make her circle the pen in this frantic manner, ramming her great head against the slats, digging at the mud, and bashing into her trough so that water sloshed across her bristly back.

"There's nothing!" Clement cried from the chicken coop. "All the hens are here!"

Papa stood in the middle of the yard, hefting his ax. Heloise could not see his face, only his outline, and he looked huge and dreadful in the darkness as all the animals shrieked, bellowed, bleated, and cried.

Faintly, far away, Heloise thought she heard more animal sounds rising in the night, from the next farmhouse over, perhaps. It was as though all Canneberges—all the world—were awake and screaming.

Then something whispered in her ear. "Come this way! Come and see!"

She knew that voice. It was the sylph. The invisible wind-being.

And her own voice inside her head urged, *Follow.*

Heloise turned toward the sound of the sylph, which was foolish, of course, since she already knew there would be nothing to see. But she did, in fact, see the ground spinning with dust and moonlight and remnant pieces of parchment. She felt invisible hands pulling at her skirts. "Come see! Quickly!"

Follow. Follow!

Evette was over by the chicken coop. Everyone was busy, no one was paying attention.

Follow, child!

Heloise caught up her skirts above her knees and ran, pursuing the wind and its luring voice. "This way! Come see! Come see!"

Under the wind-being's whispered influence she crossed the stream, hardly noticing her freezing feet or the icy water splashing up to her waist, then ran out into the fallow flax fields beyond.

Suddenly, she was aware of something beside her. Not right next to her—many yards to her left. She turned to look at it, but nothing was there. Nothing to be seen, that is, only a presence, a shadowy presence so big that it shook the air around it. She knew, without knowing how she knew, that it was same presence she'd felt in the Oakwood that morning. The shadow that sang to her.

Follow! Follow faster!

She ran up the hill on the far side of the field, the hill dotted with little leaning wooden markers. "Quickly, quickly!" urged the sylph. "I'll show you!"

Heloise's side split with pain, and her heart could have choked her with terror. But she put on an extra burst of speed and reached the top of the hill at the same moment as that dark presence did a few yards away. She saw a certain small mound, a certain well-remembered wooden marker, and there she stopped.

There she stared.

Before her, flooding her vision with a landscape far greater than anything her poor mortal eyes should have been able to hold, she saw Canneberges, the whole of the estate spreading out before her, as though she were a huge giantess standing above it all. She saw the great house of Centrecœur, except it wasn't Centrecœur as she had seen it that day.

It was an old castle surrounded by a high wall. Many bright lights blazed from each window, eerie as starlight, otherworldly, terrifying.

She saw someone riding out from the gate. Even at that distance she saw him vividly, a great red man on a great red horse, and she knew him at once: Rufus the Red. The real Rufus the Red, forefather of all Canneberges. He was too great, too awful, too full of his own redness to be anyone else.

And then she realized that someone stood beside her. Not the windy sylph, not the shadowy presence. Someone real and solid. She turned and gazed upon the most beautiful woman in all the worlds.

She was tall, taller than any man Heloise had ever met, even her own father. Her limbs were long and graceful, and her neck was long as well, supporting the most elegant face, a face that might have been carved from pure onyx, it was so black and so smooth, so completely without fault or marring. And her hair, the most glorious hair imaginable! An enormous lion's mane of black curls standing high about her head like a crown of thunderclouds, the only crown worthy of so beautiful a face.

Her eyes staring out across the fields toward the splendid red man— her eyes were the clearest blue of summer skies.

She raised up her bare arms, unaware perhaps or simply not caring to notice Heloise standing beside her. She reached out as though to catch all of Canneberges in her embrace, and there was such a magnificence of love in her voice when she spoke that Heloise fell to her knees.

"Beloved!"

Heloise thought, *I know that voice.*

Then the beautiful woman was running, her black hair trailing behind her. As lithe as a leaping deer, she sprang down that hillside and on across the fields as swiftly as the approaching horse could gallop.

So the two figures—the beautiful woman and Rufus the Red—closed the distance between them in what felt like mere moments to Heloise. She saw the great red man spring from his horse and catch the woman in his arms.

A roar like the tearing of a sundered heart rent across the sky. Heloise screamed in response but could not hear her own voice. She clapped her hands to her ears and fell over, pressing her head to the dirt, wishing, only wishing that the roar would cease! Oh, would it only cease before it tore her in half and left her bleeding! And then . . .

"Heloise, child, what are you doing up here?"

Heloise opened her bleary eyes. She lay with her head pillowed in her arms, out on the marker-dotted hilltop across the flax field. She had the worst crick in her neck.

"Heloise." Her father knelt before her, one hand resting on her back. "Are you hurt?"

The rising sun was a little too bright, and she twisted her face into funny knots as she squinted up at him. She could hardly make out his face, but she clearly heard the concern in his voice. "I—I'm all right, Papa," she said.

Her father looked at the marker nearest her head, recognized it, and his face clouded momentarily with a mixture of sorrow and understanding. Without a word he took Heloise's hand and helped her to unfold herself and rise from her uncomfortable sleeping position. Then he said, "We'll not tell Meme you came up here. Do you understand?"

For a blinking, groggy moment, Heloise did not. Then she too looked down at the stone, at the small mound. Her heart caught in her throat, and she nodded. "We'll not tell Meme," she whispered in response.

Not being a man for much talk or explanations, Papa merely shook his head at her, offered a few scolding words, and marched her back down the hill.

As they went, a breeze tugged at their hair and a voice whispered lightly in Heloise's ear: "Did you see? Did you see the princess?"

Heloise shivered and pretended not to hear.

I WOULD ASK YOU TO SEE THE SHADOW CROUCHING SO NEAR, *watching even as the girl's father helps her to her feet and leads her from the grave markers and across the field. I would ask you to picture it, but this would be unkind, for that shadow, or rather, the person contained within that shadow, cannot be seen by mortal eyes if he chooses not to be.*

Unlike the sylph, he is not invisible. He is far stealthier than mere invisibility. He simply—well, no. Not simply, for there is nothing simple about the art he practices. I should know. It was my own art once, and a fine art it is, studied and perfected over centuries of mortal years.

He lies there in the broad light of dawning day, no covering or shield for miles on either side, yet he blends into his surroundings, changing neither color nor form. It is as though his breath becomes one with the breath of earth beneath him. As though his skin, muscles, blood, and bones are made up of the grass, soil, water, and stone on which he crouches. You cannot see him though you stand beside him. You cannot see him until he lashes out . . . and by then it's too late even to scream.

But the one thing he cannot hide, at least from a more intuitive soul, is the magnitude of his presence. This is far more difficult to suppress.

So I do not ask you to see him. Rather, I ask you to feel him as he lies so still upon the hillside, pressed into the dirt, his chin mere inches from the ground, his eyes fixed upon that mortal girl and her father. Even as he watches them, another sight fills his eyes.

He looks upon the vision of the past. The same vision which the girl herself glimpsed, caught up as she was in the timeless sylph's arms. He sees the same woman running to the embrace of the great red mortal. Running to the arms of her beloved.

My beloved.

The shadow's lip curls into a snarl. Even as the girl and her father vanish inside their cottage, he rises, turns, and runs through the dawnlight, across the fields, around the bogs, and on up to the Oakwood.

A breeze follows in his wake, trailing bits of paper in twirls behind it. Watch them now, even as I do from my tower window.

EIGHT

THE SHADOW LOPED ACROSS THE FIELDS, AROUND THE BOGS, AND ON into the Oakwood.

The Oakwood was the biggest patch of forest in Canneberges, spanning gloom-shrouded acres. Up close it might seem large, even menacing, but from a distance anyone could see that it was not a big forest as forests go. Modest at best, really.

But within the shadows of the Oakwood, another Wood lay hidden. A much, much greater Wood. Bigger than all that can be seen from without, greater than anything mortal minds imagine.

The Wood Between the Worlds.

Into this Wood the shadow stepped, as easily as though stepping through a door. He knew all the gates leading from the Between into the Near World and back again, gates which were normally closed fast, preventing Faerie kind from passing through and preying on mortals. But once every generation or two of mortal lives, these gates would open.

He knew where each gate was to be found. He knew when they opened. He had made this journey to and from the Near World many times before.

So he crossed into the Wood Between. Entering the Timelessness of that vast realm was a relief to him. He hated the closeness of the Near World, the stink of coming death that so pervaded all. More than anything he hated the dying mortals who lived in that world, disgusting, crawling, time-bound things. He snarled at the very thought of them.

The Wood Between, sensing his hatred, drew back from him on all sides, the trees pulling away their branches and roots like ladies holding up their skirts. No one, not even the majestic spirits of the Wood, wanted to deal with a hatred like his.

The shadow came then to a place where great oaks sprang up from the soil like towering pillars. And they were pillars indeed, if one looked at them from a slightly different point of view, supporting high ceilings, lining great walls. But if the viewer's gaze shifted a fraction to the left or the right, he would see only forest.

The shadow saw it as he wished, unhindered by tricks or illusions. So he beheld a great house, part castle. It was, in fact, very like the shape and spirit of Centrecœur itself save that it was much larger and sometimes made up of trees and vines and moss rather than rock and stone and mortar. Its doors opened to the shadow, and he slipped inside

116

to disappear among deeper shadows still. He liked shadows. They always felt friendly to him, welcoming even. As soon as he stood among them, he no longer bothered to conceal himself but walked in sinuous, silent grace.

"Have you found her?" someone asked from the darkness.

"Of course," he replied in a voice of pure indigo.

"He's found her! He's found her!" Many voices whispered to each other on all sides. "The time has come, and he's found her again!"

Fools, he thought even as he mounted a great wide stair and hastened up to the long gallery above. What did they think would happen? Only the same that happened every time and would go on happening for all the ages of the mortal world.

But they were frightened by the Law. They did not know how to bend the Law to their own designs; that was a gift of queens, kings, and princes.

The shadow passed through the gallery, made another turn or two (it hardly mattered, for the house in which he walked rarely kept to the same shape, and one could only navigate its corridors if one had complete mastery over its doings), and came at last to a final set of doors. These were very tall indeed, taller than five men standing upon each other's shoulders. They were made of ebony, polished to shine, and carved in rich patterns of Moon and Stars and the beings of Night. No mortal hand could have rendered such carvings. No mortal hand would dare try.

The shadow rose up then and took a different form, standing on two legs now rather than four heavy paws. He shook himself out, adjusting to the new shape of his limbs, and pulled back his wild mane of black hair into a neat, thick queue of many braids. Then he pushed wide the two doors and passed through.

The floor was made of night sky. Unless it was made of polished onyx. It would be difficult to discern which. Either way, his feet made no sound as he strode across it. Curtains like the thick billowing of clouds moved gently in the enormous windows which gazed out upon a vista of more night. Overhead, on a ceiling so high that one could not guess at its dimensions, stars moved in patterns of dance and darkness.

There was little light, but he required little; his bright blue eyes held light enough in themselves. A silver brazier burned upon a stand at the far end of the room. The coals in its bowl were also silver, and their fire glowed white. They looked like the hearts of stars, though surely this could not have been possible. Perhaps they were only the dreams of stars. Perhaps they were diamonds.

Beside the brazier Mother sat upon her throne.

The throne was carved of a single block of stone, but over its surface burned fire as white as that glowing in the brazier. The flames never harmed Mother. She was herself like one stone-carved, her limbs chiseled and polished to a gleaming perfection impervious to all flames, be they enchanted or otherwise.

There was no softness to her, not like there had been in the ancient days. Back then she had boasted a bounty of glorious hair, but this was gone now, shorn away by her own hand wielding her own knife. And she vowed never to let it grow again until her victory was complete. So she was bald, and in her baldness she was more beautiful and more terrible than ever before.

He made deep reverence before her throne. "Mother," he said, "I have done your bidding. I have ventured once more into the Near World."

"Did you find her?" Mother asked. She did not open her eyes but sat in perfect stillness. Only the flames about her lips flickered, betraying the merest hint of movement. "Did you find the cursebreaker?"

"I found her, Mother," he said. "She is nothing but a child. She has only just met herself and is as yet unfamiliar with the power in her blood. She will not know what to do when the time comes. As ever, our gathering may proceed without fear."

"Well done, my son," said Mother. "Go then and take with you those whom you need. Return to the Near World and bring back our tithe."

Son bowed again. Then he turned and leapt across the room, transforming to his wilder shape within three strides. He vanished out the far doors, and soon his roaring summons echoed deep within the great dark house.

Mother sat a while longer in her perfect tranquility of darkness. Then, slowly, she raised her hands and clapped so that the white flames shot up from between them.

Out of the shadows on all sides of the room, figures appeared. Pale, shining figures of white, clad in flowing garments. They were maidens, all of the same age, and their faces were the same as well, though a keen observer may have discerned a few small variations of feature. However it was, their expressions mirrored one another: empty save for a deep, solemn compulsion.

Mother clapped again, a single burst of sound and fire.

The eleven dancers came together in a circle on the floor of sky before the throne. They joined hands, but any observer could sense that one was missing, that a twelfth figure should stand in the center of that circle.

Unseen, an instrument began to play one long, high, strange note, like a line of deeper darkness through the gloom. The line wavered, twisted, dipped, then soared even higher. Soon it was joined by the beating drums.

One of the maidens began to sing:

"Cianenso

Nive nur norum."

One at a time, as the song continued, each maiden added her voice. And as each new voice joined, so they began to move, not in time to the beating drums but in weird patterns that worked first against and then with the beat, their feet stamping, their arms waving, the soft wafting of their garments twirling around them.

Through it all, Mother sat upon her throne, her face turned to the dancers, her eyes closed. Not once did she look upon the figures performing before her with such strange grace. The lines of her face seemed to deepen like great cracks running through bedrock.

Suddenly her hand shot out. Her fingers, flame-wreathed, closed upon nothing. And she dragged it toward her face.

The sylph shrieked in surprise, its voice lost in the wild, rising music. Mother clutched the wind in her fist and squeezed. "I have honored the Law," she said. "These many generations I have honored the Law of Night."

The sylph writhed. It twisted. It felt itself being crushed, though this was impossible. It shrieked again in an agony of terror that would have broken the heart of any who listened.

No one heard but Mother, whose heart had broken long ago.

"Tell your Dame," she said, "the statutes of our Law are satisfied. She has no business with me." With these words, she opened her hand. The sylph, still screaming, whipped away from her throne, threaded through the whirling dancers, and sped from that place with all the haste of a murderous gale.

Mother placed her hands on the arms of her throne and continued to listen to the dance and never once open her eyes.

SHE CANNOT HEAR ME. IT IS MY OWN FAULT. I PUSHED TOO HARD, *depleted my strength trying to help her, trying to show her that which came before. Though I ask you, how could I resist such an opportunity? How could I resist the distant prospect provided by the sylph, offering the girl a glimpse of the truth? There was always a chance that she might understand. That she might see the story as a whole, not as a part.*

But it was too much for her mortal mind. I do not know, as I sit here at my window, if she even remembers it. For mortals are cleverer than we like to think, and they fortify their minds against that which they do not want to consider. And it is such a big, big tale for such a small, small person!

She cannot hear me. I sent my voice too far that night, and now I have little left. I must wait until Le Sacre Night.

NINE

THREE DAYS PASSED, AND HELOISE MADE ABSOLUTELY CERTAIN NOT to see her reflection anywhere. Nor did she go outside after dark unless she could drag one of her brothers along. Nor did she go up to the Oakwood alone. She made fine excuses or ducked away before anyone could ask her to.

"I'm worried about her, Meme," Evette said on the second day, while she and her mother were out in the spinning shed, spreading flax and combing out the strands in preparation for spinning. "I've never known her to be so quiet. I think she might have had a fright that night when the . . . the fox got into the yard."

Everyone insisted it must have been a fox. No one liked to imagine what else could have caused such an uproar. The serfs of Canneberges weren't an imaginative lot in any case.

Meme shrugged off Evette's concerns. "Perhaps she's finally growing up," she suggested. "Perhaps she's acquired a touch of maturity. It's about time, is all I can say."

Baby Clive began to cry just then, and Meme was busy for a few moments. By the time she returned, all thought of Heloise was far from her mind, and she asked her eldest daughter, "So, child, have you chosen who will escort you to Le Sacre tomorrow night? I saw young Briant Pigman stopped by yesterday. Didn't he take a position with the Guard at the Great House? An escort in uniform would be a fine thing, though I suppose he'll be on duty."

Evette sighed and let the topic of her sister drop, though she certainly didn't forget.

Now it was late afternoon, heading on toward evening: the evening of Le Sacre. The two sisters were up in their loft, Heloise sitting with unaccustomed quietude while Evette tugged and pulled at her thick mass of hair, taming it into its two fat braids. Afraid of what the answer would be, Evette gently asked, "Shall I pin it up, Heloise?"

Much to her surprise, Heloise grunted and nodded. It wasn't perhaps the most gracious response, but it was the first time this suggestion had received anything like an acquiescence. Evette, scarcely believing her ears, carefully wound the two braids on top of her sister's head and secured them with a few wooden pins. It would be a miracle if they stayed up all night, but it was a start. "Will you wear your new cap?" she asked.

Again Heloise grunted. She slipped a hand into her pocket and pulled out the folded linen cap with its border of cranberry blossoms. Evette arranged it over the braids, tying the strings in a limp bow under Heloise's chin. She put an extra knot in the bow. "There," she said, stepping back and smiling at her handiwork. "Don't you ever look a young lady now? I'd hardly know you!"

Heloise blushed and looked down at her hands. All that heavy hair piled up on her head was going to give her a headache, she could already tell; and the bow of her cap would never hold it all, extra knot notwithstanding. But if she moved very carefully, holding her head very still, it might last an hour or so.

"Do you want to see in the glass?" Evette asked, moving toward the cedar box tucked away in the far corner of their loft.

"No!" Heloise said hastily. She drew a breath and tried to assume a more demure tone of voice befitting her new mature appearance. "No, that's all right. I'm sure it looks fine."

Evette frowned then nodded. "It does. You look very nice."

And very nice was as good as she was going to look. Especially since her good dress was still stained with pig-pen mud and she was wearing an older one several inches too short at the hem and several inches too tight at the waist. Very nice was quite an achievement under such circumstances.

Papa called from below that they were going to be late, and the two girls hastened down the ladder to join their family out in the yard. The

Flaxmans were not well-off enough to afford a cart of their own, so they must walk the long miles between their farm and Centrecœur—for Le Sacre Night was always celebrated on the square lawn enclosed by the courtyard of the Great House itself.

Meme wore shoes. She had only ever owned one pair of real shoes, and these were too tight. She saved them to wear every year to Le Sacre, which meant she spent the whole of the next day groaning in pain at every step. But she would never dream of going either barefoot or in sandals, and she only wished her children owned real shoes themselves, too-tight or otherwise.

"Evette," she said, shifting baby Clive in his sling on her back. "Where is your escort?" She looked around as though expecting to see a farm boy or pig-keeper lad appear out of thin air.

"I told you yesterday, Meme," Evette said, bending to fix the drawstrings of Clotaire's sagging shirt and not looking her mother's way. "I'm going with all of you tonight. I have no escort."

Meme stared, mouth open. Then she burst out, "Nonsense! What can you possibly mean by that? You're eighteen! You *must* have an escort to Le Sacre this year of all years! What will people say if you show up without a young man?"

Evette continued to work on Clotaire's shirt as though it were suddenly the most fascinating task to which she had ever turned her hand. Clotaire gulped and cast about for help from his brothers, all of whom stayed well out of reach for fear Evette's determinedly ministering hand might catch one of them next. Evette smiled sweetly at Clotaire and switched from tying his shirt to rubbing dirt from his face with her finger.

"Evette!" her mother persisted.

"I don't care what people say," Evette replied softly. She straightened, taking Clotaire's hand in hers with such a death grip that he would have struggled to get free had he dared. "I'm going with my family."

Meme's mouth opened and closed several times, and everyone could see that she was working her way up to the great mother of all protests. Thank the Lights Above, Papa interceded; laying his arm across her shoulder, he drew her away beside him. "Come on," he said, and set out across the yard. "If we don't leave now, we'll never get there in time."

"But it's not decent! A girl of her age!" Meme objected even as she followed along. Heloise could not hear their father's rumbling reply, but it didn't seem to have much effect. She and her siblings fell into step behind their parents but kept a good many yards back so as to overhear as little of their argument as possible. Evette maintained her stranglehold on Clotaire's hand.

Heloise, walking a few paces behind her sister, frowned more deeply than usual. An insistent thought was working its way from the back of her mind to the forefront. For a moment she feared it might be thinking a thought she herself had not put there, as she had experienced three days before. She tried to ignore it, to shake it away.

But suddenly there it was, clear in her head: *I wonder what Evette wants for her life?*

Heloise paused. She had never considered this idea before, not once. Caught up as she was in her own angers and irritations, she had never stopped to wonder if Evette—perfect, sweet-tempered, composed Evette—might not be entirely happy with her lot, if she might not *want* to always be perfect, sweet-tempered, and composed. If she might not *want* to always do things as things are done.

If she might not want to marry any of the farm boys, pig-keepers, and dyer-lads who came courting her with posies and pleadings.

Heloise found that one of her hands had reached unconsciously to the edge of her cap to feel the flax-thread cranberry blossoms embroidered there. On an impulse, she untied the string and pulled the cap from her head so that she could study the flowers more closely. They really were quite well done, even though Evette was never permitted to use the finer thread-spinnings, only the rough stuff left over that the Great House did not want. And her needles were awkward, made of shaped and shaved bone.

Nevertheless, she embroidered with great care, working the curled petals in lovely detail. If allowed to work with good threads and good needles, she might indeed become a talented needlewoman, her skills far beyond those required of a farmwife.

"Heloise," said Evette in a voice that was almost sharp, or at least as sharp as Evette's voice ever got. "Your cap!"

Clotaire, released from his big sister's grip, gave a great gasp of relief and ran on ahead with his brothers. Evette, meanwhile, took the cap from Heloise's hands and placed it back on her head. "Your braids are already coming undone," she sighed. "I should have used more pins."

"There weren't any more," said Heloise.

"We'll get Claude to make us some then." Her sister set to rights, Evette looped her arm through Heloise's, and they continued on their way together, following their parents. Meme had lapsed into an angry silence and was pointedly *not looking* around at her oldest daughter.

"Evette . . ." said Heloise slowly. Her voice trembled, and she realized that she was almost afraid to ask the question on the tip of her tongue. She didn't know if she wanted to learn the answer, because she suspected that whatever Evette said in response would suddenly shift her out of the shape Heloise had always allowed for her in her mind. She would no longer be Evette as Heloise had always known Evette. What she would be, Heloise could not guess.

The unknown was a frightening prospect. But she couldn't *not* ask now that she'd come this far.

"Evette, if you could do anything at all in the world, what would you do?"

Evette laughed. Only one who knew her well would sense the tension behind that laugh. Heloise almost missed it, for she didn't know her sister as well as she thought. "What sort of a question is that? I can't do anything in the world. I can only do what I do."

"But *if* you could," Heloise persisted. "If you could be a . . . a . . . a great lady, for instance. Or a queen."

"That's mad," said Evette.

"It's just a game."

"We're too old for such games."

Heloise made no answer to this. She stared down at her bare, cold feet trudging along down the dirt track. Maybe it was just as well. Just as well to let Evette remain the shape she'd always been in Heloise's head.

But then Evette said, "I would make tapestries."

"What?" Heloise glanced up at her sister, who wasn't looking at her but gazed out across the eastern flax fields, away from the setting sun.

"I would make tapestries. Like the great ladies of the great houses make. Tapestries telling of our times and times of the past. Histories forever set down in needle and thread. Imagine! Imagine being a part of a work that will last through the ages, letting people a hundred years from now know who we are and what we did, and what important events transpired in our time!"

Evette sighed. There was a look in her eye, a look Heloise didn't quite understand. A look that saw beyond the flax farm, beyond even the great boundaries of Canneberges. It was not the sort of look one ever saw in the face of a peasant girl. How unnatural it seemed to Heloise, as unnatural in that moment as talking winds and singing shadows.

"I would like that," Evette finished, her voice low and tremulous. "I would like to be part of a work such as that, a work of the ages. If I could do anything."

They said no more, neither questions nor answers. But before they came in sight of Centrecœur's single tower, Heloise slipped her hand into Evette's and gave it a quick squeeze. Embarrassed immediately thereafter, she let go and fell several paces behind her sister, her head bowed to hide any thoughts that might be too apparent on her face.

TEN

LE SACRE NIGHT WAS THE MOST IMPORTANT NIGHT OF THE YEAR. THE night when every man and woman and child, be they serf or nobly born, must come together to make the great petition: the plea to Winter, the prayer to Spring. O Winter! Will you relax your hold upon the earth? O Spring! Will you gently rise in glorious rebirth?

This appeal rang in the hearts of all who passed over the drawbridge into the courtyard of Centrecœur to assemble before the oncoming dusk. Well, in most of their hearts anyway.

Heloise couldn't honestly say there were any prayers in the whole of her—heart, head, or stomach. Even the newly sprung ideas concerning her sister were crushed away as she and her family stepped onto the drawbridge, crossed the soggy ditch that had once been a proud moat, and entered the heart of Centrecœur. On the green lawn the serfs of

Canneberges gathered, waiting, surrounded by the majesty of the Great House which, rumor had it, boasted more than seventy rooms and twenty chimneys. More impressive still were the many glass-paned windows.

Heloise stared up at those windows, dark and empty, leading to dark and empty rooms, for everyone came out on the lawn that evening, even the household staff. No one remained inside to look through those windows upon events transpiring below.

Yet Heloise couldn't help the strange feeling in her gut, the feeling that someone—many someones—watched her.

With a shudder she slid between her two older brothers, Claude and Clement, who were broad enough to provide a sort of shield around her. From this barricade she gazed out upon the crowds, nodding and offering weak smiles if she inadvertently caught the eye of someone she knew. Evette was soon surrounded, both by young men (whose pride still smarted at her rejections) and by young women (who would happily catch the eyes of those rejected young men).

But a break in the crowd offered Heloise a momentary glimpse of someone far more interesting.

Tradition would have it that the Marquis and Marquise de Centrecœur must sit up all night to observe Le Sacre, doing their solemn part to help usher in the Spring. But the marquis was rarely home these days; he spent most of his time at other estates or at the king's court. And many months had passed since Madame the Marquise was last in Canneberges; she preferred to live with her own people at Bellamy House on the other side of the kingdom.

In fact, it had been so long since any of the lord's family had graced Le Sacre Night that Heloise couldn't remember one instance. But tonight, through that break in the throng, she saw a great chair (not a throne, since the Cœurs weren't royal, but throne-like enough to Heloise's eye) out on the edge of the green lawn. There sat Master Benedict, wrapped in a thick jacket and a thicker cloak.

At the same moment Heloise spotted him, Master Benedict lifted his gaze to meet hers. At first she did not think he recognized her. He looked right at her, but with an absolute blankness about his eyes that revealed no comprehension. What a vapid dullard! Heloise scowled at him.

Benedict blinked. His forehead wrinkled. Then a light dawned on the horizon of his brow. He sat up straighter, opened his mouth, and raised one hand.

Heloise ducked behind Clement and allowed herself to be lost in the crowd. She couldn't help it. The scowl was gone and she was smiling. Just a little, a *very* little smile. A very *foolish* little smile, and she knew it.

He'd recognized her! Even in her cap. Her heavy braids tugged painfully at her scalp, and she felt the string under her chin ready to give way. She didn't care. She wondered . . . did she look like such a *little girl* to him now?

There was no time to pursue this interesting speculation, however. The shawm sounded, its voice rising above all others in a long, mournful note. Just one note—the music of Le Sacre was yet to begin. But it was the summoning, and all must hasten now to their places.

Heloise felt a knot form in the pit of her stomach. She heard young women gasping and talking rapidly as they grabbed each other's hands and ran. All of the maidens newly turned eighteen in the last year, five altogether including Evette, hastened away from the rest of the crowd and stood along one end of the lawn.

There was no need for rehearsal. All knew their places on the night of Le Sacre. They knew this even as they knew when to sow, when to harvest, when to leave the field fallow. They knew like the geese on the lakes knew when to fly south and when to return. Le Sacre was the very heart of Centrecœur, the heart of Canneberges.

Heloise joined the other women and children on the opposite end of the lawn. Her two older brothers had gone to stand with other boys of their age holding torches to light the lawn. But Clovis and Clotaire waved her over, so she took a seat beside them to wait and to watch. Until this year Evette had always sat beside her. But Evette would now play her part, the most important part of the whole night.

Heloise felt her palms turn sweaty with nerves. She could still see Evette; there was just enough sunlight on the horizon. And Evette was as calm, as tranquil as ever, smiling sweetly at something the girl beside her whispered in her ear. She felt no concern whatsoever about her upcoming role—perhaps because across the way she had Heloise dying a thousand deaths for her.

Oh, great Lights Above! If she was this nervous for Evette, what would she ever do when in four years it was her turn to stand across the field? Her turn to answer the call of the shawm?

Clotaire reached a sneaky hand up and pulled at the string of her cap. Viper-fast, Heloise smacked his hand away, and he giggled, pleased with himself, and wrapped both arms around his upraised knees. Heloise started to retie her cap . . .

The sun set.

The night rose up.

And in that very moment of darkness spreading across the sky, the shawm began to play. One long, long, long note. A note of sorrow. Of cold and of binding. A note of Winter's icy hold.

The note dipped, twirling like a wind down from the mountains, like a gale blown up from the sea. It returned to the first note, held it again. Then once more it dipped and whirled. Other instruments joined their voices to its song: the sighing pipes, the offsetting beat of tabors, the gut-churning groan of ceterone and bandora.

Over all, the shawm danced its own tune, waxing more extravagant, flinging out wild notes to the sky. Just as it reached its highest, most fevered pitch—

Boom!

The copper timpani shuddered through the night, down deep into Heloise's soul. She cringed and shut her eyes, though there was nothing yet to see and she could not shut her ears. Even had she stuffed wax and rags deep into each ear, the voice of that timpani would resound through her bones.

Boom! Boom-boom!

The reverberations hung in the air long after the blows were struck. Then silence.

Heloise dared to open one eye. She saw the five maidens of proper age—just on the verge of marriage but maidens still—step into the center of the lawn, their arms outstretched, each hand touching the shoulder of another. They moved with slow steps never practiced but observed each year from the sidelines until known by heart.

It was impossible to misstep at Le Sacre. This was all part of the mystery and magic of that night.

The shawm began to play a variation on its original tune. The girls stepped in time and then out of time, forming a small circle as they moved. In a pattern of steps Heloise tried but failed to understand, she saw one girl separated from the next. This was done without forethought—this was the part of Le Sacre known as *the choice*.

Once the choice was made, the Chosen One stood in the center of the lawn. The other four girls backed away, leaving her standing there, head bowed, arms at her sides.

It wasn't Evette. It was Fleur Millerman, of all people. Heloise observed this with some surprise. For some reason she had always assumed her sister would be Chosen to begin the song. But no. Though Evette would have her turn to dance and sing, it was Fleur who, when the shawm beckoned, raised her voice to the deepening night and sang the familiar lines:

"Cianenso

Nive nur norum.

Nive noar-ciu, lysa-ciu."

No strange new words filled Heloise's head. Only the same incomprehensible language she had heard on this night every year of her life. Fleur's voice quavered and dipped out of tune on those soaring high notes of the third line. Heloise smiled, pleased that she wasn't the only one who couldn't quite sing Le Sacre.

But the life and spirit of the music moved beyond the abilities of the singer.

When Fleur began the next verse, her voice was nearly lost in the growling roar of Canneberges men suddenly throwing their voices into the song.

"Nivee mher

Nivien nur jurar

Nou iran-an."

With another *boom!* from the timpani, twenty men stepped into the field and began to dance, forming three circles, the middle circle around

Fleur. In each hand the men carried long canes; sometimes they clashed these together as they danced, and sometimes they smashed them on the ground. In the center circle, Fleur danced. Her steps did not match those of the men, and her movements went against the beat of the drums, following instead the pulsing call of the shawm.

Heloise shuddered as she watched and as the music of Le Sacre surrounded her, the solemn darkness working its way into frenzied darkness. This was an important dance. Without it, would Winter ever go? Would Spring ever come?

Fleur began to tire, more quickly perhaps than she should have. It did not matter. One of the other girls, seeing her footsteps begin to flag, slipped through the clashing, violent dance of the men and into that center circle. She took Fleur's hands, whirled about with her through one progression of steps, then Fleur ducked away, back to the edge of the lawn where there was water and food, where she could rest herself for a while. The second girl took her place and danced alone in the middle of the lawn.

All this Heloise beheld by the glow of the surrounding torchlight. Every year she had watched it, and every year it was the same. Strange, sad, beautiful, dangerous . . . and always with that sense of violence she never understood.

It seemed to her as she sat now upon the edge of the lawn—with the memory of the shadow's voice tugging at her consciousness down in that corner where she'd shoved it, hoping to forget it forever—that she understood something as never before. She saw the second girl dancing in the circle, her feet pounding out the steps, her hands waving, her body contorting.

Heloise thought, *She is meant to dance all night.*

But that was impossible. No one could dance this wild dance all night long. As each maiden tired, a new one hastened to her relief. To dance Le Sacre all night through would be . . . it would be suicide!

It would be a sacrifice.

The sick feeling in Heloise's gut redoubled. She understood. She understood now what this dance meant, what it symbolized. She didn't know if anyone else in Canneberges knew, but it made no difference. She knew. Perhaps others knew as well, and they simply didn't care. After all, it was only a symbol. They didn't really sacrifice anyone. They didn't kill the girls.

The shadows of the dancing men clashing their canes together seemed to take on life of their own, moving in wild gyrations between the pools of torchlight. The second maiden began to tire now. Heloise strained her eyes to see who the third girl would be, who it was that even now prepared to duck into that circle.

But instead she saw . . . No, she couldn't be seeing that. Not that. Anything but that. The shadows were merely those cast by the dancing men. They weren't . . . they weren't *alive*. They couldn't be.

Evette stepped into the circle. She took the hands of the other girl, and they danced around together. Then the other girl, gasping hard to catch her breath, slipped out of the circle and left Evette alone.

Heloise felt her brothers on either side of her tugging her skirts. She realized vaguely that she had risen to her feet. Indeed, she was taking a step. "Heloise!" Clotaire protested in a hissing whisper.

The shawm soared. The timpani roared.

Evette danced in the center of the lawn, in the center of the night. In the center of the turning between Winter and Spring, the center of sacrifice.

Around her the rings of movement whirled. The men. Their shadows.

"Evette," Heloise whispered, her voice lost in the shawm's wail.

Around Evette, moving in exact mirror-image of her movements, were eleven other figures, all within the center circle. They wore white— they *were* white. The opposite of shadows, they were nothing but an impression of whiteness and motion.

Heloise squeezed her eyes shut and rubbed. She must be sick. She must be dizzy. She must be seeing things.

She opened her eyes, and the white figures were solid. All young women. All like Evette. As one they moved in perfect unison with her sister, in faultless, enslaved obedience to the commanding music played.

The song swelled. Heloise felt it grow far greater, far more impassioned than it had ever been before. It surrounded her even as those shadows and those phantoms surrounded Evette.

"Heloise!" her brothers cried.

She didn't hear them. She was running. Out from among the women and the children she sped. Two tall lads bearing torches blocked her way, and she ducked between them, leaping into the ring of light.

The dancing men, intent upon their performance, did not see her. But their shadows turned. She felt the eyes of those shadows fixed upon her. Above the music, the shawm, the pipes, the tabors, she heard the shadows laughing.

A crash of canes in her ear. How close she came to being struck! She didn't care. She fell forward to avoid the whirling of the Canneberges men, darting through the center of the first circle. The gathered crowd, seeing her, began to murmur, and the musicians, for the first time anyone could recall, faltered in their playing. But the music went on without the musicians. It didn't need them, mortals that they were.

Heloise burst from the first ring and made for the center. The white phantoms were moving now, not in time with Evette but faster by far, so fast that no mortal feet could keep pace with them. Evette, unaware, continued to dance.

For the first time Heloise saw the sorrow in her face. The deeply scarring sorrow which she had never bothered to notice before.

The sorrow of a sacrifice.

"*Evette!*" she cried.

Her sister stumbled. She caught herself, not quite falling. She turned and saw Heloise burst through the center circle, running toward her, hands outstretched. "Heloise?" Evette gasped, horrified.

Suddenly she saw. She saw all that Heloise saw and more besides. She screamed.

Heloise flung herself forward, hands grasping for her sister. She caught hold of Evette's shoulder, and Evette caught hold of her head.

But then the shadows leapt within the circle and swarmed over all, obliterating the torchlight, obliterating the whiteness of the phantoms. Heloise opened her mouth, shouting in rage and terror, and felt the darkness swarm down her throat and wrap around her heart. She tightened her grip on her sister.

Then she opened her eyes and found herself lying upon the foot-trampled lawn, surrounded by a crowd of confused and angry faces.

"Heloise?" It was her father's voice floating to her from far away. It sounded furious. Distant, but furious. "Heloise, what, by Lumé's light, are you doing?"

Heloise coughed. She pushed herself upright even as her father stepped out of his part of the dance and knelt beside her. She felt paternal wrath radiating from his every movement. She didn't care.

"Evette!" she cried. "Where is Evette?"

"You're not supposed to be here!" her father growled. "You're not old enough yet for Le Sacre! Get back to your mother and leave the maidens to finish what they started."

Heloise found she was on her feet again, pushed from behind. Her head spun, her braids, having lost their pins, fell about her shoulders.

The eyes of watching Canneberges were fixed upon her—this wild-haired girl without even a cap on her head, her hair flying madly about her face. This barmy child who dared to interrupt Le Sacre, the sacred dance!

She thought she might curl up and die. But no. No, she couldn't do that. She must find—

"Papa!" she cried, whirling around and grasping her father by the hand. "Papa, where's Evette? Where did she go? They took her! They took her, Papa! We've got to find her!"

Her father glared at her. "What in Lumé's name are you talking about? Who is Evette?"

LET US LOOK AWAY. LET US LEAVE THE CHILD GASPING AND SHOUTING *and making a fool of herself. It is an embarrassing scene, and I do not like to observe it.*

For now I will send my gaze across the fields and bogs. I will look beyond into the Oakwood and, in memory if not in fact, hasten along its paths, on to the much greater Wood beyond this world. I will catch hold of a wind and follow where it flees through shadows, skirting the boundaries of night, pursuing paths so winding, so complex that they would be an impenetrable labyrinth to any mortal hero who fell upon them.

I will follow the sylph with my long gaze, and I will not be lost. Nor will it, for its purpose is fixed firmly in the center of its breezy being, drawing it swiftly and surely onward . . .

Until at last it reaches the Haven deep in the heart of the Wood Between. There the Dame dwells as she has for centuries now—though this is not so great a span of time to immortal thinking, and she still often feels a veritable newcomer. Nevertheless, she has made a place for herself, and she is known by many names and performs many roles.

ELEVEN

THE DAME OF THE HAVEN SAT AT HER HIGH DESK, HER SLIPPERED FEET
not quite reaching the ground, her back hunched as she pored over the
parchment before her. She was making a copy; before her lay some tale
of some distant kingdom, scribbled down in a hasty, unskilled hand, and
she struggled with the language in which it was written.

But slowly the document gave up its secrets to her, and as it did she
wrote them down in a much neater hand in a much clearer language. She
wrote in the language of Faerie. She was quite possibly the only person in
all the worlds—Near, Far, or Between—who remembered how.

Once upon a time, the Dame had been mortal. But that was several
centuries ago now, and she had lived in the Between for so long that her
mortality seemed to her like something from a distant dream. A dream
she must take care never to forget for fear of losing her heart and soul

entirely, but a dream nonetheless.

She worked in her library. And such a library it was, beyond all compare! For, like all the Between, it was made up of several worlds at the same time, and everything altered depending upon the viewer's immediate perspective. One moment it would seem a great, towering forest of gold-tipped pine and silver-boughed birch. The next, it was a chamber of magnificent proportions supported by tall carved pillars, with a polished floor of tiny, shining, mural stones depicting scenes fantastic, grotesque, and beautiful by turns.

But it was almost impossible to notice these strange wonders, for to step into her library is to be immediately overwhelmed by the sight of all those books. All those scrolls. All those carved tablets. Tucked away in the branches and hollow places of the tall trees, lining bookshelves, in many places piled up on the floor or leaning against the pillars. Most of them were written in the Dame's own hand. (She'd been busy these last few centuries.) Others had been brought to her from far-off places and worlds unimaginable, by people more unimaginable still.

The library was quiet, as a library should be. Now and then a gentle wind—which may or may not be living—would murmur through the branches, stir the pages, move through the Dame's long black hair then away again; and she was still at her task, a stern line between her brows as she struggled with the strange language.

Suddenly small voices exploded all around her, up in the trees and down the passages and corridors of the Haven. At first they were so tiny, she paid no attention. The beings who lived with her in the Haven were chattery by nature, and most of the time their chatter was so inane that she must either laugh or groan or send them from the library. She'd sent them away only moments ago, but they weren't an altogether obedient lot and were invisible besides. Thus many of them had simply crept between the pages of books or into the cavernous rolls of the larger scrolls and hidden there until the Dame was caught up in her work and forgot them.

They all began to chatter now, both those within the library and those without. Ten thousand little voices saying: *Look what's come! Look what's come! Look what's come to see us!*

The Dame pretended not to hear. But soon enough a dozen or more tiny hands plucked at her sleeve, and some more daring pulled at her hair and the long scarf that covered it. *See! See! See what's come!* they said in their many voices.

"I told you to go away and let me work," the Dame snapped, shaking a hand as though to wave away a swarm of gnats. But the little ones grabbed at her fingers and laughed. They were invisible, but now and then, when they were excited, their souls gleamed in many-colored lights. They glowed now so that her hand looked as if it were covered in its own miniature Aurora Borealis.

See what's coming! they cried.

The trees up above groaned, their branches moving with sudden violence, and showered leaves down in twirling storm upon the Dame's head. Startled, she leapt from her stool—then darted back just in time to place a few handy stones over her work before it, too, was strewn across the library floor. She stepped back from the desk, her hands, still covered in little gleaming spirits, clenched into fists.

"Who is there?" she demanded with no fear in her voice. Here in her library she was strong, and few could enter without her say-so.

"Please, please!" cried a voice of wind and storm. "Please, I bring a message for you, Dame of the Haven!"

She recognized the voice of a certain sylph. (She may have been the only person in all creation who could tell one sylph from the next. The sylphs themselves cannot.) "Come down to me," she called, and raised her hands.

The sylph, invited in, darted through what was, momentarily at least, an open window. It leapt into her arms like a frightened puppy. Anyone observing would have thought it strange to see the Dame standing there in the middle of the floor with her arms wrapped around nothing while a wind stirred violently in her hair and blew the scarf from her head. But she was used to this sort of thing, and she cradled the wind and crooned comfortingly to it. She sensed fear radiating from it like fever heat.

"Now, now," she said. "What has frightened you so?"

"Mother Nivien!" the sylph moaned. "She caught me and she hurt me!"

The Dame frowned at this. She knew, as everyone did, that nothing could catch a sylph, much less hurt it. At least, nothing she had ever before encountered.

But Nivien . . . it was a name she believed she had heard but one with which she was unfamiliar. The Far World beyond the Wood Between was vast beyond even her comprehension, and she had been laboring to understand it ever since she left her mortality behind.

"Who is this Mother Nivien?" she asked. "Is that her real name?"

The sylph shuddered. Granted, as a wind, the difference between its shudder and its natural state was difficult to tell. But the Dame was sensitive, and she felt it.

"Mother Nivien . . . She Who Walks Before the Night . . ." The sylph's voice dropped to the merest breath. "Queen of the Nivien Family."

"The Family of Night." The Dame's frown deepened. "Why would she hurt you?" Tactfully, she did not add the next question that sprang to her tongue: *What did you do?*

"I saw her curse," the sylph replied, wrapping itself around the Dame's neck. "I saw her curse upon her mortal kin, and I heard her Song, and it was so—"

"Wait, wait," the Dame interrupted. "Mortal kin? A Faerie Queen with mortal kin? And what do you mean, a *curse?* My great Lord forbade fey-kind from working such evil influence upon mortals long ago, back at the very founding of the Near World. Any queen of the Far World knows this well. If she dares to defy my Lord, she will suffer a reckoning!"

With that, the Dame dropped the sylph (which didn't matter since a wind can't fall) and stepped to a nearby cluster of bushes which might, from a slightly different perspective, look like a small-arms cabinet. She pushed aside the branches and plunged her arm inside, withdrawing a long, shining knife. She was much more a woman for the pen than the blade; but she had absolutely no patience for Faerie-kind who tormented mortals. She had seen too much of that, both in her mortal life and since.

The knife clutched in her hand, she strode toward the library door, ready to go to battle against any and all Faerie queens and their armies. Her invisible companions, moved with pride, gleamed and cheered in thousands of high-pitched *Huzzahs!*

But the sylph whipped around to bluster between her and the door. "No, no!" it protested. "She has honored the Law! She has commanded me to tell you, to warn you not to interfere. She has placed a powerful curse, but all according to established Law, which she has honored all these years."

"What law is this?" the Dame demanded in a voice as sharp as the blade she clutched. "What law is this that allows mortals to be persecuted? I know of no such law!"

"It is an old one, older even than sylph-kind," the sylph told her. "It's Nivien Law, the Law of the Night. If the Nivien queen places a curse upon mortal-kind, she must allow for a cursebreaker. So long as she provides for the curse's undoing, she is free by law to work whatever influence she chooses."

"A cursebreaker?" said the Dame. "Can anyone serve this role?"

"No," said the sylph. "You cannot break the curse yourself, Lady Knight. Only one of the family on whom the curse has been placed. But so long as the cursebreaker fails, the curse may live on . . . forever."

"How many cursebreakers have attempted to undo this evil?" the Dame demanded.

But the sylph did not know the answer to this. It may have known it once, but it wasn't a remembering sort of creature. It shrugged after the fashion of a wind and moaned sadly.

So the Dame, her supply of information run short, returned the dagger to its shelf and went instead to root among her many scrolls. She had not yet chronicled anything about the Family of Night, but she did not doubt that something somewhere in the midst of all these piled-up documents could give her more information.

There was no apparent order to these scrolls or to any of those lying about the library. But the Dame kept them carefully categorized in her mind (and, of course, made many promises to herself to *one day* get it all shelved and cataloged correctly, promises she'd been making for a good two hundred years at least). She set to work on a pile she mentally classified as the Dark Magic scrolls, unrolling each one in turn and studying its contents.

Suddenly, she turned and scowled up at the seemingly empty branches and shelves around her. "Make yourselves useful, why don't you?" she said.

Ten thousand tiny flutters and ten thousand pairs of hands swooped down and began unrolling scrolls and opening books, gleaming here and there as they worked.

Whoever this cursebreaker may be, the Dame was determined he or she would be given all help or information allowable. Law or no Law, this curse must not be permitted to continue!

TWELVE

RATS WERE LIVING IN THE THATCH. HELOISE WAS SURE OF IT, BECAUSE the sound of scurrying feet above her head was bigger and more awful than ever before.

Mirror.

Yes, there were certainly rats, and they'd chased off all the mice. Wicked things. She heard them squeaking now and then, and it made her shiver.

Mirror.

But she preferred that scrabbling and squeaking by far to the sound of her mother's voice rising up through the floor beneath her.

Heloise lay in the dark on her pile of straw, her woolen blanket pulled up to her chin. She stared at the empty straw pile where her sister should be, the abandoned blanket left neatly folded beside it.

Her mother's voice sounded furiously beneath her head: "I have never been so humiliated in all my life! That girl deserves switching!"

A deep rumble from Papa, probably asking Meme to hush, the baby is asleep—

"I don't care if I wake all Canneberges! How could she do such a thing? Our whole family will be talked about for months, for *years!* What young man will ever come calling on her now? We'll never be able to live this down. We'll be stuck with her for the rest of our lives!"

Rumble, rumble, rumble.

"And what was all that raving about some sister?"

Rumble, rumble.

"No, she did *not* mean Hélène. If she'd meant Hélène she would have said Hélène. She was raving, I tell you. What was that name she kept saying? Evette? Who is this Evette? *She's as crazy as your mother!*"

Heloise squeezed her eyes shut and wished for some way to squeeze her ears shut as well. She stuffed her fingers in them and curled into a tight ball, burying into the straw, roasting under the blanket. She felt as though she ought to remember something, something just on the edge of her memory. Something . . .

Mirror.

For the first time ever, possibly since the beginning of the world (or at least the founding of Canneberges, which was practically the same thing in Heloise's mind), her family had left Le Sacre Night before dawn. Well before dawn. Before midnight, even. The dance would go on, the maidens, only four of them now, taking each other's place at intervals, the men clashing their canes, the shawm sighing to the heavens. Canneberges would bid in the new season.

While the Flaxman family stormed home, Heloise caught firmly between her father and her mother.

She had protested, of course. She had argued and even tried to fight, giving her brother Claude such a punch in the arm that he would have an impressive bruise for weeks to come. But the strength of her limbs was no match for her powerful father; and her spirit was no match for her mother. She wasn't certain her ears would ever recover from the blistering of Meme's tongue.

And all the insults, all the bitter accusations, all the furious demands of "Don't you ever know your place?" couldn't overwhelm the one phrase that continued to echo over and over and over in Heloise's brain:

"Who is Evette?"

None of them had seen it. Not one of them. They all believed her sick with madness to have run out into the middle of Le Sacre like that. None of them remembered Evette.

Mirror!

Her heart raced as though she even now fled slavering predators. She needed to remember. But what? What was she forgetting? The rats scurried and squeaked, and her parents argued and growled, and the people of Canneberges went on dancing, dancing, dancing, and not one of them cared about what truly mattered. Her sister. Her sister was . . .

"No! My sister! My sister! Don't throw away my sister!"

A little girl falling, rising, running, falling again. Grey clouds overhead, grey soil under hands. Loose soil recently turned and tossed aside from the gaping hole.

So dark, so dark, it's so very dark down in that hole.

"No, no, no!"

"... my sister."

Heloise's stomach heaved as though she would be sick. But it was just a sob wanting to come out. She swallowed it back, nearly choking on it.

Then a small, secret, dangerous part of her brain whispered, *It's all your fault. Just like last time.*

Heloise was on her feet in a moment, tossing aside the blanket, scattering straw. She still wore her too-short overdress, not having bothered to remove it before crawling under her blanket. Her hair was wild, pins and braids long since abandoned. And her cap? Where was her cap? The cap Evette had made for her. It was gone ...

But it was real! Missing, certainly, but *real.* She hadn't made it up, that gift from Evette, given to her on the road to Centrecœur. She wasn't mad. She wasn't, and she would prove it to them. And when she had proven it, they would all be amazed, absolutely amazed, that she alone, out of all them, had the presence of mind to ... to ...

MIRROR!

There it was. Clear in her memory, as clear as though it had just been spoken. In the darkness of the loft Heloise whispered as though in echo, "Mirror."

The next moment she was across the loft, kneeling at the cedar box, her mother's box. She flung open the lid and hauled out the white linen wedding dress that was supposed to be Evette's. That *would* be Evette's, dragons eat it, just as soon as she was safely back home! Heloise checked all the folds. She checked them again.

She tossed the dress aside and reached into the box, feeling all around, into every corner.

"Dragon's teeth!" she cursed when her fingers found nothing. She remembered a sight she had scarcely noticed only three days ago after just coming home from the Great House: her brothers sitting quietly. Too quietly. As though they'd just done something very wrong indeed.

"They broke it. Those dragon-blasted boys broke Meme's mirror!"

THE DANCE OF LE SACRE GOES ON FOREVER. MORTALS DO NOT KNOW, *but this does not change the truth of it. Throughout that long winter night they dance their own small echo of the song, but it never ends. Even when they have finished their paces, packed up their instruments, and gone home to their beds . . . even then the song goes on. The song and the dance.*

I know. I am as much a part of Le Sacre as any of them.

If only she could hear me clearly! The strain on my spirit is so great, I feel I cannot fight this battle. If she will but come to me, perhaps then I can help her.

But she must find the mirror.

THIRTEEN

GRANDMEM NEVER WENT TO LE SACRE NIGHT. SHE HADN'T GONE since . . . well, many years ago now. She couldn't. Especially not the year she'd turned eighteen. That Le Sacre, so very long ago, she'd run away and hidden in the abandoned mill up at north-end. In those ruins she'd crouched all night, listening to the distant wail of the shawm, weeping alone, and whispering over and over again, "Forgive me! Forgive me, Cateline!"

She'd returned home the next day, offering no answer to any of the questions put to her, no explanation. At last her mother had slapped her face, called her a disgrace, and . . . that was it.

No one spoke of her absence again. No one asked her why she never went to Le Sacre.

She lay on her musty pallet this night so many years later, listening to the dark song as it soared and murmured by turns throughout the night. Her eyes were open, staring up through the many cracks and holes in her roof to the stars turning slowly in their own dance high above. But she didn't see them. It was a different dance that whirled and gyrated across the eye of her memory.

A timid knock was not enough to draw her attention away from the fantastical visions upon which she gazed. A more forthright tapping made her stir, and she blinked. Then a violent pounding and a desperate cry of "Grandmem! Grandmem, are you awake?" brought her sitting bolt upright.

"I am now!" she shouted back, her quivering old hands searching about in the dark. "I've only got me drawers on. Give me a moment to get decent."

"Hurry! Hurry, please!"

It was Heloise's voice. Why was she not surprised by this? Grandmem found her shawl and tucked it around herself; not that so flimsy a garment could do anything against the constant cold that shivered her body. But it made her feel more confident. Now why was it she'd expected Heloise to come tonight? Because she *had* expected her. She'd told herself at sunset, just as she was lying down, "Heloise will be at your door by midnight."

It was just midnight. And Grandmem opened her door and gazed down into the face of her granddaughter. Exactly as she had expected. Only she couldn't guess why.

"What are you doing here?" she demanded.

"You told me to come, Grandmem!" Heloise gasped. She took several steps back. Her grandmother looked quite dreadful in the starlight, her undergarments and long loose hair as white as a ghost's shroud, her face sagging with shadows. Heloise wasn't scared, but no one could blame her for being a bit startled. "You told me to come. You told me to bring a mirror, but . . . but I think Clotaire and Clovis broke it! I think they broke it, Grandmem, and—"

Suddenly she was crying in great, ugly, hiccupping sobs which quite horrified her grandmother, who stood in the doorway and watched this display of emotion with eyes that didn't see as well as they once had but also with an intuition that had only improved with time. She was horrified because the girl's breakdown was not unexpected, out of character though it was for sullen Heloise.

She was horrified because she recognized it. She recognized herself standing there in her granddaughter's ungainly body.

"Ah," she said, placing a shriveled hand on Heloise's shoulder. Heloise gulped, choked, then flung herself into her grandmother's arms and clung to her, still sobbing. "Ah," Grandmem said. "What is her name, then?"

"Evette!" Heloise wailed. "Evette, Evette, her name is Evette, and they've all forgotten!"

"I'm afraid I have as well," said Grandmem sadly. "Can't recall ever meeting an Evette. Other than I think there was a girl on the farm next door when I was growing up, a real brat of a thing and fat as a pig—"

"*No!*" Heloise cried, pulling out of Grandmem's arms and shouting up at her face. "*Our* Evette! *My* Evette! My *sister*, Evette!"

Grandmem nodded and adjusted her shawl. "I understand, child. I'm sorry that I don't know her. I'm sure I did once. I don't anymore though, and I can't help it." She leaned down, her cloudy eyes lost in the night's shadows. It didn't matter; Heloise felt the intensity of her gaze like the crackle of lightning heat on a dark summer afternoon. She spoke in a whisper, though there was no one around to overhear, at least as far as could be seen: "Unlike the rest of them, I believe you."

"Because of Cateline," Heloise said, choking around remnant sobs. "It happened to Cateline too, didn't it. And you're the only one who remembered."

Grandmem nodded. "Quite close to right, child," she said. "Not quite right, but quite close to it. I was *almost* the only one to remember."

Heloise felt her heart rise. The idea that someone, anyone else in all of Canneberges might not have forgotten her sister filled her with such a hope as she couldn't fully understand just then. "Who else remembers?" she asked. "Who else remembers Evette?"

"You do," said Grandmem.

Heloise thought perhaps her ears were broken or at least a little bent. "Um. No, Grandmem, I asked who *else* remembers. Besides me."

"You do," Grandmem repeated. The creases around her mouth deepened with a frown. "Where is the mirror, Heloise? I asked you to bring the mirror when you came, didn't I? I'm almost sure I did."

"It's broken, I told you. I tried to find it, but it's not where I left it, and I know Clotaire and Clovis broke something the other day, I just know it, and I think they were up in the loft, and I think they dug it out to play with, and . . . it's . . ."

Grandmem let out such a sigh and sagged so heavily where she stood that Heloise feared she'd gone and died right there on the spot. But she didn't die; she merely lost the strength to stand and sat down rather too quickly on the doorstep, groaning in pain. "Grandmem!" Heloise cried, reaching out in a futile effort to catch or support her somehow.

Grandmem smacked Heloise's hands away then bowed her head, clutching at her thin hair and skull. She groaned again, and it was a most dreadful sound. It was some while before she could do anything besides sit there and groan.

At last, however, she managed to raise her face, giving her granddaughter such a baleful glare that Heloise took several paces back. "I *told* Berthe!" she growled. "I *told* her when I gave it to her on the day she married that son of mine! I told her to keep it *safe!* I told her she must give it to her daughter one day! I told her again and again! Why does that fool girl never *listen?*"

Heloise felt her throat grow dry. "It—it wasn't Meme's fault," she said. "She kept it hidden from the boys as best she could . . ."

"Fault? Fault? Who cares about fault?" Grandmem wrung her hands then, and the menacing glare melted into an expression of sudden pleading. "Tell me, child, please tell me this: Have you met yourself yet? Have you at least done that?"

"I—I—" How was she supposed to answer such a question?

Grandmem cursed roundly by the Dragon, rattling off various bits of draconian anatomy fast enough to make Heloise's head spin. Then she demanded, "Did you ever look into the mirror and see, suddenly, that you were looking back at yourself?"

Heloise opened her mouth to answer. Her breath caught for a moment. The wink. The wave. She'd tried very hard to forget them, to ignore them. To pretend they'd never happened.

"I think . . . I think so, Grandmem," she said slowly. "I think . . . yes, I have met myself."

Her grandmother let out a sigh and leaned against the door post. "Oh, great Lights Above be thanked! Small blessings, but we'll take them."

She reached out then and took Heloise by the hand, drawing her closer. "You must find a mirror," she said. "Somewhere, somehow. The mirror holds the image long after the body is gone. Find a mirror and look inside, look somewhere your sister has been. Anywhere. It'll show her to you, and you must follow her."

Her grip tightened, and her voice became thin and small, almost like a child's. "You must follow her, Heloise, and don't stop. Don't let anything or anyone deter you. All the way to the end, and try not to be frightened. You must, you *must*. Better to die than to fail. Believe me, I know. The mirror showed me Cateline, and I almost got her back. I was close, child. I was very close. Better to die than . . . better to die . . ."

Her mind was slipping away. Her gaze, no longer fixed upon Heloise's face, wandered up to the stars, down to the ground, out across the moonlit flax fields and bogs. Her breath came from her mouth in pale, wafting curls.

"Grandmem," Heloise whispered, "who took Evette? Who took Cateline?"

Grandmem let go of her hand and wrapped both her skinny old arms about herself, rocking to and fro upon the doorstep. But she answered in a voice clear and cold on the dark air: "The Family of Night."

FOURTEEN

AS THIS DIRE PRONOUNCEMENT FELL UPON HELOISE'S EARS, A SERIES of potential reactions presented themselves before her. A distant, quiet part of herself, a piece of her soul that was always watching her over her own shoulder, considered these reactions calmly and thoroughly, all in the space of an instant.

Fear. That would be a good one. Quite reasonable too under the circumstances. Yes, fear manifesting itself in a mild hysteria would be perfectly—

Oh no? Well then. Confusion, perhaps. Confusion would fit nicely into this empty headspace where a reaction of some kind must go. Confusion followed by a series of questions: Who? What? Why? Excellent questions all, each of which would need answers sooner or later. Confusion would—

All right. Fine. But some reaction must be had, and soon now, before another breath was taken. How about numbness? Why not dissolve into a puddle of useless, numb quivering, there on Grandmem's doorstep? Plenty of advantages to this, the foremost being a lovely excuse to not actually *do* anything. That's right. Let the breath out of those tight lungs. Succumb to—

No! *No!* Oh, great Lumé . . .

Heloise exploded.

"This is all *so stupid!* Stupid! Wretched! *Stupid!*" Her voice rang through the night, momentarily drowning out Le Sacre in the distance and filling her own head with a lion's roar. She couldn't have said whom she addressed: herself, her grandmother, Evette, or possibly this Family of Night, whoever they were. It didn't matter. Rage had taken hold now, and she expelled it from her core in great gasping gusts. *"Stupid!* It's *wrong!* It's *wrong and not real and I won't!* I *won't!"* What she wouldn't, she couldn't say. It didn't matter just then. "Wretched, stupid . . . *Dragons eat it,* I won't, and *you can't make me!"*

Next thing she knew, she was halfway down the dirt path from Grandmem's shack, still shouting, though as far as she could tell there was no one to hear. She paused, still within sight of Grandmem on the doorstep, and she felt the old woman's eyes on the back of her head. She waited for Grandmem to call out to her, to summon her back with words of comfort or explanation.

But it was Grandmem's silence that reached out to her through the darkness. Silence and nothing more. No answers. No solutions.

Foolish.

There went her thoughts again, thinking things she hadn't meant to think.

Foolish!

"Dragons eat you," Heloise growled, for the rage was still hot if not as high in her head. She kicked a stone just to feel the pain as her bare toe connected with the rough surface. The stone skittered off into the long grass. Limping, she continued down the path and soon felt the night close in behind her so that she was free of Grandmem's gaze.

Foolish! Mirror!

"There isn't any mirror," Heloise said. "It was broken! Broken and gone, and I don't have it anymore! So stop thinking about it. It's over."

Over?

A long silence followed this thought. A tense sort of silence like water building up behind a dam, mounting more and more pressure until at last—

FOOLISH!!!

It was only one word. One thought. But the force of it hitting her head from the inside out sent Heloise staggering and gasping. Though she knew she was alone, she turned in place, staring into the murk around her, searching for something that might have struck her. Anything, beast, man . . . or phantom.

But all was perfectly still. Or as still as Le Sacre Night can be, with the distant moan of the shawm rising up in the distance. Though she knew it must be false, Heloise couldn't help feeling that the ground beneath her feet reverberated all the way out here, in this remote corner of the estate, with the beat of peasant footsteps performing their mad dance. In her immediate vicinity, however, there was only the emptiness of cold fields tilled but not yet sown. There was only open countryside full of the expectation of spring not yet realized. There was only loneliness.

Yet Heloise knew she wasn't alone.

The voice in her head—the voice which, up until a moment ago, she had thought was her own—whispered to her again, weakly now, as though the effort of the last blasting word had sapped a great deal of strength. It said: *Centrecœur.*

Heloise didn't pretend to misunderstand. "I can't go back to Centrecœur," she whispered. "Everyone saw me. Everyone saw how I disrupted the dance, how I spoiled Le Sacre. They'll . . . they'll . . ." What would they do? Laugh at her? Point? Shake their heads?

Did any of these reasons count in the face of her sister's loss?

Centrecœur, said the voice in her head. A voice very like her own, but much older, much sadder. Heloise wondered if Grandmem had heard this same voice. She gazed back up the path to her grandmother's shed, debating whether or not she should return and ask her. But the insistent plucking in her brain increased, impatient for her to be on her way, to waste no more time.

Mirror!

"I could find a mirror at Centrecœur," Heloise whispered. "Master Benedict said he had one."

No answer. But the silence was full of anticipation.

"Why do I need a mirror?"

Still nothing.

"All right." Heloise scowled up at the star-filled sky, scowled at the stars themselves. They didn't seem particularly intimidated. "Seriously, why do I need a mirror? It's all stupid! Mirrors and meeting myself and . . . and this Family of Night and whatnot! It's stupid, and I won't . . . won't . . ."

This time she didn't need the voice in her head to fill in the answer. She answered for herself, ". . . won't try to save Evette?"

The words hung white in the air before her face, spoken softly but with such accusation. Heloise stared at nothing, but it was herself she saw. As though she stepped outside her own body and beheld her small, scrawny, barefooted form standing there at the crossroads. Standing there in that place where the dirt track from Grandmem's house led on back to the Flaxman cottage.

And where the wider road wound away, across the fields, and on at last to Centrecœur.

Heloise knew suddenly that the seasons had turned. Spring had come. Her feet were flat upon the ground, and she felt the cold rising up through her soles, her knees, into her stomach where it shivered out to every extremity. Really, there was nothing to differentiate between yesterday's winter and this predawn spring.

But Spring had come, gently stepping into the place of Winter. Not for any work or summoning on Le Sacre's part, but simply because that's what she must do. She was Spring. She would dance her intended dance apart from all care of mortals or immortals alike.

Le Sacre soared on, lonely and dark, and Heloise knew it suddenly for the lie it was. Le Sacre did not bring the spring. How could it? It was nothing compared to the greatness of turning seasons. Le Sacre—the sacrifice—it was a lie.

It was a trap.

Heloise listened to the deep rumble of the timpani rolling across the sky, reaching out to her. There were still tales told in this region, tales of ancient days and ancient practices. Tales so blood-curdling, Heloise found them impossible to believe (though she was no less eager than the next child to lap them up in all their gory glory). These tales spoke of sacrificial drums and the satisfaction of Winter's wrath. But it wasn't Winter who had taken Evette.

Heloise stood in the cold, listening to the distant music, her eyes closed but her memory full of images. She saw again how the shadows of the dancers came alive. She saw the pale white phantoms in the circle with her sister.

"The Family of Night," Heloise whispered. At long last the question came, the reasonable question she should have asked right away: "Who is this Family of Night?"

And what did they want with Evette? What had they wanted with Cateline? Her imagination leapt in at once, offering all sorts of hideous suggestions. Heloise choked on a gasp and opened her eyes to stare down at her own blue-tipped toes.

She said, "It's not my fault."

The silence in the air offered nothing in response.

"I didn't ask for this! I didn't *do* anything!" she protested.

But no one was listening. No one but whoever it was inside her head. And that person, that voice, didn't care to answer.

"I don't know enough about what's happening. I can't be expected to do something."

Go home then.

Heloise blinked. At first she couldn't decide whether that thought had been simply hers or if it was the strange new voice that was almost hers. But she suspected the answer. No voice but her own could speak to her with such condemnation.

Go home then, Heloise. Go bury your head in the straw. Let Evette be lost.

Just like Hélène.

Heloise gnashed her teeth and hugged herself tightly. She had no tears, either mournful or angry, left to cry, but her face wrinkled up anyway in a furious, snarling expression. "It's not my fault!" she said again.

But she was the strong one, wasn't she? She'd been the hardy one from the day she was born. She was the one who never got sick or if she got sick always recovered fastest. She was sturdy and energetic, and nothing could bring her down for long. Which meant . . .

Heloise coughed out a sob and turned it into a curse. But it didn't matter. In her memory she saw that hole again. That deep, deep hole. That hole in which the thin, pale reflection of her own face lay.

"If you don't fetch back Evette," Heloise whispered, "then what is the *point* of you?"

Centrecœur, said the voice in her head.

"Centrecœur," said Heloise in the same breath. She turned her feet on the road to the Great House. To escape the accusations, to escape that remembered grave, to escape even her own strong self, she set her feet toward Centrecœur and the weird music that played on and on in the night.

Grandmem said she needed a mirror. All right then. She knew of nowhere else in all Canneberges where a mirror might be found. She would have to break into the Great House and . . . and *borrow* from Master Benedict de Cœur.

By dawn the enthusiasm for Le Sacre had worn down to almost

nothing. The four maidens trading places within the innermost circle were stumbling more than dancing; the men in the outer rings clashed their canes with little vim; even the musicians struck more wrong notes than right (though the music of Le Sacre was so strange, it scarcely made a difference).

Dawn came at last. The peasants, their ceremony complete, bowed and curtsied before the marquis's son on his throne-like chair. Benedict, in turn, did his utmost to suppress his yawns, to assume what he hoped was a lordly and gracious air. But the truth was, he could hardly keep his eyes open.

His limbs quivered in a manner he found all too familiar.

When the last of the peasant folk of Canneberges had left the lawn and vanished through the gate and over the drawbridge, only then did Benedict try to rise. This took more effort than it should have; an embarrassing amount of effort, in fact. He told himself it was because he was stiff. He'd sat up all night, after all, nodding off now and then, only to be rudely awakened by a particularly piercing screech of pipes or a particularly roaring rumble of timpani. Le Sacre Night was not a night for peace or rest, and it was only natural that he should be tired.

But it wasn't natural that his knees should quiver so. Nor that the bones of his spine should feel like running water. Though he hated to do it, he was obliged to take the arm of his manservant as they crossed the lawn to the big main doors of Centrecœur.

Doctor Dupont stood in the open doorway like a ghoul guarding the gateway to the Netherworld. He watched Benedict approach, his eyes heavy-lidded but keen.

Doctor Dupont was a thin, sallow man whose rumbling growl of a voice never quite suited him, as though he had stolen some other, larger man's voice in place of his own. He wore humble grey robes and a black mantle which gave him an appearance of pious self-discipline until one noticed that its lining was silk and the stitching exquisitely rendered by the very best of tailors. On his head was a conical hat that fit tightly across his brow, covering his ears and shading his eyes so that they gleamed out from under the brim. Benedict had never seen him without this hat, indoors or out, rain or shine.

"Hmmmmmm," he said. It was an oddly musical hum and could mean almost anything. Benedict had come to dread the sound in the months since Doctor Dupont had come to Canneberges. "Hmmmm. You are unwell, sir?"

"I'm fine," Benedict said, letting go of his manservant's arm just to prove the point. He took three paces on his own, paused, and waited for the world to stop spinning. But he fixed a firm grin on his face and hoped he betrayed none of his disorientation. "I'm tired. It's a long night, Le Sacre Night."

Doctor Dupont—who, not being native to Canneberges, had felt absolutely no obligation to stay up the whole night observing a peasant ritual—lifted his brows. The brows themselves could not be seen, hidden as they were under the tight brim of his black, peaked cap. But the cap rose up on his forehead in what would almost have been a comical gesture were the doctor's expression not so chilly. "Your man informs me," he said, "that you went riding out the other day."

Benedict shot a glare at his manservant, who stood with his hands behind his back, staring up at the morning sky, innocent as a wee lamb. Dragons blast him! There was no use denying it, however, so Benedict merely shrugged and continued on his way, mounting the stairs with care and sidling past the doctor. Or trying to, anyway.

Doctor Dupont's hand latched onto his upper arm. "Master Benedict, you know I have only your best interests at heart. Your father commissioned me, having utmost trust in my judgment and abilities. But if you insist upon such physical exertion, you will only aggravate—"

"I'm fine," Benedict said again, his voice low but his eyes flashing. "Contrary to popular opinion, I'm not standing at death's threshold."

This was a mistake. It was always a mistake to interrupt Doctor Dupont. Benedict felt the full weight of his error the moment the sharp words left his mouth. He felt the stiffness in the doctor's hand on his arm. He felt silence descend with the force of a thunderclap. He braced himself for what must follow—an extended silence followed at length by a long, slow, "Hmmmmm."

His apologetic nature leapt into play. "I'm sorry, good doctor," Benedict said. "I didn't mean to . . . well . . ."

It was no good. The error once committed could not be taken back. The doctor's brow lowered, his peaked cap sinking with it. "Away with you, sir," he said with all the authority of a king. "Go to bed at once. I will come to you anon and see what of this damage I might undo."

That was it. Spoken as a pronouncement of doom.

Benedict slipped away the moment the doctor's hold on his arm released. He hastened down the long gallery bright with morning light streaming through the new glass windows, feeling as though the specters of death pursued at his back. He glanced briefly at the staircase leading up to the Great Hall and the family rooms in the west wing of the house. As heir of Centrecœur he should be making his way up there to the grand suite of chambers belonging to him.

But when he came home from university he'd had all his things moved to a single chamber off the long gallery on the ground floor of the house. A chamber that had once been a chapel of sorts, way back when people used to believe in that sort of thing. It was gloomy but spacious, with glass windows that opened and room enough for his desk, his books, an armoire, and a big four-poster bed. Not exactly homey but . . . well, at least he didn't have to bother with the stairs.

Benedict paused in the doorway to his room, his manservant a few paces behind him. He half wanted to defy the good doctor and, rather than climb into bed, sit down at his desk and begin reworking all those lost and damaged lists of Corrilondian declensions and conjugations which had so recently been blown across Canneberges. It would take him ages to redo the work, and he was behind enough in his studies as it was, so far from university. But he felt the lightness in his head and the soreness in his chest, and he couldn't deny that the very idea of sleep was completely beautiful just then.

"Shall I help you undress, sir?" his manservant asked.

Benedict shot him a glare almost worthy of his red-blooded ancestor Rufus. "I think not," he growled. "I'll summon you when I want you again, Hugo. That will be all."

There were probably more scathing remarks he could have made if he'd had the energy to think of them. For now his tone would have to suffice.

His manservant stiffened, bowed, and turned on heel to retreat down the long gallery with an air of affronted innocence. The backstabber! He'd informed the doctor of Benedict's secret ride why? Because he came home with a few broken hat feathers? The legendary Betrayer of Destan could hardly have been more worthy of shame!

Except . . . dragons eat it, Benedict half wanted to call out an apology. It took every ounce of self-respecting resentment he could muster to shut his mouth and his door without saying another word.

His room was cold, with only a small fire on the grate, hastily set by a housemaid who'd only just dashed in ahead following the conclusion of Le Sacre. Benedict hated to remove any of the warm layers he wore. But he was a gentleman through and through, and a gentleman did not go to bed in his fine jacket.

So he slipped out of his outermost layers and, wearing only his long undershirt, crawled under the heavy counterpane of his bed. Oh, how exhausted he was! He, the lad who had once gone on a three-day hunt with Victor and the other fellows, pursuing that boar o'er field and fen, laughing and never once feeling the need for sleep. He, the student who could stay up two nights running to finish assignments just on the edge of deadlines and still impress all his tutors with his brilliance.

He felt the dull ache in his chest, the blurry numbness of his limbs. He wondered, *Is this what Grandfather felt like in those few years before he died?* The question spun around his mind a few times and made him dizzy. He closed his eyes and—

Something stood beside his bed.

Benedict felt it with a clarity he could not deny. Something stood beside his bed. Something tall. Something . . . strong.

He tried to open his eyes. He knew he was on the edge of sleep, possibly fully asleep. But he was conscious as well, conscious of the paralysis in his limbs, conscious of the leadenness in his eyes.

Conscious of something leaning down. Of a long inhalation of breath let go in a warm gust upon his face.

"He will do, I think," someone said. It was a voice of absolute darkness, not a voice he recognized. "If it comes to it, he will do."

Creeaeeeeeeeeak.

Benedict's eyes flew open.

SHE'S COMING CLOSER. I CAN FEEL THE ANGER IN HER RISING LIKE A *red tide of blood on the war-torn Mher Sea. I can feel the fear in her, the fear she does not like to admit but which is the deepest beat of her heart.*

I am sorry to see her so afraid. But I am also glad. Fear can be a strong impetus, especially such a fear as hers.

As she returns across these mortal fields, I look down from my tower, and it seems as though I can meet her gaze even across the many leagues. It seems as though she looks up and sees me where I sit.

She is coming to me. I only hope she can make it safely! But first I must help her to find that which she does not know to seek.

The saying is old and fixed in my memory for all eternity: A branch of three parts shall be the key. A branch of silver . . . a branch of gold . . .

FIFTEEN

GRIMACING, HELOISE STOOD ON THE EDGE OF THE MOAT, OR AT LEAST what passed for a moat. It was really more of a glorified drain with a number of side trenches meant to carry undesirable smells away from the house itself. It was knee-deep, cold, and absolutely foul.

In an effort not to be seen by any of the peasants leaving Centrecœur at the advent of dawn, Heloise had looped around to the north side of the house, opposite the main gate. Most of Centrecœur's outer walls were built in the castle-defense style with no windows low enough to allow for an easy break-in. But the north side, Heloise recalled, held an old chapel complete with windows all around to let in as much of the holy light of the Spheres as possible. Many of those windows had long since been bricked up or filled in with glass panes. But there still were openings big enough for a girl to fit through.

The window Heloise had her eye on happened to be not only open but also near a convenient tree growing up from the ditch and offering an ideal ladder to the intrepid climber. She had only to cross the ditch.

"Oh, dragons," she muttered, gazing down at the revolting water. A cluster of false-unicorn stalks bloomed at her feet, the sickly sweet perfume of the horn-shaped flowers only adding to the other stenches assaulting her nose. The air smelled like the dye house. Well, maybe not as bad as the dye house. But close, to be sure.

Find the mirror, child, said the voice in her head. The annoying, insistent voice which, in light of the dawning day, struck Heloise as being a likely indication of insanity or lack of sleep. But after coming this far, she couldn't prove herself a coward now.

Heloise gathered up her skirts and scrambled down into the ditch. Her toes sank into mud, followed by her ankles. Brown water sloshed at her knees. Holding her breath and willing herself not to trip or breathe or do anything but hasten as quickly as possible, Heloise sloshed across the ditch. Her footsteps made underwater *gloop* sounds that were as bad as the smell if not worse. *Ugh!*

The open window on the far side was higher than she had first thought. The foundations of the Great House were deep, so the ground floor itself was well above Heloise's head. The tree didn't offer any conveniently low branches. Heloise stood among the tree's roots, mud and muck oozing from her toes, and stared up at the glass panes winking in the sunlight above her.

192

"Now what?"

Find the mirror!

It was amazing how quickly she'd grown accustomed to the idea of a strange voice speaking inside her head; nearly as quickly as she'd adjusted to the notion of talking breezes and singing shadows. And, being Heloise, she just as quickly found herself growing short-tempered at it.

"Yes, fine, that's all well and good! But how *exactly* do you expect me to do so? I don't have wings, you know!"

If a silence can be sulky, this one had a definite sulk to it.

Well, it did no good to stand in the cold, glaring at a window that wouldn't get any closer. Using both the tree and the wall for support, Heloise began to scramble up. She found toe-holds in the stone, finger-holds in the bark, and she thanked Lumé and Hymlumé and all the starry host for the last several years she'd spent scaling the trunks in Oakwood. She was panting by the time she reached the lowest limb, but she managed to wrap her arms around it, dangle a moment, then get a leg over as well. Heaving her own scrawny weight, she gained purchase at last and paused there, her bare legs hanging out from under her hiked-up skirts, her back pressed against the trunk.

The moat seemed rather far down. Heloise swallowed, closed her eyes, and refused to look again. She wasn't afraid of heights, or of falling either, for that matter. But falling into *that* water, ending up submerged . . .*Ugh, ugh!*

At least the smell was marginally better from up here. A sweet spring breeze moved in the bare tree branches, which clicked gently against the window glass. The branch Heloise slid along toward the window wasn't as thick as she would have liked and bobbed unsettlingly at her slightest movement. But she didn't have much choice; she had to get to that window. Besides the big drawbridge gate, the only other way into Centrecœur was through the kitchen door, which would mean getting past Alphonsine Millerman and her snooty airs. No. No, that was asking too much of a girl.

With one trembling hand, Heloise reached for the windowsill. In order to catch hold she first had to pull the casement open a bit further.

Creeeeeeeak.

Then, using the window frame to support as much of her weight as possible, she slid further out along the bough. She was now far from the trunk and from any hope of help should something fall or break.

Gritting her teeth against her fear, she flung out her other hand and caught the sill. The branch waved like an unsteady sea craft under her feet as she stood up on it, putting even more of her weight into her arms and the window frame. It was dark in the chamber within. Using her head, Heloise nudged the window open a bit more.

Creak. Creeeak, creeeeak.

Now she could get her head and shoulders through and have a proper look into . . . a bedroom. Not what she'd expected. Wasn't this supposed to be the old chapel, with its high round windows on the east and west walls? She looked from side to side, and indeed, there were those round windows. Not very large, to be sure, but just where they were supposed to be.

But the rest of the room wasn't chapel-like at all. There was no lantern hanging from the center of the ceiling. There was a fire on a hearth where she'd expected an altar to be. And what on earth was a great, unmade four-poster bed doing there, taking up room where kneelers should be kneeling and chantours should be offering up prayerful songs?

It was very odd.

Find the mirror, said the voice in her head.

Heloise scanned the room quickly from this vantage but saw no mirror lying about. She'd have to get inside, take a look in that great armoire standing against the far wall, perhaps. She didn't have much else to go on as far as plans went. Master Benedict had said he owned a mirror, so she knew there must be mirrors *somewhere* within Centrecœur. If not in this room, then maybe another?

There was nothing for it. She had to get in.

Taking a deep breath and adjusting her grip on the sill, Heloise jumped. The sensation of her feet leaving the branch behind was like dropping her own stomach. For half an instant she feared her hands would slip and she would fall back into the moat. Instead she hauled herself up so that her stomach landed hard on the windowsill. "Oof!" she gasped. Her feet scrabbling along the wall, she pulled herself over and thudded on the floor below.

The unmade bed shifted. The covers whirled like the shrouds of so many ghosts disturbed in their graves. A tousled, sleepy head emerged, blinking with bleary terror, staring down at Heloise, who stared back in equal terror, unable to move even to arrange her awkwardly bent limbs.

She gazed up into the hollow-eyed face of Master Benedict de Cœur.

"Who are you?" he cried. Another series of blinks, and his vision cleared. "Iubdan's blazing black beard! You're that little girl from—"

"Oh, *hush!*" Heloise gasped, pulling herself upright and yanking her skirts down over her muddy knees. "Hush your mouth! They'll *kill* me if they find me!"

The threat of death was by no means an exaggeration, as Heloise well knew. She stood there in the pool of light falling through the window and stared at the red-headed young lord. But it was not Benedict she saw.

Only once, a year ago, had she and one of her older brothers, on a dare, ventured to the borders of Oakwood and peered out to the crossroads that marked the southernmost boundaries of Canneberges. At first Heloise had been so taken with the idea of looking out at a world *beyond* the mastery of the Marquis de Canneberges that she hadn't noticed the gibbet.

Then it creaked.

It turned.

And Heloise had run screaming deep into Oakwood, never once looking back until she was safely home and buried in the straw up in her loft. She wasn't afraid. Certainly not. When her brother Clement teased her later and called her a wet hen, she had defended her courage with complete sincerity. No, she wasn't afraid!

But she had been sick to the point of complete collapse, which was close enough to fear.

The thing inside . . . She was pretty sure it (He? She?) had still been alive.

Later on she'd overheard some of the dyer-boys talking about the wretch who had been caught trying to break into Centrecœur. There was only one penalty for a man caught thieving on Canneberges, be he egg-thief, chicken-thief, or something worse still. So, The Wretch (as Heloise always afterwards thought of what she'd seen in the gibbet) was caged and left to die at the crossroads as a warning to all traveling to and from Canneberges.

A warning which Heloise had never thought to ignore, never thought to *want* to ignore. Yet here she stood, hearing her own scolding voice echo off the four walls and the rafters overhead. And there sat Master Benedict, his hair standing straight up from his head, his mouth hanging open.

The gibbet's chain groaned in Heloise's brain.

"Well." Heloise forced herself to swallow, forced her heart to remain in her chest. "Well, that's better."

"I—I'm terribly sorry," Benedict said in a much softer voice. Then he frowned, as though just realizing what he'd said. "I mean—" Suddenly he blushed a frightful hue, so bright it was almost purple. His eyes darted to the end of his bed, and Heloise, following his gaze, saw his trousers lying there beside his coat. Benedict clamped down on the blankets on either side of his body. "What in Lumé's name do you think you're doing, climbing in through my window?" he growled, all apologies forgotten in roaring embarrassment.

Heloise stepped forward hastily, her hands upraised, not quite pleading but close to it. "I didn't know anyone was here," she said. "I didn't see anybody when I looked in."

"Because I was under my dragon-eaten *blankets*. Because I was dragon-eaten *sleeping*."

"Well sure, but it's morning now and no one should be sleeping, so I—"

"I was up all night long watching your stupid peasant dance! I can sleep the day away if I like!"

Heloise stared. She knew, rationally, that she shouldn't say any of the five things that sprang immediately to mind. Not that this morning had proven a day for rationality as of yet. Still, she didn't want to have her tongue cut out before they hung her up at the crossroads.

Thus, in the most even, mature voice possible, she said only, "Le Sacre is *not* a peasant dance. It is *Le Sacre*. It's *the most important night* of all the *year*. And *you* are a . . . a . . . ." No! No, bite it back. Heloise clamped her jaw shut and let the next several words disappear in a growl.

Benedict, uncomfortable under the force of that furious stare, framed as it was by all that wild mess of hair, glanced again at his trousers draped over the foot of the bed. He wondered if he could reach them without the girl noticing. "Why are you here?" he demanded. "Specifically, why did you climb through my window?"

Heloise unclamped her jaw just enough to let out a few words. "It was the only open window," she said, as though this were explanation enough and any simpleton could have realized it with half an effort. "I thought about knocking at the scullery, but that snooty Alphonsine would probably set the dogs on me and—"

"I'll set the dogs on you myself if you don't get out this instant," Benedict said without much conviction. He was too busy trying to slide a surreptitious hand across the counterpane.

"Don't you dare." Heloise drew herself up to her full, if not very impressive, height. "I didn't come to steal anything. I just need—"

"Hold on!" Benedict, who was bent over trying to reach the end of his bed, sat up suddenly. "You're the girl who caused the disturbance last night. You're the one who dove into the middle of the dance!"

At this, Heloise felt her cheeks burst into a blush radiant enough to rival the young lord's own. Her scowl melted away in the heat, taking with it much of her resolve. "It's not my fault," she muttered. Then, on impulse, she stepped over to Benedict's bed, picked up his trousers, and tossed them to him. "Here. You want these."

"Um." Benedict caught his trousers and clutched them awkwardly to his stomach. "Thank you."

She gave him something that might have been almost a smile under other circumstances. "I really wouldn't have startled you like this if I could have found another way in," she said. "But I had to get in. They stole my sister, you see. And everyone forgot her."

"Who stole what sister?"

Heloise glared again. A variety of possible words leapt to her tongue, words she wouldn't have thought twice about saying to her brothers. Wanting to slip out, they pressed on the back of her teeth, eager to be spoken. But one couldn't spout just *anything* at the marquis's only son.

So she swallowed back any and all curses and derogatory names and said only, "Put your trousers on, why don't you. There are ladies present."

It was the wrong thing—she knew as soon as she'd said it. Benedict, his trousers still clutched in both hands, drew himself up in bed and spoke in indignant surprise: "See here, little girl, I don't—"

Luckily for all concerned, a knock sounded at his door just then, and a deep, throaty voice rumbled from without, "Master Benedict?"

"Oh!" Heloise gasped and dove to the floor.

"No, wait!" Benedict hissed, leaning over the edge of the bed in time to see her muddy feet disappear underneath. "No, *get out!*"

He gulped the words down, however, as the door opened and Doctor Dupont entered. Benedict straightened up quickly, a weak smile upon his very red face. "Ah! Um. Good morning, doctor. Um. How are you this morning?"

It was a completely brainless thing to say considering they'd seen each another not half an hour before. Doctor Dupont did not seem to notice. He moved sedately into the chamber, his fingers steepled before his breast while his eyes scanned each corner, crevice, and shadow with a shrewdness that made Benedict's skin crawl. Only when he at last reached his patient's bedside did he speak, giving no response to Benedict's question.

"You have gone to bed as I ordered," he said. "Hmmmmmm."

This was stated almost like an indictment. What did the good doctor want? Disobedience?

"Um, yes," said Benedict. He never could maintain creditable powers of speech in Dupont's disturbing presence. "I'm a bit tired, you know. Last night. All that."

"Tired, yes. You said that before. Tired . . ."

The way the doctor spoke would make any man think he'd got the plague and even now lay in his death throes. Benedict shivered again but did not protest when the good doctor took his arm, raised it above his head, and began prodding it with his long, cold fingertips.

"Your chamber is too warm," the doctor said, despite the fact that Benedict could feel his lips turning blue with the draft coming through the window. "Heat will only aggravate the fever, which has never fully left your body. Heat will urge it back to greater life, greater strength than ever. And it will consume you. Yes. Consume."

He dropped Benedict's arm and grabbed his head, turning it so that he could stare into his ear. "No," he said at last. "I cannot see it."

"Cannot see . . . what?" Benedict asked, not at all certain he wanted to know the answer.

"The devil," said Doctor Dupont. "Once it has re-grown—as it will, for they always do—I shall be able to see the fire of it deep inside your head. I will then extract it."

There was a certain fervor in the way he spoke the word *extract*. Benedict rather hoped the fever would return and kill him before things reached such an interesting crisis.

"Have you taken your draught?" Doctor Dupont asked. Without waiting for an answer, he opened the drawer of Benedict's nightstand and withdrew a vial of yellowish-brown liquid. As he held it up to the light, Benedict could almost see his throat vibrate with a long "Hmmmmm."

"I've been sort of saving it up," Benedict offered lamely. "You know, for those bad days."

"Master Benedict," said the doctor, gazing at him through the vial, which made his face look longer and sallower than ever, "as far as you are concerned, *every* day is a bad day. Every day could be your last. You must take your medicine. It is the best to be had: ground coriander seed, tannins of nightshade, crushed blossom of Heart's Blood, and rainwater gathered on a midsummer night. All shriven according to the Old Order." He looked smug. "I know, for I made it myself." He poured a measure into a small cup and put it in Benedict's hands. "Drink."

"Um. Well, I'm quite tired at the moment, so maybe I'll take it—"

"Drink, young master."

There was nothing for it. Benedict braced himself and tossed the brew to the back of his throat. Dropping the cup, he grabbed his trousers and stuffed them into his face, barely holding back the choking cough that wanted to send Doctor Dupont's remedy spewing across his counterpane. His ears flamed hotter than ever, and his eyes watered. But by the strength of his old ancestor, Rufus the Red, he got the stuff down and kept it there.

"*Uuuuugh.*" He dropped his trousers back into his lap.

"Feeling better?" asked Doctor Dupont, ever the optimist.

"Yes, doctor," Benedict lied, and shuddered.

"Good. Very good." Replacing both vial and cup, the doctor patted his patient on the back and glided to the door. "Sleep now, Master Benedict," he called over his shoulder. "Sleep, sleep while you may. Sleep while the fever is low, before the consuming fire returns . . ."

With this intonation he vanished through the doorway like a demon, having answered a secret summons, returning to its own strange realm. The door shut behind him.

Still shuddering, Benedict sagged back into his pillows and smacked his tongue against the roof of his mouth. As if it were possible to rid himself of that foul taste! His limbs shivered and his stomach roiled, and he scarcely had the energy to react when Heloise slid around under his bed and at last emerged from down at the foot. Her hair was in her face, and she pushed it back with both hands.

"Are you sick?" she asked.

"What do you think?" he growled.

She stared at him like he'd grown a second head. "What are you sick of?"

Benedict almost answered, "Doctor Dupont." It was right on the tip of his tongue. But that would not be a good example to this uncouth urchin child, so he swallowed the words back with almost as much difficulty as he had swallowed his medicine, saying instead, "Nothing." With masterful effort, he pulled himself upright. Even with Dupont's poisons churning around in his gut, he wasn't about to let this peasant girl see him at such a disadvantage. "I'm fine, actually. Doctor Dupont gets bored now and then, and my father sent him to Canneberges to keep him out of trouble. He's only got me to experiment on, you see."

"Meme told me nightshade will kill you if you eat it," Heloise said, frowning uncertainly.

"Is your meme a nationally renowned doctor trained under the king's own physician in the court of Bellevu?"

"No—"

"Well, there you have it then." Benedict shook himself one last time. "Now will you kindly turn your back so that I may clothe myself as befits a gentleman?"

Heloise obliged. She listened to the sounds of the Canneberges heir getting dressed, and she wondered if it was possible to die of mortification, or at least of the extreme effort it took not to show mortification. But what time had she to be mortified? What did her own feelings matter just now? She must focus.

Find the mirror, child!

Yes, well, that's what she was trying to do, wasn't it? She'd got into Centrecœur, and Master Benedict didn't seem ready to call the guards and see her gibbeted. "I'm making progress," she whispered.

"All right, little girl," said Benedict, and how she would have liked to smack him for it. "I am fit to be seen. Will you kindly face me and explain exactly what brings you creeping through my window like a common thief?"

The word *thief* burned in her head. Heloise turned around slowly, twisting her face into what she hoped would be an intimidating glare. Benedict braced himself as though he wanted to take a step back, and this gave her courage.

"I am no thief," Heloise said. "I've come to borrow a mirror. That's all."

Benedict studied her. "A mirror? What in Lumé's name would you need a mirror for?"

"To admire my pretty face, obviously," she snapped. If Evette had heard her, she would have melted with shame on the spot. This thought gave Heloise both a small smile and a sharp pang. She mastered her tongue and said, "Forgive me, Master Benedict," adding a curtsy for good measure. "I cannot well explain my actions. Not so's you'd understand. I hardly understand myself."

"Try," said Benedict, which was, he thought, remarkably gracious of him. After all, the girl deserved to be tossed out the window on her ear. He folded his arms. "I'm listening."

So Heloise launched into an explanation which, were it not for her poor diction, would have impressed even the school of bards and songsters, so expansive was the imagination and passion with which she spoke. A tale of a lost sister and sinister doings at last night's Le Sacre . . . a man of less education and understanding might well have believed her.

She obviously believed herself.

"I remember," Benedict interrupted at one point. "You were shouting that name last night, weren't you? Evette. And she's your lost sister?"

"Yes," Heloise said. "But I'm the only one who remembers her. You saw her yourself last night, dancing."

"There were several peasant girls dancing," said Benedict.

"You met her four days ago. Around the back, in the kitchen garden," Heloise persisted. "She was with me when you stopped by on your horse. I introduced you to her. You spoke her name, even."

He scratched his ear, which wasn't the most lordly gesture. "I remember seeing you," he said. "I don't remember your sister."

This was actually a bit gratifying. Heloise felt a jolt of guilt at the thought. Had she ever met another young man who remembered her and not Evette? None that she could recall.

Foolish girl. What are you doing? Find the mirror!

Heloise scowled, more at herself than anything, but fixed that scowling gaze upon Master Benedict. "See here, I *know* you remember the . . . the *wind*."

He did. It was all over his face: the memory of that wind and that laugh and those moments of surprise and near-terror they had shared in the shadows of the Oakwood. Benedict's regular flush faded into pallor.

"Yes," he said slowly. "I remember the wind. It stole my whole collection of Corrilondian declensions. I'd worked for months on that list! Corrilondian is a difficult enough language to learn without having one's efforts blown out the window."

Heloise, who had no idea what a declension was and only the vaguest notion that the nation of Corrilond existed, blinked several times. "Yes. Well. It stole your de—your decl—your declat—"

"Declensions," Benedict finished for her. "And my hat. I remember that well enough. It broke the plume, and my man was in a temper about it for days. Still is, last I checked. And I remember that it . . . it laughed."

He scratched his other ear now, which Heloise took to mean he was thinking rather hard. "All right," he said at last. "All right, I'll admit there's something strange going on. I've sensed it these last few days. And just because I don't remember meeting your sister doesn't mean you never had one, I'll grant you that as well. But what do you need a mirror for?"

"Because," said Heloise, "the mirror holds the image. Long after the body and the spirit are gone, the mirror holds the image." She was only saying what her grandmother had said to her, and she didn't think it made any more sense coming from her own mouth than it had from Grandmem's. But it was all she knew. It was all she had to go on. That and the insistent voice, which was slowly driving her mad, she was sure. "I think a mirror might show me where they—where this Family of Night—have taken her. Maybe then I can get her back."

Benedict studied the girl wearing her too-short dress and peering up at him from under that tangled mop of curls. He wasn't altogether certain he liked what he saw. But he was sure that, in her mind at least, she was telling the truth. "What's your name?" he asked.

"Heloise," Heloise said. "Heloise . . . Oakwoman." Then she repeated it more firmly. "Heloise Oakwoman. Yes."

He wasn't taken in. She could see it on his face. No one was called "Oakwoman." No one ever would be. She waited for him to contradict her, to call her out on a lie.

But Benedict thought, *No. She has an honest sort of look. And really, maybe she is an Oakwoman. Just because someone else gave her a different name doesn't mean this name isn't true.*

Aloud he said, "Very well, Heloise Oakwoman. I do have a mirror. I'll show it to you if you wish."

SIXTEEN

AT FIRST HELOISE TRIED TO CONVINCE BENEDICT TO LET HER TAKE the mirror with her up to the Flaxman cottage. Grandmem had told her to look into the glass somewhere Evette had been. It only made sense to look for her at home.

Benedict stoutly refused.

"It's not as though I'm going to steal it!" Heloise protested, fists planted on her bony hips. "You know I live in south-end, and you could easily hunt me down if I tried."

"Makes no difference," Benedict replied. "You're not taking my mirror out of this house. It's too valuable."

Once Heloise actually saw the mirror, she dared not protest further. In fact, when Benedict drew it out the depths of his armoire and slipped it from its cloth covering, Heloise was hard-pressed to keep all her teeth in her mouth, so heavily did her jaw drop.

It was . . . well, it was *glorious!* A polished ebony frame of rampant lions whose claws supported the glass and whose tails made up the handle, their eyes set with small gleaming sapphires.

Heloise had heard of lions before, but she had never been able to picture them. Her father had told her they were like big cats, but the beasts holding that mirror didn't look like any cats she had ever seen. Their masses of mane coiled and gleamed, and their snarling faces looked ready to devour dragons. Indeed, they were as mystical and magical in Heloise's eyes as any dragon ever could be.

She put out her hands to take it, but Benedict snatched it away. "No, no," he said. "This has been in the family for generations and, well, you might drop it."

Offensive though this was, Heloise couldn't argue. "All right," she said slowly, her eyes fixed upon one of the lions' carved faces, which seemed to be watching her, "Evette has visited the weaver room several times. We could take it there."

"That's at the bottom of the Tower," Benedict said, "all the way on the other side of the house."

"I suppose you should lead the way then."

Benedict hesitated, waffling between amusement and irritation. Honestly, though, what could he do? Summon the guards? The girl was just a child, after all, and wild though her stories might be, he rather thought he'd like to see where they led. "Very well," he said, not quite reluctantly. "But you've got to be *quiet*."

Centrecœur was eerily silent that morning; as silent as midnight, when all the household slept. Indeed, after the long Le Sacre there were few wakeful souls to be found in all Canneberges estate. Even the beasts of the field and the starlings in the treetops tended to sleep through the first day of spring, though they had not participated in the summoning dance the night before. It was as though a soporific spell had settled like a blanket over all the estate.

Heloise felt the effects herself even as she followed soft-footed behind Benedict, out of the chapel that had become his private chamber and into the long gallery beyond. Though really, she thought, her fatigue needn't be attributed to any spell; she had spent the whole night previous up and running about, half mad with terror and fury. Was it any wonder she now felt such a tug of sleep on her eyelids?

But Heloise shook off the drowsiness as best she could. After all, spell or no spell, she had just broken into the marquis's house, right into the son-and-heir's own bedroom. While Master Benedict was being remarkably gracious about the whole thing, one never could tell where the fickle minds of the gentry might turn next.

The gibbet wasn't entirely out of the question.

This thought brought Heloise solidly back into wakefulness. She fixed her gaze between Benedict's shoulders as she followed him, watching warily for any sudden moves.

So they progressed through the lower gallery of Centrecœur and met no one on their way. Once or twice, Benedict heard footsteps coming and motioned to Heloise to duck behind a suit of armor or heavy curtains or, once, simply behind him. But it came to nothing. Heloise, peering out from whatever hiding place they currently occupied, glimpsed nothing but shadows on the wall, which always turned at the last and entered a side room or passed up a flight of stairs before drawing too near. It was like being in a house full of ghosts.

Heloise found Centrecœur overwhelming enough as it was. All her life she had dreamed of what wonders might be found beyond the high stone walls and the marvelous glass windows. Her imagination had been limited due to an equally limited range of experience. To her, the height of elegance and beauty had been Evette's embroidered cranberry blossoms on the edges of gowns and shirts; she could not have conceived of the great, heavily-embroidered tapestries lining the walls of this passage, tapestries wrought by foreign hands in foreign designs that dazzled the eye. Luxurious floors, in Heloise's experience, had meant fresh rushes scattered about; she could not have dreamed of the age-polished stone floors on which she now trod, not to mention the softer-than-grass Corrilondian rugs which startled her so much the first time she stepped on one of them that she gave a yelp and shot straight up a full foot in the air.

"Hush, you fool!" Benedict hissed, whirling about and giving her a stern eye. He had just enough of his red-blooded ancestor in him that he looked quite intimidating for a moment. But the Bellamy side took over next, and he followed up with a hasty, "I'm sorry, I didn't mean that. But you really must be quiet! They're not all asleep, you know. Doctor Dupont is lurking about here somewhere. If he were to hear you . . . well, I don't know how I'd explain you, you know?"

Heloise nodded. "Are we nearly there?" she asked meekly.

"Yes." Benedict looked around uneasily. He was jumpy with nerves, for here in the east wing, not far from the scullery and the servants' quarters, they were far more likely to meet a poor soul who must attend to some task before catching up on lost sleep. He held the mirror close to his chest, hiding the glass so that it cast no telltale gleams.

But all was still as they slipped into the narrow passage leading to the Tower and the weaver room. There were no windows here, and the passage was unlit, so it felt almost as though they stepped out of morning back into night when they made the turn. Heloise shivered and had to keep herself from reaching out and taking hold of Benedict's sleeve, suddenly afraid of losing him.

At the end of the passage was a stairway. Heloise could scarcely see it, so dark and gloomy were the shadows here. But what she saw told her it was very narrow, scarcely wide enough for Benedict to climb, and he was not particularly broad for a lad his age. She, skinny as she was, could probably slip up it if necessary . . . but it was so narrow and dark that she couldn't imagine ever wanting to. She had the uneasy suspicion that once she'd taken a few turns of the stair it would suddenly close in before or behind, trapping her forever in stone.

"Here we are," said Benedict, and she thought his voice trembled. This heartened her; it was *his* house, and even *he* was nervous while standing in this dark space. "I should have brought a candle. But this door here—it's the door to the weaver room."

Heloise saw now that beside the opening of the stairwell was, indeed, a small wooden door. "Is it locked?"

"I'm not sure." Benedict tested the latch. The door swung open almost immediately at his touch, as though it had been waiting for them. They cast each other quick glances, neither able to read the other's expression in the gloom. Then, Benedict leading the way, they stepped into the room.

It was much brighter inside, for there were windows, narrow but full of morning light. This light fell onto the tall looms on which great bolts of bright red, cranberry-dyed linen were displayed in various stages of completion. Canneberges employed a goodly number of weavers to create the linen which was its primary export.

But the weavers were asleep after the long Le Sacre the night before. The room was empty save for the great weaving looms, which seemed like giant's instruments to Heloise, used as she was to her mother's much smaller, humbler handlooms on which the rough cloth for their clothing was woven.

Benedict led the way to the center of the round tower chamber and stood in the midst of the looms. He turned to Heloise then, holding the mirror tightly in both hands. She couldn't see him very well, for the light did not fall on his face, but she thought she could *feel* the blush radiating from him. He was embarrassed. Embarrassed to be here in this quarter of the house on this strange errand. She couldn't really blame him. But she also didn't have time to worry about it.

"Here," she said, reaching out both hands. "Let me have the mirror."

He shook his head. "No, you can look into it. But I'll hold it."

"That's nonsense! How am I supposed to look into it properly like that?"

Benedict's eyes narrowed. "Properly? Last I checked, there's nothing *proper* about any of this. Or you either, for that matter." Then he blinked. "I'm sorry, I didn't mean that. I mean, I meant it, but I—"

"Fine!" Heloise folded her arms. "I forgive you, or not, or whatever you like! Just let me see the mirror."

His fingers tightened on the tail-twined handle. "Very well. I'll turn it, and you can have a look. But don't try to take it from me, or I'll . . . I'll call the guard."

Heloise huffed but nodded. So Benedict turned the glass about, holding it out toward her face. Light from a near window gleamed on its surface, making the world inside the glass look much brighter than that in which Heloise stood.

She stared into her own face. She stared some more.

She had never before seen herself so clearly! Her Meme's glass had been nothing like this, warped and spotted as it was. She had always thought it miraculous, but by comparison . . . Oh, Lumé above, there could *be* no comparison! This surface was so smooth, so pure.

"My forehead!" Heloise gasped, and then instantly wished she could take it back.

"What about your forehead?" Benedict asked.

"Well, you know. It's not fat," she muttered, then took a step closer and peered intently, trying not to see Benedict's confused reaction. "Iubdan's beard," she said then. "I'm so . . . so . . ."

"Dirty?" Benedict suggested.

She scowled up at him briefly but couldn't for long keep her eyes off the mirror itself. How marvelous it was to see herself as clearly as though she looked into the face of a friend. Of a sister.

Before she could stop herself the thought flashed through her mind: *Is this what Hélène would have looked like?*

Hélène had shared Heloise's masses of curly hair. Hélène had shared her pale eyes. But Hélène's nose was not that nose; Hélène's nose had been small and soft. It had been a child's nose, not a young woman's nose like this one in the glass. Would Hélène's nose have lengthened like this? Would it have had the same little bump, the same listing to the left?

Heloise felt tears pricking her eyes. Then she frowned. Inexperienced though she was, she knew how mirrors should work. The reflection on the other side of the glass had no tears. In fact, it looked rather scornful.

"Beast," Heloise whispered.

"I beg your pardon?" Benedict asked, drawing the mirror back. As he did so, he turned the glass just a fraction to one side.

Heloise gasped. Before she could stop herself, she leaped forward, catching his hands in hers, drawing the mirror back close to her face. She turned it again, and there! There!

"*Evette!*"

Dropping her hold on the glass, Heloise spun around and stared into the gloomy passage beyond the weaver-room door. It was just as dark as it had been a moment ago and apparently empty. Empty . . .

"You know, I'm fairly certain I've said this already, but you really must keep your voice down," said Benedict.

Heloise startled at his voice and spun back to look up at him. "Did you see her?" she asked, her voice nearly catching in her throat.

"See whom?" He held the mirror back against his chest now, as though afraid it would fall and shatter at any moment.

Heloise put out her hand. "Give it back! Give it!"

In retrospect Benedict knew he should never have put up with such language from this peasant imp. But at the time—with her great eyes blazing up at him and her wild hair standing out from her head like the rays of a weird sun—it seemed like a good idea to comply. He turned the mirror around and only muttered a small "Easy!" when she grabbed his hands again and hauled it toward her face. She turned it this way, turned it that way.

"Evette," she whispered, and a shudder passed through her body.

For there in the glass, standing in the dark passage beyond the reflected Heloise's shoulder, was her sister. Evette. Wearing the same gown she'd worn to Le Sacre, the same cap tied tightly under her chin.

All around her shone a blue-silver light. Like moonlight.

She was looking away, looking at the narrow opening of the stairwell, her head tilted as though listening to the voice of someone calling to her. She didn't look frightened or worried or . . . or anything.

She looked empty.

Evette turned slowly, her eyes still fixed upon the stairwell even as her face moved toward Heloise. Heloise, clutching the glass, staring over her reflected-self's shoulder, felt her heart racing. "Evette . . . Evette . . ." she whispered, suddenly uncertain she wanted her sister to hear her.

Evette's eyes flicked to meet hers. Only for an instant.

But in that instant Heloise saw her changed. She saw her wearing a fantastic gown of starlight, her hair long and golden down her back, her face radiantly beautiful and pale as the dead. Pale as Hélène's face down in that dark grave.

Heloise gasped again and blinked. But when her eyes opened, Evette was no longer looking at her. She wore her peasant garb and gazed up the narrow stair. Then she moved, one step at a time, each foot slowly rising, touching at the toe and settling flat, like a horse going through its paces.

"Wait!" Heloise cried and put out a hand, reaching.

Only both of her hands remained clutching the mirror frame. It was her reflected self who reached out, moving at the urge of her beating heart.

This so startled Heloise that she dropped hold of the mirror and backed away. She looked over her shoulder, though she knew Evette would not be there. She wasn't. The passage was empty of all save shadows.

But in the mirror . . . in the mirror . . .

"She's in the mirror world," Heloise said. "She's behind the glass."

Benedict, observing all, his face twisted into an expression somewhere between concern and consternation, said, "What in Lumé's name are you talking about?"

Benedict stood in the sunlight-filled scullery beyond the passage leading to the Tower. His ears rang with a garbled explanation of completely fantastical nonsense, none of which he could make himself believe. Though the scullery was empty save for himself and the girl, someone was bound to come this way at any moment. What would he do then? How would he explain his presence here, standing like a fool with an ebony-framed mirror in both hands and a barefoot peasant girl seated at his feet?

Heloise sat with her back to the wall. She wasn't crying. She was absolutely, definitely *not* crying. There may be tears in her eyes, but she wouldn't allow them to get the best of her, and she would rather turn blue holding her breath than let it out in what might be a sob. But she couldn't do anything else; she could only sit there *not* crying, for this alone took all the control she could muster.

What is this nonsense? said the voice in her head. *Get up, child! What do you think the young lord will think of you, carrying on so?*

Do you expect your sister to rescue herself?

Evette . . . Evette in that gorgeous gown . . . Evette who didn't look like Evette at all, but who was Evette nevertheless . . .

Heloise let out her breath and drew it in again. "It's not my fault," she whispered, though it came out as a choking gasp.

"See here, please, can't you take yourself back home and, I don't know, maybe have a proper weep?" Benedict suggested, his voice earnest though not very comforting. "There's no point in your sitting just here, and the household will start waking up soon now. They never sleep much past noon after Le Sacre Night. And, great Lumé above us, the apothecary is just down the hall! Do you want Doctor Dupont to come out and see you?"

Heloise held her breath again. She held it so long her ears burned. But when she let it out slowly in little puffs, she was able to reclaim some shreds of her dignity. She wiped a hand across her nose and pushed curls from her eyes so that she could glare up at Benedict. She didn't really *mean* to glare at him just then, but her face settled naturally into that expression.

He took a step back. "What?"

"I've got to look again," she said. "In the mirror."

"Because . . . you saw your sister inside."

"Yes."

"Because she's in the mirror world but not this one."

"Yes."

"Because of this Family of Night?"

"Yes."

"You're mad."

Heloise scrambled to her feet and braced herself against Benedict's disbelief. "See here," she said, "I don't need you to believe me. I don't! I just need you to let me use your mirror again. Because whether or not you believe me, I'm going to rescue my sister. I've got to! You can't expect me to go back home and forget about her, not when I've seen her!"

She thought suddenly of Grandmem. Mad old Grandmem sitting in her little shack, shivering and muttering "Cateline" over and over again. It was like witnessing a prophetic vision of her own future.

With a passion that was terrifying had she only known it, she clasped her hands, wringing them up at Benedict. "You've *got* to let me try!" she said. "Give me a chance. Give me a few days at least! You can hold the mirror if you like, but let me look again. I—I think I can follow Evette." The memory of her reflected self reaching out a hand though her own hands did not move was vivid in her mind. "I think I can get into the mirror world, and I can find her. If I can just find her, I *know* I can bring her back!"

This was false. After all, Grandmem had not brought back Cateline. But Heloise couldn't allow herself to think otherwise, much less say it.

Benedict put an arm around Heloise's thin shoulders. "Come, come," he said coaxingly. "Let's get you out to the garden at least before someone sees you. Please, little girl!"

Too overwrought to take offense just then, Heloise allowed herself to be guided down the passage, around to the scullery, and out into the kitchen gardens where, but a few days ago, she had spoken to Benedict. Once there, Benedict was able to breathe easier. He looked down at the girl, so pale and wretched-looking with her tear-smeared face.

He couldn't deny it: He felt sorry for her. Besides, if she was completely mad, what did that say about him? He had heard the wind talking too.

"Look here," he said, and she obeyed, gazing up at him with terrible solemnity. "We can't go wandering about the house today, me holding the mirror while you're staring into it. People are bound to notice. Come back tonight and"—he could hardly believe his own ears as he heard the words coming out of his mouth—"I'll help you try again. All right?"

"You will?"

Benedict startled. When her face lit up so suddenly and so brilliantly like that . . . well, she didn't look quite so much like a little girl anymore.

He blushed and scuffed one foot in the dirt. "Yes. Sure. But please just *go away* for now."

Heloise grabbed him by the hand and, before he could stop her, planted a kiss on the back of it. "Master Benedict!" she cried in the most respectful tone he had yet heard from her. "Thank you, sir! Thank you kindly!" Then she darted away across the kitchen yard, around the side of the house, and out of sight. His last glimpse of her was tangled curls whipping behind her like a battle standard.

"Oh, Lumé," he whispered. "What have I gotten myself into?"

INDEED, WHAT HAVE WE ALL GOTTEN OURSELVES INTO?

But the story must play out to its ending. We must see where it takes us afterward. So be brave, mortal hearts! Be strong and courageous!

And seek for the branch of silver. Hear me, child, listen to my words. Seek for the branch of silver . . .

SEVENTEEN

PAPA STOOD IN THE COTTAGE DOORWAY. HELOISE COULD SEE HIM long before she was anywhere near the cottage yard, and she suspected from his stance that he had spotted her too. No point in pretending otherwise.

Dragons blast it! Any other day Papa would have been up and away to the fields hours ago. But he had just danced a vigorous dance all night long—well, all night with breaks for refreshment every so often. No one could truly dance Le Sacre all night. Though the sun was by now well past the noon zenith and facing the latter half of the day, Cerf Flaxman looked as though he had only just rolled out of bed. Not unusual on the first day of spring at Canneberges.

Heloise paused at the gate long enough to see if she could spy a switch in his hand. She didn't; not that she knew what she would have done if he *had* held one.

The gate—the same gate where, but a few days before, adoring swains had swarmed around her lovely sister—creaked as she opened it. She half expected the sound to bring her bevy of brothers running to observe their sister get a good tanning (which was always great sport; Heloise was a magnificent howler). But no brothers came, not even as she crossed the yard, scattering Rufus the Red and his clucking harem as she went. Then she stood alone before her father.

"Heloise," he said. His arms were crossed, and his shoulders filled the doorway. Shadows from the low thatch fell heavily across his face. "Your mother has been weeping."

Suddenly Heloise wished there was a switch. She knew how to handle the pain of a switch. It was easy. She didn't know how to handle *this* pain.

"She is in her bed, and she will stay there today," Cerf continued. "You will not go near her."

"Yes, Papa," Heloise whispered.

"You have disappointed her, Heloise. You know how she depends upon you since . . . since . . ."

Since Hélène's death.

"Well, since you're her only girl child, she wants to see you do right by this family. She wants to hold her head up with pride."

Heloise feared for a moment that she would be sick. Right there; right then. All over her father's feet. Her stomach churned as though she'd chewed on a false-unicorn blossom, and her head went light and fuzzy. Mastering herself, she racked her brain for any explanation she might give for her recent actions.

I'm sorry, Papa. There was this talking wind, you see . . .

I'm sorry, Papa. I saw this fantastically beautiful woman kissing Rufus the Red—the ancestor, not the rooster, you understand . . .

I'm sorry, Papa. I watched the daughter you don't remember taken away by phantoms while the rest of you danced and didn't care . . .

I'm sorry, Papa . . .

"I'm sorry," she whispered.

Cerf shook his head. "It's not enough," he said. "Not for your Meme. You have embarrassed her, wounded her." His brow knotted, not quite in a scowl. Indeed, from where she stood, Heloise could almost believe his expression sympathetic or, at the very least, pitying. "I cannot stop her from saying what she thinks. I cannot stop her from thinking what she thinks. But *you*, child, can behave yourself and do right by the Flaxman name."

"Yes," she whispered, though she wasn't entirely certain what she was agreeing to.

Heaving a heavy sigh, Cerf stepped back into the cottage then reappeared to hand a bucket of slops to his daughter. "Give these to Gutrund and do your chores. Then to bed with you."

That was that. Neither comfort nor scolding but Papa's best effort at both. Heloise knew he found the boys far easier to deal with, and she felt sorry for him. He never knew how to talk to her, nor she to him. He always seemed discomfited in her presence, as though she was not quite unwelcome but not quite welcome either.

It hadn't always been that way. Only since the fever. Only since Hélène.

But Papa tried. Heloise acknowledged this in the privacy of her thoughts as she dumped the slops and scraps into Gutrund's trough and absentmindedly scratched the sow behind her ear while she grunted and rooted about for choice pickings. Papa tried. He didn't *want* to treat Heloise differently, and he disliked that he did, though he couldn't figure out how not to. He would have liked, if it were possible, to make everything all right again.

Not Meme, though. Meme didn't try. Meme didn't want to try.

"Do you blame her?" she whispered to herself. She did not need to speak the answer. No. She didn't blame Meme. Not at all. There was only one person to blame.

All of a sudden, there it was; that small, secret thought lurking in the back of her brain. Behind her anger. Behind her fear. Behind even the voice that wasn't quite her own which had plagued her since the morning of her birthday . . . This was a much deeper, much more private voice, and it was entirely hers.

If you rescue Evette, Meme might forgive you.

"Dragon's spit!" Heloise growled. Gutrund, startled by the intensity of her voice, snorted noisily and backed away out of reach. She squealed when Heloise climbed into her pen and landed with a squelch in the mud. Ignoring the pig, Heloise squished over to the water trough and stared inside, stared at her murky, rippling reflection.

"You know what to do," she said.

Her reflection mouthed the words along with her. It struck Heloise as mocking.

"You know what to do. You can follow Evette. I know you can."

Still only the mimicking lip movements. Just like any reflection.

Heloise raised a fist and smacked it down into her own watery face, splashing water over the front of her dress.

In her head, the voice not her own whispered, *Silver . . .*

All the way back to his chamber Benedict told himself that he would be too overwrought by the strange doings of that morning to possibly sleep. He suspected it was a lie, however, and his suspicions proved accurate. The very sight of his bed, mussed and rumpled though it was, drew him like a magnet.

He was asleep before his head hit the pillow, before he'd even thought to remove any layers of clothing.

Perhaps he dreamed. Afterward he couldn't say for sure. It didn't *seem* like a dream while it was happening. But then dreams so rarely do.

In his mind at least, he saw several dark figures draw near and stand around his bed. At first he thought, judging by the general aura of menace radiating from each of them, that they were Doctor Dupont, only split into several versions of himself.

But this idea Benedict's unconscious discarded as silly. Doctor Dupont, while certainly ominous, never carried himself like these figures did. One of them in particular gave such an impression of power and grace even while standing perfectly still that Benedict immediately thought of it as the Prince. Simultaneously he thought of it as the Lion. The words were synonymous in his dreaming head; he couldn't have told one from the other.

The rest of the figures—five or six, maybe more—were less majestic but equally dreadful. And all were nothing more than warm shadows surrounding his bed.

"He has my niece's mirror," said one. "He is dangerous, no?"

"Hardly," replied the Lion-Prince. "He is dying."

"They're all dying," said a third shadow. It added with a deep growl, "Mortals always die."

"This one is dying faster than most," said the Lion-Prince. "I smell it on him. We have nothing to fear from this creature."

"But he has Alala's mir—"

"*Do not say that name!*"

Each word struck Benedict's ear and turned into an animal snarl. There was a screech and, though Benedict's eyes weren't open, he saw a blur and a flash of red.

Then one fewer figure stood around his bed. None of the lesser shadows spoke, as though each was afraid of sharing the fate of the luckless shadow. At last, however, one said, "But if he is determined to help the curse-breaker, should we not dispose of him now?"

"And break the Law?" said the Lion-Prince.

"It wouldn't exactly be breaking the Law," said another voice, a wheedling, whining sort of voice that seemed to pant between phrases. "More like, sort of, you know . . . helping it along."

"No," said the Lion-Prince. His word was final.

"Besides," said a new voice, this one with a huskily feminine growl to it, "he is prime for the hunt. If she should make it so far."

Suddenly all the heads gazing down upon Benedict where he slept turned like those of so many dogs catching a sound or scent in the bushes, though more elegant. The panting one said, "Ah! She's coming."

"The cursebreaker," said the Lion-Prince. "Away with you. All of you. Now!"

A wafting darkness passed over Benedict. He felt it like silk and feathers and . . . and raw power. It was the sort of sensation one can have only in a dream, so he assumed he was dreaming indeed.

Creeeeaaak.

That sound, rather too familiar, brought him awake with a start.

He lay with every muscle frozen and tense, staring into the gloom of his bedroom, which would have been too dark to see anything save that a wash of moonlight shone through the window. It was all so strange by moonlight, and he was so disoriented with sleep that he didn't recognize where he was. At first he thought it was his room back at university, only it didn't feel quite right. He couldn't hear Victor's deep snoring or Luc's strange sleep-talking murmurs. No, this room felt empty, as empty as it had been after . . .

Oh, wait. That was over, that whole period of his life. He wasn't at university. He was back home now. He was back home, and—

Creeeeeaak.

He looked up and saw the outline of a curly head framed in the window. "Is that you?" he demanded. "Heloise . . . Heloise Oakwoman?"

"Yes!" said a sharp, familiar voice. Then, "Oooomph!" With a scramble she managed to get her torso up and over the windowsill. He heard a curse followed by a *thump* as she fell into the cold room.

Benedict sat upright. A gentleman born and bred, he felt it wasn't right for him to lounge in bed while strange young ladies—even peasant girls—fell through his window. Beyond this, he couldn't begin to say what good manners might demand in a situation such as this. Should he offer to help her up? Or simply stay put until she, like a gawky new fawn, got her feet under her?

One way or another, decisions would be easier made in the light. So, leaving Heloise to manage herself, Benedict climbed from his bed and fumbled around for a candle. The fire on the hearth was nearly gone, but a few coals still gleamed like so many devil eyes. Moving slowly, Benedict crossed the room and knelt before the hearth, holding the wick of his candle to the brightest ember until it took. He turned—

—and uttered a gulping yelp upon finding Heloise standing much nearer than expected.

"Hush!" said she, and he couldn't stop the immediate "Sorry!" that sprang to his lips in response. Heloise paid no attention to this, for her eyes, so bright in that warm little glow, were fixed upon the candle. "Is that . . . is that *beeswax?*" she asked in the same tone a beggar might ask, "Are those *diamonds?*"

"Yes," said Benedict, searching in the dark until he found a proper holder in which he affixed the candle before the hot wax could burn his fingers.

"Lumé!" said Heloise. She could have kicked herself then for sounding like such an urchin. But she had only ever heard of beeswax candles before, never seen one in use. There was a tallow chandler over in east-end, and she had once gone with her older brothers to see him at work. None of the chandler's candles had been lit, and the stink of boiling beef fat was almost as bad as the dye house (though no stink could be *as* bad as the dye house). But the lord of Centrecœur and his family, she had been told, used much finer, imported candles made of beeswax.

Heloise felt she could have stared at that candle in its gleaming holder for hours. What a thing it must be to be rich and master of all the land!

"You've got straw in your hair," Benedict said, frowning. The shadows cast by the candle made his face look comically dreadful. "What were you doing, sleeping in a haystack?"

Heloise did not grace this with an answer. Tearing her gaze away from the glorious light, she looked about the room. Her eyes, which had adjusted to the darkness as she crept over Canneberges and waded across the moat, were nearly blinded now. "Where is the mirror?"

Benedict, who'd been practically asleep on his feet when he returned to his room, had to search a bit to discover where he'd left the lovely glass. He found it at last under one of his pillows and realized he must have taken it to bed with him without noticing. Lucky for all, he hadn't rolled over and crushed it in his sleep!

He picked it up in one hand, and the gleam of his candle flickered across its surface and on the black-molded coils of the lions' manes. He thought suddenly of the shadow-figures around his bed. He knew now that they must simply have been nightmares. Strangely lucid nightmares, to be sure, but nightmares nonetheless. Still, he didn't think he would forget them anytime soon; particularly that lion-like presence who had spoken with such command.

"Come on!" said Heloise, all but bursting with her desire to take the mirror in her own two hands. She bounced from one cold foot to the other. "Please, let's hurry! Everyone is asleep, right?"

"I think so," Benedict replied, shaking away the nightmarish memory.

So he found himself stepping out of his room into the gloomy passage without, looking this way and that like a thief afraid of discovery—a strange sensation, here in his own home. Heloise kept close behind him as though afraid of losing him in the darkness. He proceeded down the hall, the candle held high like a guiding star, and the two of them passed undetected.

Once they reached the passage leading to the Tower and the narrow stair, Benedict opened the door to the weaver room and paused in the doorway. No moonlight managed to slip through the narrow window slits, and his candle hardly touched the heavy darkness inside. A gleam along the edge of the nearest loom and the soft bolt of half-woven cloth—and that was all. Everything was as dark as the dungeons below.

Somehow . . . somehow it didn't feel empty.

Heloise pressed up behind Benedict, peering around him into the chamber. She hated to enter. But what did that matter? She had gone far beyond likes and wants now. There was only *need*, and she needed to enter. She needed to look into the glass.

"Will you hold the mirror?" she asked.

Benedict, the vision of his nightmare far too present in his mind, shuddered. "Are you sure you want to do this?" he asked. "Maybe we should wait until morning."

"Yeah. When everyone's up and about, and no one's going to ask us any questions. Right."

Her sharp voice was oddly reassuring. A reminder that, however near any strange, otherworldly terrors might be, Heloise herself was nearer still and more than willing to tear him apart with her tongue if necessary. Benedict grinned despite himself. Holding the candle steady with one hand, he reached with the other into his shirt and withdrew the mirror. It was heavy, and he had difficulty supporting it one-handed.

Heloise, without thinking, put out her hands. Benedict held onto the handle but allowed Heloise to support the mirror by its frame, holding it so that the candlelight filled the glass. The room seemed suddenly much brighter, and more of the strange, monster-like looms could be seen. Of course there was nothing lurking behind them. Or under them. Or in the shadows beyond them. Because the room was empty this time of night. Absolutely . . .

Heloise moved closer to Benedict so that she could look at her face in the glass. How ghastly her reflection looked by candlelight! Her eyes peered out from great hollowed shadows under her brow, and her mouth looked as deeply lined as an old woman's. Her hair, which she had tried to tie back but which had escaped yet again, surrounded her head like a mad woman's. If she hadn't known it was herself she looked upon, she would have been frightened. As it was, she wrinkled her nose and stuck out her tongue, which rendered the hag-like visage ridiculous and therefore bearable.

Benedict, observing this childish behavior, frowned. "Do you see anything?" he asked. "Your sister?"

"No," said Heloise, and her reflection mimicked the movement of her mouth exactly. Still holding tight to the frame, she turned the mirror, bringing Benedict and his candle along with her. Gazing not at herself but at the room beyond herself, she searched the shadows among the looms.

"Anything now?" Benedict asked.

Heloise shook her head. She turned a little more and lifted the mirror higher. Over her reflected self's shoulder was the doorway to the passage, the same place she had glimpsed Evette—or what had looked like Evette—a few hours ago.

"Oh," she breathed.

"Do you see her?" asked Benedict, and glanced out the door. He saw nothing but dark, gloomy hall.

Heloise, staring into the mirror, saw moonlight.

It was impossible, she knew. There were no windows in the passage to allow light in.

Yet in the reflection, the passage was full of white luminosity, there could be no mistake. What's more (and here Heloise put her face closer to the glass until her nose almost touched the surface) there were shadows upon the floor.

The shadows of wind-stirred leaves.

She took a step backwards, pulling the mirror and Benedict along with her. "Easy," said Benedict, his candle flame flickering. She ignored him. She watched her reflected self, also stepping backwards toward the reflected doorway. She took another step.

So did her reflection.

Heloise was not very familiar with mirrors and their workings. But she felt her mouth go dry as she watched what took place. For with every step both she and her reflection took, the farther apart they drew. At first she didn't notice. After all, they were backing away from each other, so it seemed natural the space should grow.

But no. No, they were both carrying a mirror, the real mirror and the reflected mirror. No matter how many steps they took, they should remain face-to-face. Yet it was not so.

"Go on," Heloise whispered, and took another step. "Go to the door."

Her reflected self took the third step, perhaps a fraction of a moment slower than Heloise did. Heloise saw that her reflection did not hold a mirror.

"Turn around," Heloise whispered. "Turn around."

Her reflection narrowed its eyes at her and gave a short shake of her head. Heloise realized that her own eyes had narrowed, her own head had shaken. She felt her hair bouncing over her neck and shoulders at the movement. She wondered who controlled whom now.

The voice in her head whispered in response, *You are controlling you, child.*

What, both of me?

There is only one of you. Your reflection is you.

You and you.

"Me . . . and me," she whispered.

"Pardon?" said Benedict.

But she couldn't be bothered with him. Her concentration was so intensely focused on what she saw in that mirror that her hands might have broken the frame in two were it not so stoutly made. Her face was now very close to the glass indeed, but her reflection stood several paces away, still mimicking her movements but not . . . not quite.

"Turn around," Heloise said. As she spoke, she slowly turned her own head to look over her own shoulder.

And she was staring through the doorway of the weaver's room into a forest full of moonlight.

EIGHTEEN

HELOISE HAD BEEN TO THE EDGE OF THE OAKWOOD ON A SUMMER night when the moon was full, and she, Evette, and their brothers were chasing fireflies and pretending they were Faeries. Even with the moon at its fullest, one could venture only a few paces into the forest before it was too dark to see another step forward, so thickly grown were the branches overhead, blocking out the shining sky above. They would laugh and dare and venture a few steps further, but it was useless and probably dangerous.

Evette, always the practical-minded one, would call them back; and though they protested mightily, Heloise and her brothers always obeyed, secretly relieved. With the moon on their shoulders, they would return across the fields to the brightness of hearth and home, leaving the mysteries of the wood at night behind them.

On winter nights, however, things were different. The branches bare of summer glory allowed more light to stream through but cast such stark and perilous-looking shadows upon the ground that not even Heloise liked to venture in. She and her brothers would stand hand-in-hand, their breath making pale clouds before their faces, their feet, wrapped in animal hides tied to their legs and ankles with stout flax cords, slowly freezing. How far they could gaze into the Oakwood on such nights! Yet the enigma of the forest was greater than ever. Never once did they dare to venture in, and they did not need to wait for Evette to call them away.

But that was all back then. And then was suddenly so long ago. So near and yet so far . . .

This forest, Heloise thought (or would have thought had her numb mind been capable of something so coherent in that moment), was like a strange mixture of the Oakwood on both a summer's and a winter's night. For the growth was thick . . . lush and thick . . . smotheringly, soothingly, deadly thick, with vines climbing trunks and blooming with tiny flowers like stars, and leaves *shushing* together like the taffeta wings of blackbirds flocking over the fields and away to the horizon.

But the light, the lustrous moonlight, was as brilliant as a winter night, falling to the forest floor where it reflected off gleaming, knife-like grass blades and shot up to splash in white splendor across the vines, the trunks, the leaves, the branches. Everything was as clear to the eye as daylight, and yet completely unlike daylight, for all was rendered in the purest silver.

Silver. Find the silver . . .

The voice plucked at Heloise's mind. But for the moment—perhaps for an age—she couldn't acknowledge it. Her gaze passed through the shadows, through the leaves, through the sentinel-straight trees, and glimpsed the vast distances of forever.

She had to blink. If she didn't, she would die.

Her eyelids closed, blocking out eternity, her lashes brushing her cheeks. When she raised them again and dared to look, the forest was still before her and still silver. But forever had retreated, and she could comprehend what she saw. Or at least come close to comprehending.

"Master Benedict," she whispered, "do you see what I see?"

She realized then that he was not there. She could not feel his warm presence beside her as he held the mirror and the candle. Instead she felt the lack of him, which was a much stronger sensation now that she came to notice it. She turned to look for him.

Behind her was the weaver room. The great wooden looms stood as they had before, only now they too were illuminated in moonlight, and she could see them clearly, each bolt of cloth, each thread straining with the tension of creation. Almost she could see the weavers themselves, though this was silly. But maybe not so silly after all, for there was a certain timelessness here. She felt it even if she couldn't understand. In that timelessness the weavers worked and did not work all at once. The bolts of red cloth were both completed and scarcely begun.

Heloise had no time to consider this, however, for she saw suddenly a shimmering oval of glass. Mirror glass, she thought, suspended in the middle of nothing. Through it she saw her own face peering after her.

"Oh," she whispered, scarcely making a sound for fear of disturbing the moonlight. "I am my reflection."

Of course you are, said the voice in her head. *What else would you be? Your reflection is in the Between. And so are you.*

Now take the silver branch.

Heloise ignored this eager command. She was trying to wrap her mind around too many new ideas. When she tried too hard, everything went . . . wobbly. She felt her spirit shiver, and it seemed that, for the space of half a heartbeat, she stood beside Benedict in the (for want of a better word) *real* world, gazing into the mirror glass.

But that was unacceptable. So she stopped thinking about it. She closed her eyes, breathed in, breathed out. She felt the soft glow of the moon on her skin, felt the ground beneath her feet. It was warm ground. Not the cold, age-smoothed stones of the Tower's lowest chamber. No, it was dirt and little ticklish blades of grass, and shining beads of dew or possibly rain. She inhaled again, taking in the scent of a recent shower coupled with the scent of moonlight (which is similar to jasmine, but Heloise had never smelled jasmine and therefore did not know). The scent of Night.

The wobbling stopped. When she opened her eyes, she stood firmly in the forest. She felt it all around her, and even the weaver room in which she stood suddenly seemed more forest than room. The looms could just as easily be tall trees, their branches caught with luminous spider webs or fibrous vines weaving in and out of each other. If she closed one eye, she fancied even the walls would disappear.

It was terrifying and wonderful all at once.

She laughed. She must either laugh or scream, and she thought a laugh would be pleasanter just then and possibly less offensive to the forest itself. With this laugh on her lips, she turned and stepped through the door of the weaver room out into the silver forest.

She stood uncertainly among the trees. There was rather a lot of wood all around her (and her mind had not entirely forgotten that glimpse of forever, though she did her best to suppress the memory), and she hadn't the first idea which way to turn.

But she recalled her brief glimpse of Evette that morning. Evette in a gown of starlight . . . the perfect gown for this forest. Much more suitable than the peasant rags Heloise now wore.

Suddenly embarrassed that the forest should see her, Heloise looked down at herself. She half hoped, since this was apparently a *magical* place, that her own garments would have miraculously transformed into something more appropriate. No such luck. She was herself. Or her reflected self anyway. She still wore the too short gown she had worn to Le Sacre. There were straw bits all over the skirt from her long nap in the loft earlier that afternoon.

Oh, well. One could always hope.

Stop hoping, foolish girl. Start moving. Take the silver branch.

Heloise had seen that strange Evette disappear down the hall passage as though making for the narrow stair. There was no stair now, not here, only more forest. Still, it was a direction to try. So Heloise turned that way and . . . and . . .

"Hold on," she muttered. "What's this?"

The forest was gone. She stood in the windowless passage, surrounded by stone walls and wooden beams overhead. She sensed the open doorway of the weaver room nearby, and the first step of the narrow Tower staircase was before her feet. Master Benedict stood beside her, though him she could not see, only sense.

Her heart in her throat, she placed her foot on the first step.

The forest returned. She stood on flat, grass-covered ground, and her foot came down rather hard, causing her to stumble.

"At the rate you're progressing," said a voice behind her, "the next Le Sacre will have come and gone before you've taken ten paces."

Some small part of Heloise's brain tried to tell her that the voice was Benedict's. But there was no mistaking this voice for Benedict's. This voice had never, ever, in all the long ages of its existence, apologized for anything. This voice spoke to a person's gut and echoed there long after the speaker had closed his mouth.

This voice never blushed.

Heloise considered her options. She could scream, but that still seemed like a foolish idea. What would it accomplish? A laugh would be about as foolish as a scream. More so, for this voice did not sound as if it would appreciate being laughed at. She could run but wasn't certain she would make it very far in this shifting world that was sometimes forest and sometimes stone stairwell.

So she did the only thing she could think to do. Which was nothing.

"Aren't you going to look at me?" said the voice. It wasn't really a question when all was said and done. It was much more like a command.

Ignore him. Take the silver branch.

Heloise felt her limbs willing her to obey him despite her best efforts, despite the urging in her mind. She cleared her throat. Then, on impulse, she bobbed a curtsy. "You—you sound a bit frightening," she said, her voice thin in her throat, "and I'm pretty much frightened to death as it is. So if it's all the same to you, I think I'd rather not. Sir. My lord. Your Grace." None of those titles were the right fit, but she gave each of them a try just in case.

The deep voice rumbled. It might have been a chuckle. It might have been a growl. Either way, Heloise was suddenly thankful that she hadn't had anything to drink recently, since she might very well have soiled her drawers in terror.

"You may call me *Your Highness*," he said.

"Your Highness?" she gasped.

"Yes. Your Highness, for I am Prince and Master here."

Don't talk to him. He'll only confuse you. Take the silver branch and be gone.

Heloise tried to listen to the voice in her head, tried to make sense of the words. But the growl of the Prince behind her answered instead, "Ah! So *you* are here too."

"Um . . . yes?" said Heloise.

"Not you," said the Prince dismissively. "I'm talking to Sister. I know you're present. Speak to me."

I don't want to, said the voice in Heloise's head. Then, after a pause, it added, *Go on, child. Tell him.*

Heloise tried to swallow, but her throat was too dry. "She . . . she says she doesn't . . . want to."

"*What?*"

Oh, great Lumé above! He would eat her now for sure! Whatever he was, enormous and growling and terrifying, he would swallow her up in a single gulp!

Don't be silly. Ignore him. Take the branch.

But Heloise could not move.

"Sister," said the Prince, speaking so close to Heloise's ear that she felt warm breath burning her skin, "do not punish me for your sin! Do not punish yourself either. Accept the gift of our Mother and be grateful. Have no more dealings with these mortals."

"Um," said Heloise, "who are you talking to?"

A breath, deep and dark, wrapped around her from behind. "I am speaking to Sister."

"And who is she?" Heloise asked.

"The Princess of Night."

Something heavy moved just behind her. Something that made no sound, not even the barest rustle of grass, leaf, or twig, yet shook the ground where it stepped. Straining her eyes to one side, Heloise saw the enormous shadowy form of . . . of . . . She had no word to describe it. Nothing in her realm of experience fit what that form was. Nothing at all, except—

Across her mind's eye flashed the image of the two ebony lions framing the mirror.

But even as she thought this, Heloise saw the form change. Or perhaps it didn't change. Perhaps her perception altered. For the massive being she had thought she saw stepped into her line of view, and the moonlight shone full and bright upon him.

He wasn't a beast at all. He was a man. A very tall man, the tallest man Heloise had ever seen. He smiled at her. She thought her heart would stop, for it was a dangerous smile. But it was also strangely beautiful.

Suddenly Heloise hated him. She was a girl of many and extreme passions, though she was not as a rule given to hatred. But she hated this man now, hated the way he stood before her, so masterful, so powerful, without the slightest hint of ill-ease or concern. His hands hung loosely at his sides, and she hated that. He should have crossed them or put them in his pockets or folded them behind his back. Something to show some sense of awkwardness. But not him. His hands hung loose, and his shoulders were back as though he always knew exactly what to do with every muscle in his body.

He wasn't a beast. And yet he was: a magnificent beast, through and through. As much a lion as he was a man, perhaps more so.

Heloise crossed her own arms. She didn't know what else to do with them, and she felt all elbows and knees under that predatory gaze. Her hatred made her suddenly either very foolish or very brave.

Don't talk to him! the voice in her head warned.

But Heloise ignored this. She said, "I know who you are after all."

"Do you?" said he, his smile growing. Heloise had thought at first that his skin was cast in deep shadow, which was strange since the moonlight illuminated everything in this place. Then she realized that his skin was like a shadow itself. Deep black, as black as the sky in which the moon danced, yet somehow full of life and color beyond mere blackness. A true black. But his eyes were like the bright blue sapphire eyes of the mirror lions. She knew when he spoke that she had guessed his identity correctly.

"You're the one who sang up in the Oakwood the other day. The one who sang Le Sacre."

"I am," said he, and he blinked once, slowly. "I heard you sing as well, mortal creature. If you could call it singing."

Oh, great dragon-eating abomination *buzzards!* Heloise felt her whole face erupt in fiery blushes. She had forgotten about that. He'd *heard* her! He'd heard her horrid, hoarse, hideous little croakings! She would remember this. She'd remember it for the rest of her life. Every sleepless night from now until she died, she would stare up at the thatch above her and remember that this person—this lion—this beautiful being had heard her try to hit that high note and crack into a million pieces.

What's more, he knew exactly how much it bothered her. He didn't guess. He knew. She could see it in the gleam of his eye.

"So tell me, O melodious one," said he, and she would have smacked him had she dared, "have you come to break the curse?"

"What curse?" she asked before she could stop herself.

Once again he laughed. It was the most self-satisfied laugh that ever was, and he still managed to make it both beautiful and frightening. "Ah, it is almost too easy!" said he. "The pleasure is almost worth the pain you have caused me and mine. The pleasure of watching you struggle and struggle and struggle some more . . . and then fail. Always."

Not always, you great oaf! You forget who you're dealing with! There was a time I could make you turn tail and run like a cub, and don't think I've forgotten!

Heloise held her breath as the voice in her head shouted the angry words. But the shouting gave her courage, and when it was over, she braced herself and asked, "Where is my sister? You know where she is, don't you?"

"Of course I do."

"Tell me!"

He took a step toward her. She felt the ground shake again, though the form he wore was nowhere near as massive as the one she had first glimpsed. But he took another step, and since his legs were so very long, he was now directly in front of her, leaning down so that his face was mere inches from her own.

In the depths of his eyes, the black pupils in the center of the vivid blue, she saw something she could not name. The only word she could summon from the depths of her quivering mind was . . . *wildness*.

"Why should I tell you anything?" said he. "You are my enemy. You have always been my enemy. Since long before you were born. Besides, you've already asked your questions."

Heloise did not see him walk away. He was gone by the time she'd blinked and realized he no longer stood in front of her. But the ground vibrated with the heavy tread of his feet, and she thought she saw the shimmer of trees and branches withdrawing to make way for him as he passed into the silver forest.

"Wait," Heloise whispered. Then, summoning what little courage remained to her, she shouted. "Wait! Where is my sister?"

She might have shouted in a chapel, so intense was the sensation of disapproval raining down upon her from every tree, leaf, blossom, and branch. Heloise didn't care. Her hands clenched into fists, she took a stumbling step forward, then another. Then she was running up a forest trail that was simultaneously a stone stairwell. But she ignored the stairs and focused instead upon the forest, pursuing the shivering, shuddering branches, pursuing the mighty lion.

Stop, you fool! Can you not heed a word I say?

He knew where Evette was. She knew that he knew, and just then she thought she'd rather let him eat her in a few quick bites than let him get away from her.

The trees murmured. Then they growled.

Something grabbed Heloise by the ankle. She fell and landed hard upon the moonbright grasses, which stabbed at her hands like the tiny blades they looked to be. She screamed in frustration, little caring how offensive this noise might be in this silver place, and pushed herself upright. But her foot was still caught, and she saw that it was held in the twirling coil of a tree root.

She pulled hard, struggling, and managed to get herself free. Then she was up and running again, uphill now. She felt the ripple of roots in the ground behind her but refused to look back. She pushed her way through thick-grown branches only to find that the branches were pushing back, resisting her, refusing to allow her passage. All the silvery moonlight twigs caught in her hair, caught at her dress, caught at her skin, and pulled viciously.

Stop struggling! Take the silver branch!

She opened her mouth but couldn't scream again, for vines had wrapped around her chest and stomach and squeezed so hard that she couldn't draw breath to make a sound. The trunks of several trees suddenly pressed toward her. She could see every crevice of the bark, could see the strange, moving patterns of life and death.

What a pathetic effort this had been! What a stupid, pointless endeavor! How furious Grandmem would be when she learned Heloise had died so soon upon starting this venture!

A silver branch appeared before her face, its wicked, pointed ends aiming at her eye. With a last gasp she reached out and snapped the branch off . . .

Then she found that she was wrapped up not in vines but in the grasp of a long arm, and her face was not crushed against the trunk of a tree but smashed into the rough embroidery of a rich jacket. A button pressed hard into her cheek, leaving an indentation that wouldn't fade for hours.

"Are you done screaming yet?" Benedict whispered fiercely into the hair on top of her head.

NINETEEN

HELOISE PUSHED SO VIOLENTLY AGAINST HIM THAT BENEDICT LET her go—but then caught her by the arm in time to prevent her from tumbling down the narrow stone steps of the Tower. Her stomach lurched at the impending fall that did not happen, and this was enough to shock her into a more reasonable frame of mind.

She realized that she was holding the mirror in one hand.

"What happened?" she gasped, shaking off his grasp. She could barely discern the pale contours of his face in the wavering candle glow.

"You snatched the mirror and ran, that's what happened," he growled. "Then . . . I don't know. You started to bleed."

Heloise looked down at her arms and hands, realizing that they hurt. Tiny burning cuts criss-crossed her skin, a hundred little wounds from that sharp-bladed grass she had fallen upon. Where the trunks and branches had wrapped around her limbs, she saw red bruises.

"Oh!" she gasped, the pain finally catching up with her. She wobbled on her feet.

"Steady!" Benedict cried, catching her by the arm with one hand. He held onto her as her head whirled, as her blood pulsed pain through her veins. His eyes looked hollow and frightened by the light of his candle. Then he gasped, "Lumé above!"

At the sound of that exclamation Heloise opened her eyes, braving the dizzy world. Following his gaze, she looked down at her lacerated arms once more. Almost more horrifying than the wounds themselves was the sight she now beheld. For the cuts were closing. One cut at a time, yet swiftly, her skin pieced itself together, forming scars. A thousand white hairline scars. After a few breaths, even these faded.

The pain lingered a little longer. She hoped it wouldn't stay forever.

"Are you steady on your feet?" Benedict asked at last.

She nodded, and he let go of her arm. Suddenly not as steady as she'd thought, Heloise leaned her back against the cold wall of the stairwell and, pressing the mirror to her chest, sank down to sit on a step.

Benedict grunted, irritated. "What were you thinking?" he demanded, his voice a whisper so tight and tense in his throat, his vocal cords might snap at any moment.

Heloise shook her head. She couldn't talk yet. Her mind was too full even now of silver forest and strange moonlight and the sapphire eyes of a fantastically enormous wildcat. When Benedict reached out to take the mirror, her arms tightened around it instinctively and her eyes flashed a warning.

He drew his hand back. "You know you can't keep that. It's not yours."

"Oh," said Heloise, dully. She looked down then, allowing the mirror to rest upon her drawn-up knees. Her reflected face stared up at her, mostly shadows.

She shuddered. When Benedict reached out a second time, she did not resist. Indeed, it was a relief to see the wretched glass disappear under his jacket.

"Do you mind telling me what that was all about?" he asked as soon as the treasure was secured.

Heloise shook her head. She didn't know.

But Benedict wasn't about to be put off. "Come, now. You dragged me up the passage then suddenly started shouting, grabbed the mirror from my hand, and ran to the Tower stair. Do you have any idea the kind of mess I'll be in if I'm caught wandering about in the dead of night with a mad girl? Because personally I can't begin to imagine it!"

Heloise put her hands up to her bowed head and buried them in her mane of hair. One hand was closed in a tight fist, and this she rubbed on her temple, which throbbed. She shut her eyes, willing herself not to see all that she had seen. The fingers of her open hand tightened against her scalp, and she half wondered if it were possible to physically pull thoughts out of one's brain. Doctor Dupont probably had tools with which to extract unwanted memories . . .

Suddenly she realized that her tightly closed fist hurt. "Ow," she said, rather after the fact. Lowering it to her lap, she tried to make her fingers uncurl, but they resisted. She was obliged to use her other hand to pry her own fingers open.

Lying on her palm was a tiny silver branch. A leaf gleaming like the moon itself curled out from one end, unfurling even as she watched.

"Are you listening to me?" Benedict said. "I'm telling you, *you've got to go*. And never come back. I've had enough of this nonsense, and really it's not my business. You belong in a madhouse, I'm quite sure of it, and . . ."

His voice trailed off. The candle seemed suddenly to offer no light at all. By comparison to the branch in Heloise's hand, the little flame struggling on its wick might just as well have been a shadow, so insignificant did it become. For as the branch and the leaf began to shine, the narrow stairway filled with a brilliant nimbus surrounding Heloise and Benedict. Pure, silvery moonlight.

A breathless hush filled the air, broken only when Benedict whispered, "Where did you get that?"

I CAN HEAR THEM WITHOUT, THROUGH THE DOOR. IT IS A HEAVY OLD *door, a door which has served its duty for so long now that it is as much a part of the surrounding landscape of this estate as the earth and bogs and trees of Oakwood. It was built of an Oakwood oak and fastened with brass rather than iron fixtures. Thus I can lean against it without pain. I might even touch the latch, open the door a merest crack, and gaze into the narrow stairwell beyond . . .*

I hear the mortal lad. His voice rises up the spiral stair to touch my ear. "A lion?" he says, his voice brimming with disbelief. "In Centrecœur?"

"No!" says the mortal child. What a sharp-tongued mite she is! Rufus himself would be proud, if he only could know. "No, in the silver forest, like I told you!"

"Which . . . is in Centrecœur?"

Rufus would be less proud of the lad. His lineage has been diluted over the years into something elegant and refined, scarcely worthy of the Cœur name, I fear. It is difficult to believe these two spring from the same source, though it has been centuries now.

"Not in Centrecœur," *Heloise persists. Heloise Oakwoman. The sister. My sister. My daughter. My kin.* "I don't know what else to tell you! The forest was in the mirror, and the . . . the lion was in the forest, and all of it was in the house."

"And this . . . magical twig of yours. It came from this forest?"

The girl grunts. "Yes. Someone told me to take it. And the forest was squashing me, and if I didn't grab it, it was going to poke out my eye. Only it was you squashing me, not the forest . . ." *A pause. Then,* "Why were you squashing me, by the way?"

"You were screaming. I tried putting my hand over your mouth, but it didn't do much good. Besides it was a bit damp."

The silence lingers between them, an embarrassed silence, I think. At length the girl, determined to change the subject, asks that which I knew she must. "Where does this stair lead?"

"The top chamber of the Tower," *says the lad. The next moment I hear him exclaim,* "Where are you going?"

"I want to see this chamber."

But she cannot. Not yet. I see her shadow cast by the candlelight rounding the bend. She herself will follow soon after. But she does not

yet have the three-part key. I know the law. I know what will happen if I am caught breaking the law . . .

So I shut the door and lean against it, my ear pressed to the wood, listening.

"You can't," says the boy. *Good boy that he is.* "No one goes into that room. It's locked."

"You mean you've never tried to get inside?"

The mortal girl's voice is much nearer now. So close to me, separated only by a few inches of wood. Yet she is worlds away.

"No," says the lad. "It's been locked for ages. I told you."

The silence that follows could be interpreted any number of ways. But I suspect the mortal girl is giving the boy a certain look. A look of extreme annoyance. A look that would be as comfortable on my own face as it is on hers.

"You mean . . . you've never tried?" she asks. "Just to get a peek?"

"Um. Well."

"Oh, please! Aren't you even curious?"

"Well, I mean, I've thought about—"

"But you've never tried?"

The lad growls. In that moment he sounds more like his great ancestor than I have yet heard him. "The room is locked," he says again.

"Where's the key?"

"No one knows."

"No one?"

So they begin an argument that will prove useless. At least for now. Although I admire the girl's determination, the lad is right. They haven't a key, and they will not gain access to this chamber until they do. She has only the first part of the three-fold branch.

I step away from the door, step back into the chamber which has become my whole world. Let them pursue their plots and plans. I can do nothing more until moonrise tomorrow.

I turn.

I pass through the heavy branches of flower-laden trees.

I sit at a window that isn't a window so much as a break in the trees. Around me all is green and gold and lavender. But my view is of the moonlit landscape of Canneberges. So far away . . .

The power of mortal magic increases around me.

TWENTY

NEVER BEFORE HAD HELOISE WALKED TO AND FROM CANNEBERGES SO
many times in such a short span of days. As a rule, her life only brought
her within sight of the Great House once a year, during Le Sacre.
Otherwise, work on the broad grounds of the estate filled her hours, and
she scarcely had time to think about the family for whom she labored or
the mighty comfort in which they lived.

But once more she found herself scrambling out of the shallow moat
and bounding away from solemn, inward-looking Centrecœur and off
across the fields and bogs. On most any other night she would have
thought the world around her looked strange, even frightening,
unfamiliar as it was by solitary moonlight.

After what she'd seen tonight . . . no, nothing to be found on the
grounds of Canneberges could scare her.

She felt spring in the night around her. The air was as cold as late winter, the ground as hard beneath her feet. But the night birds were home from their southern travels, and she heard them singing soulfully to one another through the darkness. Yes, spring had certainly come. A deadly spring.

It wasn't fear so much as trepidation that slowed her pace when, at long last, she drew within sight of her family's cottage. How sore were her feet, how tired her eyes! She had slept but little the afternoon before. It had been difficult to sleep with the memory of Evette in that starlight gown so vivid and awful in her mind.

Now she knew she must sleep. She must, or she would drop dead to the ground and never move again, and what would become of her sister then? What would become of her Meme, mourning the loss of three daughters even if she did not know it was three she had lost?

So, though she dreaded climbing up into her empty loft and seeing the even more empty place where Evette should be, Heloise crept across the cottage yard, tiptoed through the door, past the low beds upon which her brothers slept around the hearth, and slipped light-footed up the ladder.

There it was—that awful empty place.

Heloise shuddered. She curled up, not in her own pile of straw but in Evette's. She drew Evette's blanket over her head and pressed its woolen scratchiness to her nose, breathing deeply. Was that her sister's scent? No. Just the scent of sheep. Heloise wept.

She woke in the morning with dried tears crusting her face and nose, and her brother Clovis perched at the top of the ladder, pounding the loft floor with his fists so that it vibrated.

"Wake up! Wake up, Heloise!" he shouted cheerfully, grinning like a fiend when her head appeared out of the straw and her fierce eyes shot daggers his way. "Meme says you're to go up to Oakwood again today and not return until you've carried three full baskets to the south-end dye house."

"Rrrrumph!" Heloise kicked the blanket from her legs, scattering straw as she did so. "Got to feed Gutrund," she muttered.

"Nope. Meme says you're to go right away. *I'm* to feed Gutrund." Clovis made this declaration with such delight, Heloise thought he must be a natural-born Pigman.

"Is Meme gone to the spinning shed?" she asked, pulling bits of straw from her hair and attempting a braid. She'd never learned how to properly tame her own hair. Why bother? Evette had always been on hand to see to such things. Not that Evette had ever had much success with Heloise's mad curls either.

"Yes, and she's got Clive with her," Clovis said. He slid down the ladder before her and indicated the stewpot over the coals. "We left some breakfast for you."

So Heloise's day passed. She ate; she gathered her basket and paring knife; she made her way up to Oakwood and stepped into the shadows beneath the leaves, thinking suddenly how tame this forest felt compared to the one in which she had walked the night before. How friendly were her oaks as well, welcoming and even generous as she harvested their bark. They wouldn't crush a girl just for trying to walk between them. They wouldn't snatch at her feet with their roots.

Heloise sat on one high limb with her legs swinging and gazed through a break in the foliage out across the expanse of Canneberges. From here she thought she could catch just a glimpse of the Tower's rooftop. From that high, unoccupied chamber, someone could probably survey all the estate grounds with ease.

"I wonder if Meme hates me?"

The words slipped out before she could stop them and hung in the silence before her. Heloise gripped her knife harder. No. She couldn't think about that right now. She couldn't allow this sudden rising anger in her heart. Besides, who was she angry at? Her mother?

No. Not Meme. She couldn't be angry at Meme . . .

Three baskets of oak bark to the dye house meant three separate trips back and forth from the Oakwood. The walk to the dye house wasn't short, and by the time she completed her third delivery, the sun was already high. She paused just out of range of the dye house's stench, her empty basket on her hip, and considered the prospect of returning home. Meme would probably be out of the spinning shed by now, preparing a meal for her husband and sons.

"And me," Heloise whispered. "But I'm not hungry."

What a lie that was! Still, Heloise meant to return to Centrecœur that night, and she thought it pointless to walk all the way back home and make a pretense of going to bed when she would only be sneaking out again a few hours later. Better to not return at all. Papa would worry, but Meme would assume she was having herself a good sulk somewhere and would tell him not to go out searching.

So, her basket still on her hip, Heloise set out for Centrecœur once again.

Benedict lay in bed. He didn't like it. Evening had not yet turned into night; there was still plenty of light in the sky. He should be up and hard at work, for he was only getting farther behind. How could he expect to return to university and keep pace with the other lads if he didn't push himself? That dragon-blasted wind had ruined weeks' worth of efforts!

But he couldn't quite make himself rise.

Doctor Dupont had looked in upon him a few hours before, tapping his fingertips together and nodding solemnly as though heeding some secret voice of wisdom and doom which Benedict could not hear. He'd checked inside Benedict's ear again, but apparently the fires of fever and the fever spirit had not yet returned. Which was good, Benedict supposed. Except that it seemed to prove the value of the doctor's awful prescriptions, which was not good.

Still, once Benedict downed his dose, the doctor had left, and Benedict was free to sleep.

In his dreams he thought the shadow figures watched him. But they said nothing, and really, what were dream shadows going to do to him anyway?

He woke at dusk and stared at the canopy above his bed. He tried to think, but nothing happened, so he simply stared, counting his heartbeats as though each one would be his last.

Someone had brought him a platter of food and left it on the table at his bedside. Nothing much, he saw upon dull inspection. Doctor Dupont prescribed a strict and unsatisfying diet of fish broth with "healthsome" herbs. Benedict didn't mind the healthsome herbs so much (though *healthsome* seemed to be synonymous with *bitter* in Doctor Dupont's vocabulary), but he would have liked it better if the fish were still in the fish broth.

"Are you going to eat that?"

"Heaven help me, no," said Benedict. He turned his head on his pillow to look at the girl perched in his window. There wasn't much point in being surprised at seeing her, so he didn't bother. "You can have it, if you like boiled fishy-water."

"Is there bread to go with it?"

"I didn't look."

Heloise swung herself down from the window, a more graceful

entrance than her previous two, though she exposed rather more of her leg than was quite decent. Benedict, always the gentleman, shut his eyes until he heard her stomping footsteps round the foot of his bed and approach the table and food platter.

"There's a bun," she said. "Looks a bit hard."

"Help yourself."

Heloise hesitated. It didn't seem quite the thing, to eat in front of the lord's son. But her stomach growled, and the bowl was still steaming.

She dunked the bun in the broth to let it soak then ate with a will. Benedict observed her from the corner of his eye as he lay there in bed. Peasants apparently weren't picky about what they ate. Nor how they ate it for that matter. Lumé, did she not know what a spoon was for?

Heloise finished sipping the last of the fish broth from the bowl itself and wiped her hand across her mouth. "When does everyone bed down for the night?" she asked.

"Soon after sundown," Benedict replied.

"But you're already in bed?"

"As you see."

She made a face at him. "My Meme says that those who go to bed before the sun aren't worth a bowl of pottage come dawn." She paused before adding, "I think it's supposed to be a rhyme."

"I shouldn't wonder," said Benedict. Slowly he sat up. His trousers were nowhere in sight, but he lacked the energy to be bothered at the moment. His limbs felt shivery, and a certain numbness throbbed in his veins. Nothing much, nothing worth complaining about. He closed his eyes and leaned his head back against the carved headboard, which proved singularly uncomfortable.

Heloise watched him, her eyes keen and quick. Benedict was a pale man by nature though blessed with an abundance of freckles. But behind the freckles lurked more than paleness, she thought. Behind the freckles was . . .

"Here now," she said, taking a step forward and frowning sternly. "I thought you said you weren't sick."

"I'm not." Benedict opened one eye and squinted at her. "I'm fit as a fidget."

"No, you're not. You've got—you've got—" She stopped. For a moment she feared her knees would give out, so to keep herself from landing on the floor, she sat down hard on the edge of his bed, too stunned in that moment even to be surprised at its delightful softness. She stared at the cold color behind his freckles, and she knew exactly what she was looking at.

"You've got the Winter Fever," she said.

"Technically, it's got me," said Benedict. Then, because he was Benedict, he added, "Sorry. That's not very funny, is it?" He opened both eyes and gave her a hard look. "I say, you're not—Oh, dragon's teeth, you're not *crying?*"

"I'm not," Heloise snapped and angrily brushed the two tears away. "I'm not. It's just . . . I didn't know the gentry folk got our sicknesses."

"Don't be daft," said Benedict. He reached under one of his pillows and produced a handkerchief which he handed to Heloise. "Here, blow your nose. You look ghastly."

Heloise *honked* loudly, glaring at him as she did so. "How'd you get it?" she asked. "The fever, that is."

He shrugged and leaned his head against the uncomfortable carvings again. "It went around at university," he said. "All my mates . . . well . . . It struck our hall, and three were dead before the Black Tops—that's what we call our professors, you see—knew what was happening."

Suddenly he was talking. Suddenly he was spilling out names he hadn't spoken in months. He said things he'd scarcely allowed himself to think, all of it pouring from his lips in a quick tumble he could not have suppressed had he tried:

"Henri, Giles, and Luc. They were dead so fast, I didn't have time to think about getting sick myself. And then I was sick. And so was my best mate, Victor. And Victor died. And I survived, and they packed me up and sent me home. Sent me here. My father was away at court, and he didn't come back when he heard. My mother, when she learned I was coming, removed to her people's house, the Bellamys', you know. Father doesn't want to see me sick. Mother doesn't want to catch my sickness. But they sent Doctor Dupont at the recommendation of the king's own physician. So that's something."

His voice was heavy and dull, but the words continued to fall from his tongue. "I haven't heard from any of the lads since. I told Serge to write to me, but he hasn't, and that was four months ago now. I sometimes wonder if it spread to the other halls. If Serge got it too."

Benedict shuddered again and shifted in his bed, trying to find a comfortable position. He had never spoken of these things. Not to anyone, not to his manservant and not in any of his stiff and formal letters to his parents. Certainly not to Doctor Dupont. Indeed, he'd intended never to speak of that dark time again, of his loss. What did it matter anyway? It couldn't be long before he too was dead and joined his fellows.

Yet here he sat in the gloom of dusk, listening to the echo of his own words poured out into the ear of this grimy peasant girl who sat on his bed and watched him with such wide, knowing eyes.

He realized there were tears on his own face. "Blast it all," he growled.

"Here," said Heloise, offering back the used handkerchief.

"Thank you. I've got one," Benedict assured her, and fumbled under his pillow for a spare. He didn't use it, merely mashed it up in one tight fist. "They say it hasn't left my body. Not really. The fever, I mean." His voice was little more than a whisper. "They say it's gone into . . . *hibernation*, I think is the word Doctor Dupont used. But it'll wake up one day, and I probably won't survive next time. I don't know when that'll be. Doctor Dupont thinks it's a miracle I've lasted this long."

"Doctor Dupont is a dragon-kissed idiot," said Heloise.

The vehemence of her voice startled Benedict, and he looked up sharply at her dirt-streaked face. She gestured furiously, as though wishing the good doctor was in smacking distance even now. "He thinks you've got a fire devil in your head, and that's just stupid! The Winter Fever isn't a devil. Any simpleton knows that!"

"I thought all peasants believed . . ." Benedict stopped himself, realizing how desperately condescending he sounded. "Um. So you know about the Winter Fever then, eh?"

"It killed my sister."

"What?" Benedict frowned. "Hold on. Aren't we wandering about with mirrors and dealing with other worlds to *rescue* your sister? You're not, as it were, trying to"—a cold chill ran up his spine—"raise the dead, are you?"

Heloise didn't answer this. One hand clutching Benedict's handkerchief, she wrapped her arms around her skinny body and stared at the pattern on Benedict's thick counterpane. It was a pattern of running deer. She wondered vaguely what they ran from.

"It came when we were small and took many of the little ones that winter," she said softly. "But I was always the stronger one, from the time we were born. I came first, and I was stronger, and I cried, and I ate more. I took all her strength. Hélène didn't cry, and she ate very little, but she was so good. And I wasn't. I couldn't be. I'd got all the strength; Hélène got all the goodness. When the Winter Fever struck, I was so strong, it couldn't catch me. But Hélène . . . she died in two days."

She was buried in the graveyard where all the Flaxmans were

eventually laid to rest. A younger Heloise, small and strong, hadn't understood. She'd never known anyone to die. She'd cried and screamed at her mother, standing over that shallow grave.

"*Don't throw away my sister!*"

How hard had her small fists struck her mother's weeping body? Not hard, she was certain. She was strong, yes, but still not yet six years of age. Surely she couldn't have caused more than the smallest bruise. Yet her mother had crumpled before her on the ground, wailing like a lost soul in the depths of the night.

"*Cruel child!*" her father had growled, dragging her back even as she continued to shout and scream for Hélène. "*Have you no sense? Have you no pity?*"

Heloise realized that she was no longer staring at the pattern of deer. She was gazing into Benedict's eyes and he into hers. She saw there, deep down in his gaze, the death of Victor, his best mate. He saw the death of Hélène. Two more dissimilar souls could hardly exist. But in the face of death, they were kindred.

"Heloise Oakwoman," said Benedict, and his voice trembled with the intensity of his words when he spoke. "We're going to find your sister. We're going to find Evette. Do you believe me?"

"Yes," said Heloise. "We're going to find her all right."

TWENTY-ONE

AN AWKWARD SILENCE FOLLOWED THESE BOLD DECLARATIONS, because while both parties spoke with passion, one was a dying youth and one a ragged peasant girl with straw in her hair and no shoes. Neither was the stuff of heroes and legends, and both knew it. So, though their eyes burned bright for a moment, at the next moment each looked away from the other, Benedict to study the canopy above his bed, Heloise to study his counterpane. A low fire in the hearth provided the only warmth and almost the only light in the room, which fell more deeply into night by the moment.

"Where's the branch?" Heloise asked to fill the silence as much as anything.

"What branch?"

"The silver branch I showed you last night. The one I brought back from the forest."

"Oh. That. I put it in the armoire with the mirror."

Heloise waited for what she felt was a patient interval before prodding, "Aren't you going fetch it?"

"I'm not wearing my trousers." Benedict scowled at her but without malice. "And I don't have the strength to get out of bed just now. You get it."

"*Really?*" Her eagerness propelling her, Heloise sprang to the floor before Benedict could change his mind and hastened across the room to the great armoire. It was an enormous paneled structure, as big as the entire Flaxman fireplace and hearth, built of solid oak harvested from the Oakwood itself and carved by a master craftsman of Canneberges. It had to be a century old or more. All three of its doors were adorned in patterns of wood thrushes and cranberries, and the handles were polished brass.

Heloise, recalling from which section Benedict had taken the mirror the day before, put up her hand to the middle door. She paused, however, suddenly unwilling to open it. One could almost believe whole kingdoms were contained in such an old and enormous trove! After her visions of the day before, this was not such an odd thought as it might have been.

"It's on the middle shelf. You'll see it right away," Benedict called from across the room. He was hardly visible in the evening shadows now, for the light from the fire couldn't quite reach his face. Heloise, looking

278

over her shoulder, could discern only a vague lump in the bed. But she knew she herself was fully visible in the firelight. Unwilling to let the marquis's own son see her hesitate, she grasped the brass handle firmly and swung the door open.

The middle portion of the armoire was made up of a row of shelves upon which many fine things rested. Heloise glimpsed these out of the corners of her eyes: elegant belt buckles, embroidered and fur-lined gloves, bottles of ointments the purposes of which she could not begin to fathom (hygiene not being a particularly important aspect of life in the Flaxman household). These and many more treasures, like a whole dragon's hoard belonging to one young man . . . and yet none of these could capture her attention.

For the silver branch resting atop the ebony-framed mirror's glass was the only sight truly worth gazing upon in all that chamber. Possibly in all Canneberges.

It didn't look like a real twig. Or rather, Heloise decided at second glance, it looked more real than real. As though some master silversmith had formed every little twist and turn and knob and bump with expert care. Its unfurled leaf, the most delicate filigree, as fine as spider webs, gleamed unnaturally bright.

Reflected as it was on the surface of the mirror, the branch's silver light filled the whole armoire and nearly blinded Heloise with its brilliance until her blinking eyes had a chance to adjust.

"It wasn't doing that when I put it in there," Benedict said. He sat upright and, his blankets wrapped in a bundle around him, shuffled down to the end of his bed to gaze over the massive footboard. "It looked fairly normal. Silver, but normal. It didn't glow." He glanced nervously toward his door. "Lumé! I hope no one sees the light and comes knocking."

Heloise, having no answer to this, reached out one hand which, despite her best efforts, shook. But she plucked up the silver branch. Strange—she could have sworn it had been much bigger the night before, when it aimed right for her eye! Yet she knew it was the same branch.

She took up the mirror with her other hand. The room was cold, but both branch and glass felt strangely warm. Not hot, not uncomfortable to the touch. They simply felt as though they had not been sitting in the cold space in which she stood. The early-spring chill of Canneberges did not affect them.

She held the branch up between two fingers, turning it slowly. It seemed to her, though she could not have said why if asked, that it was somehow *incomplete*. Not simply that it had been broken off its tree; it seemed to her that it was meant to be part of a whole, the shape of which she could not quite guess.

It was a puzzle. But then, everything was a puzzle these days.

Since she couldn't guarantee that her pockets sported no holes just then—Evette was always the one to check and make certain Heloise was properly mended and put together—Heloise tucked the silver branch into the thickness of her braid. The braid itself was partially undone but still secure enough. She doubted the little coiling twig would easily work itself free of the tangles. Besides, she rather liked the idea of wearing shining silver in her hair. She wondered if it made her look like a Faerie.

Then she lifted the mirror by its handle and looked into the glass.

"Oh, dragons!" she cried, whirling around to stare at Benedict.

He, wrapped in his blankets, frowned back at her. "What's wrong? What did you see?" He shivered, and not from cold. "Is it . . . is your forest in *here* as well?"

"Um," said Heloise. She didn't like to answer. She didn't want to tell him that in the mirror world, yes, his reflected bed stood in the middle of a green glade, the four posters each themselves tall trunks of trees, the canopy a sweep of green branches all intertwined.

But more than anything she didn't want to tell him about the six shadowy figures standing all around him—in the mirror world, but no less real. Figures that were not merely shadowy but truly shadows themselves, needing no bodies to cast them.

She didn't want to tell him. She didn't want to know it herself. In fact, she would willingly have scrubbed her eyeballs with lye soap just then.

"You look ill," said Benedict. "And that's something, coming from me."

She did indeed look very strange with the silver glow from the branch lighting up one side of her face, leaving the other half cast in darkness. Both of her wide eyes were visible and bright, however. He knew without being told that whatever she'd seen must be terrible.

"Maybe," he said as gently as he could, "you should put the mirror down. Maybe you shouldn't attempt to . . . to do whatever it was you did last night. Leave it for now. We can try again later."

Heloise could hear him talking. She could even discern a few of the words above the wild hammering of her heart in her breast. Her immediate response was, *Yes! Listen to him! He makes a good deal of sense. And he is the marquis's own son, so he must know a thing or two, and he's got all that book-learning and those decl—declat—those things he'd written on all that paper! He knows what he's about, and yes, he'd be well worth paying attention to, don't you think? So put the mirror down, put it back, shut the armoire, and go home. Just go home. At least for tonight. You can try again later, just as he says.*

But it didn't make a difference. Because no matter how much her brain pummeled her with these ideas, no matter how madly her heart pounded, the quiet voice that wasn't hers was already there, whispering a counter thought:

You can't leave Evette with them.

That's just what she'd be doing if she went home now. Because she'd seen those shadows before, she'd seen them on Le Sacre Night. She'd seen them, along with the white phantoms, take hold of her sister and drag her away.

They had her. They held her. Somewhere in their strange forest realm.

You must return to the Between. You must find the second branch, the branch of gold.

So without answering Master Benedict, Heloise turned her back on him and held up the glass. Though all was dark on that side of the chamber beyond reach of the firelight, in the glass she saw pure green, rich and warm, so lush she could almost hear it humming the song of its own greenness.

The shadows around the bed were gone. The bed itself was gone. But the four tall trees standing in place of the bedposts were still there, as was the canopy of leaves.

"Heloise?" said Benedict.

She didn't answer. She was looking at herself. Only she saw herself standing in the dark, fire-lit bedchamber, her face cast in silver-and-red glow, her hands holding something just out of sight which she knew was the handle of the mirror.

But her own hands held nothing. Because she now looked on herself from the mirror world.

"I am my reflection," she whispered. Then, "This is getting easier to do."

She turned away from the little oval of glass. She didn't need it and didn't want to be distracted by it. Lifting her gaze, she sought some glimpse of the sky through the greenery above her. But the trees stood so close together, their branches so entwined, that there was no sky to be seen.

It should be much darker. No sunlight could shine through foliage that thick, and yet all was bright as midday. But search though she might, Heloise could discover no light source. Perhaps the brightness was all in her own mind. Or perhaps the trees themselves gave off light.

Well, none of that mattered. She couldn't remain here turning in place and expect to get anything done. She wasn't certain how much of her Benedict could see or hear. Obviously, when she'd screamed in the moonlit forest last night, she'd screamed in the real world as well. And those cuts had been real as well, though now even the scars had disappeared.

Just in case he could hear her, Heloise spoke out loud: "I'm going to go exploring. Just a little ways. I'll . . . I'll be back. I suppose." She couldn't promise for certain. After all, in a forest this big, how could she expect to find her way back to any one particular spot?

With a shrug, she set off in a direction that appeared less thickly grown than the rest. Indeed, as she pushed her way past a low-swinging bough (wondering, as she did so, if she was stepping through the door of Benedict's room), the ground beneath her bare feet shifted. Tree roots rippled beneath the soil, pulling back and away. Grasses skittered and slid, flowers ducked and danced, and Heloise found a path of warm brown dust spread before her, as clear as though someone had cut it ages ago.

"Well," she said, "I think I'll go *this* way."

Rather than pursuing the path, she turned and pushed her way firmly among the trees. She heard the forest murmuring around her, frustrated vibrations that struck her bones rather than her ears. But she resolutely pushed through boughs and ducked under branches, wading through grasses and ferns that came up to her knees, sometimes up to her chest.

Every second she expected the trees to surround her again and crush her. But this time, much to her relief, they only grumbled. The further she plunged, the more the forest withdrew, no longer presenting an enticing path but at least not interfering with her efforts.

Good girl. Very good. Now, find the branch of gold.

It was warm. Heloise decided to focus on this fact above all others. It was warm. Blisteringly warm. Damp as well, like the most humid of days at the height of summer in Canneberges, down among the bogs . . . but ten times more so. Yet there were no bugs, not even one. No living thing moved or breathed anywhere so far as she could discern.

Other than the forest itself, which was far more *living* than anything she had ever before encountered.

But even this thought she chose not to dwell on. She focused on the warmth and how uncomfortable it was. She focused on the sweat rolling down her spine so that her garments stuck to her skin. She focused on these things with desperate intensity as she moved through the tall grass and pushed leafy limbs from her face.

She didn't think about the fact that she was in a forest while still in a house, and that none of this was really possible. Because, possible or not, it was happening. And she had to find her sister.

You must find the branch. The branch of gold.

A gurgling, shushing, lulling voice called to her from a near distance. She turned her head to one side so that her ear might better catch the sound. It was like rain, but not really. Definitely water, though.

Having no other clear goal in mind, she decided to pursue it. Once more the trees permitted her to pass, and within a few paces she found herself standing in a sort of avenue, as finely tended as the main roadway leading up to Centrecœur on which the marquis and marquise themselves traveled to and from. The trees on either side of her were stately, but of a variety she did not know. Their trunks were pale, almost lavender-hued, and the leaves arching overhead were richly golden. Not golden like autumn, but golden like the buttons on Master Benedict's fine jacket, glinting. They glinted so profoundly that one could almost hear *glint* as an actual sound as light struck each leaf and bounced to the next.

"Branch of gold," she whispered. But even if she were to stretch up as high as she could reach, she could never grasp any of those branches, and, skilled though she was at climbing, these trunks were too tall and smooth. Even the lowest limbs were beyond her reach.

Keep going. You'll find one. I promise.

The gurgling song of water continued to beckon, and it seemed to come from the end of this avenue. So Heloise continued on, taking one step, then a second.

But as she took the third, she realized that she wasn't alone.

She couldn't see them, at least not when she looked at them directly. But as the leaves overhead went *glint, glint, glint*, the light they cast struck the air and left impressions.

Heloise blinked. While her eyes were closed, just for that small instant, she saw the lower gallery of Centrecœur in the middle of the dark night, and moonlight shining through the windows along the wall fell upon twelve figures dressed in white not many paces ahead of her.

Heloise's eyes opened again from their blink. The figures were gone, as was the hall. She walked the golden avenue of trees, one foot just come to rest, the other about to rise. But the air ahead of her still bore the impressions of twelve young women.

She closed her eyes again immediately. This time no image of Centrecœur appeared; she saw only the inside of her eyelids. She wanted to curse but was too angry, so it came out in a sort of splutter.

Grabbing her skirt in both hands, she ran up the avenue, pursuing that which she could not see. The glinting leaves cast strange shadows on the ground before her, and had she given them more than a passing glance they would have made her dizzy. But she was so intent upon her pursuit, she could scarcely spare a thought for anything else.

Then, though she knew it hadn't been there a moment before, she came to an abrupt halt before a waterfall.

Its liquid voice filled her ears to brimming, and she stood with her mouth open, staring. How it could have manifested itself so suddenly she could not begin to guess. But then, this forest didn't follow any of the rational rules by which Heloise had thought the world worked, so really she shouldn't be surprised.

The waterfall itself was tiered, dark stones beneath the water forming a set of stairs that would have been perfect had they not been quite so slick and had the water not run over them quite so fast. At its base a churning pool bubbled and sparkled. Heloise expected a river or stream flowing away but saw no sign of one. Perhaps the pool was very deep and thus never overflowed the banks upon which Heloise now stood. The waterfall itself was tall. She stared up its great height and blinked again.

With her eyes closed, she saw a broad stairway cast in moonlight and stone leading up to the Great Hall of Centrecœur above. Twelve girls dressed in white climbed that stairway. One turned and looked back at her.

"*Evette!*" Heloise cried.

Don't try to follow! Leave her alone!

Heloise stood a moment in frozen indecision. Then, despite the voice roaring commands in her head, she plunged into the pool—which was foolish considering she didn't know how to swim. Just then she didn't care, and fortunately the pool proved shallow, rising only as high as her knees. She waded forward, little noticing how cold the water was despite the heat in the air. She reached the waterfall and stood before its heavy white churning. The first tier was no more than a step, so she lifted her foot and took it.

"Ouch! Dragon's teeth!" she yelled. The step was slippery, and she nearly hit her chin as she fell, which surely would have jarred several teeth loose had she not caught herself. The whole front of her dress was now soaked through. But she grabbed the stone under the water and pulled herself up.

You foolish, foolish child! Take the branch and be away! Why can you never listen?

Despite the white rushing, Heloise managed to climb five steps. Her knuckles pale with the effort of gripping and supporting herself on wet stone as water poured in a never-ending stream into her eyes and mouth, she braced her arms and legs and reached for the sixth step.

You've got Rufus's own stubbornness about you. Open your eyes and see what's before you!

A low-hanging bough extended over the water, a gleam of gold against the moist air. She caught hold of it and pulled, feeling for an instant the strong support it gave her.

Then, with a crack, it broke off in her hand.

Heloise fell, and the waterfall pushed her back several steps. But she caught herself with one flailing hand even as her other hand remained firmly clasped around the broken branch. Water poured into her gasping mouth, and she choked and gagged and felt what it might be like to drown.

Let go! Let go and be on your way!

Heloise clung to the stone, refusing to fall any further. No! She couldn't allow that. She must get to the top of the stair! She must—

Something caught the top of her head. Long, muscular fingers wrapped around her skull, tangled in her mass of curls. A heaving tug, a jolt of pain, and Heloise found herself rising up out of the waterfall's flow to stare into the face of a strange, horrible being.

At first she thought the face was a skull. But that couldn't be. It couldn't be! It must be a mask. The body was tall and black as pitch, but the forest's golden light made each glossy limb gleam with an odd speckling, as though there were spots just beneath the surface. The shoulders were massive, the neck thick and powerful, and yet the body itself was thin, willowy, and weirdly feminine.

One long arm stretched to its full extent held Heloise by the head as bright gold eyes flared at her from behind the skull's hollow eye sockets.

"Where do you think you are going?"

The voice poured through grinning sharp teeth that never moved, only grinned, and it spoke the same, incomprehensible language of the Le Sacre song. But even as before, the words struck Heloise's ear and broke apart, shifting in her mind to find a shape she could understand.

"Where do you think you are going, mortal creature? Stealing our bounty as you go!"

The stranger's other hand, black and speckled as her bare neck and massive shoulders, darted with the lethal swiftness of a wolf driving in for the kill, caught the branch Heloise clutched in her hand and, with a sharp twist, snatched it away.

"Alala, you silly child," said the voice behind the teeth. "Will you

290

always place your trust in such doltish creatures as these?" The strange woman held up the branch, claw-tipped fingers twirling it so that it gleamed before Heloise's gaze. Heloise wanted to reach out, to try to snatch it back. But both her hands clutched at the long fingers holding her by the head as she struggled uselessly to be free.

The strange woman laughed. At least, it might have been a laugh—a high, chortling, coughing gulp of a sound, closer to a laugh than to anything else Heloise had ever heard. It froze the blood in her veins despite the humid heat of the air.

"Here, mortal beast," the woman said through her laughter. "Fetch!"

With that she tossed the golden branch down into the pool below. Heloise twisted in the grasp that held her, saw the little *plop* . . . and watched the golden glimmer vanish under the bubble-churned surface.

The woman let her go. Heloise fell hard onto the steps, and water poured into her face. After the fact she reflected that this would have been a good moment to pause and consider a reasonable course of action. But reason had no place in this realm.

Get it back! Get it, quick!

Heloise whirled about, the stones of the steps grinding painfully against her back and bones. She flung herself down into the pool.

Before it had been shallow, no higher than her knees. Now, as she plunged in a rush of white bubbles and froth, she realized that it was very deep indeed. So deep that she felt the strength of depth as though it latched hold of her arms and pulled.

Her eyes were tightly shut, and she plugged her nose with one hand. But that was no good. What did she hope to accomplish? She couldn't swim, to be sure, but she could hold her breath and try to look. The water stung her eyeballs, but that wasn't so bad. She forced her eyes open and peered into the darkness below.

It was strangely clear. Impossibly clear. All around her, silver light glowed, and she realized that it came from the small silver branch caught in her hair. Below her, the golden branch, turning gently as it sank, lit everything as clearly as a paper lantern on a summer evening. She could see every bubble, every eddy in the water. She could see the smooth stones around her like the walls of a well.

A moment of choice so brief it could hardly be called a moment flashed through Heloise's consciousness. She could struggle and flail to reach the surface, or she could do what seemed to come naturally and . . . sink.

Suddenly she knew that she would rather die than let that golden branch get away from her.

So she sank. She kicked and waved her arms, and somehow this helped the sinking. The weight of the waterfall pressed upon her, pushing her deeper. Her rate of sinking was faster than the branch's, but she was still far out of reach. She rotated her body, her legs tangling in her sodden skirts, and went headfirst down into the gaping depths, her eyes filled with silver and gold light.

One hand outstretched. Oh, the pressure around her head, in her ears, in her bones! It crushed her, compressing her like a newly washed cloth being run through a mangle. But she reached, and she kicked, and the waterfall urged her further down to her doom. Her fingers strained, and she thought her bones must break in the weight of water.

The branch gleamed brighter. Then, just as her hand closed around it, the light went out.

And Heloise found herself lying halfway on the bank of the shallow pool (which was now only a few inches deep), coughing and spluttering even as the waterfall rained down from above. She spat out what seemed like a whole well's worth of water and lay shuddering with her face in the golden grass.

A foot as enormous as a knight's helmet came down into her line of vision. Black and velvety, boasting giant claws that ever so gently tore the ground beneath it.

The Lion-Prince spoke: "So you've met Aunt now, have you?"

TWENTY-TWO

RATHER TO HER SURPRISE, HELOISE FELT A SURGE OF RELIEF THAT filled her body and expelled itself in a great sigh. Possibly a hundred or more reactions would be considerably more appropriate in this particular situation.

Nevertheless, as she lay there on the brink of that pool which had, only moments ago, been unbearably deep and seemed likely to prove her final grave but which was now scarcely more than a puddle—as she felt the pound of a waterfall on her legs, a waterfall which she knew even now poured down the staircase of Centrecœur—as her one hand clutched the golden branch and the other wiped spit from her face, she felt nothing but relief that the Lion-Prince had appeared in his lion form which, though more dreadful, was far less intimidating than his man form.

She didn't much like the idea of lying face down, drenched through and bedraggled, covered in her own spit before the gorgeous, princely being she had met in the moonlight only the night before.

Gracious, child, don't start sighing over him! He's not worth it, I tell you, and he'll only confuse you more if he catches on.

"I'm not sighing!" Heloise muttered even as she pulled herself out of the pool and glared up at those strangely blue eyes set in the even more strangely ferocious face of the Lion-Prince. She spat again and sat up, trying to think of something witty and biting, something that would begin to express just how thoroughly she *wasn't* sighing over *anyone*, certainly not under these circumstances.

All she managed was to gasp through another cough, "Is—is your aunt that skull-woman?"

Don't bother asking him questions! He'll only twist them anyway. Get up and be on your way.

"Skull-woman?" said the Lion-Prince, tilting his massive head to one side. A breeze played through the luxurious silk of his mane, which was so black that even the golden light shining down upon it seemed to lose itself in the blackness, rendering it blacker still. He snorted, which was a far more majestic sound coming from a lion than it would be from anyone else. "That was a mask. You should see Uncle. His face really *is* a skull. And yes, she is Aunt. My aunt. Sister's aunt."

The shudder seemed to begin in Heloise's gut and work its way out to every extremity, even to the ends of her sodden, heavy hair. She was obliged to wait for it to pass before she could say anything. Then, pushing her hair back from her face with the same hand that clutched the branch, she said, "I think you're lying. I think you're trying to scare me."

"I don't need to try," said the Lion-Prince, and his expression, were it not so disdainful, might have been amused. "Nor do I need to lie. But you'll find out for yourself soon enough. You'll have to go on the Night Hunt with both Aunt and Uncle in order to break this curse."

The shudders wouldn't stop. Heloise's whole body quaked as if she were cold, though the air was warm and steaming around her. But her ears were quick, and she pricked them at the Lion-Prince's words, and her eyes shot briefly to his face. "A curse?" She scowled at him. "I still think you're lying."

Oh, great dragons and imps! It would serve you right if I left you to him. Are you even listening to me?

"I am not lying," said the Lion-Prince. He took a seat then and gazed idly over her head as though she were nothing more than an unavoidable nuisance. "I never lie."

Which was probably a lie as well. "Besides," Heloise continued, ignoring the irritable growling of the voice inside her head, "if you're not lying—if there really is a curse—I suspect *you're* the one who set it. So you certainly wouldn't want me to break it."

"Of course I don't want you to break it," said the lion, and he might have rolled his eyes at her if it weren't so undignified a gesture. He continued to stare up at the waterfall, speaking to Heloise as though she were invisible. "For your information, I didn't set it either."

"Who did?"

That's two questions. If you must ask them, don't waste them. But you would be wiser not to ask at all. He's not to be trusted, even when he speaks the truth.

The Lion-Prince looked as though he didn't want to answer. As far as Heloise could tell, he had no reason to. After all, though he had answered a few questions of hers the night before, he'd given her no useful information. Then he'd refused to say anything more but had stormed away into the forest, leaving her to be crushed by ferocious trees. She half expected to watch him rise now and pad away into the golden gloom, his shadowy mass vanishing into deeper shadows.

Instead, albeit with extreme reluctance, he said, "It's a curse more powerful than anything I can do . . . yet. Not even Father could do it, and he was always among the greatest of our number."

You'll notice he hasn't answered you. But he must. Force an answer from him.

"Who is Father?" Heloise asked.

Is that what I told you to do? Truly you are a dunce!

The Lion-Prince gave her a momentary glance then, and his eyes glittered with an expression she didn't understand. "The King of Night. Be thankful you don't know him. Be thankful you never will. You'll be dead and dust long before any of us sees Father again."

He resumed his intense contemplation of the waterfall over her head, the tip of his long tail twitching.

Heloise, the irritable voice in her head plucking away at her nerves, scowled with thought. Then she grinned and drew herself up. "So if you did not set the curse, and neither did your father . . . what does your mother want with my sister and with Cateline?"

Well done! Maybe you're not such a dunce after all . . .

To her delight, the Lion-Prince actually looked surprised. He shot her a glance then quickly masked his face with a bored expression. Too late. She'd startled him with her accurate surmises. A small victory, but she'd cling to it.

"You have to answer me, don't you?" Heloise persisted. "You don't want to, but you have to. Otherwise, you'd have left by now. Or . . . or eaten me. But you're not supposed to eat me. Why not? Did Mother send you to help me? Does *she* want the curse broken?"

Clever child! Not quite right, but clever. My Rufus would have loved you . . .

"Never," said the Lion-Prince, and his lip curled in a snarl. "And it never will be."

He stood then, so enormous that Heloise could scarcely take in the whole of him. Indeed, she suspected that there was more to him than she was actually *able* to see, that she would need a different set of eyes entirely if she were to begin to comprehend the power before her. Yet his voice was oddly young, even petulant.

"Mother wants nothing to do with your sister, with any of your sisters. Throughout the ages she has wanted nothing to do with them. She cannot bear even to look at them. But she will take them, for they are hers by right. And she will go on taking them until your line is dead and gone and there is no one left to take. They will be hers for all time, little mortal; they will be hers long after you have forgotten, long after you *are* forgotten."

He turned his back on her and moved away into the surrounding forest. The shadows and lights falling from the trees above swayed over his mighty form but seemed unable to touch the absolute darkness of his hide. He called back over his shoulder even as he disappeared:

"You have asked more than your share of questions, mortal beast, and I have answered what I must with truth. Go on the Night Hunt with Aunt and Uncle if you want more answers. But it will do you no good!"

Heloise, seated where he'd left her, realized that she no longer sat on the edge of the pool. Indeed, the further he got from her, the darker her surroundings became. Darker and smaller and closer, and all the golden light faded away. She was cold too. Not just shuddering, but truly cold, with goose pimples running up her arms and neck as icy air breathed against her wet body.

The forest was gone. Or mostly gone. She found herself at the foot of the staircase in Centrecœur in the middle of an early spring light. The stones around her captured the cold and held it close, and the floor beneath her was like ice.

"Heloise?" Someone spoke near to hand.

The forest vanished entirely, and she knew she was back in the mortal world.

"I hope you'll notice," came Benedict's voice from the darkness behind her, "that I am *not* asking how you managed to get sopping wet between my room and here."

Something thick and rich-smelling wrapped around Heloise's shoulders. It should have felt lovely and warm, but instead it seemed to squeeze her own soaking garments more tightly against her shivering skin. Heloise tried to shrug it off, but Benedict caught it and pressed it to her shoulders. "Here now! You'll catch your death if you're not careful. What good will that do your sister?"

Heloise bowed her head, momentarily winded and unable to protest, as though she'd just run a mile at breakneck speed. All was too dark for her to see much after the brilliance of the golden forest, and the gold branch, suddenly smaller than it had been, was hidden in her hand and offered no light. Minutes passed before her eyes adjusted well enough to notice that she wore the counterpane of fleeing deer around her shoulders, deliciously elegant and acquiring large damp patches where Benedict held it against her.

As she sat there, relearning to breathe and wishing she knew how to force her limbs to warm themselves, a sound plucked at her ear. At first it was so faint, it was difficult to believe she truly heard it. But the longer she sat there counting the moments in heartbeats, the more certain she was that her ears—or possibly her reflected ears somewhere beyond the mirror glass—did indeed discern the voices falling through the ceiling above:

"Cianenso

Nive nur norum.

Nive noar-ciu, lysa-ciu"

Her eyes lifted to stare at the wooden beams crisscrossed overhead. Benedict, his vision better adjusted to the darkness, watched her. "Do you hear something?" he whispered.

"That's the Great Hall up there, isn't it?" Heloise whispered.

"Yes," said Benedict. Then, though she hadn't asked, he added, "It's old, as old as this gallery and the tower. From back in Rufus the Red's day." He turned his head, listening intently. But the only sounds to reach his ear were those of a lordly house plunged into sleep.

"Le Sacre," Heloise whispered. "They're singing Le Sacre."

Her shoulders hunched beneath the counterpane, and her dripping hair looked strangely lank about her face, giving her a more fragile appearance than Benedict would have thought possible. Slowly she curled into herself, her head low between her shoulders, curled into a ball of wet misery.

"Heloise?" Benedict said, giving her an anxious shake. "Heloise, are you all right?"

Then, as though this moment of fear and vulnerability had never happened, the girl sat upright and tossed back the counterpane and her wet hair. She held out both hands, and when her fingers opened to reveal what lay in her palms, Benedict saw in one the silver branch and in the other a gleaming gold branch, larger than the silver and equally as bright.

"Did you get that in the mirror world?" he asked.

Heloise nodded. She stared at the two branches, studying them, each twist and curl.

"By the way," Benedict said, uncertain whether Heloise would even hear him, so intense was her concentration, "where is the mirror? You had it with you, and—"

"Oh, dragon's teeth!" Heloise gasped, closing her fists and turning in place on the stone. Her gaze cast about for the ebony frame and the shimmering glass. "Isn't it here?"

"Are you . . . sitting on it?" Benedict suggested, and Heloise immediately leaped to her feet. Then she kicked the counterpane aside, searching beneath its folds. But not until they checked the shadows at the foot of the staircase itself did they find the mirror lying facedown upon the stones.

Benedict picked it up and with great trepidation turned it over. Both sighed in relief to find the glass unbroken. "Lumé love us!" Benedict said. "When I saw you fall down the stairs, I rather thought the mirror'd had it." He paused. "I mean, I was worried for you too, of course . . ."

Heloise shook this off as the nonsense it was. "May I see?" she asked, and he turned the mirror around so that she could look into the glass. She saw her own face or what she assumed was her own face, for it was difficult to say in the gloom. Nothing else. No golden forest. No strange path, no waterfall, no pool.

Yet she still heard—or almost heard, like the echo of a memory or a dream—Le Sacre falling softly from above.

"Nivee mher

Nivien nur jurar

Nou iran-an."

Much to her embarrassment and frustration, Heloise suddenly wanted to scream. She was cold. She was frightened. And she was so, so, *so* angry. Angry at the Lion-Prince for telling her only so much but leaving her more confused than ever. A curse? What curse? And why? Why? Why was she able to walk in her reflection? Why did the lion call her his enemy? *Why did there have to be women wearing skull masks, with husbands whose faces were real skulls?* This was all completely beyond the utmost edge of ridiculous. She felt a scream welling up in her breast, and if she didn't do something soon, all Centrecœur, possibly all Canneberges, would suffer a sudden and rude awakening.

The voice in her head offered no word or warning.

The murmur of the incomprehensible Le Sacre still in her ear, Heloise turned her back on Benedict so as not to see his confused, pale face. Just then there could be nothing more appalling, more galling than confusion. Particularly from him. She was confused enough herself, feeling the heaving bile of bewilderment in the back of her throat, and she couldn't bear even a fraction more. She clenched her fists so tightly, she felt the sharp contours of the twigs digging into her skin.

Then, frowning even more deeply, she opened her hands again and looked at the two branches. She had seen it before—she knew she had. But she hadn't understood what it was she saw. Even now she wasn't absolutely certain, but . . .

She took the two branches and held them up to each other.

Like two lovers reunited after a long absence, the silver branch and the gold reached for each other. The stems entwined, the leaves quivered and brushed each other, and the gleaming of moonlight and sunlight made solid was suddenly so bright that it filled the whole of the long gallery.

"What in Lumé's name is that?" Benedict gasped, standing close enough to gaze over her shoulder.

Heloise held up the two branches. But they were now not two but one, fastened together and forming a new shape, a shape she felt she almost recognized but not quite.

"I don't know what it is," she said. "But I think it's time I visited Grandmem again."

TWENTY-THREE

GRANDMEM WATCHED THE FIGURE APPROACH ACROSS THE FIELDS. She sat in her doorway, gumming her morning carrot and slouching like a wilted blossom on a thin stem, and she knew who was coming. Who but Heloise would venture out to see her at this cold, early hour with the sun only just beginning to rise?

Her granddaughter's progress was odd and awkward. Heloise had never been what one would call a graceful child, at least not by ordinary standards of grace and gentility. But she had a certain galloping energy that might in due time pass for grace, especially if she learned to forget her own self-awareness.

This little figure, however, was entirely lacking in energy, though she shuffled along with great determination and equal consternation. The morning was still too dark for Grandmem to discern the cause until

Heloise was well up the path to the humble shack.

Then Grandmem asked, "What have you got on your feet?"

Heloise raised a fisted hand in greeting. "Slippers, Grandmem," she said. "They're slippers."

"Those aren't proper shoes now, are they?"

"No, I don't think so," said Heloise, not one to claim expertise where footwear was concerned. "I tried on some of his shoes, but they were much too big. These are too big as well, but we stuffed stockings in the toes, and they're quite warm."

So saying, Heloise drew near enough for her grandmother's bleary eyes to take in the whole of her. She wore a young man's tunic, several times too large for her skinny frame, and the bedroom slippers adorning her feet slapped with each footfall and wanted to slide off. They were, nonetheless, extremely fine. Or had been before Heloise slipped her muddy toes into them and trekked across half of Canneberges.

The tunic was also fine, too elegant for the likes of a flax farmer's daughter. Heloise had protested when Benedict drew it from the depths of his wardrobe, claiming she daren't touch it, much less *wear* it. But, as Benedict had practically pointed out, it wouldn't do for her to race across the night-shrouded fields and bogs, soaking wet and barefoot on a night as cold as this. She'd be sick by dawn and dead by dusk.

Heloise insisted this was a gross exaggeration. "*You're full of bog-dregs!*" she'd declared. Still, shivering as she was, she agreed at last to exchange her damp clothes for Benedict's offered garments and hastily changed into them while he stood outside the door. Benedict had hurled the slippers out the window, just managing to clear the soggy moat so that they landed in the cluster of false-unicorn plants on the far side. Then, with her shift and outer dress in a bundle under her arm and the two joined branches clenched tightly in one fist, Heloise had dropped down into the mud, waded across, wiped off her feet and calves as best she could, and pulled on the slippers, thus ruining them forever.

They were very uncomfortable, Heloise thought. Why would anyone ever want to bother with shoes? Big though they were, her toes felt constricted, and she couldn't feel the ground properly to test its various merits. But she stood bravely and, after a wave to Benedict at his window, set off through the night for her grandmother's hovel.

So she appeared now, clad in garments far too elegant and far too large for her body. The tunic hung sack-like, caught at the waist by a simple leather belt that was more beautiful by far than the flax-cord belts worn by everyone Heloise knew. The hem of her garment reached well below her knees, and rabbit fur lined its sleeves, which Heloise didn't like (she liked rabbits well enough but preferred them wearing their own coats).

She blushed as Grandmem looked her up and down, embarrassed at the old woman's disapproving inspection.

"Your father was here last night," Grandmem said around her carrot. "He asked if I'd seen you."

"Really?" Heloise couldn't keep back the startled question. She'd known that her parents would note her absence, but she hadn't thought they would care enough to go looking for her. Well, Meme probably didn't care, if she'd noticed at all. But Papa . . . well . . . She couldn't decide whether or not she was pleased.

Grandmem continued her study of Heloise's strange outfit. "I hope, dear child," she said, interrupting the tumble of Heloise's thoughts, "that what I'm seeing does not mean you have turned into a thief."

Her father forgotten, Heloise blushed hotly. "No!" she protested, and tossed her damp garments down at her grandmother's feet. "I got wet, and Benedict—that is, Master Benedict de Cœur—that is, well, he loaned these to me."

Grandmem rolled the carrot to the other side of her mouth and gummed it thoughtfully. Her tired eyes traveled up and down her granddaughter's fine raiment and took note of her clenched fists. "Hmmmm," she said, which wasn't really saying anything but was merely a sound to fill the silence between them. "Hmmmm."

"I'm not lying, you know," Heloise growled. "He's helping me. Master Benedict, that is. He's been loaning me his mirror."

"Ah," said Grandmem, again without communicating anything she might be thinking. "Ehh."

Heloise felt irked. Irritation being her natural state, she didn't notice it at first. But as she watched her grandmother sitting there in the rising morning light, she suddenly found that she was indeed quite irate and ready to focus all her ire upon the frail old soul before her. After all, hadn't she done what her grandmother asked? Hadn't she risked her neck (and continued to risk it, since Grandmem wasn't the only person who would cry thief if Heloise was spotted in Master Benedict's clothes) to fulfill this fool's errand that she didn't half begin to understand?

Silly child, said the voice in her head. At this distance from Centrecœur the words were faint, few, and strained, as though whoever spoke must struggle to speak them.

But they were sharp. Sharp enough to bring Heloise up short, mid-sulk, and force her to look both at herself and at her grandmother again. And she thought, after all, what *did* she expect from the old woman? A pat on the head and a "Who's a good girl then?" Grandmem wasn't the head-patting sort, thank the Lights Above. Besides, what adulation did she think she deserved? Was there any special honor in doing the only thing she could possibly do?

After all, she was the *strong* one. If she didn't act strong, what was the use of her?

As she stood staring at her grandmother with these varied thoughts sifting through her brain, Heloise frowned suddenly. She frowned as she noticed something she had not been able to see even a moment before.

Her grandmother was angry. Angrier than Heloise had ever seen her. Angrier than Heloise had ever been.

This anger manifested itself in neither word nor deed. Grandmem sat gnawing on her carrot with her one good tooth, studying Heloise's odd garments, and the new sun illuminated her face in gentle softness.

But there was no softness to be seen in the core of her eye. The anger rose up from inside of her and strengthened with each passing moment until Heloise feared she would be knocked flat with the force of it.

Grandmem drew a deep breath. She let it out in a long, long gust. As she did so, it seemed that some of the anger (not all of it, for there was far too much) blew from her body. She spoke then in the same quiet, easy tone she always used:

"I had no one to help me."

Heloise felt as though she'd been struck in the face. At first she couldn't understand why her heart heaved in her breast so, why she felt that sudden rush of tears prickling in her eyes. But it came to her within three painful heartbeats.

Grandmem had been alone. She had been all alone. No friend at the Great House to assist her, no grandmother to believe her, no support. Just herself and her reflection in a mirror glass—not the bright, clear mirror Heloise had been using, but just that old, dingy thing. She'd had no help, no one to tell her what to do or even what to try.

She had me, the voice whispered faintly in the back of Heloise's head. *But she forgot.*

And she failed.

Heloise knew then that whatever else happened, she dared not fail. Not when she had Grandmem helping her on one hand and Benedict on the other. If she failed . . . Oh, the shame would be too much! Too much to bear! And the anger, the same anger she saw simmering in

Grandmem's stone-still face even now, the anger would be destructive. She would not survive it.

She did not know if she could even survive the pressure now weighing on her shoulders.

Grandmem raised a quivering hand and passed it over her eyes, gently swiping wisps of white hair back behind her ears. She blinked once or twice, and now, though the anger was not gone, it was at least better hidden. "So, Heloise," she said, stretching one stiff leg out before her and gently shifting on the doorstep. "So you tried to climb the stairway, did you?"

Heloise drew a long breath of her own and let it out in little shuddering puffs. But when she spoke, she too tried to make her voice as natural as possible. "Yes. It was slippery. And the pool didn't stay put! That is, it was shallow one moment and—"

"—and deep the next. I remember," said Grandmem. "You shouldn't try to climb the stair again, not on the mirror side. I attempted it three nights running and nearly drowned myself each night for my efforts. You'll not follow your sister to the top, no matter how you try."

Heloise felt her knees betray her. She felt them giving way before she fell, and she even made a paltry effort to prevent them from buckling entirely. But it was no use. She was so tired and damp, and her knees simply could not support the heaviness in her heart. She sank to the dirt, little caring just then how she dirtied Benedict's tunic. "Then it's hopeless," she whispered.

313

Grandmem gave her a sharp look. Then she took the carrot from her mouth, leaned over, and bopped Heloise's head with it. She wasn't one for head-patting, but head-bopping suited her rather nicely.

"Sit up straight, girl," she said, as imperious in that moment as any dowager queen. "I'll not have you despair in front of me. That's my lot, and I've a right to it after what I've been through. But you—you haven't failed. Not yet. And you have help that I had not, so we'll see to it you *don't* fail, won't we?"

"But how can I succeed?" Heloise wailed. Then, reinforcing that wail with a louder one, she added, "I don't even know what I'm supposed to succeed at! I don't know what I'm doing or why. Some curse? That's what the Lion-Prince said, but he won't tell me what the curse is or why we're cursed or anything useful!"

"So you've met the Son, have you?" said Grandmem, leaning her head sideways against the doorpost. A funny twist tugged at her mouth. "He's a pretty one, isn't he?" At Heloise's subsequent blush, the old woman uttered a disdainful "Ha!" and gripped the carrot tighter.

She said no more, so Heloise, rubbing at her cheek as though she could rub the blush away, asked, "Who is the Lion-Prince? That is, whose son is he?"

"He's Mother's Son," said Grandmem.

"All right." Heloise wanted to spit, but knew she'd end up with her ears boxed if she dared. "Who is Mother then?"

"I don't know," Grandmem replied. "I never met her. I never made it up the stairs." She closed her eyes then. The sun was brighter now, and perhaps its warmth comforted her. All the many gathered wrinkles of her face smoothed under its rays, and Heloise, for the first time she could remember, thought she might almost glimpse the young woman Grandmem must have been at one time. A young woman not all that different from herself.

"I tried three nights to climb those stairs," Grandmem said. "Each time I knew it was impossible, but I tried anyway. Because I didn't want to face the truth. Son told me what I had to do. But I couldn't accept it. Not at first.

"On the fourth night, however, I knew that I must do as he said. I must run the Night Hunt with Uncle and Aunt. If I wanted to find answers, I must join them. And I tried. Oh, believe me, Cateline, I did try!"

Heloise, sitting with her knees up, her elbows propped on them, and her hands, one clenched in a fist, hanging limply from the wrists, frowned at this. Had her grandmother lost her head? Did she not remember to whom she spoke?

"I told myself there are things worse than death," said Grandmem. "I told myself that it would be better to die than to fail. So I made my way to the forest of diamond, and I prepared myself for the Hunt to follow. I prepared myself to die. For I believed that I must be the prey they hunted.

"I was wrong. And I could not join them. Not when I saw who it was they pursued. Not when I saw what they did to him."

Grandmem shuddered then and hunched over. She was motionless for a moment. Then her body heaved, as though trying to cough up a sickness in the gut. It heaved again and a third time. But the spasms passed, and Grandmem sat up slowly, both hands covering her face. She rubbed her eyes, rubbed her cheeks, and at last settled her hands down along her jaw, supporting her face.

"Grandmem," Heloise urged, "who did they hunt? Please tell me."

"Marcel Millerman," her grandmother replied softly. "He still lives about these parts, runs the east-end wheat mill. He was just a miller-boy back then, nothing much to look at, nothing much to mind. But Cateline . . . well, she smiled a certain sweet smile for him. When she was taken, he forgot her and was left despairing without knowing why."

"But . . . but they didn't kill him," Heloise persisted. "In this Night Hunt, I mean. He's still alive."

Grandmem shook her head. "No, child. No, they did not kill him. Much worse than that."

Heloise face twisted into something between a frown and an incredulous smile. "What's worse than death?"

Grandmem did not meet her eye. She only shook her head and whispered so that Heloise had to lean in to hear her: "I couldn't stand it. I couldn't join them. I couldn't watch what they did to him. They promised they would cease their evil games if I left. So I walked away, I left the forest of diamond, and I never once returned."

A single tear rolled down Grandmem's faded cheek. "Did you face the silver forest and its crushing, Heloise?"

"Yes, Grandmem," Heloise said.

"And you passed through the golden forest to the waterfall staircase, I know."

"Yes, Grandmem."

"Did you retrieve the two branches, the one of silver and the other of gold?"

In answer, Heloise sat up straighter and held out her hand. She turned it palm-up, uncurling her fingers. Even in the brightness of morning, the two little branches gleamed with magical brilliance.

"I think something's missing," Heloise said as she displayed her find. When her grandmother reached out to take it, she almost snatched it back. This impulse she suppressed, and Grandmem took up the two branches, holding them so that the morning sunlight played on the little twists and curling leaves. Were it not for the distinct gold and silver glimmerings, it would be easy to think the two had always been one, so naturally did they fit together.

"Beautiful," said Grandmem. "It is very like the one I had. But see here?" She pointed with one gnarled finger at a space beneath one of the two curled gold leaves. When Heloise leaned in to look more closely, she saw a small cut in the stem, so small as to be unnoticeable if one didn't know to look for it.

"What is it?" Heloise asked.

"It's for the diamond branch," her grandmother replied. "The one you must gather. The one I failed to gather. For I could not finish the Night Hunt. When I returned to our world, failure burning inside me, I told myself I would go back the next day to try again. But the next day dawned, and I did not go. Nor the day after, nor the day after. It was a year or more before I finally dared try again. But by then . . . it was too late."

"Too late?" Heloise asked fearfully.

Grandmem's eyes, which once were blue, were almost gray now as they gazed down upon the dirty, frightened, angry face staring up at her. She feared her bitterness might pour from her tongue and poison the child.

But no. If the child was poisoned, the poisoning itself had taken place long ago. Ages ago. Back when this curse was set in place as payment for a sin Grandmem could not guess. What a vile sin it must have been to merit so great a price!

"When I looked again," Grandmem said, "gazing into my little dark glass, I saw only my face looking back at me. Everything else was gone. Whatever power I once possessed over the mirror had fled me. Perhaps because I was too afraid. Perhaps because I was too old.

"But know this and know it well, Heloise, daughter of my son: The powers you now possess will not last forever. They will forsake you in the end."

"Grandmem," said Heloise, "why could you not finish the Hunt?"

"If I were to tell you," her grandmother replied, "you would never try."

TWENTY-FOUR

IN THE DEPTHS OF THE WOOD . . . BEYOND THE GOLDEN FOREST AND
the silver . . . beyond the edges of imagination . . . in the vaulting
chamber of green growth and solid stone ever changing, always true . . .

. . . the Dame of the Haven slouched in the middle of an enormous
pile of scrolls and growled, "Dragon's aching teeth!"

"Where?" said the sylph, and wafted about her with interest, looking
without eyes into the various corners of the library. It could see the
Dame's invisible helpers. Having no eyes can be a great advantage when
it comes to spying invisible beings. They ducked away from the sylph's
gaze or made faces at it, but it wasn't particularly interested in them. "I
don't see any dragon teeth."

"No, no," said the Dame, rubbing her forehead. Realizing how bad
her posture had become while sitting cross-legged on the floor, she drew

herself up straight. Her back clicked painfully. Just like a mortal's.

Heaving a sigh, she pulled her feet under her and stood. They had, of course, gone to sleep while she sat, and she swallowed a few more curses as the blood rushed down through her veins, tingling uncomfortably. While waiting for both numbness and tingling to subside, she cast her gaze upon the mess littering the floor around her. Scrolls and volumes and missives galore.

But not a single written word about the Family of Night.

That was the problem with Faeries, she thought. Or one of the many problems. Because they did not die, they felt no need to write things down. Anything important they would either remember or get someone to remember for them. All the rest . . . well, what did they care? If they forgot it, it couldn't have been that interesting. Thus there were few scribes to be found among Faerie folk, few who would bother themselves to learn the difficult language of pen and ink and parchment.

She frowned suddenly. Pen and ink and parchment, or perhaps . . .

Stepping carefully over her various piles, narrowly avoiding crushing priceless documents beneath her heel, the Dame hastened to a far corner of her massive library. She climbed a staircase that spiraled up a tall, proud elm, pushing aside branches as necessary and peering into the grooves and crevices of the trunk. But not until she neared the top did she find what she was looking for.

Tucked away in a deep hole in the elm's trunk was a stash of wax tablets. They were bound in wood and closed to protect the delicate wax inside. They contained some of the oldest writing to be found in all the worlds, Near, Far, or Between.

The Dame selected one bound with a cord of blackest midnight. Indeed, the cord itself might have been spun from strands of the Black Dogs' own hair, so absolute was its blackness. She carefully slipped the cord free and, hefting the heavy tablet to support it on one arm, used her free hand to open it.

The wax slab inside was covered in writing, Faerie writing set down with a sharp stylus in precision that could only come from a Faerie hand. The words themselves were so old that at first the Dame could not understand them. She frowned and narrowed her eyes, as though she could somehow scare the wax into submission.

Slowly, resentfully, the letters took the shape of understanding. They formed new ideas, vivid ideas, playing them out before her mind. She read them with difficulty, but they offered up their secrets at last.

As she came to the end of what the Faerie scribe, whoever he or she was, had written down, she realized she'd been holding her breath and let it out in a long gust. Then, very carefully, she closed the wooden binding and slipped the black cord back into place.

The sylph stirred up scrolls and wafted the pages of open books, gently, for it did not wish to inspire the Dame's wrath. Seeing her face as she descended the stairs, it gave a glad little cry. "Did you find something?" it asked. It was a flighty creature and couldn't quite remember what it was they had been looking for. But it loved the Dame and wanted her to be happy, and it thought it saw, if not happiness, at least *satisfaction* in her eye.

"I did," said the Dame, sitting down at her desk and drawing a fresh sheaf of parchment to her. She did not open the tablet but kept it at her elbow in case she needed to reference it again. With a dip of her pen she set to work, drafting Faerie letters with the care a royal artist might employ while painting the king's own portrait. Every line was meticulously drawn, graceful, and purposeful.

When she had finished and the ink was drying, she turned on her seat to address the sylph, who was chasing invisibles up among the branches of the ceiling. "Dear sylph," she said, "do you recall the Time in which you left the mortal girl?"

"Yes," said the sylph, wafting down to her at once. Then, "No." Then, "Maybe?"

"You must find her. In her own Time," said the Dame, putting into her voice all the sternness she could muster, which was considerable, despite her lovely face. "You must bear this message to her, and it must reach her where she was when you left her, not a year before, not a year later. If you return to the wrong Time, it may be that you return too late. Do you understand?"

It didn't. But it wanted to. The Dame, even as she rolled up the scroll and tucked a shining starflower into the securing cord, prayed that it would want to hard enough. "Away with you then," she said, "and help the mortal girl if you can."

So the sylph planted a breezy kiss upon her face and darted to the open window. It vanished into the vastness of the Wood Between, and the Dame heard it laughing as it went. She could only hope it would remember the errand on which she had sent it.

Otherwise, her only labor was to wait and see what might come about.

TWENTY-FIVE

HELOISE WAS TIRED. SHE COULD NOT REMEMBER EVER BEFORE BEING this tired.

Her clothing was still damp, but she couldn't go home clad in Benedict's garments. So, after dropping the tunic, the belt, and the slippers on the floor of Grandmem's shack, she donned her shift and slipped into the overdress, making faces as she did up the laces. She hated the clammy feel of coarse, wet fabric on her skin. But there was nothing else to be done.

When she finally arrived home, her mother was already up and bent at work over the hearth fire, stirring the great pottage pot. "Well," she said when Heloise's shadow fell through the doorway, "so you deign to turn up, do you?"

"Sorry, Meme," Heloise said. She hadn't the energy to invent an excuse or explanation. Her feet dragging, she tried to step around her mother and slip up the loft ladder.

But Meme caught her by the ankle. "Get down here," she said. "You may think it fun to drive your father and me half mad with worry. You may think it a lark. But you'll not have your larks and your laziness too. Get down and feed the pig and chickens. Then you'll go to the pond and bring up the retted flax. All of it."

Heloise opened her mouth to protest. The bundles of flax down in the retting pond were heavy, and normally she had Claude or Clement to help her fetch it up to the spinning shed. But the look in her mother's eye was not a look to argue with.

"Yes, Meme," Heloise sighed, and jumped down from the ladder, staggering several paces with fatigue.

She couldn't bother herself to scratch Gutrund after she dumped the slops in the sow's feed trough. She couldn't bear to look at her reflection in the water trough; the very idea made her shudder. Rufus the Red and his harem were furious at being kept waiting for their feed, and rooster Rufus was not one to restrain fury when it took him. He aimed a series of sharp pecks at Heloise's feet and landed several of them. It was enough to make Heloise half wish she'd kept the slippers, just for the protection.

These tasks complete, there was nothing for it but to make her way down to the retting pond. This was a bit of a walk, following the stream down to a low place where the water pooled in dark murkiness.

Sometimes it seemed to Heloise that Canneberges was made up entirely of low places and murky pools. But the cranberry bogs were at least full of health and growth.

The retting pond was meant for rot.

The stink of rotted flax rose up to greet her as she approached. Usually Heloise didn't mind it; to the stinks at the dye house, nothing the retting pond offered up could compare. But today, after she'd just worn Benedict's sweet-smelling garments, the stink struck her as particularly loathsome. A few weeks ago her father and older brothers had bound great bundles of flax together and left them in the shallow pond to decay. The rot gradually ate away the outer sheath of the stalks, freeing the fibers inside.

The bundles of flax were slimy and dirty after several weeks of lying in pond scum. Heloise could not think of a single task she hated more than fetching retted flax.

The water was cold. But the early spring was already warmer now than it had been a few days ago, so stepping into the pond was disgusting, not painful. Heloise squelched down, feeling mud squeeze up between her toes, and grasped the nearest of the bundles. She hauled it up onto land, grimacing at the stench of it. But the stalks had broken, and the fine white fibers hung like the limp hair of drowned maidens, ready to be cleaned, combed, and spun.

Blinking the exhaustion from her drooping eyes, Heloise hefted the bundle up across her shoulders. Just as well her garment was already soaked through, she decided as she plodded back upstream toward the cottage and the spinning shed. By the time she finished hauling all the bundles, she would be as drenched as she'd been the night before when she climbed out of the strange pool.

This thought passed through her mind like a dream. She scowled and shook her head, not wanting to consider it. Everything that happened last night and the night before and the night before that . . . all those weary nights, they were so distant suddenly. Here in the real world were rotted flax and spinning sheds and bare cold feet on bare cold dirt. Here was the reality of her life, the life she had always lived, the life she always would live. Far from forests of silver or gold. Far from the sons of lords and tall, proud lion men. Far from—

Far from Evette.

Evette whom everyone had forgotten. Even Grandmem. Evette, who possibly never existed.

Heloise paused, panting, feeling the soggy flax stalks dig into the back of her neck and shoulders. Her eyes stared on up the path to the cottage, but her vision was far away. She saw again the waterfall that was also a staircase. She saw the white phantoms and her sister, one of twelve, clad in a gown of brilliant starlight.

But that wasn't Evette. Evette would never wear such a gown, would never be happy in it.

Her stomach clenched in a painful knot. Heloise closed her eyes. She didn't want to see that memory, however brief; that memory of her sister on the stair, looking over her shoulder. That memory of a glimpse so swift it might never have happened.

That glimpse of sorrow. And dread. And fear.

"Evette," Heloise whispered. The weight of retted flax seemed to double, bowing her shoulders. She braced herself. Simply keeping on her feet was a monumental effort in that moment. "Evette, what are they doing to you?"

All manner of ideas flitted through her head, ideas half-formed and dreadful. They passed before her mind's eye so quickly, skittering and growling like so many nightmares come suddenly to life. They resolved themselves at last into a single image:

A face wrapped in a shroud so thin that the delicate child's features could still be seen. A gaping grave beneath a cloud-covered sky.

"*Mortal! Mortal child!*"

The voice calling in the distance could not reach her. Heloise stood like one frozen, staring at the image that was only in her mind but more real than all the reality surrounding her. More real than the very ground upon which she stood.

"*Mortal child! I see you!*"

A wind stirred the treetops. It blew along the surface of the stream. It caught in the bundle on Heloise's back and tugged so hard that she dropped it. Thus abruptly returned to the present, Heloise gave a scream of surprise and wrath as the cords securing the bundle burst, and rotted flax littered the path. "Oh, dragons and monsters and griffins and *things!"* she shouted, too tired to be eloquent just then. She whirled about, glaring up at the empty air and cried, "Is that *you?"*

"If you mean me, yes, it is," said the sylph, which was probably the most reasonable response one could offer to such a question.

Heloise crossed her arms and kicked at a clump of wet flax. "Look what you made me do!" she snarled. "You're useless, do you know that? You dragon-blasted sylph-beast! Why don't you go away again? Go blow down a tree or drag in a storm or whatever it is wind-spirits do."

The sylph laughed. Delighted once more to be among mortals, it whipped through Heloise's hair and tickled her under the chin. "I have something for you," it said. "Open your mouth!"

Heloise did not obey, but the sylph tried to stick something between her teeth anyway. She spat and slapped at the breezy being, which did about as much good as one might expect. But her hand connected with something solid, and she found herself holding a parchment scroll.

"For you!" said the sylph. "A gift from the Dame."

"A gift?" said Heloise, staring at the scroll. There was a white flower tucked into the securing cord, and it gleamed as bright as her silver and gold branches, brighter even. Like a star fallen from the heavens themselves. "A gift from who?"

"From the Dame," the sylph repeated. "I told you."

"What dame?"

"*The* Dame!" The sylph laughed again as though Heloise were truly the funniest, most foolish thing it had ever encountered. "The Dame of the Haven. She bade me carry this message to you, for your support, she said. For your encouragement."

Heloise, her mouth gone dry, tried and failed to moisten her lips. "What is it?"

"A gift," said the sylph, and again, "I told you."

"But I can't read," said Heloise.

To which the sylph replied with great delight, "Neither can I! It is a mortal magic. Do you know anyone who works such enchantment?"

Heloise nodded slowly. "Yes. I think I do."

Benedict propped his elbows on his desk, held his head in his hands, and pretended not to sleep. It wasn't much of a pretense, but as long as he kept on telling himself that he was working, he didn't mind so much when his brain slipped into a doze.

If he tried to lie down in bed, he knew he wouldn't sleep at all. He would stare up at the canopy over his head and wonder how long now until he crawled beneath that canopy for the last time . . . and died.

Like Victor.

His head came up, and he drew a sharp breath, his eyes struggling to focus on the world around him. Then he cursed and sagged back in his hair, shoulders slumped. Victor. How vivid his friend's face had appeared before his waking mind. Vivid and yet surreal.

Victor as he had last seen him, standing before the simple pine coffins of Henri, Giles, and Luc. Coffins which were ready to be loaded into fine carriages and sent home to their families on various estates across the kingdom so that their remains might be elegantly interred in the tombs of their forefathers.

Victor, who was always at the forefront in the maddest of all their games, stood beside those coffins as the winter snow fell silently on his dark cloak. He lifted eyes already bright with oncoming fever to meet Benedict's gaze.

"*It could have been us, Ben,*" he'd said. "*We could be the ones in those boxes.*"

Only a week later, his words became a prophecy fulfilled. A fourth carriage set out through the university's gates, bearing shroud-wrapped Victor home to his grieving father. Or so Benedict was told. He had been too sick in his bed at the time to know. It was nearly a month before he learned of Victor's fate; nearly a month before he learned that a sad, snow-filled afternoon spent standing before the coffins of their dead mates would encompass his last memory of his best friend.

Benedict realized he was staring blankly at the documents before him on his desk. He was recopying all that the sylph had destroyed nearly a week ago. Corrilondian declensions. A labor like no other, for Corrilondian was considered one of the most difficult of the Western languages to learn, full as it was of strong Eastern influences. Victor had hated it and goaded Benedict many a time for his obsessive study of it.

"*When the next war with Corrilond finally gets going,*" Victor would say, "*you won't be better able to kill Corrilondian warriors by conjugating verbs as quickly as they do!*"

To which Benedict always laughingly replied, "*A good ambassador to Corrilond might be the key to keep that war from starting, don't you see?*"

Victor would then feign complete dismay at the idea, for it was always the way of boys among the great houses of the kingdom to pretend a longing for warfare and bloodshed; to pretend so hard that sometimes the longing turned real. Benedict played along to a certain extent. He listened to Luc and Giles tell gory stories passed down by their grandfathers of long-ago battles along the border, and he cheered with Henri and Victor when they made bold declarations of future warlike prowess, promising decimation of all that was Corrilondian and, therefore, evil. Why, he even made some declarations of his own, which were toasted among his fellows, and he wondered now if he had lied, or if they had lied, or if any one of them had really known what he believed about war and death.

Now they were all dead. Even Benedict, really, though he remained upright and breathing. There was no need for a war to prove their courage. They had died gasping in pain, burning up from the inside out. And he had gasped the same as they, and he had cried out in fevered delirium, and he had learned just how far from glorious death was.

He had looked into Death's own face as he stood on the threshold of life's end. But Death had blinked, and Benedict had revived. For a time at least.

He shivered, though the air pouring through his window wasn't as cool as it had been a few days before. Spring was already warming in Canneberges, promising a sweltering summer to come. It didn't seem to matter; Benedict suspected he would shiver for the rest of his life, however long or short that life might be.

He stared at the Corrilondian declensions so carefully categorized by his own hand: number, case, and gender. The Corrilondian language had many forms of gender—those for people, male and female; those for animals and objects, male and female; those for ideas, including ideas *about* people, animals, and objects; and those for immortals.

It was confusing enough without random spirit-wind-monsters destroying his work. He picked up his quill and penknife, trimmed the nib, and reached for his inkwell.

"Master Benedict!"

Benedict paused, his quill in midair. He looked over his shoulder to his open window, half expecting to see Heloise's curly head framed by sunlight. But the windowsill was empty.

"Master Benedict, are you awake?"

"Lumé love me," Benedict muttered, rising from his chair and stepping toward the window. "It's *midday,* you daft girl! Someone will see—*Arrrrrrgh!*"

This last was as much a cry of rage as of dismay, for, with a sudden *bang* as it burst through the window and all but shattered the panes of glass, a tremendous wind exploded into his chamber, roaring around the bedposts and laughing like a maniac.

"Oh, dragons eat—" Benedict cried, but didn't bother to finish. He dove for his desk and, even as the sylph swept down upon him, tickling and pinching, flung himself over his work. He spilled the inkwell but managed to put his hand down fast enough to redirect the ink flow away from his documents. The last several lines he had written were probably even now emblazoned upon his linen shirt, but he didn't care! At least some of it would be spared.

"Get out of there!" Heloise shouted from beyond the window. "Get out of there at once, you wicked thing!"

The sylph, still laughing, planted a blustery kiss on Benedict's furious face and darted away again, out into the spring day. Benedict heard it giggling as it darted up the side of the house to play on the roof among the chimneys.

Benedict wondered briefly: If he were to curse the wind-spirit in Corrilondian, would he use the gender form for ideas or for immortals? Then he shook the thought from his head and picked himself up, surveying the damage. The inkwell was practically emptied onto his floor, but he turned it upright anyway and grabbed a blotter to wipe his umber-stained hand even as he approached the window. He poked his head over the sill and scowled down at Heloise, who stood in muddy water up to her calves, holding her skirts up with one hand and what appeared to be a parchment scroll in the other.

"What in Lumé's name do you think you are doing?" Benedict demanded in a whispered shout (which is like a shout, only not so loud). "Did you bring that wind back here on purpose?"

"Of course not," said Heloise, scowling up at him from beneath her matted curls. "Don't be an ox-head."

Benedict said, "Forgive me," before he could stop himself. Then added, just to show he wasn't a man to be pushed around, "I'm *not* an ox-head," which made him feel far more foolish. He wanted to slam the window shut and stomp back to his desk, turning a deaf ear to any protests Heloise might make.

But Heloise, he did not doubt, could make some noisy protests. And the last thing he needed was to call attention to himself or any of his recent doings, particularly where this wild girl was concerned. So he leaned further out, his stomach resting on the sill, and asked, "Why are you standing down there in broad daylight?"

"I can't climb the tree while carrying this," Heloise said, waving the parchment scroll. As she did so, the little starflower gleamed brightly. "Take it, and I'll be up in a smidge."

Benedict obeyed almost without thinking, for the shining starflower had caught his eye, and he was interested to see it up close. He leaned out over the sill, stretched out his long arm, and caught hold of the scroll. Stepping back into the room where the shadows made the flower seem brighter, he studied it even as he half listened to the grunting mutters of Heloise as she scrambled up the tree and fell into his room. It was a beautiful blossom indeed, more beautiful even than the silver and gold branches Heloise had brought back with her from the mirror world, for it seemed more fragile somehow.

Heloise picked herself up and approached Benedict. "Open it," she said.

"Where are my slippers?" Benedict asked.

"At my grandmother's house. Open it."

Benedict frowned but did as he was told, slipping the cord and blossom free and handing both to Heloise. "What is it?" he asked even as he unrolled it.

"I don't know," said Heloise. She added in a mumble, as though she didn't want him to hear but couldn't deny the truth, "I can't read."

Benedict shot her a quick glance then fixed his gaze on the characters written on the golden parchment in his hand. He frowned. They were like nothing he had ever before seen. As different from Corrilondian writing as Corrilondian writing was different from his own language. More so, perhaps. He could get no sense of whether they should be read right to left, left to right, up to down, or possibly in zigzags. He didn't even know if he held the scroll the right way around and tried turning it several angles.

"What does it say?" Heloise asked. He felt her eager gaze fixed upon his face and realized, rather to his surprise, that he didn't like to disappoint her. She had come to him with so much confidence in his abilities, confidence he knew he didn't deserve. After all, what had he done for her other than let her wander about his house in the middle of the night and use his mirror? But she trusted him, and he didn't like to damage that trust. Though really, he asked himself, why should he care about the opinion of one scrawny peasant girl?

It didn't matter. He cared. He cared very much, and it was with reluctance that he opened his mouth to tell her that he couldn't make heads or tails of anything he saw . . .

Only, suddenly he could.

The words remained the same upon the page, but in his mind they shifted. They took on shapes and forms, creating a sense of understanding that was possibly an illusion but just as possibly genuine. He stared unseeing at the page, his mind fixed on the images in his head, and he read those images far more clearly than he had read anything else in his life.

In his mind he saw:

To the Cursebreaker—

> *A three-part branch will prove the key*
> *To set the captives flying free*
> *'Tis more than me, 'tis more than thee,*
> *The spreading branches of this tree.*
> *Search ye for the branch of three.*
> *Hope lies with the branch of three.*

The message went on from there in a slightly different tone:

I do apologize for the above, although it is the best help I may offer you. Faerie-kind has a great love for verse and rhyme, even of the cheapest variety. When they can be made to put down anything in writing, it is often only in poetic form. Take whatever help from this you may. It might be nonsense, but I wouldn't assume as much if I were you.

Let me assure you of two more things. Firstly, they cannot kill you without breaking their Law, nor can they prevent you from attempting to break the curse.

Secondly, you are stronger than you think.

I can say no more without risk of breaking their Law myself. So remember. When you have finished your task, I will come for you. Wait for me, Cursebreaker.

That was it save for the signature, which was a blooming starflower exquisitely rendered. Or rather, exquisitely rendered in Benedict's mind. On the page it was nothing more than a strange but elegant assortment of lines and squiggles.

Benedict blinked, and the images and sensations were gone from his mind. He turned wide-eyed to Heloise. "Who is Starflower?" he asked.

"I don't know," said Heloise. "Why? Does it say something about a starflower?"

"Did you try looking at this yourself?"

"I told you, I can't read."

Benedict's brow formed a tight frown. "I don't . . . I don't think it will matter," he said, and turned the parchment around for Heloise's inspection. He watched her face and saw exactly when the written characters made themselves as clear to her as they now were to him.

"I've heard rumor of this," Benedict said, though he doubted she was listening to him, caught up as she was in what took place inside her head. "I've heard about this sort of writing. It's cropped up around the world here and there, writing that anyone can read, no matter their language or scholastic abilities. They say it's written by the hand of Faeries. I used to think the idea foolish, but after recent events . . ."

Heloise gasped and turned away from Benedict. Startled, he glanced at the parchment, but it was quite still now, still and dull, revealing no secrets. Had she seen something he had not?

"Heloise?" he asked, putting out a hand but not quite daring to touch her shoulder. "What's wrong?"

She shook her head, her dirty curls bouncing like a whole hedge caught in a windstorm. He heard her take a quivering breath like a sob. Was she crying?

"Who sent this to you?" Benedict persisted. "Is this from . . . from the mirror world?"

"I don't know," Heloise muttered. Then, pulling herself upright and giving her head another shake, she turned and addressed herself to Benedict. Her face was drawn and pale, but full of a fierce determination and no trace of tears. "I don't know who sent it," she said. "I don't know what it means, except . . . except . . ." She swallowed hard, and her eyes were bright. "Except I know I must gather the third branch. I must go on the Night Hunt with Uncle and with Aunt."

TWENTY-SIX

HELOISE COULD NOT BEGIN TO IMAGINE HER MOTHER'S REACTION upon discovering the bushel of flax lying strewn on the path between the spinning shed and the retting pond. She only knew she dared not return home that day while waiting for nightfall.

Since they couldn't very well pull out the mirror just then when anyone could come knocking on Benedict's door, Benedict suggested Heloise get some sleep. Not *on* his bed, which would be both improper and rather too conspicuous. Instead he gave her a pillow and blanket, and she made herself reasonably comfortable *under* his bed, in company with a forgotten stocking and a small warren of dust rabbits.

She was surprised at how quickly she fell asleep and how thoroughly she slept. She half-woke a handful of times: Once when Doctor Dupont wafted through like an ill wind, dosing Benedict before wafting out again.

Once more when Benedict's manservant went round the room, tidying odds and ends and asking Benedict whether or not he felt up to taking his supper in the dining hall that evening.

By that time Benedict was in bed himself. The bed-ropes sagged under his weight, making the cramped space in which Heloise lay more cramped still. She couldn't hear Benedict's voice very well through the feather mattress, but she heard his manservant's grunt of disapproval. The good man left eventually however, shutting the door behind him. A few minutes later, someone else delivered the young lord's evening meal on a platter.

When the door shut this last time, Heloise heard Benedict shifting up above. His bare foot slid to the floor just in her line of vision. A few creaks and groans of the bed-ropes, then half of Benedict's face appeared, peering into the darkness where she lay. "I think you can come out now. Are you awake?"

"Yes," Heloise muttered into the pillow on which her head rested. She'd never slept with a pillow before, and she rather hated to leave it. But she hadn't come here to luxuriate in the amenities of the gentry. So, rubbing sleep from her eyes with the heel of her hand, she slid and scrambled along the floor, chasing dust rabbits before her, and emerged from under the bed. Benedict, rather to her surprise, sat on the floor cross-legged, clad in his trousers and long undershirt, which covered his knees, but no jacket. Instead a fur-lined robe draped across his shoulders.

He blushed at her startled expression. "Forgive me," he said. "I'll put

346

on my jacket if it makes you more comfortable."

"No, no," said Heloise hastily. She'd seen him at greater disadvantage before, after all. She crossed her own legs, tucking her cold bare feet under her skirt, and noticed that he had brought the platter down on the floor with him.

"Fish broth and healthsome herbs?" Benedict offered.

They ate in near silence. Neither spoke of the mysterious adventure Heloise intended to find and face that evening. Neither speculated on what it might be, what it might mean. They simply ate and sat in mutual ignorance that was as near to sympathy as anything might be. When their eyes chanced to meet, both tried to smile. Both failed miserably.

When the food was gone, Heloise rose and brushed off her skirts then offered a hand to help Benedict to his feet. He gave her an odd look for this but accepted the help. By this time the room was growing dark. Their eyes, however, accustomed to the dimness, felt no particular lack. They stood for a moment, hand in hand, looking at one another and sharing a great unspoken fear.

"I'll get a light," Benedict said at last. Leaving the platter and empty bowl on the floor, he fetched a candle, lit it at the hearth, and placed it in a holder. Heloise, meanwhile, pulled the silver and gold branches, intertwined into one, from the depths of her pocket. They did not shine this evening but lay dull and quiet in the palm of her hand. She gave them a half-hearted shake, but it made no difference.

Benedict, turning to her and holding up the candle, saw the

expression on her face. "Here now!" he said sharply, crossing the distance between them, and put out a hand to touch her arm. "Remember what the message said. They cannot kill you. According to some law of theirs, you're safe from them."

"Yes," Heloise whispered. "But you know what? Try as I might, I can't think what they'll do that could be worse."

"Nothing," said Benedict. "Nothing's worse than death. Right?"

But they both knew this for the falsehood it was.

The sun set, and Centrecœur was quiet. Another hour, and everyone had finished their day's work and gone to their beds. A half-hour more, and Benedict opened his bedroom door, looked up and down the hall, then stepped out and beckoned Heloise to follow him. She held the mirror tight in both hands, pressing the glass against her breast so that it might not catch and reflect even a trace of candlelight.

They had discussed where to begin the night's exploration. If Heloise was to find a forest of diamond, she needed to enter the strange mirror world from a different point in the house itself. After some debate, they agreed to begin this evening's venture in the dining hall, which was located in the west wing of the house, far from where any of the household staff slept. It was as good a spot as any, and they were unlikely to run into anyone.

The dining hall was a long room, long enough to encompass the extensive table. Built on the ground floor, the room boasted two massive staircases, one on each end, leading up to the private family apartments above, none of which were currently occupied. Chairs lined the walls, pulled back from the table when no diners were present. Though the ceiling was low, the room had a cavernous feel, and Heloise shivered and drew nearer to Benedict, and he drew nearer to her as they entered. A fireplace along one wall was like the gaping mouth of some great, deep-throated beast.

"Well," said Benedict, standing just inside the doorway with his candle held high, "are you ready to try?"

Heloise shook her head. But aloud she said, "Yes," and lifted the mirror. Turning so that the light of Benedict's candle would be cast onto her face, she gazed upon her pale reflection.

Then she turned her gaze to look beyond her reflection.

There stood the forest. Dark as a moonless night, so that Heloise could only just discern the black trunks and branches of the trees. But it was the forest all right, not the dining hall reflected in the mirror. She tilted the glass, searching for a glimpse of white, of a starlight gown.

Nothing. Only more forest, and herself standing in that forest.

"Heloise?" Benedict said. His voice sounded as though he was about to make some reasonable protest, urging her to put the glass away. She couldn't allow it. She couldn't bear it.

She blinked.

When her eyes opened, she stood in the forest, gazing through a small window at her own face.

Welcome back to the Between, child. Are you ready to take the diamond branch?

The voice passed through her head, weirdly familiar after these several weird days. Heloise refused to acknowledge it. She wasn't altogether certain the voice was or ever had been helpful.

Turning away from the sight of her own face, Heloise braced herself against the darkness of the forest. Squaring her shoulders, she took a step. Then another. Then, clenching her hands into fists, she strode boldly forward and—

"Ouch!"

—walked into a tree she could not see.

Sitting down hard, Heloise cradled her nose in her hands and squeezed her eyes shut. She felt the bizarre *swooping* sensation that meant her presence in the mirror world was unstable, felt for a moment the warmth of Benedict standing close by. But she shook this away, focusing her mind, and the forest surrounded her. Her nose throbbed but wasn't broken, and it only bled a little. The dizziness passed as well. "Dragons eat it," she muttered, opened her eyes . . .

. . . and nearly choked as her heart leapt painfully up into her throat. For the forest was not dark anymore. Oh no! No, indeed! It was not dark at all.

It was alive with brilliant, refracted light.

Every tree—and there were more trees than she could begin to count—looked as though it had been carved from the most perfect, clear stone. But they weren't stone. They were leafing, growing, root-plunging, and alive, so very alive that she could feel the life buzzing on the edges of her vision, vibrating her senses. But they were also perfectly still, as though time itself had been frozen in this faultless moment of life.

The light came from their hearts. It shone out from the inside of each tree and bounced off the surfaces of surrounding trees until it was all too bright, too pure, almost too much to be borne. With so much light, there was scarcely any room for shadow.

But the shadows present were far, far darker as a result.

Heloise sat where she had fallen, blinking at the world around her. She had heard tell of diamonds, heard them spoken of as one hears rumor of angels or heaven. She knew they were stones, and Clement, her older brother, had once held up a piece of uncut quartz and told her that a diamond was like it only better. Stronger.

This forest was nothing like quartz. But Heloise did not doubt that she looked upon a forest of pure, living diamond.

For some moments she couldn't move, even as the voice prodding in the back of her brain reminded her that she would accomplish nothing by sitting there with her mouth open, staring at the beauty surrounding her. She'd never be able to absorb all of that beauty anyway.

You must take the diamond branch. Complete the three-part key.

So, after picking herself up and dusting tiny motes of diamond dust from her skirt and then from her hands, Heloise approached the nearest tree. Its branches were set high on the trunk but so heavy that they bent down close enough for her to reach. She grasped hold and twisted.

It was like trying to twist a block of granite.

Heloise frowned and put up her other hand as well. Bracing herself, one foot on the tree trunk, she pulled harder. But she could have pulled until the bones in her hands and wrists snapped; it made no difference.

Remember, child, said the voice. *Remember what the Dame told you. You're stronger than you think!*

"I'm stronger than I think," Heloise whispered. A third time she took hold of the diamond branch. Every muscle in her body heaved and strained with the effort to break it off, even just a small twig, a single leaf.

But the diamond would not give.

Heloise cried out in frustration and fell back. Her hands were cut and bleeding, shaking with pain. She tucked them under her arms, warm blood staining her dirty gown.

Never mind, said the voice. *You'll have to pursue the Night Hunt after all. I'm sorry. I'm so sorry.*

"Sure you are," Heloise growled. Because there was nothing else for her to do, she set off through the shining forest. The light cast her shadow dizzyingly around her, first one direction then another, with each step she took. Before she had taken many paces she was squinting, for it was all too bright, too lovely, and too disorienting.

She sensed somehow that it was night here in the mirror world, or whatever version of night this mirror world had. But this could have been a mistaken impression; anything outside of this diamond light was bound to feel as dark as nightfall. Still, she clung to the impression as she walked.

The air felt as though it should have been cold. But it wasn't. It was as still as a winter's midnight, but it was a living stillness, not a sleeping stillness. The refracted light leaping from tree to tree built up an intense energy, leaving the air warm. Yet the atmosphere struck Heloise more like winter than summer, for there was not an insect to be seen nor a trace of floating pollen or seed pods.

Something moved.

The motion caught the tail of Heloise's eye. Her first impulse was to turn and look at it, but this impulse she squelched, and instead held herself perfectly still. She felt her heart throb painfully against her breastbone, and this angered her. "Don't be foolish. Don't be frightened," she whispered to herself. "They can't kill you, remember?"

Another movement, this time catching the tail of her other eye. There were two of them then, whatever they were. Or perhaps one that moved very fast, hidden by the brilliance of the diamond light? No, no, it had to be two. Aunt and Uncle.

And there she stood, practically blind, a helpless target to any skull-headed men—

No! She would *not* think about what the Lion-Prince had said! He had probably lied to her anyway just to scare her. No one, not even the strange, otherworldly beings who lived in this mirror world, could go around with *skulls* for *heads*. Masks, certainly. Very good masks even. But not *real skulls.*

Still . . .

Heloise kept her face pointing forward, her chin level. She didn't want the shadows, whoever or whatever they were, to think she was looking about for them or, worse still, looking about for some escape. Slowly she slipped her hand into her pocket and took hold of the silver-gold branch hidden inside. It was small, but it was sharp.

She drew it out, clutching it dagger-like in both hands, and dropped into a defensive crouch.

Someone laughed. Right behind her. A heaving, hideous, gulping sort of laugh that made any listener feel simultaneously idiotic and terrified.

Heloise ground her teeth, awkwardly spinning her crouch to face that laugh. Her foot caught in her own skirts, and for a moment she listed to one side, pinned down by her own knee. The laugh sounded again, this time to her left. Heloise lashed out with the silver-gold branch, yelling wordlessly. But there was nothing there, not anymore.

Pulling her skirt free, Heloise scrambled to her feet, one arm still extended, the small branch held like a knife. The curling, glistening leaves brushed her hand and wrist, and they were warm with vitality that was incongruous to metal. But Heloise scarcely noticed this. She turned about, her head always straining to look over her shoulder, her shoulder always moving in an impossible effort to keep anything from being *behind* her. Her own shadow, cast wildly by the light of the diamond forest, chased her; sweat flowed in streams down her temples and dripped down her forehead into her eyes.

Another laugh echoed off the trees, galloping through the shadows, circling round and round. Then a form as tall as a giant (or so it seemed to Heloise) approached through the shimmering light. It was like watching a heat-vapor turned living and dark, so indistinct were its contours. Yet it walked with a strange litheness almost akin to grace had it not been simultaneously ugly. It was impossible to say whether the silhouette was animal or human. Both at once, perhaps. All Heloise knew for certain was that it was female.

Her hand holding the branch shook. Realizing this, Heloise clasped her other hand tightly around the first, steadying it. Her eyes blazing, she shouted at the approaching figure, "Are you Aunt?"

Another laugh. The darkness between the shining lights shifted, and the shape was definitely human now, or close to human, but so tall that it would have stood a head or more taller than Heloise's father. As the creature drew nearer, either her form became solid where it had been vaporous, or Heloise's vision clarified. The woman's neck was so thick and her shoulders so powerful that she might pull the load of five oxen without strain. Once again Heloise stared up at the great figure, cringing despite her best efforts under the empty-eyed gaze of that white skull mask. The mask grinned at Heloise in the diamond light.

The woman spoke in that voice as strange as her laugh. "I am Aunt. I am Sister. I am Wife. I am Family."

"Not my family," said Heloise. "You've taken my family. And I want her back." She cringed again, cursing herself but unable to help it, when another laugh burst through the clenched teeth of the skull-mask grin.

"Not your family?" said the woman. "Indeed, would that it were true!"

She began to circle Heloise, who turned in place so as to keep the sharp, pointed end of her silver-gold branch between them. This didn't seem to worry Aunt in the least; the skull mask went on grinning even as it had, even as it always would. She moved with a heavy tread, her feet coming down hard upon the ground, grinding diamond dust with loud crunches at each step. Her head lowered, and Heloise sensed eyes studying her through the mask's empty eye holes.

"Have you come," Aunt said at last, still circling Heloise as she would her prey, "to hunt with Uncle and with me?"

Heloise recalled the tale her grandmother had told—the hunt of Marcel, the miller lad for whom Cateline had smiled a special smile. But Evette had no special smile for any boy in Canneberges. So surely this hunt could not be as awful as that one. Perhaps Aunt and Uncle would be unable to find a proper prey. Perhaps . . .

Perhaps nothing. She could reason and she could hope, but the fact remained: She must continue what she had begun.

"Uh," said Heloise. "I—I don't intend to hunt anything. Or anyone, for that matter. But . . . but I'll follow your hunt if that's what I have to do. To get Evette back."

"To get *what* back?" said Aunt.

"My sister."

"Oh. That thing."

Suddenly, to Heloise's horror, a tongue shot out from between the mask's teeth. A long black tongue that licked across the sharp edges once, twice, then disappeared.

Heloise's stomach heaved, and she thought she might cough up all the fish broth and healthsome herbs she had eaten in recent history. Her face went green with the effort it took to keep her stomach contents in place. But she brandished her branch and took a step forward, half expecting that rictus jaw to open wide and devour her even as she did so. Nevertheless, she put all the force and fury of her spirit into her voice as she demanded, "Where is my sister? Where have you taken her?"

Aunt laughed again. She crouched, and her limbs changed. Or rather, Heloise's perspective on them changed, for Aunt was always herself, unchanging as the sun and the sky. Heloise knew as she gazed upon the powerful creature before her, with its great spotted shoulders and its sturdy forelimbs, that this was as much Aunt's true form and self as the womanly body she had appeared in but a moment before.

Heloise had never heard the word *hyena*. She had no frame of reference from which to understand what she looked upon. It was too strange, too ugly . . . and yet there was so much power in its ugliness. Nothing like the power of a lion. This was a strength far more raw, far less majestic.

Aunt still wore a mask upon her face, a skull-shaped mask with a jutting muzzle. Once again the black tongue shot out between the cage of teeth, licking the cavity where a nose should have been.

"Come, little mortal bane," said the hyena-woman. "Let us join Uncle in the Night Hunt!"

TWENTY-SEVEN

THEY PROGRESSED THROUGH THE FOREST, HELOISE ALWAYS JUST A few paces behind the loping form of Aunt. Sometimes the light cast by the diamonds was so bright, she lost sight of her grotesque guide entirely. But within a few paces, the light would shift and Heloise would see the broad-shouldered creature which, in an instant, might transform into the shape of a woman. Then back again. Then back again.

Heloise stopped trying to keep track.

Before they had gone far, she sensed that someone had joined them. "Uncle," she whispered, and could not stop herself from turning her head, from trying to spot him . . . from trying to see if he indeed had the head of a skull as the Lion-Prince had claimed. But if it was he, she could not see him, no matter how close he came. He kept the light of the diamond trees close about him like a shield. If Heloise tried to look too closely, she would be blinded.

A weird duet of laughs filled the forest around her. They were so alike, it was impossible to say which laugh belonged to which monster. As they ran, they never seemed to stop laughing. The sound got into Heloise's ears and wriggled its way deep inside her head until she almost felt like laughing herself. But she wouldn't.

Soon it was no longer a laughing duet, it was a whole chorus. The light of the diamond forest flickered with more shadows as a dozen more hyenas joined the chase.

What were they hunting? Heloise wondered, but the voice in her head offered no answers. The image of the fleeing deer embroidered into Benedict's counterpane flashed across her mind's eye. Would she be expected to participate in the kill? To feast on newly dead flesh?

Her stomach heaved again. She recalled Grandmem on her doorstep in the morning sun, doubled up and gagging upon a memory so hideous even all these years later.

Aunt was near to hand, fallen back a few paces to run alongside Heloise. Her black tongue hung over the skull's sagging jaw.

"What are we chasing?" Heloise demanded, afraid to hear the answer but determined nevertheless.

"Chasing?" said Aunt, turning to glance at her through the skull's empty eye-sockets. "We chase nothing. We hunt only that which is already dead, and we feast upon that which remains."

Heloise came to a stop, clutching the silver-gold branch tightly in her fist. She did not think she could go a single step further.

This did not matter. In that moment the diamond light of the forest dimmed before her vision. Straight ahead, as though seen through a tunnel of alternating lights and shadows, stood a strange figure the like of which she could not have described even to herself. It was man-like but warped, bent, and . . . and writhing, somehow. Like liquid or smoke made just solid enough to stand on two feet.

Though *stand* wasn't the right word at all. For this creature, whatever it was, was braced as though it had died upright while receiving blows of the most extreme agony.

It stank. Far beyond the stench of retted flax. Far beyond the stench of the chandler's tallow caldrons. Far, far beyond even the stink of the dyer's yard, so far beyond that the comparison could scarcely be made. It stank like the very breath of Death himself. Like some treasure, once beautiful, left out to rot and decay.

With a manic, gluttonous cry, the shadow of Uncle, who had been just out of sight, surged forward, nearly knocking Heloise from her feet with the force of his passing. She saw a thick neck topped with a skull that may or may not have been living. She saw powerful forelegs and shoulders more massive even than Aunt's.

So the beast that was Uncle fell upon the dead, smoke-like creature and tore into it, worrying it, savaging it even as it stood there, defenseless in its death. It should not be possible to tear out lashings of twisted darkness, but Uncle did just that, gulping down mouthfuls while uttering hideous, guttural sounds that Heloise could not stand to hear.

He was joined a moment later by others of his kind, laughing, roaring monsters who ripped into the . . . the *thing*, whatever it was, from all sides. They pushed it from a standing death to a kneeling death and slashed with their teeth into the back of what Heloise considered, for want of a better word, its neck. Black flecks of what might have been blood, or might have been something else entirely, stained their muzzles.

Heloise could not think, could not find the strength or courage to make her mind work. She stared unblinking in the light of the diamond trees at the gorging taking place, a gorging she could not understand.

Then Aunt, standing beside her, grinning though she did not join the carnage, spoke in a low growl: "Do you recognize this dead thing? Do you know who it is we have hunted down? Do you know upon what we feast?"

It came over Heloise in a terrible rush. She recognized it. She recognized . . . *him!*

She blinked.

When her eyes opened, Heloise was not in the diamond forest anymore. She stood in the dark dining hall of Centrecœur, clutching the mirror in her hands, staring not into the glass but over it. Staring at Benedict.

He stood like one struck numb. His eyes were open and fixed upon her, but his vision was far away. His face, pale with sickness, pale with near-death, was ghastly in the glow of his one small candle.

Suddenly he moaned and dropped the candle, which sputtered out in its own pool of hot wax. Benedict sank to his knees, moaned again, then was silent. Utterly silent even as he buried his face in his hands, frozen, bowed down, bent almost to the breaking point.

"Benedict!" Heloise cried, nearly dropping her mirror as she rushed to him. She felt his arms, felt his chest, put her trembling hand to the back of his neck. But there was nothing. No tearing animal wounds.

He grunted. His body convulsed beneath her touch. She put down the mirror and grabbed his hands in both of hers, struggling to pull them away from his face. "Benedict! Benedict, what's happening to you?"

Heloise heard the memory of her own voice asking her grandmother about the Night Hunt and the miller boy upon whom Aunt and Uncle had preyed. "*Did they kill him?*"

"*No, child. No, they did not kill him. Much worse than that. Much worse . . .*"

Heloise wept without realizing it. At the sight of the young lord so utterly broken, so lost in pain, she could not help herself. She clutched his hands harder and, half afraid she would hurt him, pried them at last from his face. It was too dark in that room to see him well, so she grabbed his cheeks, turning his head toward the window.

His eyes gleamed in the pale light. But they were the eyes of a dead man.

"What are they doing to you?" Heloise whispered, dropping her hold on him and falling away. Then, cursing herself for her cowardice, she fumbled around in the darkness. Her hands found the mirror, and she took it up swiftly and stared into it, nearly blinded by the brilliance of the diamond forest within. She shook her head fiercely . . .

. . . and she was back among the trees, surrounded by the sounds of slaughter and savagery. Aunt stood before her, grinning through her mask, her great shoulders drawn back and her arms crossed over her chest.

"Do you understand, mortal beast?" she asked. "Do you understand what we do?"

"No! I don't understand!" Heloise cried, but even as she did so, she stared at the black, writhing form. It had grown. In those few moments since she fled the forest it had grown, and more monsters had come from all corners to feast upon its pain.

The voice in her head whispered at last, *They feast upon the shadow of his despair. Here in the Between it is made living, though it is a dead sort of life. And the more they feast, the greater it will become.*

I'm sorry it has come to this.

"You can stop it, cursebreaker," Aunt said, bending so that the snarling muzzle of her mask was level with Heloise's face. "You can put an end to this even now. Walk away. Leave the Between, leave this forest. Never return."

Heloise blinked again.

She stood in Centrecœur. Benedict lay prostrate on the ground, weeping, groaning, convulsing in agony he could not comprehend. It was her fault. She had led him into this. He had wanted nothing more than to help her, though he had no reason to. He had been a true friend to her, believing her madness, aiding her in a quest not his own.

This was his thanks. Even now, what sights did those dead eyes of his look upon? What dreams now ripped to shreds?

Before her vision flashed the memory of that dark day, that dark hole dug in that dark ground. And the pale dead face of her sister. Her heart. Her goodness. Buried and lost forever . . .

"I am stronger than I think," she whispered, and lifted the mirror.

"What will it be, cursebreaker?" Aunt demanded as Heloise appeared in the diamond forest. "Will you continue this madness of yours in the face of his suffering? Are you so cruel as to allow this innocent to bear the punishment for your family's sin?"

Heloise swayed where she stood, feeling the strange wobbling of the world around her wanting to push her back out again. How easy it would be to slip back into her own world and never return! To accept the loss of Evette, whom no one else remembered in any case. No one would miss her. No one would know of Heloise's failure. Not even Grandmem, who couldn't possibly live much longer. Who would blame her for making this choice, for saving the kind young lord who had done nothing to deserve this pain! No one would fault her, no one would know, except . . .

"I would blame myself," Heloise hissed through clenched teeth.

She turned away from the shadow, from the laughter, from the gory sounds of gorging. She marched to the nearest of the diamond trees, its heavy boughs bending down to her, sharper than any sword, stronger than any steel.

Take the diamond branch, said the voice in her head, thin and strained with anxiety and need.

"I'm stronger than I think," Heloise said.

She took hold of the lowest branch even as she had before. And she pulled.

"What are you doing?" Aunt snarled behind her. The monsters looked up from their prey, and Heloise felt the force of their many, awful gazes boring into her from behind. "What are you doing?" Aunt demanded. "You cannot break the diamond! Give it up!"

"Give it up!"

"Give it up!"

"Give it up!"

The monsters chortled and roared. The brilliance of the forest swam with shifting, racing shadows swarming around the edge of Heloise's vision. She felt them close in, felt the potent wrath of their spirits.

"You cannot break the diamond!" Aunt shouted and laughed. The others joined in her laughter, mocking and threatening all at once.

Heloise pulled again. She lacked the strength in her mortal limbs. But these weren't her mortal limbs.

She was her reflection. Her reflection was her.

"I'm stronger than I think!" she cried, adjusted her grip, and twisted with all her might. All the might of her sister, her dear, dead Hélène, whose strength she had stolen since before they were born. And such a strength it was, coursing through her veins, through her bones, through every sinew and muscle!

She felt fire, the fire of strength which had always been hers but which she had never known until this moment. The branch groaned, cracked. The diamond shivered with life and energy and sudden heat far more vital than stone.

"Hélène!" she gasped and then, "Evette!"

A branch of silver . . . a branch of gold . . . a branch of diamond adamant . . .

The branch broke off in her grasp. Heloise staggered and fell on her back, both hands gripping the strange, many-sided contours that gleamed with their own inner light. Suddenly it was the only light to be had, for the shadows swarmed down upon her, their laughter turned to screams of rage, eyes flashing red with hatred.

Heloise rolled onto her stomach then up to her knees, then her feet. She clutched the diamond branch inexpertly in the way she thought perhaps a sword should be held, the sharp ends faced away, the broken stump gripped in both hands. The shadows spun dizzyingly around her, a whirlwind of fury. She could scarcely make out distinct forms. This didn't matter.

With a wild yell equal to any of theirs, Heloise flung herself at the nearest shadow, swinging the diamond for all she was worth. It connected with a crack that didn't come from the unbreakable branch itself, and she felt a shudder roll up her arm even as the monster she'd struck roared in pain.

She didn't pause even a moment to triumph; there were still far too many. With another yell, she whirled and struck again. They pressed in so close upon her that she could hardly move without striking something. She saw a bright red stream trickle down the brilliant diamond, and it made her sick to see. But she redoubled her energies, swinging again, thrusting and striking at anything that moved.

Someone shouted beyond the howls of the monsters, a voice she recognized distantly as Aunt's:

"Away! Away! You cannot touch her! Remember the Law!"

A last blast of angry roaring, like the final gusts of a raging thunderstorm, was enough to throw Heloise hard onto her knees. But she braced herself, clutching the diamond branch, her eyes squeezed tightly shut.

Suddenly they were gone. All the monsters and their fury. She felt the warmth of the diamond forest's glare upon her, and the force of a single angry glare. Opening her eyes, she looked up into the face of Aunt.

Aunt, who no longer wore her mask. Who stood before Heloise, weirdly fey, with skin black and speckled, and eyes the bright blue of a summer sky. Whatever glamour of terror she had worn before had dropped away, and the truth of her beauty was more terrible still.

"Very well, cursebreaker," she said. "You have taken the diamond branch. Proceed as you are determined."

She took a step nearer, then a second. She knelt before Heloise, her face luminous and yet so dark. Tears coursed down her cheeks, and the expression in her eyes was enough to break the heart. Heloise could not bear to look, but neither could she bear to look away. Though she did not understand why, she felt tears well up in her own eyes and a tremendous sorrow in her spirit.

"Hélène," she whispered.

In the same breath, the fey woman whispered, "Alala."

She took Heloise's face between her enormous hands. Claws tangled in Heloise's hair, but the woman's grasp was gentle. She spoke in a voice that might have been a growl were it not so full of desperate pleading.

"Understand this, mortal beast: The end of your journey will be death and only death. Remember what I say! Should you succeed, you will kill her. Our beloved Alala. You will kill her, and she will be lost to us forever."

Then she was gone. So swiftly, so completely that Heloise did not even feel the wind of her passing. She knelt alone in the diamond forest, clutching her branch. Her chest heaved with exertion and terror not yet relieved, and her blood boiled with anger and with . . . something else which she did not understand.

With a ragged "Ohh!" she squeezed her eyes closed and bent forward until her forehead pressed into the ground. She felt it change, the warm earth breaking away and leaving behind cold tile. When she sat up again, she was back in Centrecœur.

Benedict lay beside her, illuminated in the light of the diamond branch she held. His face was fixed, his mouth wide in a soundless scream. His eyes, glazed over, stared into nowhere.

TWENTY-EIGHT

SOMETHING HORRIBLE HAD HAPPENED. BUT WHAT? HAD HE FORGOTTEN an important exam or tried to give an ill-prepared speech before a crowd of ill-tempered Black Tops?

No. No this was more horrible than that.

Why was it dark all around him? Perhaps he lay in bed on a moonless night. But no, he could not feel his bed underneath him. He couldn't feel anything except . . .

"*Benedict!*"

Had word arrived from his father, his mother? Some bad news that could sink such dread into his heart? But what could either of them say that would cause this feeling? This feeling rising up inside, greater, stronger by the moment, ready to choke him in panic, in dread.

"*Benedict, wake up!*"

They hadn't the power over him to cause this sensation. They did not love him, he knew. He had known as much for years, and he no longer feared the truth. Yet, why had they not come to him when he . . . when he lay . . .

"*I think someone is coming!*"

Oh! There it was. There was his answer.

The pine boxes. His dead friends. Victor's pale face, already full of fever.

His own body. What was this covering his own body? This red lattice of rash like gripping veins of poison. The fingers of a crimson Death clutching him by every limb, across his torso, his back. All else is blackness, blindness, save for this scarlet, ugly fever, this scarring. Just like what he had seen on Luc, on Giles, on Henri. It had gripped them. It had taken them. It took Victor. Now it would take him too . . .

"*Wake up!*"

No. No, he had survived the Winter Fever. The rash had faded, leaving him pale and wasted, but his body lived on.

And his spirit? What remained of his spirit in the face of the future he now saw before him? A future of looming Death at every turn. A future which at any moment could mean the return of the clutching rash, of the pain, of burning—

"*Wake UP!*"

Benedict gasped and sat up suddenly, his hand flying to his face, which smarted from a sharp slap. He drew in breath for a shout but found

372

the shout stifled by two hands pressed hard across his open mouth.

A strange white light illuminated the dirty, wide-eyed, terror-filled face of the peasant girl.

"Lumé love us!" she hissed. "Don't make a sound! Someone is coming, and we've got to hide."

Benedict stared at her, unable to think. What in the name of Lumé, Hymlumé, and all the starry host was he doing? In the dining hall! In the middle of the night and—

"Hush!" Heloise hissed again, grabbed him by the hand, and pulled. In her other fist she gripped a small branch which gleamed with an unnatural light. She stuffed it under her arm, stifling the glow as best she could. "Don't say anything, just come with me."

"See here, little girl," Benedict began.

But then he heard an all too familiar voice speak beyond the door. "Is someone within?"

It was Doctor Dupont.

Memory washed down upon Benedict in a roaring flood. Not full memory just yet, but enough. He turned a desperate glance over his shoulder and saw the light of a candle gleam beneath the heavy door of the dining hall entrance.

With a smothered cry, he staggered to his feet and followed Heloise's lead. She dragged him around the long banquet table and right into the vast dark mouth of the fireplace on the other side. Benedict, who had seen that fireplace alive with a bonfire-like blaze, would never have dreamed of entering that yawning darkness to stand on the ashes of long-dead embers. But just then his brain could concoct no reasonable thought or idea of its own save the vague notion that obeying Heloise was his best bet if he didn't want to be found.

They crouched in deepest shadow at the very back. Heloise sat on the gleaming branch to hide it beneath her.

The door to the dining hall opened. A hand, weirdly pale in the glow of the taper candle it held, appeared, followed soon after by the solemn face of Doctor Dupont, more ghoulish than ever when lit by that single light source. His eyes searched the room, ineffective against the weight of gloom and darkness.

"Is someone within?" he asked again, like the intonation of an ancient priest performing some secret rite. Which was a stupid comparison, of course, and Benedict silently cursed himself for thinking it. After all, Doctor Dupont was just a man; an odd man of odd habits, but hand-selected by his own father as the best possible minister to Benedict in his illness.

Nevertheless, a chill like ice trickled down his spine as the doctor moved into the room and glided around the table, holding his candle up before him. Its light passed within inches of their terrified faces, and Benedict feared they must certainly be discovered.

But the good doctor moved on beyond the fireplace toward a certain elegant armoire that housed much of the Cœur family's fine silver, including two elegant chalices from back in the day when holy habits and sacraments were still practiced in Centrecœur.

This armoire was not meant to hold wine, which was stored in the cellars. But as Benedict watched, Doctor Dupont withdrew not only one of the two chalices, but also a bottle of an expensive vintage imported all the way from Southlands beyond the isthmus of the Six Towers. The ease with which he uncorked and the slosh inside the bottle as its contents were poured into the chalice told Benedict that the bottle was already half empty. Great Lights Above! Good Doctor Dupont was nothing short of a thief. A drunken thief at that.

Heloise's hand clamped down hard on Benedict's arm, reminding him that he would be wise to observe this thievery in silence, suppressing the indignant wrath that bubbled up on his tongue. He ground his teeth but allowed himself to be drawn deeper into the dark corner of the fireplace, his eyes sparking with fury as he watched the doctor down not one but two full chalices of wine. Then, as solemn and long-faced as ever, the thief used a square of linen to wipe out the chalice before replacing it on the armoire beside its mate. He tucked the now empty wine bottle into the depths of his sleeve, picked up his candle, and wafted back across the dining hall.

Heloise made no sound, but a sudden stiffening of her hand shot up Benedict's arm like a shout. Though she said nothing, and he could not see her face to help him guess what her sudden fear might mean, he cast his gaze about the room and saw what she must have spied but an instant before.

Beneath the great table was a gleam of silver and gold, faint but growing brighter by the instant; the two branches joined as one.

One slight turn of his head, and Doctor Dupont would see it. One pause in his stride, one stumble, and the glow would surely draw his eye. Benedict and Heloise huddled together in the fireplace, neither able to breathe, their gazes flicking from the little branch to the shadowy form of the doctor outlined in reddish gold by his candle, and back again. It seemed impossible that he could miss it, so bright was its brilliance by the time he had crossed to the open door.

Yet the good doctor stepped from the room and shut the door with a soft *clunk* behind him.

"Dragons!" Heloise breathed and sagged heavily against Benedict's arm. The next moment, however, she scrambled from the fireplace, exposing the diamond branch as she did so. It had shrunk somehow, just like the other two, but it was still more radiant than any candlelight. She snatched it up, closed it in her fist, then hastened across the room to duck under the table and retrieve the other branch as well. There she sat, both fists tightly closed over her treasures, her back against one of the massive table legs.

She didn't think she would ever move again. Her strength—however great it was—was sapped dry.

Benedict emerged from the fireplace and crossed the room with some hesitation, for it was very dark with the light of both branches hidden in Heloise's fists. But he found his way and knelt before her. "You saved me," he said.

Her mouth moved, but she was obliged to try three times before she could utter a response. Even then, it was only, "Yes."

"I don't remember what happened," Benedict persisted. He passed a hand over his face. "At least, not completely. I do know . . ." He shook his head and heaved a long sigh. The images in his head were too strange, too convoluted. All he saw with clarity was the fever rash killing his mates, marring his own skin, disfiguring and agonizing.

But it was gone. It wouldn't come back, not yet. Eventually, but not yet.

"I know you saved me, Heloise," he whispered. "You risked everything, and you pulled me back from some . . . some darkness I don't understand. I—I can't—"

"Shut your mouth!" Heloise whispered, her voice sudden and harsh. Horrified at the sound of her own words ringing still in her ears, she bowed her head and pressed her clenched fists into her eyes. She couldn't push out the memory of those awful beasts tearing into that black living-death. That image would never fully leave her, nor the image of the red blood staining the diamond branch, nor . . .

Nor the image of Aunt's face wet with tears.

Look at the branches, said the voice in her head. *Look at what you hold.*

But she was so tired! Her fear and fury had been too great. How could she ever overcome them? How could she go on?

She wept. She realized this suddenly and with a curse. Tears spilled down her cheeks, and she hadn't taken a breath for some moments because of a sob choking in her throat. With a gasp and a moan, she buried her face in her arms.

"Lumé love us," whispered Benedict. Then his arms were around her. She lowered her arms and pressed her face into his shoulder instead, allowing him to pull her close. She cried for reasons she could not name, or at least did not like to name.

Benedict whispered, "I'm sorry," though he had nothing to apologize for that she could think of. It was just his silly, stupid way, and she wanted to scold him for it. But she couldn't because she was crying too hard. He whispered, "I'm sorry. I'm so sorry, Heloise," and patted her shoulder and her hair. "I'm sorry this has happened to you. I'm sorry all of this, whatever it is, has fallen on your shoulders."

But the voice in her head had no such patience.

Sit up, girl! Sit up and wipe your nose and behave with some decorum! Whose child are you? Is this what the blood of Rufus the Red has come to over the generations?

"I'm not of Rufus the Red's blood," Heloise muttered through her tears.

"What was that?" said Benedict.

Of course you are! growled the voice in her head. *Do you think family lines follow but one course throughout your mortal history? Sit up, and remember you're the daughter of warriors. Sit up and look at what*

you hold in your hands. And come to me. Come to me!

Heloise sat bolt upright, staring into the dark rafters of the ceiling above. With a loud sniffle, she rubbed her sleeve across her nose.

"What's wrong?" Benedict asked. He could just discern the basic outline of her shape before him, could see that she was looking up. He glanced up as well but saw only more darkness. "Did you hear something?"

Heloise didn't answer. Instead she slowly uncurled both her fists.

The branch of silver and gold gleamed like the light of the sun and moon entwined. While the branch of diamond sparkled like all the stars in the heavens.

"Another branch," Benedict whispered. His eyes, filled with the light of diamonds, shone in awe. "I've never seen anything like it! It must be worth . . . a king's ransom. Three kings' ransoms!"

Much more than that, foolish boy.

Heloise didn't bother to answer. She held up both branches, lightly touching them to each other. And, just as she and Benedict had seen before when the gold and silver branches were united, so they saw again. The first branch reached out to the new one, caught it, twined about it. Gold, silver, and diamond stems blended into one long, curling branch of indescribable beauty.

It was whole. Somehow Heloise knew that it was now the shape it was meant to be.

"What is it, do you think?" Benedict asked.

Heloise, though she couldn't say how she knew, responded immediately and with absolute conviction: "It's a key."

They did not need Benedict's snuffed candle to light their way—the Faerie branch was light enough. So Benedict tucked the candle stub into his pocket and followed Heloise into the gallery, out of the west wing of the house, past the chapel that was his room, and on toward the old east wing. Heloise moved with surprising confidence for one who had not set foot inside Centrecœur until a few days ago. She might have been born to the Great House, so easily did she navigate its corridors.

Benedict made no effort to take the lead but followed her in silence. He spoke up only when they neared the east wing, whispering, "Remember, the apothecary is just down the passage. If Doctor Dupont is still awake he might see the light."

Heloise snorted. "He drank enough to put him to sleep for days!" she said, and urged Benedict on with a glance.

So they came to the narrow stairway winding up the lone Tower of Centrecœur. Heloise went first. The heavy closeness of the stairwell was enough to smother much of the light. Benedict hated to follow but hated still more to be left behind. If Heloise was right—if the branch she held really was a key, despite not looking like any key Benedict had ever before seen—he didn't want to miss this opportunity to discover what lay behind the locked Tower door.

So they proceeded up the stair, Heloise easily enough, being small and slight; Benedict with more trouble the higher they went, for the passage got narrower and narrower. Any marauding Corrilondians of historical times who tried to fight their way up this stair would have had their work cut out for them! A defender well supplied could fend off all assailants for ages while waiting for aid from king and country.

The folks of centuries past must have been much smaller people, Benedict decided as he ducked his head and squeezed his shoulders through the passage. Heloise reached the top long before him and stood on the topmost step, tapping her foot and scowling as he finally rounded the last curve.

The wooden door stood behind her. It was blackened with age and fixed with brass. By the light of the silver-gold-and-diamond branch, it looked strangely ominous.

"Were you right?" Benedict asked. "Is the branch a key?"

"I don't know," Heloise said. "I haven't tried it yet."

They stared at each other for a long silent moment, each waiting for the other to urge action, neither certain they wanted to pursue the course set before them. Then, without another word, Heloise turned suddenly and stuck the diamond end of the three-part branch into the heavy lock.

Without a sound, the door swung open.

Benedict, standing farther down the stair, could see nothing save for a light falling suddenly upon Heloise, illuminating each of her tangled curls in such sharp detail that she seemed suddenly more real than real. "Wait!" he cried, and tried to catch hold of her arm.

He was too slow. Heloise stepped through the doorway, and before Benedict could take a single step, the door shut behind her. He stood alone in utter darkness at the top of the Tower stair.

TWENTY-NINE

ALL AROUND HER THE TREES WERE LADEN WITH FLOWERS SO THICKLY blooming that it was impossible to see more than the vaguest impression of what lay beyond them. They hung like a curtain of white and rose and lavender, and long tendrils of stems and leaves curled around them in shades of green and blue. Each blossom was exquisite in its design and proportion so that, though they grew in great clusters, not a single one was lost in the crowd.

It was too much. Too much splendor too distinctly rendered in too many colors and brilliant lights. A single one of those blossoms would be enough to fill the eyes of a longing poet or lustful painter to the fullest. In such profusion, the glory of them was . . . deadly.

Mortal eyes were not meant to behold such beauty and survive. Heloise took one desperate glance and shut her eyes as tightly as she could. She stood with her back pressed to the shut Tower door, feeling its fastness behind her.

"Greetings, mortal child."

Someone approached. Heloise could hear the soft murmur of stirring in the boughs, and she felt the silken kisses of petals falling on her face and arms.

"I am glad you have come," said a voice like the sound the night sky would make if it could sing with the stars; deep, dark, and enigmatic beyond mortal comprehension. It was full of kindness and profound sorrow.

"Who are you?" Heloise asked.

"I am Princess Imoo-Alala, Daughter of the House of Night," said the voice.

It was the voice she had heard in her head since the morning of her fourteenth birthday. Heloise blushed, suddenly horrified that she had ever mistaken such a voice for her own. She couldn't think of anything to say, so she stood clutching her three-part branch, leaning against the door, and wishing she'd had the good sense to stay on the other side, in her own world.

"Why do you not open your eyes?" the voice asked, but in a way that let the hearer know she knew the answer to her question already.

"It's—it's all too beautiful," Heloise admitted, suddenly ashamed of her poor, ragged dress, her dirty face and feet, her . . . her mortality. It was wrong for one like her to stand in this place. "It'll kill me to look."

"If you look with your mortal eyes, perhaps," said the voice of Princess Imoo-Alala. "Though perhaps it will only render you mad."

"I don't want to go mad, if it's all the same to you."

Two fingers, soft and cool, touched Heloise, one gentle fingertip pressed to each eyelid. Heloise felt her heart jolt in her breast at that touch. Then she felt a certain—she couldn't describe it. It was as though something which had lain dormant inside her all her life suddenly stretched, yawned, and opened its eyes.

"You may look now, child," said Princess Imoo-Alala. "I have called up your Faerie blood."

The two soft fingertips left her eyelids, and Heloise stood still as if frozen for several ramming heartbeats. Then, afraid of what she might see, she opened first one eye then the other.

"Oh," she breathed. "It's *you.*"

Before her stood the woman she had glimpsed on the hilltop near her parents' cottage: the woman with the onyx-black skin, with the wild mane of thundercloud hair. The gloriously tall woman, taller than any man Heloise had ever met, taller even than the beautiful Lion-Prince.

She stood before Heloise, clad in a sleeveless gown of brilliant saffron edged in blossoms like those growing from the trees surrounding them. The hue of that gown made her skin seem even darker, even more luminous, and her eyes were the most brilliant blue, bluer than the sapphire eyes of the carved ebony lions on Benedict's mirror.

It was no wonder, Heloise thought suddenly, that Rufus the Red had loved her so dearly.

Wait. Where had that thought come from, so clear in her mind, in her heart? She couldn't explain it, and yet she knew and understood it for absolute truth.

"I saw you before," she whispered. "In . . . back in Canneberges."

"Yes," said the princess. "In Canneberges of six hundred mortal years ago." She bowed her head, gazing down at Heloise from her towering height. Blossoms from the tree branches draped through her hair like a veil of shining gems. "The sylph, you understand, is not bound by linear streams of time the way you are. I could not speak to it directly, but I urged it, spirit to spirit. At my urging, it caught you up briefly in its arms and carried you back to that moment long ago; that moment when I and my beloved Rufus pledged our troth and I gave to him my greatest gift . . . and committed myself to the fate before me."

Heloise could not speak. Her mind scrambled to comprehend that which was said to her. *I traveled through time.* But no, she couldn't think about that. *Rufus the Red married a Faerie princess.* That she could consider, at least briefly, for she had heard of such things in stories and tales around friendly hearth fires on cold winter evenings.

Then she thought, *Benedict has Faerie blood.*

"He does indeed," said Princess Imoo-Alala, as though reading Heloise's thoughts. "But in the male line, the blood does not manifest in the gifts of the Fey. In the female line, however, every few generations will boast a single girl-child who has the power, or the potential power. It need only be summoned to life. As I have summoned yours. As I summoned your grandmother's power when she was your age. And her grandmother's before her."

Heloise stared at the princess. It was difficult to do anything else, for Imoo-Alala was so lovely. But as she stared, Heloise noticed something; not once, as they spoke to one another, had the princess's mouth moved. Though they stood face-to-face, the voice Heloise heard spoke directly inside her head.

"Why are you doing that?" Heloise asked.

"Doing what?"

"Talking inside my head still."

"Because," said the princess, "I have no physical body with which to speak in person."

She was a ghost. Heloise saw this now with a clarity that might have come from her awakened Faerie vision. Or perhaps she had realized it all along but hadn't wanted to acknowledge the truth. Imoo-Alala stood before her, but her tall, powerful form was only a shade, an illusion perhaps. A trick of the many magical lights and shadows falling through the trees, shining from the blossoms.

"Are you . . . are you dead?" Heloise whispered, wondering if she should be afraid.

Those eyes like the morning sky overflowed suddenly with the sorrow which never fully left the princess's face. "I am not dead," she said. "More is the pity!"

She extended an insubstantial phantom hand. The fingers were so long, so tapering, and each was tipped with the most delicate, polished nail shining like a small crescent moon. Heloise hesitated before accepting that hand, surprised when she did so that she felt solid substance when she knew there was nothing truly there. Perhaps it was her Faerie perceptions, or simply her own mortal brain filling in what it thought should be in place of what wasn't.

Or perhaps none of this was real, and she had gone utterly ever-blooming mad.

"Walk with me," said the princess. "I will show you this beautiful heaven to which Mother banished me for my sin. And I will take you to your sister."

"Evette?" Heloise gasped, her heart leaping to her throat.

"Yes," said Alala. "Evette, and all the lost sisters of our line. I will explain to you as much as the Law permits, and I will help you as I may."

They proceeded into the forest, away from the Tower door. The curtains of blossoms parted before them, and twirling petals fell at their feet, casting displays of glittering lights in their path. All was so bright with color that Heloise at first thought they moved through daylight. But the farther they walked, the more often she glimpsed the sky through the twining tree branches above, and it was a deep purple spangled with a few distant stars, which seemed to dance and whirl in their nightly patterns. So it was night. Or twilight. Or maybe the very edge of dawn.

As they walked, Alala spoke, her deep voice filling Heloise's head and heart.

"I married Rufus the Red, a mortal man, against the wishes of my family. Ha! That is to put it far too lightly. When I say I married against their wishes, I mean I went against all that they hold most dear and true and Faerie. For to give my heart to a mortal was to give up my immortality. Among my people there can be no fate more dreadful nor any sin more dire.

"Father would have killed me for my choice. In his mind it was the only right thing to do; I was doomed to die anyway, and he sought to prevent me from birthing a brood of half-blood children, mortals who might possess Faerie attributes, thus polluting the line of the Family of Night forever. Indeed, though I had no wish to die—the new mortal life granted me was so brief a span of years as it was—I could not blame Father for his fury or his actions.

"But Uncle, at great risk to himself, stood up to Father. As a result, his face was destroyed, leaving only the skull-like visage you glimpsed in the diamond forest. A simple glamour could disguise his hideousness easily enough, but he wears his scars with pride, for he faced Father and survived, and there are few indeed who can boast as much. Uncle prevented Father from killing me, momentarily at least, and I was able to escape back into the mortal world, to the arms of my beloved.

"Soon afterward, I am told, Mother learned of Father's attempt on my life. In a great rage, she turned on him. The battle which ensued was mighty and dreadful; even in the mortal world, I felt the effects of it quake in the very marrow of my soul. It ended with Mother's death—her first death, mind you, for Faerie Queens are graced with three lives and may return from death twice before their souls are taken across the Final Water. Mother died . . . and Father was imprisoned in a secret place of which even I do not know.

"So my life was spared, and I was permitted to continue in the short existence I had chosen. I bore a daughter, then a son, then two more daughters by my husband. They retained some likeness to their Faerie kindred, being tall and strong-limbed, dark of skin and bright of eye. But they were each of them mortal, even as I had now become.

"On the day my eldest daughter—Ayodele by name—turned eighteen and came of age to wed, we held a great dance in Canneberges. It was the last night of winter on the verge of spring's dawning, and we wore our brightest clothes and fairest jewels—and though none of these compared to the treasures I had enjoyed in Mother's demesne as a Princess of Night, the love I felt for my husband and my children was a greater treasure by far. Already I felt the effects of Time upon my body, the thinning of my skin, the thickening of the blood in my veins. It was a terror to me sometimes but not on that night. On that night I knew only joy, and I rejoiced in my decision to wed my love and spend my days with him and our offspring.

"We danced that night to a mortal song, all of us joining in a series of rings, our hands clasped, our faces upraised to the sky as we sang and laughed. My eldest daughter danced in the centermost ring, held in the arms of the young man she had chosen for her husband. I saw in their eyes the same love I shared with my Rufus, and all of my heart wished for their future joy and happiness.

"But, as you have already guessed, my wish was not to be fulfilled.

"Before the first of our dances ended, a new song began to play. I do not know if others heard it; I do not think so. I believe it played for my ears alone. It was a song I had heard a few times before in my long, long, immortal life: the Sacrificial Dance. The one you know as *Le Sacre*. I recognized the pounding, pulsing, sighing beat of it, and I knew that my Family had come to Canneberges.

"I stumbled in the dance. When Rufus asked me if I was ill, I made some excuse and slipped away into the shadows on the outskirts. I searched the night surrounding us, feeling the nearness of my Family but unable to see them.

"Suddenly Mother's hand slipped into mine. I knew it at once as hers; no child forgets the grip of her mother's hand. She was alive again, reborn to her second life. How glad I was to see her! How glad and how horror-struck all in the same instant.

"'My daughter, my Alala,' she said to me even as the music of the

Sacrificial Dance filled the air around us. 'I have come to rescue you.'

"'I'll not return to Nivien,' I told her, though I did not withdraw my hand from hers. 'I will not leave my husband or my children.'

"'No indeed,' said she, and her expression was one of deepest sorrow. I have never seen another face so sad, though sometimes I wonder if my own face reflects her sadness now. I saw then how she had changed. Mother was always the most beautiful of our people, a Faerie Queen incomparable among the queens of the Far World. But the sorrow of her second life had changed her. I saw that she had shaved away her glory of bountiful hair, leaving her scalp bald and even scarred where the knife had cut her skin.

"'No indeed,' she said to me, 'for you may never be what once you were, my darling child. But I will save you from the very jaws of Death. I will not let you go down to the Final Water at the end of your mortal life. I will rescue you. I will keep you forever safe. My own . . . my daughter . . .'

"Her words struck fear into my heart, for I suspected even then what she had purposed to do. 'Mother!' I cried, 'I chose this fate willingly! I am not afraid of Death, and I will gladly pay the price of my mortality.'

"It was too late. She had slipped from my grasp, melting into the darkness. I sensed rather than saw her moving through the night toward the dancing circles. And suddenly I felt my Family around me—Mother, Uncle, Aunt, Brother, my many cousins and kindred. All were gathered,

392

invisible to my mortal eyes. They could not disguise, however, the intensity of their souls, which shouted to me above even the swelling music of Le Sacre.

"I knew what Le Sacre meant. I wanted to pretend otherwise, to lie to myself. But I had heard the same song used for similar purposes in the past. I myself had helped to perform it, helped to sing it in ages long forgotten.

"Nevertheless, as I ran through the darkness toward the laughing voices of my family and the gathered celebrants of Canneberges, I lied to myself again and again.

"It was all for nothing. Even as I came within sight of the dance—even as I gazed out from the shadows into that central circle where my oldest daughter whirled in the arms of her true love—I saw the shadows of my people surround her. The music reached its climax; my daughter turned and saw those who set upon her. I heard her scream . . .

"The next thing I knew, I was waking in my husband's arms. Rufus begged me to tell him what I had seen, what had frightened me, his fearless wife, so that I should fall down in a dead faint. I would not answer him. I demanded only to know where our daughter was.

"'Our daughters are here,' he said, indicating my youngest two.

"'But where is Ayodele!' I cried.

"'Who,' said my husband, 'is Ayodele?'

"So I knew the worst had come to past. The Family of Night had stolen away my child, leaving behind not even the memory of her in the hearts of her family. I alone recalled her existence.

"Such a fury came over me then, a fury I know you have felt yourself, mortal child. In this rage, I could have torn down all of Centrecœur with my bare hands! Instead I made my way to the Oakwood, which stood even then in the south of my husband's great estate. I passed into those trees, shouting for Mother, for Uncle, for Brother, shouting their Faerie names, which I will not tell you, for they are sacred among my people. I did not care for their sacredness just then. I shouted them as loudly as I could, for all the ears of Canneberges to hear if they liked!

"Brother appeared before me, massive and young and beautiful as ever. Looking at him, I felt the full weight of my mortality upon my shoulders, for I was no longer young, though I was still beautiful.

"'Why do you call my name, Sister Alala?' he demanded.

"'I want my daughter back!' I growled and wished that I still had the power to take my other shape so that I might claw him across the face. 'Give her to me!'

"'I cannot,' he said. 'She is ours now by right.'

"'By what right?' I demanded. 'You know as well as I the Law of the Lumil Eliasul. He will not allow Faerie-kind to prey upon the mortals He so loves. You will bring His wrath down upon your heads. You will bring about the destruction of Nivien. I myself will journey to the Farthestshore, and I will plead for justice!'

"I want to say Brother looked ashamed. I want to say that perhaps he even felt a true sorrow for me in my anguish. We had been close once, bonded in both rivalry and affection.

"Nevertheless, he said to me only, 'Mother has provided for a cursebreaker. The Law is satisfied.'

"He would say no more, though I pleaded, cajoled, and threatened him with violence. At last he left me weeping in the Oakwood, alone.

"But I knew Brother had not lied. He would never lie to me. And I knew that a cursebreaker would be found among my own children, for this is the way of Faerie and Faerie law. So I watched my son and my two daughters. I watched for the power of Nivien to manifest itself in one of them.

"My youngest daughter, on the morning of her fourteenth birthday, discovered she could understand the languages of trees. She also remembered, suddenly and painfully, the sister she had lost. She came to me at once, telling me of her new abilities and wanting to know what had become of Ayodele.

"My youngest daughter, my sweet Adanna, my pride and my hope. What joy it was to see the powers of Nivien reborn in her body, giving her strength and purpose beyond that of her two remaining siblings! How I longed to see her break this curse, to restore my eldest daughter to me, and to spare me the fate Mother had planned . . ."

The princess's voice faded inside Heloise's head as they journeyed on through the forest. Heloise, who had been so intent upon the story that she had scarcely noticed the landscape through which they passed, found her gaze now wandering. She realized that they had not progressed very far, though they had walked all the while Princess Imoo-Alala talked.

But when Heloise turned her head to look back over her shoulder, she saw the Tower door still half hidden by the flower-laden boughs. They did not wander or journey in circles. They simply made no progress, no matter how far they went.

It struck Heloise then that perhaps this world was very small.

"Yes," said Alala, once again reading her thoughts. "It is a small world indeed. Nothing more than a pocket world crafted with secret, powerful magic. Its existence depends on the curse Mother set in place, and its boundaries fit within the realm of her mind. It is a world of her imagination, you might say."

Heloise almost tried to understand this but thought better of it. Instead she asked the question which throughout Alala's tale had burned upon her tongue. "Where is Evette?"

"We are coming to her soon."

"And Cateline?"

"Her as well. My Ayodele is with them too, and many more besides. You will see."

At this, Heloise frowned. "But you said your youngest daughter was going to break the curse that snatched away Ayodele. You said—"

The princess turned her beautiful face to look down on Heloise, effectively cutting off anything she might have said. Indeed, Heloise could not say a word in light of that dreadful sadness. It reminded her of . . .

Of Meme. Of those stolen moments when Meme thought no one watched and her face fell into lines of such age and mourning, it cut Heloise to the quick to see it. Meme who never once forgot Hélène, not for a day, not for a moment.

"Ayodele was never restored to me," Princess Imoo-Alala said. "And my Adanna, in time, lost her Faerie powers and became wholly mortal. She retained only her memories of her lost sister and her own failure to break the curse. She died before I did. I sat at her bedside when she was still young, and I held her hand even as her spirit slipped away to the Netherworld and beyond. Her last words were . . ."

The princess stopped. Her grip on Heloise's hand tightened, though Heloise knew a ghost should not be able to have such a grip. Though Alala did not speak with her mouth, Heloise felt the struggle inside her head as the princess sought to finish what she intended to say. "Her last words were 'Forgive me, Ayodele. I tried.'"

Heloise heard Grandmem's voice clearly in her memory as though the old woman even now spoke: "*I tried. Oh, believe me, Cateline, I did try!*"

So the curse was unbroken. Six hundred years, and it remained unbroken! How many sisters had been stolen away? How many curse-breakers had set out on this same, hopeless quest? How many had lost their powers in the end and faded into despair?

Heloise stopped in her tracks, unable to make herself take another step, so heavily did the weight of those years and those failures press down upon her heart. She stared at the silver, gold, and diamond branch, the key that looked like no key she had ever before seen, which she held in her hand. Somehow she had thought it was all she needed. Fetch the branch of silver, fetch the branch of gold; finally, fetch the branch of diamond, and all would then be well. Was that not what the verse sent to her by the Dame had implied? *A three-part branch will prove the key to set the captives flying free . . .*

"This is only the first step," said Alala, reading her mind. She placed a gentle hand on Heloise's shoulder. "The key brought you here. And here I may, by our law, show you what has become of the sister whom you seek to free. But I cannot tell you how the curse may be broken."

"Do you know?" Heloise whispered, glancing up quickly at the princess but unable to hold her gaze.

Alala nodded solemnly. "I do. But if I tell you, I will break the law, and the curse on my line—on your family—will be fixed until the End of Days."

The Princess of Night turned then and, with an elegant sweep of her arm, drew back a curtain of blossoms and vines, revealing a meadow full of white light like moonlight, surrounded on all sides by trees of silver, gold, and diamond. From these trees hung enormous tapestries of fine cloth, finer than the softest linen ever woven in Canneberges, soft and sheer and delicate as the threads of a spider's web.

Sitting before these tapestries were the pale phantom figures of twelve young maidens, all of the same age. They sat in absolute silence, unaware, perhaps, of anyone else around them, and they stitched away with bright needles and gossamer threads, creating pictures in silk, elaborate pictures which Heloise did not at first discern.

For her eyes were fixed upon one particular figure sitting apart from the rest.

"*Evette!*"

Alala touched the top of her head with a warning hand. "Hush, child. This is an enchanted place. She cannot hear you in any case."

THIRTY

HELOISE APPROACHED HER SISTER FROM BEHIND, SOFTLY WHISPERING, "Evette?" But the Princess of Night had spoken truly: The twelve maidens existed in a silent world all their own, visible but unreachable. Heloise put out a trembling hand and tried to touch her sister's shoulder. It was no use. Her fingers clutched at nothing more than cold, still air.

Evette, unaware of her presence, stitched at her tapestry, her head tilted to one side, a line of concentration between her brows. She might have been sitting at the family hearth on a spring evening, quietly embroidering an edging of cranberry blossoms around the neck of some humble peasant garment.

Only here, in this other world, she was as pale in face and form as the shroud-wrapped memory of Hélène.

Heloise blinked back tears. She longed to catch her sister in her arms, to hear Evette call her *dearest* in her most appallingly patient voice. Then together they should leave this place, arm in arm, Evette chiding her gently on the state of her gown and the dirt on her face, following up these remonstrations with questions about the family and Gutrund and Rufus the rooster.

Instead Heloise turned to Alala, who stood behind her, her hands folded, her eyes gently veiled by her long lashes. "How many others have come this far?" she asked, afraid to hear the answer. "How many cursebreakers collected the three branches and came to you?"

"Of the twelve who set out," said Alala, "you are the seventh to come this far."

"And none of the others succeeded. None of them broke the curse." Heloise could have smacked herself for the quaver in her voice. She would not, *would not* cry in front of this beautiful woman, this beautiful great-great-great-something grandmother of hers! She would not disgrace the blood of Rufus the Red.

"It is a powerful curse," said the princess, her voice kind but full of a darkness bordering on despair. "Of the six others who came to me, three perished in their attempts to free their sisters. The other three . . . wished they had perished."

"But wait!" Heloise cried, scowling. "That's not right. I know they, your family . . . they cannot *kill* the cursebreaker." She recalled the horrible moment of so short a time ago, when she stood surrounded by furious, ravening monsters, and the voice of Aunt, shouting out, "*You cannot touch her! Remember the Law!"* The monsters, so many of them, enough to have torn her to bloody shreds in mere moments, had left her alive, had abandoned their prey.

Whoever the Dame of the Haven was, she had been right: The Faerie law forbade the Family of Night from causing her harm.

But Alala, reading Heloise's many swirling thoughts, said, "Child, child, they cannot kill you. But they need not interfere should you kill yourself."

"Why would I do that?"

The princess shook her head slowly. "I may not tell you. You must find other means of discovering your answers. I may only tell you my own story."

She took Heloise by the shoulders, turning her so that she would look at the tapestry upon which her sister worked. "See what she creates by the skill of her hand," Alala whispered. With another pressure, she turned Heloise to see the eleven other maidens and their work. "See what they create together."

For the first time Heloise forced herself to study the images depicted in the tapestry. They were far more vivid, far more detailed than any of the thick tapestries she had glimpsed during her wanderings through Centrecœur. Unlike those tapestries, these images were wrought on thin, delicate fabric. The slightest breeze made each tapestry shiver and dance as it hung from the low tree boughs.

When they shivered and danced, the figures picked out with needle and thread danced as well.

Dancers, Heloise realized. Each tapestry depicted a series of dancers. Some were elegant folk dressed in rich garments of days gone by. Some were peasant folk clad only in rags. But they all danced in forms and movements which Heloise recognized.

They danced Le Sacre.

Stepping away from the princess, Heloise moved to the first of the tapestries. The girl who sat at work over it was very like Imoo-Alala. Though her form was pale and ghostly, Heloise could see that, in her own world, she must have possessed the same dark skin, the same wild mass of hair that was not unlike Heloise's own tangled mane save that it was more carefully arranged. She was probably quite tall, just like the princess, for even seated as she was, her head came as high as Heloise's own.

"Ayodele," Heloise whispered. For an instant she half wondered if the maiden paused in her work, if a flicker of interest crossed her face at the sound of her own name spoken by a strange voice. But no. She could hear nothing, lost as she was, far from all she knew, all she loved.

Heloise studied her tapestry. She saw the ringing circles of dancers—noblemen and women in the inner circles; burghers and merchants of repute in the middle rings; peasant folk in the outer edges. And outermost, stitched in black silk, were shadow figures clashing sharp weapons together in the same way the men of Canneberges clashed their canes as they performed Le Sacre.

In the very center of the tapestry stood the perfect image of Ayodele herself, rendered in exquisite, impossible detail. She held the hands of a young man who stood a good head shorter than she, and Heloise could see the adoration shining in his eyes as he gazed upon his bride-to-be.

Ayodele's poor young betrothed, who lost his love and forgot her more than six hundred years ago. But here in the tapestry, they lived on together, dancing for eternity in silk.

Heloise proceeded to the next tapestry, the next maiden hard at her silent labor. This girl was similar in appearance to Ayodele but much shorter, and her hair was not quite so thick and wild. She too depicted Le Sacre dance, and when some wind which Heloise could not feel stirred the silk, the figures seemed to move and whirl and stamp their feet. The third tapestry and the fourth were more of the same, as were the fifth, the sixth, and the seventh. Each maiden shared a resemblance with those nearest to her, but Heloise suspected that often several generations passed between them, and in these cases, the differences were more pronounced than the similarities.

By the time she came to Cateline, the disparity between her and Ayodele was so great that few would have believed a blood connection. Ayodele was the daughter of a princess; Cateline was the offspring of peasant farmers.

Yet there was a touching, if rough sort of beauty about this girl. A beauty not unlike Evette's; a beauty of sweetness, of good humor, of kindness, which softened plain features into something lovely.

"Cateline," Heloise said, though she knew the square-faced, curly-haired young woman could not hear her, "my Grandmem never forgot you. Your sister. She loves you still."

Tears sprang to her eyes, tears for Grandmem as much as for herself. For Grandmem had never come this far, she knew. Grandmem had never had one last opportunity to look upon the face of the sister she longed to reclaim. Or perhaps that was easier. Perhaps it was better not to see this glimpse; to come so close and still to—

But no. She could not think that thought, she dared not. Heloise wiped an angry hand over her face, dashing away any trace of weeping before turning to Princess Imoo-Alala. "Why?" she demanded. "Why do they sit here like this, stitching these images? What is the *point* of it? What does your mother want from them?"

"A mortal magic," the princess replied.

"A what?"

Before Alala could answer, however, a sighing, mournful sound filled the whole of that small solitary world. The sound was like a voice, but the voice of someone or something Heloise could not imagine. A single, low, melancholy note, like a plea or a summons.

At first Heloise could do nothing but stand with her mouth open and her ears filled to bursting. She could not say if the note went on playing in her heart or if she heard only the echoing memory of it. She felt an urge to follow it, and it was all she could do to hold her ground.

Movement caught her eye. She turned her head this way and that, watching as each of the twelve mortal maidens set aside her work, rose from her low seat, and stood. Evette rose last of all. Though Heloise hastened to her, staring into her face, Evette's gaze was faraway, unaware of her sister's nearness.

A second note played, the same as the first, but longer, more compelling. The maidens, led by Ayodele, proceeded across the clearing, pale wraiths of mingled loss and sorrow. "Evette?" Heloise whispered, and tried in vain to catch her sister's hand. But Evette moved with the others, passing from the meadow and into the trees.

Forgetting Princess Alala for the moment, Heloise hastened after them, keeping pace just behind her sister. They moved much faster through this tiny world than Heloise had when walking beside the princess. Within a few paces they came to the Tower door, which opened for them, revealing the forest of silver beyond.

"Evette! Wait!" Heloise cried, though she knew it was useless. Her sister passed through the door, following but a step or two behind Cateline. But when Heloise tried to pursue, the door shut firmly in her face.

"Dragons eat it!" Heloise cursed, grabbed hold of the heavy latch, and hauled the door open. Rather than a silver forest, she found herself gazing out into the dark, narrow passage of the stairway. Benedict stood a few steps below her, staring up at her with large, frightened eyes.

"Heloise?" he gasped.

"Dragons!" Heloise cursed again, and slammed the door.

She turned around, her back against the wood and brass, and stood there in that pocket world of light and blossoms. Her breast heaved as she drew great breaths to fill her lungs, struggling to calm her racing heart. Then, clenching the three-part branch in her fist, she stomped through the trees, shoving branches and blossoms from her way, and marched back into the clearing.

Alala waited for her, surrounded by the twelve tapestries. She held herself like the Lion-Prince had—her hands at her sides, her arms loose, her shoulders back, her head high. No trace of awkwardness, only elegance and grace. She was a sight to behold, a figure of simultaneous beauty and dread.

Heloise paused but a moment. Then, shaking the branch like a weapon, she hurried across the meadow and stood in the shadow of the princess. "What is a mortal magic?" she demanded.

"It is a magic worked by mortals, as the name would suggest," Alala replied.

"Yes, but what does that *mean?*"

The princess didn't so much as blink an eye in the face of Heloise's impotent wrath. She turned away slowly and moved amidst the tapestries to sit on a stone seat Heloise had not noticed before. A seat before a windowsill. Heloise saw that the window looked out upon . . . upon Canneberges!

Wonderingly, she drew nearer to Alala, gazing over the princess's shoulder at the vista spread below them. She recalled that they were still in the upper Tower, even if the chamber was full of this small forest and groves. This, then, was the solitary window at the very top of the Tower, the one from which she had sometimes felt a prickling sensation that someone watched her. A sensation which, she now realized, was entirely correct.

Heloise gazed out at the moonlit fields so familiar to her. From this high vantage, she felt she could see all of Canneberges, all the way to Oakwood and beyond to that dreadful crossroads where the gibbet stood.

Shivering, Heloise closed her eyes and turned away. When she dared look again, she fixed her gaze only upon Alala's calm face. "Please," she said, "what is this mortal magic and what does it have to do with Evette?"

Alala said, "I will tell you. Listen."

"I loved my Rufus well through the short years of our life together. But the loss of two daughters—one remembered by no one but myself—cast a pall over my days, a shadow I could never lift or shake. My Rufus grieved with me for the death of our youngest, but he never understood the true depth of my pain. How could he? For him, death was a natural part of life.

"But for me, such loss was strange and dreadful. Though I was now mortal, I had lived many long ages as a Faerie, and I could not forget the ways and beliefs of my people.

"The death of my husband was the final blow. Though I had still one daughter, one son, and their growing families to love, I found I could take little joy in the days ahead of me. I began to realize the gift of mortality, to look upon this existence as the end. And what would follow after death? The beginning . . . .

"Old age fell upon me with a suddenness I never could have expected. After all the centuries (as mortals count time) of my existence, I came at last to my weakened, sickened, final days. But as I lay me down upon my deathbed, my children and grandchildren gathered on each side, I found that I no longer feared death. I feared only Mother's promise made to me on the very night she stole Ayodele:

"*I will not let you go down to the Final Water at the end of your mortal life. I will rescue you.*'

"I had suspected even then what she intended. Over the years since that night, I had had plenty of time to speculate further. As, with great difficulty, each breath left my lungs, I felt a dread unlike any I had ever before known welling up in my heart.

"Rufus! Brave, red-blooded Rufus! How I long to be reunited with you. To see you again on the Farthestshore. And Adanna—dear Adanna, my courageous girl. Have you found the peace you craved? Would you have welcomed me with open arms and led me into that new Beginning?

"But even as I drew my last breath, even as I expelled it and, with the expulsion, left behind my frail, mortal body—I knew it was not to the Final Water my spirit would fly.

"Instead, I opened my eyes and found myself standing in this world. This beautiful world of flowers and twilight, of soft spring air and crisp autumnal whispers—a world so like the world of my immortal youth. My Mother's imagining of perfection, a haven to house my soul forever. To keep me alive and close to her.

"I saw where I had come, saw the restoration of my physical form, incorporeal and yet real—and I screamed with rage and despair!

"'Mother! What have you done?' I demanded. 'Why have you imprisoned me here?'

"'I told you already,' Mother said, appearing before me and smiling, though her eyes were sad. 'I told you I would rescue you. I will not let a Princess of Night be lost to death and whatever lies beyond the Final Water. Here you will be safe, my love. Here you will be near to me forever. I will never lose you.'

"I wept. I pleaded. I screamed and shouted. I tried to make her understand that though this life must end, a beginning awaited me on the Farthestshore. She could not understand, immortal that she is. I could not make her understand no matter how I tried.

"When at last my ranting calmed, she took me by the hand and led me to this selfsame meadow. There, to my surprise and delight I beheld none other than my oldest daughter! Seated there upon a low stool, her hands busy—as they often were back in her own world—with needlework.

"'Ayodele!' I cried and ran to her . . . only to discover, alas! She was not fully present in this world. Indeed, she was held in some prison of mind or matter (it hardly makes a difference which in Faerie), unaware of all around her, all time, all thought, all hope or fear. She worked upon her tapestry.

"'It is a great magic, this magic of mortals,' Mother said, standing back and watching as I tried in vain to catch the eye of my daughter. 'They put down in words or pictures all their memories so that when they die, the memories live on, passed down from generation to generation. It is a weird sort of enchantment, but powerful.'

"I saw then what Mother had done. She had stolen my mortal daughter and harnessed her abilities, abilities beyond those of Faerie-kind. Ayodele stitched at her tapestry, depicting the Sacrificial Dance—and with every stitch she made, she held my spirit close.

"For there I was in the center of the image, invisible at first glance, but present. The dancers themselves became the folds of my gown, the sky and stars my face, my skin, my eyes. A perfect portrait of me, caught in the magic of mortal memory—and worked to evil purpose by Faerie hands.

"I whirled upon Mother. Though once I had loved her dearly, in that moment I believe I hated her for what she did to me and to my child. 'It cannot work forever!' I declared. 'Mortal magic does not last throughout all time. It will fade away and be forgotten, and then I will be free.'

"'No indeed,' Mother replied. 'For you have begun a line of children who will carry your memory down through the ages of this world. You will see, my darling Alala. My plan for your rescue is strong, and it will not be broken.'

"She left me then in this prison she had crafted for me with such tender care. Though I explored its every corner and crevice for some sign of weakness, I found none. The most made available to me was a single window—a window to the Near World, with a view that looked out upon Canneberges.

"So through these long centuries I have watched the generations of my line. I have watched sisters stolen. I have sent out my voice to whisper in the ears of the cursebreakers, to aid them as I can. I have learned many a secret and studied the law which binds me.

"And here I remain, neither dead nor alive. A prisoner of Mother's love. A prisoner of mortal magic."

As Alala told her story, Heloise gazed out the window upon the nighttime landscape of Canneberges. The moonlit fields and peasant cottages, the dye houses, the bogs, all those things so familiar to her, displayed in unreal detail before her new Faerie eyesight. She clung to the sight as she might cling to a lifeline; for out there, in that world beyond this one, was the reality she knew, the reality she had always known, and she longed suddenly to be Heloise Flaxman again, with Heloise Flaxman's small troubles, hurts, and irritations.

Heloise Flaxman, with Evette always at her side.

Alala finished speaking. Heloise felt the princess's clear eyes fixed upon the side of her face, but she couldn't make herself look back. Instead she turned away, moving from the window back into the meadow surrounded by the twelve fluttering tapestries. Six hundred years, and still they remained incomplete! Either the maidens were very slow seamstresses or time moved at a different pace where they dwelt.

Odd, though . . . Evette could not have begun her work until a few days ago, and yet . . . Heloise approached the final of the twelve tapestries, her sister's handiwork, and saw that it was as near to completion as Ayodele's. It vividly depicted the peasants of Canneberges performing Le Sacre, and Heloise recognized each face. There was her father clashing canes with Alphonsine Millerman's oldest brother. On the outskirts of the dance stood the lads with their torches, among them Claude and Clement. She even saw Meme with baby Clive in his sling and Clotaire and Clovis sitting at her feet.

The tapestry fluttered again in that strange wind which Heloise could not feel. As it moved, she saw how the images and the landscape shifted and whirled—she saw how they took on a new shape and became, however briefly, a perfect image of Princess Imoo-Alala herself, caught forever in mortal memory by this mortal magic worked by Evette with such skill.

Evette, who now had her dream come true.

Heloise scowled at this thought, her fist clenching the three-part branch tighter than ever. This was so wrong, so evil! Such a cruel way to twist the simple desires of a kind girl's heart, to . . . to . . . to *punish* her for wanting to be something more than she was! This, of all the cruelties wrought by the Family of Night was, Heloise decided, the absolute cruelest. And to Evette, of all people!

For a moment she was so lost in her anger that her Faerie sight clouded over with a red haze. But then she felt Princess Imoo-Alala's hand on her shoulder, and the princess whispered softly inside her head, "Look again. Look at what your sister has done."

Drawing strength from that ancient, ageless voice, Heloise breathed deeply, shook her head, and did as she was told. She looked at the tapestry, which hung motionless again.

She saw little red cranberry blossoms.

They were rendered so small compared with the hugeness of the tapestry, it was easy at first to miss them. But there they were, picked out in bright scarlet thread, bright as the finest thread brought up from the south-end dye house, brighter even.

Heloise stepped closer. The tapestry hung in another realm or world, but unlike her phantom sister, it displayed every color in brilliant hues. The cranberry blossoms edged the border even as they edged the border of Heloise's own shift and the linen cap her sister had given her on her birthday. Following that trailing edgework, Heloise's gaze traced the top of the tapestry, down the long side.

Then the cranberry blossoms led her gaze into the heart of the tapestry, like a path drawing her eye. They trailed delicately through the many dancing feet, and Heloise could almost hear the Le Sacre song playing as she followed those blossoms, followed Evette's sure hand. The rest of this work may be wrought of magic . . . but the only magic in those blossoms was Evette's humble sweetness, her eye for simple beauty.

The blossoms led to the centermost ring where Evette danced. Except it wasn't Evette who Heloise saw depicted there in silken detail.

Heloise gasped and took a step back, then another, then a third. She stepped back far enough that she could take in the whole of the image, the many dancers, the stones of Centrecœur, the green grass of the lawn.

But in the center she saw herself; her own wild head of hair, each curl rendered in perfect clarity with threads of gold and brown and copper. She saw herself dancing Le Sacre, her hands upraised, her feet stamping the ground until they bled drops of blood as bright as the cranberry blossoms. On her face she saw . . . she saw . . .

"How many died, did you say?" she asked. "Trying to save their sisters?"

"Three," Alala answered. "And the other three wished they had."

Grandmem's voice in her memory spoke with shuddering truth: *"Better to die than to fail."*

Heloise whispered in echo, "Better to die . . ."

416

Her image in the tapestry gazed out at her from the swirling dance. She saw that her face was twisted with pain.

The candle stub in his pocket was cold and dead as a stone, and Benedict hadn't thought to bring a flint with him. So when Heloise carried her three-part branch with her into the Tower chamber and the door shut behind her, he was left at the top of the narrow stairwell in absolute, pitch blackness.

He wasn't scared of the dark. He wasn't scared of many things. But the Tower was very old, and he suspected that many men had died on this narrow spiral staircase in battles of ages past. When the wind moved outside, one had the strong sensation that the whole structure was going to crumble to the ground, dragging with it the sighing souls of ghosts long dead.

"Iubdan's beard," he growled. He couldn't say how long it had been since Heloise vanished into the room. He'd fumbled his way up to the door and tried the latch, but it was locked again. Several heartbeats passed, and they seemed to count by hours.

"Heloise?" he called softly, wondering if she could hear him through the heavy wood. Probably not, but he daren't raise his voice. He didn't want it to echo down the stairwell and capture someone's attention. He tapped gently on the wood with his knuckles. "Are you in there?"

The door swung open, and Benedict was blinded by the brilliant light shining out. He vaguely discerned a scrawny form crowned in wild hair. "Heloise?" he hazarded.

"Dragons!" she snapped, and it was definitely her voice. But the next moment, she slammed the door, and he was plunged again into darkness.

Well. She was alive. That had to be good, right? And there was definitely something in that chamber, something beyond stone walls and cold floors. So maybe that was good as well?

Benedict sat down on the top step. It was very cold, which, despite Doctor Dupont's advice to the contrary, he didn't think was good for him. He was so tired, though he knew there was no chance he would sleep that night even if he left Heloise where she was and made his way back to his bed. No, he would have to wait for her. He had to make certain she was . . .

Perhaps he dozed off; not in sleep exactly, but in a sort of numb daze. In that daze the cold felt strangely pleasant, a sweet cooling on his skin which still bore the memory of that red-lattice rash and that inside-out burn. It was so dark up here, one had to wonder if this was what it would be like to die. Henri, Giles, Luc, and Victor—is this what they felt, deep down under the earth, wrapped in their shrouds?

The door opened again. It swung so quietly on its hinges that Benedict didn't notice and remained where he sat, gazing into the darkness.

Then Heloise growled behind him, "You're blocking my way."

Benedict spun around on the stair, gasping, "Oh, forgive me!" on reflex. He nearly slipped down several steps in his haste to rouse himself, to rise. Somehow he got himself upright and made room for her, though there was little enough room to be made. Briefly he glimpsed the chamber behind her—and there was no light, no warm glow such as he believed he'd seen when she first entered. There was only a pale square of moonlight falling through the window upon a cold, bare floor.

Heloise, her face illuminated by the silver-gold-and-diamond branch, scowled at him. Or rather, not *at* him, he decided the next moment as she slipped past, drawing the door shut behind her. This was an expansive sort of scowl aimed at the general world, at whatever chanced to fall under her eye.

Heloise stomped down the stair, and Benedict, compressing himself into the smallest shapes he could manage, squeezed after her. "What did you see?" he asked, eager to hear her answer but just as eager not to be overheard by anyone else. When she refused to reply, he reached out and caught her by the shoulder. She stopped moving, frozen in his grasp. At first he thought she was angry, never a bad supposition where Heloise was concerned.

But then he thought, *She's frightened. She's more frightened than I have ever seen her.* And he had seen her dissolve into a quivering lump of tears, sobbing even as he held her. But that had been . . . nerves, maybe. Or another manifestation of her ever-present anger. A touch of fear, to be sure, but nothing like this. Nothing like this dread so palpable that at the merest touch he felt a jolt of terror shoot up through his bones and tingle in his brain.

"What did you see?" he whispered, putting his head down close to her shoulder and ear so that he need not speak too loudly. "Did you find your sister? Did you—"

"I learned what I must do," Heloise answered. She seemed to shrink under his hand. "I learned how to rescue Evette."

"How?"

She turned her head to the side so that she could look at him. The three-part branch illuminated only half of her face, leaving the other half in deep shadow save for the eyes, both of which shone with brilliant force.

"I must dance Le Sacre," she said. "I must dance it all night through."

THIRTY-ONE

THE SYLPH WOUND ITS WAY WITH DEEP SIGHS AND LOW WHISPERS across the rooftops of Centrecœur, around the chimneys, over the eves. It felt the pulse of Nivien wrath, the potent power of the curse shimmering over all of Canneberges. The memory of Mother's hand grasping its breezy body made it shudder, and it found itself creeping with unprecedented caution up one side of the house and down the other, skimming along the fetid moat and through the clusters of false-unicorn flowers. Its memory was too short for it to recall why it was there exactly—but it recalled Mother well enough.

And it recalled the Dame of the Haven's final injunction: "*Help the mortal girl if you can.*"

"Help her, help her, help her." The sylph repeated the phrase to itself as it blew ripples across the surface of the moat and, rounding a corner of the house, approached the window through which the mortal girl had disappeared. But how could it help her? What help did she need? Perhaps it should catch her up, carry her away to the Haven, and deposit her before the feet of the Dame herself. That would be helpful. The Dame was kind, and she would take good care of the mortal.

With this thought half-formed in what passed for the sylph's mind, it crept up the tree, skipped along the branch, and pushed at the window. It was shut and fastened. With one really good blast the sylph could probably get it open. But some sense almost akin to reason kept it quiet. Rather than blasting, it peered quietly through the glass and into Benedict's room.

There sat the mortal girl and another of her kind (sylphs struggle with the concept of gender, so this one thought of Benedict as "the other her") on the floor before a flickering hearth fire.

"Help her, help her," the sylph whispered again. But it had already forgotten its intention of moments earlier, and no new idea presented itself. What could it do to please the Dame? What could it do that wouldn't also incite the rage of Mother?

So it wafted outside the window in a tangle of uncertainty, while Heloise and Benedict, unaware of their invisible observer, pursued their heated, low-voiced discussion.

"You know it's impossible," Benedict said. He sat cross-legged, wrapped in his cloak, and couldn't help the occasional shiver that started in his gut and unfurled itself through his veins and limbs. He ignored it as well as he could and leaned closer to Heloise, seeking a better view of her face behind her curtain of hair. "No one can dance Le Sacre all night through. You'd faint from exhaustion before you made it halfway."

Heloise shook her head. She held the three-part branch in her lap and turned it gently so that the firelight would flicker first on the silver then on the gold then on the diamond twists and leaves. "I don't think so," she said. "I think, since it's a Faerie dance, I'll be able to keep going."

"Because you're part Faerie yourself?"

Heloise's gaze flicked to his face. "You are too," she said. "We both are, from way back when. We're both from the line of Rufus the Red and the Princess of Night."

Benedict stared at her, his mind spinning with these new thoughts and ideas. Just a week ago if anyone had told him a story so daft, he would have laughed outright. But now . . .

"So we're some sort of cousins?" he said. Though he was surprised to realize it, he found he didn't like the idea. At first he thought this was pure snobbery, the distaste of learning his blood was not so far removed from that of this dirty urchin girl. But on second thought, no. No, that wasn't the reason he disliked the idea. Not even close.

He blushed and scratched his ear. "I suppose six hundred years is a bit of a gap. Not much family connection by this time, right?"

Heloise paid him no heed. She seemed to be studying the branch with an intense fixation, though in reality she didn't even see it. Her

423

mind was too busy forming thoughts, making connections, considering all she had learned both from Princess Alala's story and from conjecture. Since leaving the Tower behind she hadn't heard even the faintest murmur of the princess's voice in her head, and she half-wondered if she was alone now. If, having told her tale, Alala's role was finished, leaving the rest up to Heloise to figure out on her own.

Well, she would figure it out. She'd managed to come this far, hadn't she? Sure, she'd had help along the way, but she'd done it. She was the strong one. Stronger than she thought, even. Strong enough to dance a Faerie dance. She knew the steps well enough. Every girl in Canneberges knew the steps of Le Sacre.

The Sacrificial Dance.

Perhaps that was the secret to breaking this curse: death. A willing death, a sacrifice, so that her sister could be free. A death for a life. Alala could then be liberated from that beautiful pocket world, liberated to die at last and pass beyond the Final Water. A death for a death. There was a strange and awful symmetry about the idea, a sense of rightness that fit with the rest of this weird adventure. Perhaps she was meant to die.

Except . . .

"Three died," she whispered. "Three wished they had died."

If the other cursebreakers had tried to dance Le Sacre as she even now intended to do, their deaths had been insufficient. Three had given their lives, and the curse had lived on. In Mother's eyes, a mortal death could never suffice for the life of her beloved daughter.

What was the answer then? Le Sacre for sure, but not the sacrifice?

She felt Benedict's gaze on the side of her head. She looked up at him, scowling. "What?"

He turned away toward the fire, and his cheeks were brightly flushed. "I was just wondering," he said softly, "if all the . . . the cursebreakers of your family . . . if all of them were like you."

Heloise sat still as a statue, still scowling. But her mind exploded with sudden thoughts, sudden ideas. With the memory of something Alala had said—said almost in passing, but certainly said: "*My youngest daughter, on the morning of her fourteenth birthday, discovered she could understand the languages of trees.*"

Heloise had thought nothing of it at the time beyond the fact that Adanna and she were so much alike, both discovering strange abilities on the same morning of their lives. And yet . . .

"She had a different gift," Heloise whispered.

"Pardon?" Benedict glanced at her again.

"Adanna," Heloise persisted. Suddenly excited, she reached out and grasped Benedict by the arm. "The Princess of Night's youngest daughter. She had a different gift! She didn't have the mirror magic! Oh, why didn't I think of it before?"

Then she was on her feet, pacing the length of Benedict's room to his bed and back again, her bare feet making no sound on the cold floor. As she paced, she muttered, not to Benedict but to herself: "We all have Faerie gifts, but they're not all the same. Grandmem had the mirror

425

magic like me, but she never even made it up to the Tower. She never saw the tapestries, she never learned about the dance. Who knows if any of the others had mirror magic? Who knows if those who did knew about Le Sacre? I might be wrong, but—"

But she couldn't be wrong. This must be the answer!

"I am my reflection. My reflection is me."

Benedict got to his feet, holding his cloak at his throat. He put out a hand as Heloise passed near him and restrained her by the shoulder. He meant to be gentle, but she whirled upon him and wrenched against his grasp with such force that he had to tighten his grip. "I'm so sorry," he said, his voice low and urgent, "but you really *must be quiet.* It's almost dawn, and the housemaids will be up soon. If they hear you, if they find you—"

"Don't you understand?" Her voice nearly strangled her in its effort to keep from shouting. But she couldn't express what she needed to say in a whisper, so it came out in a garbled gasp. "Don't you *see?* I am my reflection! And my reflection doesn't die! I was squashed by trees, I was drowning in a well, and I didn't die! Benedict"—in her excitement she completely forgot to call him 'master,' and her eyes sparkled with a bizarre combination of triumph and terror—"I *can* dance Le Sacre all night through!"

With that she started toward the door. But Benedict's grip on her shoulder restrained her, and she came to a halt. "Let me go," she hissed.

"No," said Benedict. "You can't go out there now. The household will be rising soon, and they'll find you. You've got to hide until nightfall."

For a terrible instant he half expected her to bite him or claw at his eyes, so fierce was the expression that flashed across her face. The instant passed, however, and she sagged in his grasp. "Fine," she said. "I'll wait. It's got to be all night, anyway. No use in starting now. I'll wait until sundown."

So the sylph, watching through the window, saw Heloise accept a pillow from Benedict and crawl under his bed to hide. Benedict himself scraped his fire until it was nothing more than a pile of glowing embers. Then he climbed into his bed and buried himself under the covers.

Silence fell upon the room. At first neither of them slept. But as the moments slipped into hours, both eventually slipped into unconscious exhaustion. The sylph kept watch and whispered to itself again, "Help her. Help her . . ."

HELP HER. HELP HER.

The prayer in my heart rises up, even as it has for many generations now. Help her. Please! Let her succeed. Let this one, this brave young fool, discover the power of the three-fold branch and learn the truth of her sisterhood.

But she'll never succeed on her own. She's strong, but not strong enough. They were all of them strong, and all have failed.

Oh! Help her. Please, help her.

And help me as well.

THIRTY-TWO

HELOISE WOKE UP WITH A START, A SINGLE THOUGHT BLAZING BRIGHT in her head:

They're going to be so mad!

At first she couldn't decide whom she meant exactly. The thought was there, brilliantly present in her mind, but without clarity. She lay quite still, staring at the corner of the soft pillow on which her head rested. A decoration of candlewicking depicting a pattern of running deer adorned its edge, similar to the design on Benedict's counterpane. Heloise stared at those little deer rendered in elegant curls and knobs, wondering yet again what they fled.

Slowly her waking thought crystallized into more solid substance. *They're going to be so mad. Meme and Papa. The boys too.*

Could she blame them? She hadn't been home now for another full night, and what would Meme be thinking or guessing of her behavior? Nothing good, that was certain. If she wasn't careful, Papa would raise a hue and cry across all the south-end, and they'd start dredging the bottoms of the deeper bogs, and her brothers would go plunging into the darker reaches of Oakwood, calling her name . . .

But what could she do? If she went home now there would be only questions and scoldings, and they'd probably set one of her older brothers to watch her like a hawk. She'd never slip back to Centrecœur, never have a chance to try her plan. No, she couldn't go home. She daren't risk it.

They would forgive her, though. When Evette was safely home among them, and they remembered, and they held her in their arms and wept with joy . . . then they would forgive her for everything. Everything.

Even Hélène.

Lifting her face from the pillow and rubbing her eyes hard with one hand, Heloise gauged the light pouring through the window onto the bedroom floor. She guessed the time at mid-afternoon already, well into the day. She whispered, "I have to dance all night." Which meant beginning at sundown.

Suddenly wide awake, she scrambled out from under the bed and, moving stiffly, stood up. Benedict was nothing more than a series of odd lumps under his blankets, but she could hear him snoring. Feeling altogether wicked for taking such liberties with the son of the Marquis of Canneberges, Heloise reached for a lump she thought likely to be his shoulder and gave it a shake. "Wake up, sir."

"Rrrrrmph," said Benedict, and she realized she had grabbed his head.

She let go, backed away, and folded her arms. "Master Benedict," she persisted, determined despite her embarrassment, "I must be off. I have to be ready to dance when the sun sets."

Benedict made a series of noises both pathetic and grouchy before finally emerging from his blankets and blinking blearily at her. "Where— where are you going?" he stammered, forming words with difficulty through a haze of sluggishness.

"Up to the Great Hall," she said.

"What?" He sat upright, still blinking, but more awake than he'd been a moment before. "Why?"

"It only makes sense," Heloise persisted. "I saw Evette and the others—the phantom girls I told you about—climb the waterfall stair the other night. Remember? I tried to follow them, but I couldn't make it up the falls. Grandmem warned me not to try again, but she said, '*Not on the mirror side.*' So I've been thinking, and what I need to do is climb the stairs in *this* world. Before I look in the mirror. That way I will be there waiting when Evette and the others arrive."

Benedict nodded, though Heloise could tell by the half-empty expression on his face that he was still too much asleep to make sense of her words. Eventually, though, they seemed to line up properly in his head. "And you think . . . you think you're to dance Le Sacre there? In the

Great Hall? Or rather, on the mirror side of the Great Hall?"

"I heard them singing," Heloise said. "The other night after I tried to climb the falls and you found me wet at the bottom of the stairs. I heard them singing through the ceiling, and I think they were dancing. Last night . . . remember I told you that I saw Evette and Ayodele and Cateline and all of them pass from the Tower chamber out into the silver forest. It was like they were answering a summons. I heard a note of music play, as though the Family of Night was calling them. I think Mother makes them perform Le Sacre every night."

"You think so," Benedict said, "but you don't know. This is not what the princess told you, is it?"

"No," Heloise admitted. "The law doesn't permit her to tell me much except her own story. It's just what I believe. But I'm right. I know I am. I've got to be."

Despite the confidence of her words, Benedict could see the doubt in her eyes. Doubt combined with that same dreadful fear he had sensed in her on the Tower stair but a few hours ago. She masked it well, but he saw it shimmering behind her scowling determination.

"If we go to the Great Hall now we run the risk of being caught," he said. "The household will be up for hours yet. I don't know how I'll explain you to them should they find us."

"You won't have to," Heloise said. "I'll go alone. If they catch me I'll . . . I'll just . . ." *I'll end up in a gibbet!* "I'll say I got lost. Or something."

"No, that won't do." Benedict sighed and rubbed his forehead, which was wrinkled in concern. "I don't know how they'd react if they caught you sneaking around, but I can guarantee it wouldn't be pleasant. You'd better stick with me."

He blushed then and couldn't meet her gaze, which struck Heloise as odd. But she didn't have time to worry about such things at the moment, so she shrugged and said, "All right. Fine. We'll go up to the Great Hall and hide until sundown. Then I'll dance."

Then she would break the curse. Somehow.

They would hide in the old minstrels' gallery, Benedict decided as they prepared themselves for the next stage of their adventure. The gallery overlooked the Great Hall, but it had been ages since anyone but rats or spiders went up there. They should be safe enough if they were quiet and lay low for a few hours. Heloise, who had no idea what a minstrels' gallery was but who hated to appear ignorant, agreed to this plan without question.

With a candle in his pocket and the lion mirror hidden close to his breast, Benedict led the way from his room into the long gallery, Heloise keeping pace behind him. Though Heloise felt a strong sensation that something was following, watching them through the windows—

something invisible, perhaps—they met none of the household staff on their way.

They came to the big stairway, which Heloise had not yet seen by daylight. What a massive structure it was, with two enormous rails, the newel posts carved as rampant lions, one male, one female. Though she did not look into the mirror, Heloise could almost hear the rush and roar of the waterfall which even now, on the other side of the glass, poured in torrents down stone tiers.

But not on this side. Gripping her grimy skirts in both hands, Heloise followed Benedict as he mounted the stairs, his long legs taking two steps at a time. She tried to mimic his stride but hadn't the length of limb and was obliged instead to take shorter, faster steps in order to keep up.

At the top of the steps, a heavy wooden screen blocked Heloise's view of the Great Hall. She wanted to peer around the screen, but Benedict beckoned her instead to a humbler stair which led up to what she assumed must be the minstrels' gallery. This proved to be a landing which looked out upon the Great Hall from above. In the glory days of Rufus the Red, feasts held in the hall would have been graced with sweet music falling as though from the heavens above as musicians plucked and played upon their instruments.

It was quite a gloomy little alcove now, thick with spider webs and the droppings and gnawings of rats. The floor did not feel entirely stable either, and it creaked ominously as Benedict crossed it to sit along the far wall. Heloise moved to join him but first crept to the rail for a quick glance down at the hall.

"Oh, Lumé!" she whispered. She had thought she'd seen greatness when she walked with Benedict in the long gallery down below, hung with its tapestries and brilliant with its glass-paned windows. She had thought she'd glimpsed grandeur in the massive dining hall with its yawning fireplace and massive table. But none of those sights had prepared her for Rufus's Hall.

It was so red! Redwood rafters supported the vast arched ceiling, and pillars as thick as a grown tree's trunk and painted a brilliant scarlet rose up at the far end to frame the lord's dais. The floor was of treated redwood with patterns of crimson wrought into fantastical depictions of the sun or of a series of red stars.

On the dais stood Rufus's chair. Not a throne, for he was no king; a mighty chair from which he passed judgment on his people or took counsel from his trusted advisors as the threat of Corrilond loomed and he sought to protect king and country from disaster. All happening six hundred years ago . . .

Behind and above this seat, hung upon the wall, was a huge mirror of perfect, clear glass. It too was framed in redwood. It was as tall as Heloise herself, taller even. It reflected the whole of the hall so that the space appeared double in size.

Heloise had lived a small and simple life, her world made up of the immediate needs of *now*. She rarely stopped to consider the past (which was painful in any case) or the future (which was frustrating to contemplate and therefore better ignored).

But standing here in the gallery, gazing at all the redness of the Great Hall below, she was struck suddenly by the enormity of History. History which was her own. History which made up as much of her purpose and existence as her name, as her dreams, as her hopes and fears. She was part of a much greater whole. She was part of Rufus. Of Alala. Of Ayodele and Grandmem and Adanna; of all the warriors who had fought against invading Corrilond and of all the farmers who had plowed the fields of Canneberges for centuries.

"A mortal magic," she whispered.

"Psssst!" Benedict beckoned to her. Heloise, with a last glance over her shoulder at the great shining mirror, hastened to join him in the shadows by the wall. "I'm sorry," he said, making her roll her eyes. "But you need to stay out of sight. I don't think anyone comes into Rufus's Hall often, but you never know, and you're a bit conspicuous standing at the rail."

"Fine!" Heloise said, and drew her knees up to her chest. She lapsed into silence which Benedict did nothing to disturb.

So they sat together, and the hours passed by. Other than the occasional creak of the gallery floor as one or the other of them shifted to a more comfortable position, all was as still as a grave. Through the long windows on one side of the hall (which had within the last century acquired shiny new glass panes), the sun deepened in the sky. Spring lengthened out the days, and Heloise was glad. Even a week earlier, night would have fallen much sooner.

She had never before feared nightfall. Now she sat with her back to the wall, watching the gloom deepen, and she trembled.

"Master Benedict," she said suddenly, her voice creaking with disuse, "I have a question for you."

He sat with one leg out before him, the other bent at the knee, his head leaning back against the wall. His eyes were closed, and he did not open them to look at Heloise when she spoke, saying in answer only "Yes?"

"Are you afraid to die?"

For a time he didn't speak. Both of them felt the looming presence of his impending doom, the shadow of the Winter Fever that was never far from his thoughts. The shroud which covered the whole of his life, the whole of his future, however long or short it may prove to be.

He said at last, "Always."

Even as he spoke, the long, sighing note of summoning moaned from an unseen instrument. Benedict did not hear it, or did not seem to, for he sat in the same position, unmoving, un-startled. Heloise, however, jumped in her skin, for it sounded to her as though the instrument had been played right next to her ear.

She stood up and paced to the gallery rail. She looked out upon Rufus's Hall, at the mirror hung behind his chair. Where before she had seen the hall itself reflected in redoubled splendor, now she saw . . . she saw . . .

"Night," she whispered.

The sun sank to the very rim of the horizon, casting the Great Hall into intense gloom.

"Master Benedict," Heloise said, turning to him and holding out her hand, "I need your mirror now."

Le Sacre was about to begin.

THIRTY-THREE

THE FLOORBOARDS CREAKED LIKE THE BREAKING OF BRANCHES IN A high wind as Heloise crossed the gallery. In the profound silence following that single note of summons, even her own breathing filled her ears like the gusts of a summer storm. So she held her breath and tried to keep her footfalls as light as possible as she made her way down the steps from the minstrels' gallery.

The heavy screen separated her from the Great Hall. Though earlier she had been eager to look out, now she felt as though this was the final shield between her and . . . and who could say what evil forces? Her hands shook, and she pressed Benedict's mirror hard against her heart, afraid she might drop it in her fear. With a quick, sharp inhale of air, she opened the screen door and stepped into the hall.

The sun's dying rays fell through the long windows at a strange angle, and the red floor was alive with burning light. But the light was of a sort that promised to go out at any moment, and the shadows all around seemed like predators ready to leap. Though she could not see them, Heloise knew that on the other side of the mirror glass, many invisible figures stood in those shadows, black figures like shades themselves. A great, dark audience, come to watch the dance.

She couldn't allow herself to look at the big mirror beyond Rufus's chair. So, her head bowed to stare at her own feet, she hastened out to the center of the floor, under the heavy red ceiling beams.

"Heloise!" said a cautious voice, not loud but carrying in the silence of the hall. She turned to look up over her shoulder at the minstrel's gallery rail. There Benedict leaned out to watch her from above. He said no more but raised his hand and clenched it in a fist, a symbol of encouragement.

How strange all this must seem to him, unable to see what she would see, unable to hear what she would hear. He should have called her mad and sent her running with dogs at her heels long ago! Yet there he stood, supportive and helpful.

Heloise felt her heart go out to him in sudden gratitude. She raised her own fist and clenched it in response. Then she turned her back on him and lifted his mirror to her face.

The shadows along the walls were suddenly full of indeterminate shapes—perhaps animal, perhaps human, it was impossible to say which, for either form was equally true, equally vital. Out of the darkness gleamed a host of brilliant, star-like eyes.

And every gaze fixed upon Heloise.

Heloise stood on the far side of the mirror. How easy it had become to step into her reflected self and so to pass into this strange world! Her powers must be growing with practice, and this idea gave her courage. She spun slowly in place, there in the center of that hall, and saw that it wasn't a hall anymore, or not completely. But neither was it a forest. The floor under her feet was black and gleamed with the reflection of lights from above. When she looked up she saw sky, deep blue but with a thin line of red rimming its borders. In the very highest, deepest vaults the stars gleamed, and they seemed to spread out and increase in number even as she watched.

It was too much, too . . . too *big* a sight. It might kill her to try to take it in, to understand it. So she focused her gaze instead on the far end of the hall.

There was the dais framed by tall pillars which, when Heloise blinked, momentarily became oak trees. On that dais, instead of Rufus's chair stood a black throne. It was empty. But even as she watched, Heloise saw a shadow (whose shape she could not determine) slip up the dais steps, a small light held in its hands—not a candle, but a white flame cupped in two dark palms. This the figure dropped into a silver brazier that stood beside the throne. The brazier lit up at once in a brilliant white light, like a cluster of stars held together and made to shine upon command.

The silence was profound. But, though there was no disturbance in the air, nothing to catch her ear, Heloise felt a change take place behind her. A movement perhaps, a small vibration that touched her bones. Turning around, she saw that the screen through which she had passed was now a thick-grown grove of oak trees, and the minstrels' gallery where Benedict had stood moments before was now intertwining branches. But there was a door—a huge, huge door, taller than five men, built of a blackness so deep it may have been the spirit of night made solid. Fantastic shapes decorated its panels, shapes Heloise could not quite discern.

The door opened. The tallest woman in the world—taller by far than Princess Alala—stepped through, her hand resting on the arm of the magnificent Lion-Prince. Though the prince was himself as beautiful as ever, clad in rich garments, his bountiful hair caught back in a long queue of braids, no eye could bear to look upon him when *she* was present.

She was so great, so majestic that she overshadowed the prince with ease. Her face was black as night, but with skin so luminous that the contours of her high cheekbones caught the light and made her shine like a polished stone. Her head was shaved bald, and as she approached, moving with a silken tread, Heloise could see the little cuts and nicks where her shaving knife had sliced her scalp. But this marring only added to her majesty, for she wore her scars like a crown.

Her eyes were closed fast. They looked as though they might never open.

Heloise did not doubt for an instant upon whom she looked: Mother. The Queen of Night.

Together, Mother and Son progressed up the great length of the hall. They were coming right toward her, Heloise realized suddenly. She cast about, wondering if there was anywhere she might hide. But this was foolish—there could be no such place in that hall where shadows and shining eyes lurked. She could not hide, not here.

So, even as Mother and Son approached, Heloise simply ducked a few paces to one side. She thought perhaps she saw a flicker of movement in the Lion-Prince's eye as though he saw her, though he did not deign to acknowledge her presence. She blushed, knowing how small, how dirty, how . . . how *mortal* she must look to him!

Mother allowed Son to guide her up the dais stairs, taking each step slowly and with extreme deliberation so that she never once faltered or stumbled. Before she sat, she put one hand out to the brazier of shining white flames. To Heloise's horror, the flames shot up her arm and swiftly engulfed her. But though she flamed bright, the fire did not hurt or harm her. She wore it about her like a rich gown, and when she sat upon her throne, it too was soon covered in flames.

It was all so strange. So beautiful and so strange. Heloise could have stood there in the center of the black floor and stared for an age of mortal lives upon that sight.

But then the sun set. The music began to play.

It was the song and soul of Le Sacre. Heloise recognized it at once. But the instrument playing those familiar yet bizarre opening notes wasn't the shawm. It was what the shawm makers dreamed their instruments could be, a dream that would never be fully realized no matter how they labored to perfect their skill. The sound this instrument produced was living, moving, like water and earth and sky and flame, all combined into a single voice.

The song was sorrow. The song was life. Heloise closed her eyes and allowed the music to fill her up from the inside out, rushing through her veins, rushing through her spirit. The soaring melody flowed down in a whirlwind then rose again like a fountain of magma erupting from the deeps of the earth.

Other instruments began to join—she heard the wind-like sighing of pipes. She heard the rock-grinding groan of ceterone and bandora. The first instrument, carrying still the dominant melody, rose even higher than before, flinging out notes with wild abandon, rushing toward a brilliant, explosive crescendo.

DOOM!

The drum that beat was no timpani. Its voice was much greater, much deeper. This drum was the drum of the sky itself, and Heloise thought her bones would break at the force of the reverberations striking her from all sides. She fell to her knees, and as she did so, her eyes flew open.

Around her stood the twelve maidens. Twelve sisters through time. Each was dressed in a gown of shimmering starlight. Their faces were pale, empty, and exactly alike. Yet Heloise could tell them apart, for she guessed in an instant which one was Evette standing with her arms upraised directly in front of her. She tried to speak, tried to cry out her sister's name. But her voice was lost in the roar of the drum:

Doom-doom! DOOM!

This time when the drum sounded, Heloise braced herself. She knew how this song went. She knew each beat, she knew each measure. When the echoes of that final *doom* faded, she knew there would be a long silence.

She got to her feet. There in the center of the circle of white phantoms she stood. Outside that circle were other circles made up of fierce black figures bearing sharp weapons, not canes. Her fellow dancers, she knew, prepared to perform Le Sacre.

The twelve sisters reached out to one other, each hand touching the shoulder of the nearest maiden. Their gazes fixed unseeing upon Heloise. The music did not play, but they moved with slow, careful steps in a rhythm heard inside their heads.

The instrument-that-wasn't-a-shawm played again, a new variation on the first tune. Heloise knew it well. She knew what would happen. The maidens moved in time and then out of time, and their circle tightened around her. The choice must be made. And Heloise must be chosen. She closed her eyes again, standing perfectly still even as the phantoms drew near. She felt them close to her and, though they did not speak, she sensed their desperation.

Save us! Save us! Save us, sister!

The circle parted. The maidens dispersed into the surrounding shadows and disappeared.

Heloise stood in the center of ringing shadows—the Chosen One who must sing the opening lines. She knew her role like the beat of her heart. She listened to the melody, listened to the progression of notes.

Lifting her hands above her head and raising her right foot in preparation for the first step, she opened her mouth and sang:

"Cianenso

Nive nur norum.

Nive noar-ciu, lysa-ciu."

In her mortal body she had never been able to make her voice hit those high notes. But here in this world she sang them with ease, each word pouring from her throat as though they had always waited there, ready to be sung.

In her head the words shifted. She heard herself singing:

"Night comes to fall

Upon the forest,

Night so hopeless and so pure."

She went on to the second verse. But she could not hear her own voice now, lost as it was in the enormous, all-consuming darkness of the Night rising up all around her. Together with the Faerie-folk of Nivien she sang:

"Nivee mher

Nivien nur jurar

Nou iran-an."

And she heard:

"Evening comes to promise

All my children

Of a deeper night."

She began to dance. The steps came to her as though from practiced memory. She had watched them performed every year upon the lawn of Centrecœur. So she danced the wild paces, the strange rhythms. The heavenly angels who watched over her birth had not seen fit to gift her with particular grace of form or movement, and yet the magic of Le Sacre dictated that she would not misstep. Or perhaps there was no magic.

Perhaps it was only that her belief in magic was strong enough to generate such confidence inside her.

However it was, she danced against the beat of the drums, following instead the manic beckoning of the shawm-like instrument, her hair and skirts whirling about her like the rush of the pipes, her hands clapping with fervor to the pulse of the ceterone.

The Faerie folk around her sang:

"Shadows of the Night,

Dance with me,

Dance with your arms entwined.

Shadows of the Night,

Sing with me,

Sing with your voices combined."

The Lion-Prince did not join the dance. Sometimes as she twirled, Heloise caught a glimpse of him through the gyrating darkness and movement and music. He stood beside Mother's throne, his bright eyes watching her every move with the intensity of a stalking predator.

Mother sat wrapped in white fire, her eyes closed, refusing to look upon the mortal beast or the phantom maidens before her.

The music's tempo increased—faster, faster, wilder, wilder. The drum beat with a dangerous urgency, and Heloise fled before it, chasing the shawm's melody. Like a deer fleeing through the forest, fleeing from the hunter's spear and bow, so she moved and danced. Her mortal heart raced in her breast, and she knew that were she even now in her own world, in her own body, she must be gasping with exhaustion. On the lawn of Centrecœur, another maiden would prepare to take her place.

But this was not Centrecœur. Here in the center of the whirling People of Night, she was without aid.

You are stronger than you think! she told herself, each word pulsing in time to the ceterone. *I am my reflection. My reflection is me.*

Somewhere, on the far side of the mirror glass, did her mortal body stand in the center of Rufus's Hall, clutching the mirror frame? Did Benedict, in the gallery above, watch her sway and move her head in time to music he could not hear?

Faster! Faster! Wilder! Wilder!

Voices of the Night, sing with me! Promise a deeper Night!

The music staggered and stumbled, falling into a heavier, slower cadence, a rhythm of exhaustion. Heloise felt her heart beating far too quickly, throwing off the movement of the shawm melody and the drums. But she adjusted her pace accordingly. How weighty did each step become, pounding into that black floor as though she would crush it beneath her heel!

Her sisters—sisters of centuries gone by—surrounded her again. She glimpsed their faces half hidden behind their twirling hair. She glimpsed their apprehension. On Evette's face she saw great fear. But this must have been imaginary, for their expressions were still, their eyes blank.

451

Perhaps she felt the truth beneath the outward form. Or perhaps she saw only her own anxiety, her own fear, reflected more clearly than in any mirror glass.

The shawm-like instrument dominated all, soaring above the rest of the music like a wind suddenly rising among the tree tops. The trees surrounding that dark hall rustled and moved suddenly as though under a heavy gale. Leaves fell and darted, whirling among the dancers like dancers themselves. The Faeries of Nivien, formless wraiths, clashed their weapons together, and Heloise thought she saw a flash of crimson blood. Her heart flinched, but she did not falter.

You are stronger than you think! She wondered briefly if Princess Alala spoke in her head. But no. No, she was alone here, alone among these dreadful figures, alone with Le Sacre. There was no one to help her, not now.

But she would succeed. Already she had danced longer than her mortal body would be capable of doing. She did not tire, for her reflection did not need what her body needed. She could succeed. She could keep going all night long. She could dance Le Sacre until the sun rose upon the horizon.

DOOM! roared the drum.

Mother, seated upon her throne, tilted her head to one side.

Then she stood.

A gasp rose amid the dancers. The music froze as though caught suddenly in the grasp of Time and restrained. Only the shimmering strains of the shawm-like instrument could still be heard upon that dark air.

Heloise went on dancing. She could not stop. She must dance Le Sacre all night through! She must, for this alone could break the curse! She knew it. She *knew* it, and she could not be wrong!

Around her the other dancers made no movement. Even those caught in the most dreadful contortions held themselves with such perfect stillness that she might have believed they were turned to stone. But their eyes watched Mother.

The Queen of Night descended the dais stairs, trailing fire behind her like the train of a long robe. Her feet moved to a rhythm all her own, a stately rhythm more graceful than any dancer's tread. She passed through the bizarre figures of her people as though they were insubstantial as ghosts.

Heloise, still dancing, watched her approach. *She cannot kill me,* she told herself even as she raised her arms again and clapped her hands. The silence caught the sound of her clap and smothered it into nothing. *She cannot kill me, for it would break the Law.*

Mother stood before her, her head still tilted, her eyes still closed. She spoke, and white flames shot from her tongue:

"Do you think I would let you cheat Nivien Law?"

Heloise gasped. The black Hall of Night was gone. She stood in Rufus's Hall upon his red floor, surrounded by his red pillars. Night poured through the windows, and moonlight fell upon the towering form of Mother, who was so much bigger here in the mortal world. Fire flamed about her body, no longer white but red.

She opened her eyes.

For a moment Heloise saw her reflection. She saw it twice over, trapped in the depths of two round onyx mirrors, so enormous, so furious. Her reflection stared out at her from behind Mother's gaze.

She saw them move of their own accord. She saw them, both of them, raise their hands and slap against the confines of the black orbs in which they stood. She saw her own mouth forming a scream, and she heard herself scream in response. "*NO!*"

Mother blinked. When her lids rose again, the reflection was gone.

Heloise collapsed in a faint upon the floor of Rufus's Hall.

BEFORE THERE CAN BE A BEGINNING, THERE MUST FIRST BE AN END.

But how can there be an end if one never truly begins?

I fear for her. I have always feared for her, for each of my brave girls. I fear she will realize now the truth of what she must do and, in the realization, turn and run. She will regret forever that choice, though it is the choice of a rational mind.

What would I have her do? March into certain death with certain knowledge that death is insufficient? Others have done so before her, three brave young girls. Dead. Gone.

Beyond the Final Water . . .

THIRTY-FOUR

AT FIRST SHE WAS AWARE ONLY OF AN EXTREME DISCOMFORT stemming from her neck and shooting through her shoulder. She tried to move, to adjust her position in order to relieve this discomfort, and in so doing discovered that she was paralyzed. A moment later she knew it was merely the heaviness of a deep sleep, so deep that her body was slow to catch up with her awakening consciousness.

Then she felt the cold, hard floor underneath her, not the prickly straw or woolen blanket of her loft bed. So she wasn't home. But where in Lumé's name was she?

"Heloise?" whispered a voice she did not at first recognize. "Are you alive?"

She groaned. Then her eyes flew wide and slowly focused on Benedict's face above her, pale in the moonlight. Over his head arched the great red rafters of Rufus's Hall and the railing of the minstrels' gallery. He held her with one arm under her shoulders so that her head and neck lolled at an uncomfortable angle, and with his other hand he pulled hair from her face and mouth.

Heloise groaned again and, summoning what control she could over her half-conscious body, put up a hand to push Benedict away.

"Iubdan's beard!" His voice was hushed but tense. "Oh, great Iubdan's beard! You're alive. I saw that . . . that person! That fire-woman! She appeared right here, right in this hall, and I saw her. She didn't touch you, but you fell, and I thought she'd killed you! I can't believe it. I mean, I didn't doubt you before, not really, but . . . Iubdan's beard and mustache! That was beyond anything I've ever—"

"Dragons eat you," Heloise muttered and turned sharply where she lay so that he lost his tentative hold on her and she fell hard upon her shoulder, her face pressed into the floor.

"Sorry!" Benedict said, but when he reached out to her again, she shrugged and shook her head violently, so he backed away. She lay where she'd fallen, breathing hard, giving her memory a chance to catch up with the rest of her mind, even as her body rediscovered use of its limbs.

Somewhere beyond this world, music played. Here she lay on the floor, not dancing, while Le Sacre sang on through the night. She closed her eyes and clenched her teeth, forcing back the scream that wanted to burst in furious frustration from her throat.

Heloise hauled herself upright, shook the hair from her face, and addressed herself to Benedict. "Where's the mirror?" she asked.

For a moment he looked as though he wouldn't answer her, and that moment was in itself the most dreadful of all. Then, drawing a deep breath, he turned and picked up the ebony-framed glass from the floor behind him. Without a word he handed it to her.

Heloise lifted the mirror in both hands. She stared at the dark and shattered glass. It could hardly even be called glass anymore, so ruined was its surface. She tilted it so that the moonlight coming through the window might fall upon it. Even then it did not shine. It was as black and blank as a broken stone.

"No," Heloise hissed through her teeth. "No, no, no, no! This isn't right!" Still clutching the mirror in both hands, she scrambled to her feet. Ignoring Benedict's whispered protests, she ran across the Great Hall, sprang up the dais stairs, and darted around Rufus's great council chair. The pale light through the windows only just reached the huge mirror glass hung on the wall at the back of the dais, barely enough to reveal any reflection.

But Heloise took hold of the big, heavy frame, stood on the tips of her toes, and stared into the lower half of the glass. She saw the shadow of the back of Rufus's chair. She saw taller shadows that were the framing pillars of the dais. She saw the high, looming shadows of the rafters in the ceiling, and she even saw the smudge of shadow that indicated the reflected minstrels' gallery.

But where she stood there was no shadow, no indistinct form. Though this glass was as unbroken and smooth as it had ever been, it held no trace of Heloise's reflection.

Benedict approached from behind her. She saw his reflection, indistinct but certainly his. "What's wrong?" he asked.

Heloise stood still, holding his broken mirror in one hand, her other hand grasping the big mirror's frame. She couldn't look around. She couldn't bear to face him. But she whispered, "They took it from me. She took it."

"Took what?" Benedict asked, his voice very low as though he feared to be overheard. "Heloise, what did they take from you?" He put out a hand to touch her shoulder.

Heloise, seeing the movement in the mirror, darted out of his reach, moving around so as to keep Rufus's chair between them. Her eyes were bright and fey in the darkness, and for an instant they shone with an otherworldly blue gleam.

Then she dropped his mirror—his broken, dark, useless mirror— into the seat of Rufus's chair. She descended the dais steps in a single jump, landing hard on the floor below and falling in a half-crouch. But she was up again in a moment and dashing across the hall. She heard Benedict's half-whispered protests behind her and paid no heed. The moonlight seemed to chase her, and she fled it for the darkness behind the heavy wooden screen.

She left the Great Hall behind, left Benedict where he stood. She raced down the great staircase, almost certain that her feet splashed in the water of the falls though she felt no wetness. Surefooted despite the darkness, she continued at full speed down the long gallery, little caring if she met anyone, if startled eyes saw her. Her face was set, her eyes intent, and she turned neither to the right nor the left.

She came to the Tower and ran up the stairs, taking two or three at a time. Gasping for breath by the time she reached the top, she nevertheless fell upon the door, pounding it with her fists. "Alala!" she cried. "Princess Alala! Let me in! Let me *in!*"

Nothing. Not a sound, not a glimmer of an impression that anyone heard her.

"Dragons, dragons, dragons!" Heloise cursed, plunging her hand into her pocket. She drew out the three-part branch, which did not gleam or shine but looked dull in her hand. One would never know it was anything more than a random twig plucked from the forest floor. With another biting, "Dragons!" she shoved the branch into the lock and twisted. For a moment she feared the branch would simply break. Then she felt the bolt give way.

The door did not open silently as it had before. Heloise had to put her shoulder to it and shove with all her might, and even then it groaned and screeched and protested noisily, as though it had not been opened in a century or more. Her feet scraped on the stone stairs, and when at last the door swung wide, she fell into the room. Into the silent stone chamber, with its close walls and its single window. Onto the bare, hard floor, a wooden floor, dangerously rotted in places.

Heloise braced herself with her hands out before her on the floor, like an angry cat prepared to fight. Her eyes darted to every shadow, but there was nothing to be seen—no life in the shadows, no faint hints of trees or blossoms. No tapestries. No mortal maidens. No Faerie princess.

"Heloise?" Benedict's voice called cautiously up the stair. No doubt he was trying even now to squeeze his way up after her.

Heloise rose and, placing each step cautiously—half afraid that she would plunge through the floor and down any number of stories to some un-guessable landing below—she crossed the room to the window. It had no glass, only an empty space gazing out over the night-filled landscape. Heloise saw Canneberges before her even as she had glimpsed it when she'd stood at this same window the previous night. But then she had looked through Faerie eyes, and she had seen the land in brilliant detail. Now she had only her own mortal eyes with which to see, and she could discern only moon-tipped lumps and formless plateaus.

Along the horizon she saw the dark outline of the Oakwood.

"Alala?" she whispered. "Are you here?"

She felt nothing. No voice in her head. No whisper, no faint impression of a presence. It would be all too easy to think she'd imagined the pocket world she had walked in the night before.

Yet somehow she knew, without knowing how she knew, that Alala stood beside her.

"She took my mirror magic," Heloise said. "I can't enter the world beyond the mirror. Not anymore. Mother took my magic."

462

Silence filled the room. Absolute silence made all the more absolute for the struggling grunts and grumbles of Benedict as he sought to climb the narrow stair. Heloise strained her ears, strained her heart, strained the unconscious senses of her soul and will for any sign, any word. Anything!

But she was alone. No voice to guide her. No help, no hints.

She turned slowly from the window and stared into the dark chamber, gazing upon the spot where Evette had sat and worked upon her tapestry, creating the magic of memory, her efforts serving to capture Alala forever in Mother's ensorcellment. So they would continue till the end of days, spinning mortal magic in a Faerie realm, each stitch securing more power for Mother, each tug of the needle affixing the binding . . .

"No," Heloise growled. "I'm not through just yet."

Benedict appeared in the doorway. He saw the outline of Heloise's wild hair against the window, but he could not see her face. "What is this?" he demanded. "Have they gone? Did you break the curse?"

Heloise did not answer. Heedless of the creaking, rotted boards beneath her feet, she stomped across the chamber and shouldered her way past Benedict, moving swiftly down the stairs. "Where are you going?" he whispered as loudly as he dared.

"To the Oakwood," she called back over her shoulder.

"Why? What for? Are you coming back?" He tried to pursue her but couldn't keep up. He thought she had outdistanced him and vanished, but then he felt a cold hand touch his in the darkness.

"I don't know if I'll be back." Heloise's voice rose up from a few steps below. "I don't know anything. But I'll try. Wait for me and keep your window open."

She was gone. Benedict stood alone in total darkness, his head and shoulders bent to fit in a too-small space. The memory of that burning woman engulfed in red flame seared his mind with a branding scar that would never fully heal.

Grandmem sat in her doorway while the dawn rose up around her. She held her customary carrot in one hand but did not chew it. Her hands hung limply in her lap. She merely watched the horizon, her faded eyes seeing little, her heart feeling much.

She muttered, "Oh, Cateline! She failed. I know she did. She failed her sister even as I failed you."

She bowed her head. Though her ears discerned the faintest breeze of a laugh, she paid it no heed. Only when a distant voice sang like a chant, "*Help her, help her, help her,*" did Grandmem murmur as though in response:

"Help her. Lights Above us, help her!"

When at last she found the strength to raise her head again, she saw a distant figure running with awkward, loping strides. A gawky young person who did not use the dirt paths and roads but cut directly across the newly tilled fields, sprang over lumps of earth and ditches, and splashed through the shallow edges of the cranberry bogs.

Heloise darted past and never once turned her head to see or acknowledge her grandmother. She ran without pause all the way up the road leading into the Oakwood. Grandmem, watching her progress until she vanished from sight, heard again the sighing whisper on the wind, "*Help her . . . help her . . .*"

Just as the sun cast its light in full morning splendor upon the fields and forests of Canneberges, Heloise plunged into the ever-present darkness of the Oakwood.

She had run much of the way from Centrecœur. The distance between the forest and the Great House was too great for her to run the entire way, but when she could run no more, she'd walked or trotted and so made good time. Here at the end of her journey she ran again, as fast as she could go, along the familiar paths she had trod many times before.

But when she came to the place where only a week before she had first heard the shadowy Faerie language sung—when she came to the dark fir tree where the Lion-Prince had hidden from her sight and watched her as she worked—there she leapt over the ditch and left the path behind, plunging into the deeper forest.

She could not run now. The growth of trees and underbrush was too great, even at this time of the year before spring's green growth had thickened. Broken branches and nettles clawed at her bare feet, tore the skin of her legs. These she ignored save for the occasional grunt of pain.

Patches of sunlight fell through the new green foliage, casting dappled patterns upon the forest floor. Heloise avoided the light and made always for the darker shadows.

She began to shout: "Imoo! Prince Imoo!"

What was it Alala had told her? "*I passed into those trees, shouting for Mother, for Uncle, for Brother, shouting their Faerie names, which I will not tell you, for they are sacred among my people.*"

Sacred, secret names with which they did not wish to part.

Heloise paused to cup her hands around her mouth. "*Imoo!*" she bellowed at the top of her lungs. She did not know if it was the Lion-Prince's name or even part of his name. It was only a guess, a hopeless, foolish guess. But if Alala was Princess Imoo-Alala then perhaps it would be close enough. "Prince Imoo, Son of Night!"

"Cease your braying, mortal beast. I am here."

A shudder of change passed over Heloise. She felt a shift, an alteration in the trees. Nothing overt—nothing she would have been able to describe clearly in words. But she knew in an instant that she no longer stood in the Oakwood. No, this was a different Wood entirely. A solemn, timeless, forever realm, the Between of all worlds, Faerie and mortal alike.

The Lion-Prince stood behind her. She couldn't hear him, not even the depths of his breathing, for after his initial speech he had gone completely silent. But he could not disguise the intensity of his presence, and she knew that his magnificent lion's muzzle even now rested in the air but an inch or two behind her ear.

"You must answer me three questions each day," Heloise said, and she was careful to allow no sense of inquiry in her voice, to make her statement as firm as possible. "I've thought back upon our meetings, and you answered me three questions each time before you left. You didn't want to, but you did. Which means it's part of your law. You *have* to answer me."

The Lion-Prince said nothing. For all she knew, Heloise stood in the middle of that forest, surrounded by trees, speaking only to herself.

She swallowed a lump of fear and continued, "Your Mother broke the law."

The silence was neither acknowledgement nor acquiescence. It was silence, pure and simple.

"She broke the law," Heloise persisted. Then because she couldn't help herself, she added, "Didn't she?"

"No," said the voice of the Lion-Prince, a low growl in her ear.

Heloise felt her bones quiver as though they'd been turned to water. With an effort she remained upright and forced her shrinking voice to speak. "She did! She stole my magic! I know the law, or enough of it, anyway. The . . . the . . . the Dame of the Haven sent me a message. She said that you could not kill me or prevent me from trying to break the curse! I was dancing Le Sacre, and I was going to make it through the night. I know I was. I was well into the dance, and I wasn't going to die. I'm stronger than I think! Your Mother broke the law when she stopped me and stole my magic."

The Lion-Prince said nothing. But his previous answer remained echoing in Heloise's ear: *No.*

She had to use a question. She had to know. "How can she steal my magic from me and *not* break your law?"

"You cheated," said the Lion-Prince. "And now you have but one question remaining."

A series of gasps and protests leapt to Heloise's lips. But many of them could have sounded like a question, and she couldn't afford to lose her last one so foolishly. So she held them inside, struggling with equal surges of rage and despair pulsing from her heart and rushing through her veins. In a voice as low and steady as she could manage to make it, she said, "I am my reflection. My reflection is me."

Silence. But she felt the heat of the Lion-Prince's breath on the back of her neck, stirring in her hair.

"It's true. I did not cheat. I used the mirror magic, but it was *me. I* entered your world to dance Le Sacre." She hated to say it, hated to use her final question on something she felt she should be able to discern for herself. But though she stood with her fists clenched, her mind racing through every possibility, she could reach no conclusion. So she whispered,

"How was I cheating?"

"You are your reflection," said the Lion-Prince. His voice seemed to fill with a slow, dangerous smile. Heloise felt it even though she could not see it. "Your reflection is you. But your reflection is not the *whole* of you. It is but a part, a very small piece. You risk nothing when you move inside it. Without risk, you can never, *never* break the curse Mother has placed upon your family. You will never kill our Alala."

His words sank into her head and simmered there. But with each passing breath, the heat of them rose until it brewed to a boiling point. Sweat dripped down Heloise's face, though the air was still and mild. Her breath came in little panting gasps.

"They died," she said before she could stop herself. "Three of them. Three of the other cursebreakers who tried to dance—they died. They came to your hall, and they danced, and they gave their lives. They risked everything *and they died!* How is that not enough? Why did their deaths not count?"

She spun around then, but the Lion-Prince was not there. She knew he was still near, however. His enormous presence had not gone, though she could not see him. She wrung her hands and shouted into the great Between, "How many deaths does she need? How many mortal lives will satisfy her? Am I to be but one of dozens? Is that the answer? I must die along with the others, along with who knows how many more? Tell me. Tell me!"

"You have already asked your three questions," said the Lion-Prince.

He appeared suddenly before her as though he had stepped out of thin air. But he wasn't a lion; he was a man, tall, beautiful, wild, and deadly. He gazed down upon her with an expression she could not read. Terror roared in her head until she could not think, could scarcely breathe.

But the quiet part of her brain, the still place behind her fear, nudged her consciousness. *He could have gone. He doesn't need to be here. He has fulfilled the law, yet here he stands.*

Heloise stared up at the Lion-Prince, meeting his eyes. Though but a moment before she would have shrunk into nothing under his gaze, she met it now, strength for strength, knowledge for knowledge. For she now knew something he did not want her to know. Or perhaps . . . perhaps he did want her to know and was only afraid to tell her himself.

"You want to set Alala free," Heloise said. She knew it for truth as the words left her lips. "You want me to break this curse. You want to liberate your sister from Mother's prison so that she can die."

A muscle tensed along his cheek, and for a heartbeat the prince looked more like a lion than a man. "Immortals cannot die," he said. "It is too dreadful an end. Sister must live on. Forever!"

"But she's not immortal anymore," Heloise said. "She's mortal, and mortals are meant to . . . to . . ."

She stood alone in the Oakwood. The vastness of the Between was gone, and the confines of her own world surrounded her. The Lion-Prince had vanished as though he had never been, and her words fell unheard into the gentle spring air: "Mortals are meant to die."

THIRTY-FIVE

BENEDICT SAT IN A CHAIR DRAWN UP CLOSE TO HIS COLD HEARTH, staring into the grey embers. Occasionally he used a metal-tipped poker to stir up the ashes, but it was no use; the fire was long dead, never to be revived. His room was as cold as a tomb.

In his mind's eye, however, bright flames swirled—red flames surrounding a tall, slender body of polished black. And Heloise before that figure, so small, so helpless . . .

His hand tightened around the poker. He wanted to get up, to pull on his boots, to steal his horse and ride out even as he had done a few days ago. She'd gone out to the Oakwood. But why? Benedict recalled the wind spirit they had met together out there, and wondered what other strange beings might dwell therein. It couldn't be safe. She couldn't be safe.

But she'd told him to wait. To keep his window open. She was counting on him to be there when and if she returned.

A chill wind blew through the open window behind him, breathing down his neck and shoulders. He drew his cloak tighter but could not prevent the shiver that ran through his limbs. For an instant he feared it was the shivering that never stopped, the shivering that belied the raging fever burning from the inside out.

A knock at the door startled him from these gloomy fears, and he nearly dropped the poker as he sat upright. "Who's there?" he called.

"It is I, Master Benedict."

The voice was like the intonation of a sepulchral spirit. Well, probably not *quite* that bad. But close enough that Benedict shivered again, this time for a rather different reason. With a forlorn sigh, he said, "Enter," and sagged back in his chair. He didn't bother to look around as the door opened and Doctor Dupont's footsteps crossed the floor. It was amazing how ponderous a tread such a thin man could produce!

The doctor scanned the room from beneath heavy lids and raised a single brow at the sight of his charge sitting up in his chair. The bed lay rumpled, half-heartedly made, and did not look as though someone had recently slept in it. "You are awake, Master Benedict?"

"As you see," Benedict muttered, still without turning around. He nearly apologized for his rudeness the next moment, but after what he'd been through recently his apologetic spirit wasn't as keen as usual. His mouth remained shut. By the sound of the heavy footsteps he guessed when the doctor approached the bedside table, then heard the slide of the drawer opening, the clink of the vial and cup being removed. A *glugging* sound told him that Dupont poured more of his brew than usual. Benedict closed his eyes and muttered, "Dragons eat it," between his teeth.

The doctor approached him from behind. A pale hand holding the cup appeared before Benedict's face. "Your draught, Master Benedict."

Benedict looked at it. He sighed. Then, accepting his fate along with the cup, he tossed the medicine to the back of his throat and downed it all in a gulp. The next several moments were spent doubled up and gagging, stuffing the corner of his cloak against his mouth to keep everything where it was meant to be. A few brown droplets spattered among the dead hearth ashes, but with a brave effort Benedict managed to get most of it down.

Doctor Dupont observed all in solemn silence. When Benedict's convulsions subsided, he took the cup and returned it to its drawer. Benedict hoped he would leave then, but no such luck. Instead, the doctor returned to his side and, without a word or warning, grabbed him by the head, tilting it sharply so as to peer into his ear. Benedict had suffered this indignity many times before and only uttered a small groan of protest.

"Hmmmmmmm," said the doctor, and turned Benedict's head the other way to peer into his other ear. "Mmmmmm, hmmmm."

He possibly imagined it, but Benedict could have sworn he smelled

Lord Cœur's fine vintage on the doctor's breath. He grimaced and asked, "No fever spirit?"

Rather than answer, the doctor said, "Where were you last night, young sir?"

It took tremendous willpower not to pull himself from Dupont's grasp and spring to his feet. Instead he sat very still, his fingers tightening on the arms of his chair as though to hold himself in place. "I was—I was in bed," he said. But he wasn't a good liar and he knew it.

Doctor Dupont let go of Benedict's head and moved slowly to stand in front of him. He pressed his palms together before his breast as though in an attitude of prayer. Behind his heavy eyelids, his eyes were bright. A little too bright.

"One of the guardsmen came to me this morning," he said. "Young Briant, a dull-witted but quick-eared sort of lad. He knocked on my door, interrupted me in the middle of my work." The doctor's voice dropped an octave lower, though this shouldn't have been humanly possible. "I do not like to be interrupted in my work."

Benedict knew how the heroes of old must have felt when the Dragon stirred in his slumber. He bravely stood his ground—or sat his ground, as the case may be—and said nothing.

The doctor continued, "Guardsman Briant claims that he heard you last night."

The blood rushed from his head, leaving Benedict pale and dizzy. Yet he held the doctor's gaze and managed a quiet, "Oh?"

"In the Great Hall. With a girl."

"Oh," said Benedict again. His brain, sluggish from lack of sleep, sifted through several possible answers as quickly as possible. None of them seemed worth speaking, even in the privacy of his head. But he had to answer promptly or he would appear all the more guilty. "Doesn't sound much like me, does it?"

The doctor's brows lowered, dragging the whole of his tight cap forward. He said nothing beyond a deep "Mmmmmmmm."

"Truly," Benedict persisted, hating how weak his voice sounded to his own ears, "I've been in bed. Don't have much energy for traipsing about in the night. And I don't know any girls."

Victor would have been much better at this. Victor had spun stories for the Black-Tops that convinced everyone of his veracity, himself included, until the lies he told might as well have been truths. Victor would have laughed at Benedict and his paltry attempts at deceit, would have laughed at the way his paling then blushing complexion gave away every emotion.

Doctor Dupont did not laugh. He merely observed. But the way he observed made Benedict want to crawl under his bed where Heloise had spent the whole of yesterday. Once he got there, he might never come out again.

"I feel it is my duty to warn you, young master," said the doctor at last, "that such carryings-on cannot be conducive to your future or health. Any association with a young woman is sure to awaken the fire spirit sooner rather than later. When it wakes again, it will kill you. Yes. It will kill you as it kills all whom it indwells. I will have to be swift to extract it if there is to be any hope of saving you."

The doctor took a step toward him and leaned down so that his thin face was level with Benedict's. The smell of wine on his breath was beyond doubt. Benedict thought, *This man is mad. I don't care what his credentials are. I don't care if Father trusts him. He's out of his dragon-eaten mind!*

But he dared not say anything. He sat motionless and met the doctor's gaze, eye for unblinking eye. Carefully he said, "I will keep that in mind, good doctor. Thank you."

"Mmmmmmm." The doctor straightened, and his eyes narrowed to shiny slits. Without another word he turned and wafted from the room, his somber robes rustling in his wake. The door shut with a decisive *clunk* behind him.

Benedict sprang from his chair and, despite his fatigue and grogginess, rushed to the door and locked it fast. He then stood staring at the lock and muttered, "I'll write to Father. As soon as . . . as all this . . . is over, I'll write to Father and ask him to remove Doctor Dupont." He didn't know if he'd mention the theft—Lord Cœur had a strict and rather awful approach when dealing with thieves. But somehow he must make his father understand that the doctor's treatments were *not* working out for the best, would ask him to send someone else . . .

Only, what would he do if Doctor Dupont followed up his letter with a letter of his own that explained in fine-sounding medical terms how Benedict's complaints were but the product of his sickness-weakened mind?

"Master Benedict."

"Beards!" Benedict exclaimed, whirling about, his eyes wide and startled. There sat Heloise in the open window, her hands clutching the frame, one leg sliding through. How long had she sat there? Had she heard the whole exchange with Doctor Dupont?

"Get in, quick!" Benedict strode across the room to offer his assistance, but she scrambled through before he reached her. She stepped out of his path as he hastened to lean out the window and look this way and that and even up along the wall of the house. As far as he could see, no one was about. But this didn't mean she hadn't been spotted. If one of the guardsmen believed he was keeping company with a peasant girl, gossip would surely have spread throughout Centrecœur by now. Thank the Lights Above, the house servants gave him wide berth, afraid as they were of catching his illness.

He pulled his head back in and shut the window. "We can't keep doing this," he said, turning to Heloise, who stood now in the center of his room, her arms wrapped tightly about her skinny body. "You can't keep sneaking in this way. Someone's going to catch us, and I don't—"

He broke off abruptly. His gut, full of Doctor Dupont's brew, churned violently, and his whole body shook with the foulness welling up inside him. With a groan he sat down on the floor, his head between his knees, and waited for the dizziness to pass.

Maybe the doctor was right. Maybe the spirit was waking up. Maybe associating with Heloise, taking part in her mad plots and schemes, had shaken something loose inside him, and the fever would return. He squeezed his eyes shut, wishing to all the heavenly hosts that he'd never met—

But no. He couldn't wish that. Not even when he tried.

A cold hand touched his forehead. He didn't look up when Heloise sat down beside him but remained in the same attitude, his head bowed.

"You're warm," she said.

"No, you're cold," he replied, and she couldn't deny it; her fingers were icy. Benedict shrugged and glanced up at her with one eye. "I'll be fine. Where were you this morning?"

"Down at the Oakwood. Did the doctor make you drink more nightshade?"

"Tannins of nightshade," Benedict said. "And a lot of other things. Shriven and whatnot."

"You should stop taking it. It's going to kill you."

"Well, the idea is that it'll kill the fire spirit inside me before it kills me." Benedict stretched his legs out before him and leaned back against the wall beneath the window. "Someone heard us in the Great Hall," he said, his voice low as though he did not want even Heloise to hear him. But her quick ears caught every word, and he felt her tense beside him. "One of the guardsmen, Briant. He told Doctor Dupont."

"Pigman!" Heloise growled the name like a curse. "Briant Pigman, the stupid oaf. Once a Pigman, always a Pigman; doesn't matter if they dress him up in armor and give him a pike!"

Startled at this passionate outburst which he did not understand, Benedict raised both eyebrows. "Well, the point is," he went on, "they'll be watching us now. Watching me. We can't keep on as we've been."

Heloise studied him closely. He felt her gaze on the side of his face, and he couldn't make himself meet it. "What are you saying?" she demanded.

Benedict rubbed at one ear as though he could even now reach inside and pull out whatever evil spirit lurked within. "I'm saying," he whispered, "that you need to go away and not come back."

For a long moment neither spoke, neither moved. Then Benedict sat up straighter and turned to Heloise with a hasty, "Forgive me, I didn't mean for it to sound like that!"

She was pale. Very still and very pale. Her expression was . . . nothing. Completely blank. Her gaze didn't move from his face.

Benedict hurried on, stumbling over his words as he tried to get them out. "I don't mean you should *never* come back. I just mean, not for a few days. A few weeks even. Give some time for the attention we've attracted to die away. I'm not saying you should give up trying to save your sister, I swear it!"

Slowly Heloise drew herself together and stood. Though she was as barefoot and ragged as ever, a scrawny peasant girl with dark shadows under her eyes from both fear and lack of sleep, she loomed above him with all the imposing force of a short, dirty-faced warrior. Benedict had no trouble whatsoever seeing great Rufus's red-blooded spirit flash in her eyes.

"I don't care what you swear," she said. "I don't care what you believe or don't believe. I'm not going away. I'm not leaving my sister."

"Please, Heloise, be reasonable," said Benedict, gathering himself and standing with some difficulty. But even when he looked down upon her from his superior height, he felt at a disadvantage. The force of her stare alone could skin him alive. "It's just for a few days. I promise. But if we try to—"

"We're not trying anymore!" Heloise cried. Her hands rose in fists, and for an instant he thought she would strike him. Instead she caught at her own hair and tugged as though she would pull it all out. "I'm not *trying* again. I'm *doing.* I'm going to dance Le Sacre tonight. I'm going to do it *myself.* No mirrors. No magic. I will find a way into their world, and I will dance their dance, and . . . and . . ."

"You'll die," Benedict said softly.

She did not reply. But the longer her silence lingered between them, the more surely he knew he'd stated exactly what she was thinking.

"You'll die," he persisted. "You cannot physically do what they want. You cannot dance their dance. Maybe they won't kill you, but they'll let you kill yourself. Then who will break the curse?"

She dropped her gaze and stared down at her feet. "I've got to do it," she said.

"You don't even know if this is how the curse is broken!" Benedict reached out and took her hand, but she pulled away, turned her back on him, and crossed her arms. A forest of shields could not have been more impenetrable than her stance and attitude. But Benedict wouldn't give up easily. "Heloise, what did that fiery woman do to you last night? What did she say? Did she *tell* you that the curse would be broken if you danced Le Sacre all night?"

Heloise shook her head.

"What about the . . . the princess you met? In the Tower. Did *she* tell you as much?"

Again Heloise shook her head, one short, quick shake.

"Then this could easily be a ploy of theirs to kill you without breaking their law! If you kill yourself, they're not to blame, and then you can do nothing more to end this curse. You'll just be . . . dead." Benedict stepped around to stand before her again, trying to make her meet his eyes. She ducked her head, refusing to look at him. Were those tears on her cheeks trailing white lines through the grime?

"You've got a life ahead of you," Benedict said. He knew better than to touch her, but he reached out to her with his voice, trying to compel her to hear reason. "You're strong. You're healthy. And you're brave. You're the bravest girl I've ever met. And while, granted, I haven't met many girls, I think you might also be the bravest *person* I've ever met! You've come this far all on your own, and I—I think—well, imagine how much more you could do with your life! Don't throw it away."

She didn't move. Another tear ran down her cheek and dripped off her tucked-in chin.

Benedict went on, his voice more urgent than before, "It's not your fault. You know how many others tried and died. It did no good. Why should you give your life needlessly? What's the point of it?"

In his memory he saw again the caskets which held the bodies of Henri, Giles, and Luc. What was the point of that? Young, brave lads they'd been, and Victor too. Full of bright ideas and mad schemes and vows of honor and courage! Each one a perfect representation of the kingdom's pride, a bright hopeful light for the future. All dead. All gone. All for nothing.

"Nothing," Benedict growled. He shook his head, and his jaw clenched in an effort to keep back what he very much feared might be a sob rising in his throat. Only when he could be sure of his voice again did he say, "Don't do it, Heloise. There's no use. Go home and live your life."

But Heloise, her gaze fixed upon the floor, stared back into her own past. She stared into her sister's grave.

With one hand she wiped away the tears on her face then reached into the pocket of her gown, grasping the three-part branch in a tight fist, just to feel its sharp contours poke into her skin. She was stronger than she thought. But no, that wasn't true. She *knew* she was strong. She'd always been strong—stronger than Hélène because she'd taken Hélène's strength. Perhaps that strength would prove enough. Perhaps not. But either way . . .

"If I don't try," she said, raising her eyes to Benedict's white face, "what's the point of me?"

He opened his mouth. For a moment she feared he would make protests, stupid protests, saying things she didn't want to hear and couldn't bear to hear in any case. Her mind was made up. He could help her or not, it made no difference.

And he knew it.

Benedict drew a couple of long breaths. Then, very quietly, he said, "All right then. What do you need me to do?"

"I don't know," Heloise said. She sagged as she spoke, and the determination in her face and stance sagged as well. In a moment of vulnerability she felt the full weight of her ignorance, and it was crushing indeed. "I don't know if there's anything you can do. I need to find a way back into their world. A way that doesn't involve—"

Suddenly a roaring gust blew at the window, pounding like a small body hurling itself at the glass over and over again in an effort to break through. A laughing fey voice cried out from beyond:

"I know! I know! I can help you, mortal girl!"

THIRTY-SIX

"OH, *NO!*" BENEDICT CRIED AND LEAPT FOR THE WINDOW TO MORE firmly secure the latch. Much to his horror, Heloise leapt a split second later, crying out, "Wait! Let it in!"

He was fast, but her hand knocked his away with surprising force, and before he could move to prevent her, she flung wide the window. The next moment both were knocked from their feet as the sylph, cackling like a fiend, gusted hugely into the room. It struck the far wall, bounced off, and whirled around the bed posts, tossing covers and pillows about like so much dandelion-down. Then it roared across the chamber and jumped into the fireplace, and the air filled with a cloud of ashes that stung the eyes and burned the nose. Benedict could do nothing but lie flat with his arms over his head, his eyes squeezed as tightly shut as possible, and curse through clenched teeth.

But Heloise, the moment she could get her feet under her, sprang up. "Stop it at once!" she barked, and held out her arms. "Come here!"

Much to her surprise, the sylph not only heard her command but also, with a yelp of delight, obeyed it. She found herself standing, swaying for balance, with her arms full of wind as the many fingers of the wind-creature played in her hair, tugged on her ears, and wrapped themselves around her neck. Size was apparently no issue with the sylph; while a moment ago it had been great enough to bend a tree in half, it was now nothing more than a breeze, almost pleasant were it not for the strangeness of its giggling voice.

"Mortal girl! Mortal girl!" it cooed, pulling on her curls with its invisible hands. "I can help you! Help you, help you! The Dame said to help you, and I will!"

"No, you won't," Benedict, still prostrate on the floor, growled. "You're a dragon-eaten nuisance, and we certainly don't need—"

"Don't listen to him," Heloise said, which was rude, she knew, but she hadn't the time to worry about rudeness just then. She looked earnestly into the empty whirling in her arms. "You know a gate into the Faerie world, don't you? You came through one yourself."

"Many gates!" said the sylph. "Many gates, to and fro. From the Near World into the Between. From the Far World into the Near. So many gates! So many worlds! So many Times!"

"Many gates, yes," said Heloise, trying not to be impatient. She rather doubted impatience had any worthwhile effect on this creature. "But is there one close by? A gate to the Between?"

"Yes!" cried the sylph, and swirled up so enthusiastically around her that Heloise was momentarily lifted off her feet. "Yes, there is a gate! A gate close by, so very close! Just up above!"

"Up above? In the Great Hall?"

"Up above. Over and up. Follow me!"

With that, the sylph caught Heloise by her arms and dragged her across the floor so hard that she would have fallen had the wind not held her up. The door stopped it, however, for it did not know how to work a latch, and it let go of Heloise in order to hurl itself at it. Heloise landed flat, only just catching herself in time to keep from striking her nose rather painfully. The door, solid oak though it was, rattled in its frame.

Benedict scrambled up and hastened to Heloise's side. "Are you out of your mind?" he snarled even as he helped her upright. "You can't trust this . . . this *thing!* It's one of them, one of those Faerie creatures, and it's as likely to hurt you as help you. More likely, I should think!"

Heloise gave her head a vigorous shake. "It brought me the letter from the Dame, and that proved helpful, didn't it? And it must know a way to and from its world. It must! How else did it get here? I don't think it's one of the Family of Night; it's nothing like any of them that I've met."

Benedict opened his mouth to protest. Before he could put the words together, however, there flashed across his brain the memory of the tall, stone-black woman wrapped in her garments of flame. He had to admit, even if only in the privacy of his own head, that truly she was nothing like this merry, mad little creature.

"You know I'm right," Heloise said, studying his face with far more acumen than he appreciated. "We've got to try. *I've* got to try."

Stepping through the whirling wind, Heloise reached for the door latch. Before she could touch it, however, Benedict interfered, catching her by the wrist.

"Wait," he said. "I've got—"

Before he could finish, he found himself caught up in a strong set of invisible arms and flung from his feet across the room. By some luck or good fortune—perhaps by the intention of the sylph—he landed on his bed and, with a groan of the bed-ropes, bounced off of it and landed in a pile on the floor. He lay stunned, staring up at his own spinning ceiling.

"Dragons blast you, stupid thing!" Heloise cried even as she hastened around the bed. At first Benedict wondered if she meant him, so fierce was the gaze she fixed upon him. But then she whirled about, addressing herself to the air. "What'd you do that for?"

"I was helping you," said the sylph, its voice surprisingly meek and coming from up on top of the canopy. "The mortal was going to stop you."

"I'd like to see him try!" Heloise snapped. She bent then and offered Benedict a helping hand, which he accepted, albeit reluctantly. Once he was back on his feet, she let go and folded her arms again, her feet braced as though for a fight. "All right, out with it," she said. "I assume you have an idea, and you'd better tell me quick or I'm on my way."

Any peasant overheard speaking to the son of her lord that way would have spent the night in the household dungeon and received five lashes in a public display of punishment for disrespect. It was the law. It was a law which hadn't been enforced for decades, for not a man, woman, or child in all Canneberges would ever have thought to speak to their betters in that tone of voice.

But Benedict, rather to his surprise, found he didn't mind. Not at all, in fact. It was rather nice to be spoken to like—well, like an equal. Like a friend.

He blushed and mumbled, "I'm sorry. But I do have a thought: If we're going to ally ourselves with this invisible being, we should make use of its invisibility."

"Yes?" said Heloise. "Go on."

Thus permitted, Benedict continued. "We don't know but that my room may even now be watched. Doctor Dupont could have staged the household guards at intervals up and down the gallery or even in the Great Hall itself. So if you could convince your . . . friend . . . to go before us and give a signal if all is clear, we might actually be able to get you to this gate successfully, without being caught."

Heloise considered the merits of this suggestion, her face tightening into a knot of concentration. Then, without replying to Benedict himself, she looked up at the canopy. It was shivering with the sylph's presence, and the embroidered deer on the dark, heavy fabric seemed to run and leap with movement. "Did you hear him, sylph?"

"I heard him!" said the sylph.

"Did you understand him?"

"Yes!" Then, "No." Then, "Maybe?"

Heloise sighed. She went over Benedict's scheme again, then Benedict himself tried to explain it. After the third or fourth time through, the sylph finally offered a cheerful "Oooooooh! I understand now!" which inspired no confidence in either mortal heart.

Benedict persisted, however, saying, "When you get up to the Great Hall, if you have seen *no other mortals at all* on your way, knock on the floor four times. Like this." He knelt and tapped on the floor with his knuckles to demonstrate. "But if you have seen any mortals between this room and the Great Hall above, you must knock three times, like this." He demonstrated again.

Silence overhead. Not even the canopy moved or shifted.

"Wind?" Heloise said, her eyebrows rising on her forehead. "Are you there? Do you understand?"

"Yes!" said the sylph, and darted down to plant a gusty kiss on Heloise's forehead. "I understand! I will knock on the floor, and I will see the mortals, and I will show you the gate!"

With that it hurled itself again at the door like an eager puppy desperate to go out. Heloise and Benedict exchanged glances. Heloise shrugged. They could stand there explaining for hours and never know if any of their words got through to what passed for the sylph's brain. And they didn't have hours to spare.

So Heloise opened the door to Benedict's room, and the sylph darted out into the long gallery, smothering its giggles into little hiccupping gasps, for Benedict had done his best to impress the need for silence upon it. Heloise and Benedict stood in the shelter of the doorway and watched the ripples in the gallery rugs, the only sign they could discern of the sylph's passing.

Then it was gone, and they stood in expectant silence.

"Do you think it understands?" Benedict whispered at length.

"Doesn't matter," Heloise replied. "I'm going no matter what."

Benedict gave her a sidelong glance. "You know, there might not be a gate up there at all. We're only guessing and hoping. It might all be for—"

"Shut your mouth," Heloise said in a small, small whisper. He almost didn't hear her, but he saw the movement of her lips. He saw the desperation in her eyes and hadn't the heart to continue his protests and warnings.

For he saw too that she was half-hoping he would be right. If he was, then she wouldn't have to go through with her dangerous purpose.

He had no words of either comfort or argument. So he did as he was told and shut his mouth, and they waited for a sign from the sylph overhead.

At last they heard through the ceiling above, faint but unmistakable: *Tap, tap, tap.*

"Three taps," Benedict whispered. "It must have seen someone—"

Tap, tap, tap. Pause. *Tap, tap, tap.* Pause, *Tap, tap, tap, tap, tap, tap, tap, tap . . .*

Benedict groaned and smacked his face with his palm. "Lumé's crown! What is *that* supposed to mean?"

"Be thankful it remembered to tap at all," Heloise said. "It doesn't matter anyway," she added, even as she had said before. "I've got to try. You can wait here, and—"

"I'm going with you." That was the end of that argument.

Benedict led the way as he had the previous several nights, Heloise following close at his heels, the idea being that she could somehow hide behind him if they were set upon by any of the household. It was a foolish, useless idea, but the only one they had, so they clung to it as they might have clung to a spell of invisibility.

Rather to their surprise, they successfully made it to the great stair and crept on up as swiftly as they could. They stood at the great wooden screen and listened to the ongoing tapping of the sylph on the other side, straining their ears and other senses for any indication of watchful eyes and waiting hands.

Heloise peered through the doorway. The great red Hall of Rufus was empty so far as she could see. She spotted at last a bit of broken railing, taken from the decrepit minstrels' gallery no doubt, which the sylph was using like a drumstick, enthusiastically tapping the floor in all manner of weird beats and rhythms.

492

"Oi!" Heloise whispered as loudly as she dared. "Stop it, now!"

The sylph gave a squeak of joy, dropped its stick, and sprang across the room to Heloise, nearly knocking her flat with the force of its approach. "You came!" it cried, as delighted as though it had not seen her in years, and showered her with kisses.

"Yes, of course," Heloise replied, trying hopelessly to push it away. "Where is the gate?"

"This way, this way!" said the sylph, and both dragged and pushed her into the Hall. "This way, behind the chair!"

Heloise frowned. For behind the chair was nothing except . . .

"I can't use the mirror," she said, and stopped in her tracks, which took a quite a lot of strength with the sylph still urging her on. "I need a gate that I can get through. *Me*. In *this* body. I don't need a mirror. I can't use a mirror."

The sylph continued to pluck at her hair and skin. "There is the gate! See the gate?" it said. Heloise realized that, invisible as it was, it probably had little to no concept of mirrors.

She cursed then, bitterly. All her plans, all her fine aspirations—all her worked-up self-sacrifice—and for what? Not for nothing. It couldn't be for nothing!

"There has to be some other gate," she said. Her voice rose as she spoke, mounting with the pressure of panic inside her. "There *has* to be. Somewhere close. Tell me where the gates are, wind!"

"The gate is there! Behind the chair!" the sylph persisted. "As long as you know it's there, it will be a gate for you. If you do not know, it will not serve and you will remain in your world. But I have told you, so you know, and you may pass through the gate!"

With that, the sylph left her, darted across the floor, whipped around behind Rufus's chair, and blew against the mirror glass, which gleamed and shivered, looking insubstantial for a moment. Was that the green of forest Heloise glimpsed or only her imagination seeking to show her things she wanted—and feared—to see?

The sun was setting. She hadn't much time now.

"See the gate! See the gate!" said the sylph.

What other choice did she have? How she loathed the idea of approaching the glass, of seeing the absence of her reflection as she gazed inside! But she was out of options. She had to try.

She took a step.

"Wait!" Benedict's hand came down upon her shoulder. She didn't turn and lash out at him, didn't shrug him off . . . and she hated herself for it. Was she waiting for him to protest? To restrain her? Did she want him to convince her, finally, to back down? To give up?

Was she such a coward?

"Heloise," he said, his voice uneasy in her ear, "let me go. Let me do it for you."

"What?" She couldn't speak the word out loud. Her mouth moved without sound.

"I'm dying anyway," he went on. She felt his hand tremble on her shoulder. "I haven't much time, a year, two years maybe, and that's at best. So let me try to do this. For you."

A stillness, a quiet bubble, surrounded her from the inside out. A complete emptiness of thought, reason, or resistance. Nothing but silence, no thought, no emotion.

Then the fire roared to life in her head.

Heloise whirled about, smacking Benedict's hand away. For a moment he feared she would fly at him, so intense was the rage in her eyes. "This is *my* task!" she cried. "Mine, and only mine! *I* will die for my sister! I am stronger than I think! I took all the strength from Hélène, and I'll make up for it now! I will rescue Evette, I will dance Le Sacre, and if I die, I die, but *I'll be the one doing it!*"

She ran out of words. She ran out of breath. Her face went red with the effort needed to draw air into her lungs. At last she managed a great gasp then stood there, fists clenched, and stared up at Benedict as though he were her first and greatest enemy.

He stared back, his eyes bright with emotions she could not read. He opened his mouth, closed it, and ground his teeth together.

Then, to her surprise, he answered in a low voice, "I understand."

So that was it. He wouldn't fight her. He wouldn't restrain her or argue or anything more. No more protection, no more grasping, gasping hope for reprieve. He understood.

She must go.

Heloise turned away from him and started across the hall. Each step was a battle, but each battle she won. The sylph, still shivering by the mirror glass, beckoned her with its voice, "The gate! The gate! I'll show you the gate!" and she followed its beckoning.

Before she'd gone five paces, she heard Benedict speak softly behind her. "You matter, Heloise," he said.

She didn't stop. She didn't turn.

"Whether or not you believe it. Whether or not you rescue your sister tonight," he said, his voice reaching out to her as the distance grew between them. "You matter. You matter . . . to me."

Another step. Then another. The Great Hall was so terribly long! But she kept walking, and she would climb those dais steps.

"You reminded me what it means to live. I thought I was dead and done, but you taught me otherwise. I . . . I'll never . . ."

She could hear what he was going to say: *I'll never forget you.* It caught in his throat, but she heard it as clearly as though he'd spoken the words. But he could not say them, for what did they even mean? They both knew he wouldn't remember for long. *Never* and *forever* meant little to a dying man. And the Family of Night might steal away the memory of her once she was dead. They might steal away her memory as they stole the memory of Evette.

She approached the dais. She couldn't see the mirror from this angle, hidden as it was behind Rufus's chair. But she felt it waiting for her; she felt the worlds beyond its glass. Perhaps the sylph was right. Perhaps it was a gate after all. It felt to her like a gaping mouth ready to gobble her up and gulp her down, never to be seen again.

"I *thought* so!"

The deep, deep voice filled the hall as it had not been filled in centuries, rising up to echo among the rafters like the ghosts of lords and mages and courtiers of the past. Heloise whirled around and saw the gaunt form of Doctor Dupont step through the doorway of the screen. His hand was upraised, one long finger pointed and trembling, first at Benedict, who stood staring at him in opened-mouthed terror, then at Heloise.

"I thought so!" he said, striding toward Benedict like a marching minion of the Netherworld. "I thought I would find you here! There was too much truth about the guard's warnings, though I wanted to disbelieve him. You *are* carrying on with this peasant wench. Just as I feared! The worst, the worst."

"Doctor!" Benedict protested, raising both hands and backing away. "It's not what you think. Not in the slightest! You've got to believe me, and you've—"

"Believe you?" The doctor drew back as though stung, and his heavy-lidded eyes widened momentarily. "How can I believe you? It is not you who speaks! The evil spirit indwelling you forces you into these wicked acts! Forces you to disgrace the name of your father and forefathers."

"What? No!" Benedict cast a desperate glance toward Heloise, who stood frozen, one foot on the dais steps. "No, you've got it all wrong. I don't have a spirit inside me, and I'm not—"

"Lies!" cried the doctor. He raised a fist in a summoning gesture, bellowing as he did so, "Guards!"

At the doctor's cry, three of the five household guardsmen stepped into the room behind him. They were armed with their pikes, and their gazes fixed, not on Benedict, but on Heloise. On the intruder.

"Seize her!" the doctor cried. "Seize that wicked child, and restrain your master before he does himself an injury!"

The guards hesitated, uncertain exactly how to follow both commands at once. One of them took a threatening step toward Benedict then paused when the others didn't follow.

Suddenly a wild laughter filled the hall, resounding from all sides, and accompanied by a wilder roaring of wind. One of the guardsmen was lifted off the ground, and he bellowed and kicked and lashed at nothing with his pike while the others looked on, gaping.

Doctor Dupont screamed, his voice higher pitched than Benedict had ever before heard it. He pointed at the poor, struggling guard and cried out, "See! See there! It's witchcraft, I tell you! It's the evil spirit come to life! We must stop it, we must extract it from our young lord!"

His voice was almost inaudible, lost in the thunderous voice of the sylph. But the other two guards, understanding the doctor's gestures more than anything, hurled themselves at Benedict as the probable source of their comrade's distress.

Just before they fell upon him, Benedict turned to Heloise and shouted, "*Go!*"

Heloise stared at him, her mind a storm of indecision. Then, plunging her hand into her pocket, she drew out the three-part branch. As the sylph's laughter and the doctor's screams filled her ears, she darted behind Rufus's great chair and approached the mirror. She lifted the branch, and the diamond end gleamed bright. She saw no hint of her lost reflection, only the solid surface of glass.

She plunged the branch at the mirror even as she leaped up to grab hold of the redwood frame. The glass shivered and rippled like water.

Heloise fell through into the silent Wood Between.

SHE'S IN! SHE'S THROUGH! O LIGHTS ABOVE BE THANKED!

But now . . . Oh, now . . . I've watched them die. I've watched them live. For years now, I've seen them suffer, one by one. And every time, the end is the same for me and for my daughters.

The three-part branch will be the key.

I see one, I see two . . . but where is three?

THIRTY-SEVEN

"DRAGONS," HELOISE MUTTERED, AND THE WOOD AROUND HER shivered in disgust at the sound of her voice, like a fine lady who has just happened upon something dead. Though the silence remained absolute, Heloise felt the trees draw back their limbs as though gathering up skirts. She felt the ripple under her hands and knees as roots moved and shifted below the ground. The trees pulled away and left her in a small clearing as bright as daylight.

Daylight . . .

"Dragons!" she growled again, pulling herself upright and clutching the three-part branch like a weapon in one hand. "Dragons, dragons, dragons!" Daylight was the last thing she needed! The sun had been on the very verge of setting! Night was supposed to fall, and Le Sacre was supposed to play, and all of this would take place in the Hall of Night!

But this was not that hall. She had stepped out of her world, to be sure, but not into the right *other* world.

"What am I supposed to do now?" she asked the disapproving trees. None of them would deign to answer. Though they had no faces that she could discern, they gave off the strong impression of not looking at her. They drew together so thickly that she could not see a place to pass between them. She was, for all practical purposes, imprisoned in this brilliant little clearing, the shadows of crisscrossing branches at her feet like the shadows of the gibbet's bars.

She closed her eyes, willing the image of the gibbet to leave her head. But then, in the darkness behind her eyelids she saw Benedict's pale face, desperate and full of coming death as his own guards bore down upon him from behind. What would happen to him now? What would Doctor Dupont do to him?

Would she ever know?

"It doesn't matter," she muttered. "I'm here now. I must finish this task."

She waited a moment longer, her mind straining for any sign or whisper that might be Princess Alala. But the princess had not been present inside her head since their meeting at the top of the Tower. Her role was played out.

The rest of this burden fell upon Heloise's shoulders alone.

Heloise opened her eyes and stared at the surrounding trees. Had they drawn closer, moving in, ready to crush her even as the silver forest had?

But that couldn't be right. The law forbade the Family of Night from preventing her attempts to break the curse. But were these trees in any way governed by the Family of Night? She rather thought not.

The sun would set soon. Or would it? Here in this world the air was full of a strange sort of Timelessness—as though yesterday, today, and tomorrow had somehow become confused for each other . . . no. No, that didn't make sense. Heloise had no words, no reasoning that could clarify what she felt, standing caught in this place. Somehow she knew that the Night would wait for her. She had only to find her way out of this clearing, find her way back to the Great Hall.

Moving around the periphery of her slowly shrinking cage, Heloise put her hands into the leaves, pushing on tree limbs and trunks, testing their resistance. They didn't like it. Several of them lashed back at her, and she came close to losing an eye—a true danger since she had come here in her real body, not in her reflection. But one tree shivered at her touch and, rather than resisting or fighting back, simply pulled away, creating a little space.

The memory of the crushing silver forest all too present in her mind, Heloise nevertheless took the step and pushed against the next tree and its branches and leaves. She used the hand holding the three-part branch, vaguely thinking that perhaps the trees would recognize something of their own. As she pressed forward, she found more space opening before her, reluctant but passable.

Ahead of her she glimpsed something—something big. A shadow on four legs. Another few paces, another glimpse, and she knew she saw a massive head of black mane.

Her heart ramming in her throat, Heloise leaped forward, pushing against the trees more urgently than before. They gave way now without resistance, and soon she was running, chasing after not the shadow itself (for it had vanished) but the idea of where the shadow might have been. The path became clearer beneath her feet, gold earth, bare of grass and ferns and fallen leaves. Her dirty soles pounded without a sound, and her breath came in voiceless gasps.

Was the Lion-Prince leading her? Had he come to find her, to guide her through this endless forest?

It didn't matter. All such thoughts and speculations vanished as she found herself standing before two massive oak trees. Only they weren't oak trees at all; they were pillars to which the chains of a drawbridge were attached. Heloise recognized it at once. It was the same drawbridge she had crossed with her family when entering the protective walls of Centrecœur.

Somehow she had come back around to the Great House itself. Only it was the Great House of dreams or nightmares, like Centrecœur in essence, but much bigger, much wilder, much stranger. Across the drawbridge Heloise glimpsed a lawn like the dancing lawn upon which her family had danced Le Sacre each spring for generations uncounted, though this lawn, unlike the forest in which she still stood, was dark with the gloom of swiftly approaching night.

Sudden movement startled Heloise, and she turned to her right. Out of the trees stepped none other than Aunt wearing both her woman's shape and her skull mask. She passed Heloise without a glance or word, proceeding over the drawbridge and into the darkened landscape beyond.

Another movement, and Heloise turned in time to see Uncle, flanked by two of his great-shouldered, spotted monsters. Here, in the golden light of the Wood, Heloise saw clearly that his face was indeed a skull, the white bone polished to shine. But though the sight was gruesome and strange and otherworldly, Heloise recalled Princess Alala's words: "*Uncle, at great risk to himself, stood up to Father. As a result, his face was destroyed . . .*"

Thus, though his appearance was horrifying to her mortal eyes, Heloise felt her heart beat in sudden response at the sight of him. She saw that he was a hero in his own way, a being willing to sacrifice himself for the sake of one he loved. She could not hate him. She could fear him—and indeed, as he passed close by her, it took all the strength in her spirit to keep her feet firmly planted—but she could not hate him.

Uncle disappeared over the drawbridge as well, his two beasts pacing close behind him. More dark beings appeared from the Wood and flowed past Heloise in a steady stream. She saw them both as people—beautiful, dark-skinned people—and as animals. Both forms were true among this strange Family of Night, and it was impossible to view one form without thinking of the other.

All progressed across the drawbridge, through the gate, and into that darker world beyond. So Heloise, adjusting her grip on the three-part branch, stepped forward and passed with the shadowy Faeries into their world.

She found herself standing, not on the grass-grown lawn but in the looming Hall of Night.

She recognized it at once; she would never forget this place as long—or as short—as she lived. The endless ceiling above, darkening with dusk. The polished black floor gleaming with reflected lights so that her eyes swam at the sight of it. And the dais before her, where the black throne of the Queen of Night waited with a brazier beside it. Someone had already lit the coals inside, and white flames reflected brilliantly off the chair's many angled surfaces.

Heloise felt the hugeness of that hall in a way she had not experienced when walking in her reflection. For now she was herself, her dowdy mortal self wearing an ash-filmed, peasant-spun gown and her own flimsy body. It did not matter if she was stronger than she thought, not here. No amount of mortal strength, even blessed as it was with Faerie blood, could be a match for this immortal world.

Brilliant blue eyes watched her secretively from the shadows. Whenever she turned her head, trying to meet one of their gazes, the eyes instantly blinked and disappeared. She felt terribly alone as she walked on that hard, cold floor. She had not noticed how cold it was when she was here before.

A certain sensation of heightened attention alerted Heloise, and she turned to see Mother appear in the doorway. It was no longer the drawbridge gate but the same enormous doorway Heloise had seen the last time she came to this world. Beyond it Heloise saw only more shadows, no glimpse of the green-gold Wood and its resentful trees.

Mother stood alone, a black figure only just discernible from the lesser blackness behind her. She waited patiently, as though Time itself would bow to her if she so willed it. Heloise could not guess how many seconds or minutes—or hours—passed. None of those gathered in the hall dared breathe or move as they watched the Queen of Night.

At last the Lion-Prince emerged from the darkness behind her. As he approached, he shifted from his mighty lion form into that of the prince. Heloise watched as he smoothed back his hair, bowed to his mother, and offered her his arm. Even as they had the night before, the two of them proceeded across the hall. Mother's eyes were tightly shut, and Heloise could only pray they would remain so. The memory of her own reflected self caught within the endless darkness of Mother's gaze would haunt her forever.

But Mother gave no sign to indicate she was aware of Heloise's presence. The Lion-Prince led her across the hall, and they passed within a few feet of where Heloise stood trembling. Neither turned. Neither spoke. Neither paused.

At the dais Mother mounted the steps, stopped before the brazier, took up the white fire with her hands, and allowed it to cover her completely. Heloise wondered if she would ever understand this incomprehensible fey ritual. Did the Queen of Night seek to purify herself somehow? To absolve herself of some sin? There was no way to know, no way even to guess with certainty.

Mother took her seat upon her throne. As she did so, the sun set.

The shawm-like instrument began to play.

The high, sighing, soaring strain filled Heloise to the brim of her spirit. She realized suddenly that she had never before heard this song. Not truly, not completely. Her reflection had heard it only the night before, but that time had not been so . . . so *real.* So ancient and so compelling. She knew then how wrong she had been to think, even to imagine that dancing Le Sacre in her reflected form would suffice! How could she truly dance when she could not truly feel?

How could there be a sacrifice without the whole of the heart and soul involved?

The song played on, moving through her heartache, moving through her fear like a weaver pulling the various threads, tightening them, crushing them together in the taut rack of the loom. Hearing the song played in this place as it was meant to be played was a beauty beyond anything Heloise had ever hoped to experience.

She knew now exactly why no mortal could survive this dance. It had nothing to do with the length. It had everything to do with the truth. For this song sang the truth of Death. There can be no truth more deadly.

The shawm-like instrument flung its voice maddeningly high, joined even as it crested the very peak of its range by the other, lesser instruments. Heloise's gaze rose to that place where, in her own world, the minstrels' gallery would be found. But she saw only the crowned heads of oak trees and glimpsed no sign of musicians or their instruments. It was as though the Night itself played this melody, these complex harmonies.

DOOM!

The drum sounded. Heloise felt it shiver her bones, and she gasped as she fell to her knees and bent double in sudden agony. She had not expected that; which was foolish, she now realized. The drums . . . the drums would beat her with their truth. The drums, not the shawm-like instrument, would slay her.

The twelve maidens appeared. Heloise, still shuddering with the pain of that single drumbeat, at first saw only their feet, which were bare like hers. Their gowns were not the beautiful starlight gowns she had seen when she came here in her reflection. They wore only rags, tattered rags.

Heloise sat upright, still clutching the three-part branch in her hand, and stared at the girls who surrounded her. She saw Ayodele. She saw Cateline. Then she saw Evette. She could not tell if they saw her, for their empty gazes were fixed upon an unseen mark straight before them.

Doom-doom! DOOM!

Heloise tried to scream, but pain clutched the sound in her throat so that it could not escape. Her bones shook in her body. But she knew this song. She knew each rising and falling note. She knew each beat, each moment when the drum would sound. The echoes of the drum faded, followed by silence.

Heloise gathered herself. She had no use for the glittering, three-part branch, so she stuffed it into the pocket of her gown. Holding herself as straight as she could, she raised her arms as she had seen the Chosen One do every year, every spring.

The maidens—her sisters—performed their silent paces, following the rhythmic beatings of their own hearts. When the shawm-like instrument began to play again, Heloise's eyes filled with tears at the plaintive sorrow of its voice. She held perfectly still, even as she had the night before.

Evette danced before her, her eyes unseeing but her face wrung through with pain and sorrow. Did she know Heloise was near? The dance drew her closer. With a turn and a sweeping motion of her arm she came right up beside Heloise, their faces so close they were nearly touching.

"I'll save you, Evette," Heloise said, though she did not know if it was a promise she could keep.

The circle parted. Evette and the others dispersed and vanished into the shadows. Heloise stood still, waiting for her moment, the moment when she must sing. She opened her fists and reached to the blackness of the ceiling-sky above as though begging a boon of the heavens themselves.

When her moment came, she opened her mouth and sang:

"Cianenso

Nive nur norum.

Nive noar—ugh, arg, bleh!"

Her face flamed red with embarrassment, an odd and yet completely natural emotion here in this most terrible slice of time. For in her mortal body she hadn't the skill she needed to hit those high notes. She hadn't the range or the training. So her voice broke, and she feared that the song itself had broken . . . that she had failed Le Sacre and Evette already.

But the music went on. Even as she recovered and forced the next words from her throat, the black figures around her joined their voices with Le Sacre. She heard their Faerie words shift in her head as they sang:

"Evening comes to promise

All my children

Of a deeper night."

The dance beckoned. Heloise obeyed. Last night, she had moved as though she could not make a wrong step. Tonight, she was awkward, uncertain. She knew the dance, she knew the paces, but she was only herself, and she'd never done this before, not really, and never in front of such an audience. She saw the strange formations of the Faerie folk as they ringed her and danced in their many circles, weapons clashing and flashing in the light of the stars and the white fire of Mother's throne.

The drum roared.

Heloise gasped again, though she had known this was coming. The booming shattered her, and she stumbled. But she did not fall, not this time. "I'm stronger than I think!" she said, though her voice was lost in the music. She forced herself into the next pace, and the next after that.

The drum sang: *Doom, doom, doom!*

Heloise screamed at each beat, but her feet went on moving. Her hands went on clapping and forming the signs and figures in the air. Sweat rolled down her face and trailed white streaks in the dirt. She felt the music killing her. No mortal could dance Le Sacre all night through. Not the true Le Sacre. No mortal could survive the music.

No mortal could survive the drums.

> *"Shadows of the Night,*
>
> *Dance with me,*
>
> *Dance with your arms entwined."*

So sang the Family of Night. They danced, but she knew they also watched her. They watched to see the pain overcome her, to see her give up and flee this place. Because she could . . . she still could! The door was there, open and waiting. She could even now burst from the rhythm she followed and fly away from here. Back to her own world, back to her own kind. Back to a realm where nightmares did not manifest and dance with weapons upraised.

"I'm stronger than I think!" she shouted, and this time she could almost hear herself above the wild melody.

But the drums sounded again, and her strength could not match theirs. She screamed as the bones in her body broke, one by one. But the music held her in its thrall and forced her to continue the dance even as her limbs hung at weird angles of anguish.

Suddenly Evette was there. She stood unmoving beyond the gyrating shadows of the dancers. Her gaze fixed upon Heloise, seeing her for the first time. Her eyes were wide, her hair loose and limp around her shoulders.

As though unexpectedly possessed of power hitherto unknown, she broke from the circle of maidens and entered the central circle where Heloise swayed and stamped her mangled feet. Evette's mouth moved, forming Heloise's name, screaming it as she ran, but no sound came. She plunged through the whirling of bright blades and strong limbs, even as, in their own world, Heloise had darted through the dancing peasants with their canes on the first night of spring.

Heloise watched Evette approach. She saw her sister draw near, saw her reach out both hands as though to catch her.

DOOM! roared the drum.

Heloise felt her own heart burst in her breast. She fell to the floor, broken and smashed beneath the weight of Le Sacre.

THIRTY-EIGHT

I'M DEAD, HELOISE THOUGHT. THEN SHE THOUGHT, *I'M CONSCIOUS.*

The third thought came more slowly, though time didn't seem to matter here. She could take an eternity to think up whatever she wanted to, and no one would complain. Nevertheless, as the idea tickled its way into her consciousness, she struggled to force it out, to understand it as quickly as possible. At last, there it was:

I've always been dead.

Why had it taken the whole of her life to realize this?

She had no body, at least none that she could discern. But then, it was so dark here, it was impossible to discern anything much. But she was conscious, aware of herself, aware of her name, which meant she still had some form of existence.

All right. Good. She was dead, but she wasn't gone.

So . . . what next?

The Final Water, she thought. She didn't bother to speak out loud since she wasn't entirely certain she had a mouth anymore. Besides, there was no one to hear her. At least, she hoped not.

Suddenly the darkness seemed much bigger, much closer, and much more . . . full. How could she know if anyone was out there or not? After all, if she was dead, was it not likely she had gone down to the realm of the afterlife? The Netherworld. Yes, that's what it was called. The Netherworld, where the souls of the dead wander. Which meant there were probably quite a lot of souls around her, whether she could sense them or not. The souls of those who could not find . . .

The Final Water. I need to look for the Final Water.

That's what the dead were supposed to do upon entering the Netherworld. At least, according to tradition. Who could say if that tradition was right or not? Heloise had never spoken to a dead person— save for Princess Alala, of course. But Princess Alala had never made it that far into her death and therefore could not vouch for tradition.

What else had her traditions taught her? Very little, really. She knew only that she was supposed to search for the Final Water and, if she found it, must try to cross over. Some who sought to cross made it safely to the far side—Farthestshore, as it was so named. Some who set out for that shore ended up washed away forever, down to the Dark Water, which was below . . .

Below what? What did that even mean? Seriously, now that she was dead, couldn't some special illumination be provided so that these strange ideas would make better sense than they had during her life? It didn't seem fair.

Another thought pulled at her consciousness. But she couldn't bear to think it, not yet. When that thought came in fullness of clarity she would step beyond the mere darkness of the Netherworld.

She would step into hell. And that she could not face. Not yet.

She wasn't certain how to walk without a body, but she made an effort. After all, it wasn't as though her body would be useful anymore. She considered what was left of it with a cold detachment that can only come after death. What a mangled, broken thing it had been when her spirit finally slipped free of it! Every bone crushed by the pounding of the Le Sacre drum. All her muscles twisted, all her joints swollen. There had been a lot of pain. She remembered the pain. Why would anyone want to remain in a body that could feel so much hurt? It didn't make sense. None of it made sense.

I've always been dead, she thought. *Trapped in a body of death.*

It was clear to her now. No wonder immortals hated mortals so much! No wonder Father had wanted to kill Daughter for making her evil choice. No wonder Mother wanted to protect her child's soul in a pocket world of her own invention. No wonder they had cursed her family line.

Mortals are meant to die.

What a terrible truth it was.

Her path was lonely. Though she suspected there were countless other souls all around her—perhaps even within touching distance had she known how to reach out to them—she walked alone. Wasn't that the truth everyone spoke in hushed whispers around the sickbeds of the dying? "*We all die alone in the end.*"

Like Hélène.

But Hélène should not have been alone. Hélène should have died with her sister, and then the two of them should have entered this realm together, even as they had entered their life together. And Hélène had been so young! So young, so innocent to be sent down into this darkness alone to wander in search of the Final Water.

Hell was near. Heloise couldn't allow herself to think these thoughts, or she would be lost. She must simply search. She must not think that other thought; that thought whispering, nagging, calling to her from the darkness just two steps behind. She could not allow herself to think: *What is the point of—*

"Dragon's teeth!" Heloise spoke the curse aloud, surprised that she was able to. Immediately she wished she hadn't, for, according to other, older traditions, the paths of the Netherworld belonged to the Dragon. Would speaking his name, even in a curse, wake him from his thousand-year sleep to fall raging and flaming upon her?

A silly notion. If the Dragon did exist, as this world of his appeared to do, Heloise rather doubted he would wake from his ancient sleep just to persecute one dead peasant girl.

Or maybe she wasn't dead. Maybe she was still clinging to life, and all this experience was nothing more than a strange nightmare conjured up by her dying body?

Maybe when she truly died, there would be nothing.

"*Heloise!*"

Now she knew that she could still feel emotion. Fear, in particular. Up until this moment, despite the frightening truth of the death around her, she hadn't feared anything. There had been no reason to fear. The worst had already happened.

But when she heard her own name called out from some distance she could not imagine, through some darkness she could not guess . . . then she knew that she could still fear. Then she knew what fear truly meant.

"*Heloise!*" called the voice again. Her soul lurched with terror, and she would have fled had she only known which way to run. But running here in this dark world didn't seem like a good idea. She might run straight into the mouth of the hell that pursued so close at her heels. Then she would never find the Final Water.

So she remained where she was . . . standing, for want of a better word. She listened as the strange voice called out a third time then a fourth. "*Heloise! Heloise!*"

Was it someone from the living world? Now there was an idea, and one that calmed some of the raging fear. Did her physical body hang onto life by a thread? Did someone on the other side seek to summon her back? But, no. No, this wasn't a voice she knew. It wasn't Evette, wasn't Alala, wasn't Benedict. It certainly wasn't her Meme.

Not a living voice then. Who among the dead would call her by name?

A light appeared, a distant, winking glimmer. Or perhaps only very, very small? It was impossible to say which, for it was the only thing visible in all this darkness, and Heloise had nothing with which to compare it, to gauge its size or distance. But it was definitely light and . . . and it was *something*. Something upon which she might fix her spirit, something toward which she might direct her wanderings. Like a guiding star in the winter sky it shimmered.

With hell so close at her heels, what choice did she have, really?

Heloise pursued the light. As she did so, the path beneath her feet seemed to straighten, to gain in substance. Soon she felt almost . . . *solid*. Though that wasn't really the right word, for she didn't have a body. She felt more *real*, however, as though her soul had increased its essence. With that increase came strength, and she was able to move more swiftly.

A sense of landscape rose up around her—a landscape of vast, blank emptiness, to be sure, but still a landscape. Rolling gray hills. No growth or greenery, just grayness. A sort of wind touched her, though it may simply have been the motion of her own passing.

The light continued to shine. It wasn't a big light, Heloise realized as she came nearer to it. It was quite small, actually, little more than a candle's glow. But unlike a candle, it burned with a steady beam that never wavered, casting an aura of whiteness that drew her like a moth.

At last she saw a break in the empty landscape: a single stone jutting up from the ground. *A gravestone,* she thought, though she didn't know why, for it was unlike the markers in the sad little plot above the Flaxman farm where Hélène's remains rested. But she knew it was a gravestone without knowing why she knew, and she didn't see much point in second-guessing herself. Not here.

Besides, there was no thought left for the stone when one looked at that which sat atop it: a lantern of silver filigree, from the heart of which shone the light. A perfect white light, purer than starlight, purer than moonlight. Warmer, deeper. Like the light of nearly forgotten hope.

"*Heloise!*"

The voice had been silent for—well, not for some *time*. There was no *time* here. But there had been no sound since Heloise first glimpsed and pursued the light, and she had almost forgotten both her fear and her curiosity as to who might call her. Now the voice cried out again, and she remembered the fear.

But as she stood in the glow of that lantern, she found that fear couldn't affect her as it once had. She stared into the light, and she allowed herself to wonder.

Then she put out a hand (surprised to discover that she had one; perhaps she hadn't until this moment) and lifted the lantern by its handle. It swung from the end of her arm (she had one of those too) as she turned toward the voice.

She saw the Final Water.

Heloise had heard many people speak of the Final Water back in what she had once thought of as her life. When Hélène died, her Grandmem had whispered to her, saying, "*Not to cry, child. Be thankful your sister is not trapped here, unable to move on. She has surely found her way to the Final Water and beyond . . .*"

The words had meant very little to Heloise, nothing more than a vague impression of what life after death would hold. She had never bothered to try to imagine it, for what was the use of that? Life was full, life was busy; life was consumed with the struggle for survival. There would be time enough after death to consider such odd, vague concepts.

But this was after death. Now she not only considered, she *saw.*

The Final Water stretched before her, more endless than endless, more boundless than boundless. She had thought she glimpsed forever when she first entered the Wood Between. But that small forever would be lost in but a drop of the hugeness upon which she now gazed.

She had never seen an ocean during her lifetime, but she had heard tell of oceans. Once an old, weathered man with a strange, rolling gait had passed through Canneberges, begging bread at the doors of the peasant cottages. A sailor, he had claimed to be, and he told tales of the sea. None of these tales had fascinated Heloise so much as the very idea of the ocean itself. Water that went on beyond the horizon . . .

This wasn't an ocean, she knew at once, even though she had never seen one. But she had seen streams, and one time she had walked beside her older brothers, following a stream all the way to the river. She knew what a river was.

And she knew, in that first, eternal instant of a glance, that the Final Water was a river. Greater than any ocean, but flowing forever from a source she could not name to a destination she could not guess.

"I can't cross that," she said. She spoke the words like a confession of some dire sin. But there could be no denying the truth. Never, in all the millennia of all the ages of all the worlds stacked up on top of each other, could she ever swim that flowing torrent; not even if, while standing here upon the dark shore of the Netherworld, she could glimpse the hope of the Farthestshore beyond and, so inspired, strive after it. She was stronger than she thought—but she was not that strong.

The lantern in her hand felt suddenly heavy. She wanted to set it down. She almost did. But she knew that once she let go of the handle, the darkness would return and she would wander lost again, lost from the Final Water. The heartbreak was agony beyond all the pain of her tortured death, but she knew she would rather stand there gazing out upon the impossible than never see it again.

"*Heloise!*"

The voice was much nearer now. So near, in fact, that Heloise almost thought she recognized it. "Who's there?" she called back, and lifted the lantern higher.

The light shone out across the Final Water and captured in its brilliant beams the form of a boat approaching. A tall boatman, cloaked in a long white robe with its hood pulled low so that his face could not be seen, stood in its stern with a long pole in his hands. This he used to push the boat along. The currents of the Final Water were terribly strong, yet he seemed to navigate them with ease, so he must be stronger still.

In the prow of the boat sat a small figure. Or not so small, Heloise realized as the boat drew nearer. The figure was about her own height but seemed much smaller compared to the vastness of the boatman. The light was so bright as it fell upon the strange person's face that Heloise could gain no solid impression of who or what it was.

Soon the boat crunched against the pebbled shore. While the boatman remained where he stood, his long pole firmly fixed, the figure in the bow leaped out, splashed through the shallows, and waded up onto the gray, featureless landscape where Heloise stood.

I should run, Heloise thought. *I should run before I'm caught.*

But behind her waited only hell. So she stood her ground and clung to the lantern even as the stranger approached. The lantern's light, which had at first been too bright, became gentler, clearer, illuminating the stranger's face, and Heloise saw . . .

She saw herself.

It was her face, her own face, as clear as it had been when reflected in Benedict's mirror. The same bright eyes, the same smattering of freckles. The same wild mane of curly hair, color indeterminate but possibly gold. The same protruding collarbones and soft, round cheeks as yet un-hardened with age. It was her own face, except . . . except for the nose. The nose was different. Yes, it boasted that same bump in the middle, but it listed, not to the left, but to the right.

The stranger—her own living image—stopped but a few paces from Heloise. While Heloise's brow was naturally stern, this one's brow was smooth and clear, and her eyes were bright with a cheerful smile.

"Hullo, Heloise," she said.

"Hullo, Hélène," said Heloise.

THIRTY-NINE

"WHAT DO YOU HAVE IN YOUR POCKET?" HÉLÈNE ASKED.

Heloise heard the words. But she couldn't understand them. She stood with the lantern before her, its light forming a sort of barrier between herself and the image of her dead sister—the image that wasn't even right! Not even close! This wasn't Hélène, not really. How could it be? Hélène was only five years old when she died. When she was wrapped in that thin shroud. When she was laid to rest in the cold ground without even a pine box to cradle her.

"Don't throw away my sister!" Heloise had shouted. But they'd tossed the dirt in on top of her anyway, and Hélène was gone.

She certainly wasn't the young woman who stood in the white light of the lantern there on that dark shore, with all the looming blackness of the Netherworld on one side and all the looming hugeness of the Final

Water on the other.

So this must be a trick, Heloise decided. Some evil trick, some lure set to ensnare her, to prevent her from trying to cross the Water on her own. Perhaps a final spell from Mother, or even a poisonous illusion sent by the Dragon himself. It couldn't be real.

"You're dead," Heloise said. "I mean not *you.* You're not her. And she's dead. And I don't know who you are."

"Don't be silly," said Hélène. "I'm quite alive, as you see. But you're dead, I'm sorry to say. What do you have in your pocket?"

"If you're not dead, then you can't be her," Heloise persisted. "I saw you die. Her die, I mean. I was there beside her. We shared the same bed. I got up, but she never did. And she's gone, long gone. And it's . . . it's . . ."

And it's my fault.

In that moment, hell caught up with Heloise. It closed in from behind her, and she realized, even as it overwhelmed her, that it had always been only a step or two in her wake. Throughout her life it had followed her, needing only death to claim her fully. It wrapped around her, a miasma of loathing, regret, and aching confusion.

Hell asked her again and again: *What is the point of you?*

She had lived when Hélène had died. She had been the strong one, the one who took all Hélène's strength since before their birth. Yet what good had she accomplished? Had she rescued Evette? Had she liberated Alala or Ayodele or Cateline or any of the prisoners? Had she been strong enough to dance Le Sacre through the night? No. No, no, and no again. So what was the point of her, really? What was the use?

The Chosen One. The gifted one. The strong one.

She deserved hell, and it caught her even as she dropped the lantern, dropped the light—

A hand caught hold of hers. And suddenly, hell could not be hell anymore, because she was not alone in it. Someone held onto her, someone knelt before her, grasping her hand. She had shut her eyes so that she would not see the blackness where the light of the lantern had been. But through her self-imposed blindness, she heard her sister speaking:

"I'm not dead, Heloise. My mortal body died, and my mortal life came to an end. But *I* am not dead! I am alive. I am living even now. I was dead before I died. But when I died, I came alive."

"It's my fault," Heloise whispered. But her other hand sought in the darkness, and Hélène caught it in a tight grip as well.

"It's no one's fault," Hélène said. "It is the way of mortality. It is our burden and it is our gift. The Faerie folk don't understand it. They can't because their lives go on and on and on." She squeezed Heloise's fingers, urging her to an understanding she could not grasp. "Before there can be a Beginning, Heloise, there must first be an End. I've suffered my End. I've entered into my Beginning."

Slowly, afraid of what she might see, Heloise opened her eyes. Rather than the blackness of hell, she saw her sister's face before her. A homely, comfortable peasant girl's face. Nothing transformed or transfigured. Nothing radiant or angelic. Just a girl, a pleasant, plain girl with a crooked nose and tangled hair and a smile that would not surrender.

"I was sent from beyond the Final Water," Hélène said through that smile. "I was sent from the Farthestshore to meet you here, to show you the truth you have overlooked because you could not help but overlook it. And that's all right, Heloise. You're not expected to save the day. You're only expected to try and try and, when all else fails, to try again."

"I did try," Heloise said. "I . . . I tried to dance Le Sacre. I tried to save our sister. I wasn't strong enough."

"Of course not. A branch alone will bend and break. It is the branch of three parts that you need. Now answer my question: What do you have in your pocket?"

"I'm dead," said Heloise. "I don't have pockets anymore."

"Check it anyway," said Hélène.

Obediently, Heloise slipped one of her hands free of her sister's grasp. She felt along her waist, surprised, somehow, to discover her own body and the fabric of her ugly, simple gown. And yes, a pocket. Of all things, here in the Netherworld she did indeed have a pocket.

Her hand sought down inside and closed upon the three-part branch of silver, gold, and diamond. This she withdrew, and it gleamed in her fingers, reflected brilliantly in Hélène's eyes. It wasn't as bright as the lantern, but it was bright enough. At the sight of it, hell itself retreated, and Heloise found herself kneeling upon the shores of the Final Water, one hand still held in her sister's firm grasp.

"Here it is," said Heloise, holding it up.

"Do you see now?" asked Hélène.

"I—I don't know what I'm supposed to see."

"You're still looking with your mortal eyes. You don't have to do that here." Hélène leaned in closer, her smile eager and urgent at once. "Look at it and see the truth. Remember what your sister has done for you."

Heloise obeyed, though she did not understand what was asked of her. She stared at the branch of silver, gold, and diamond entwined into a single shape. She recalled when she'd gathered each one—the silver branch in the crushing forest, the gold branch from the waterfall, the diamond branch during the Night Hunt. Each alone was complete.

Yet when brought together, they were made whole.

"Three together," Hélène whispered. "Three branches. Three sisters. Three quests."

Remember what your sister has done for you.

In her heart, Heloise recalled the voice of Princess Alala saying, "*Look at what your sister has done.*"

A tapestry. An embroidered picture of memory, of pure mortal magic.

A magic so strange and so strong, it can hold onto the spirit long after death.

Heloise saw her sister's tapestry, unique among the twelve. For while all of the other eleven maidens embroidered themselves in the center of Le Sacre, dancing with their true loves, Evette had instead depicted Heloise.

"*They put down in words or pictures all their memories so that when they die, the memories live on, passed down from generation to generation.*"

Heloise danced Le Sacre, there in the silken image. Surrounded with Evette's red cranberry blossoms, her hands upraised, her feet moving forever in time to the music. Forever captured in memory, dancing Le Sacre all night through.

There was more to the picture. Heloise saw it now, though she did not remember seeing it at the time. In Evette's tapestry she saw all twelve maidens picked out in lifelike detail. She saw Ayodele and Cateline as well as Evette. And in that image . . . in Evette's image . . .

They did not dance. They ran away, each in her own direction, free of Le Sacre's binding.

"*Imagine,*" said the voice of Evette in her memory. "*Imagine being part of a work that will last through the ages, letting people a hundred years from now know who we are and what we did, and what important events transpired in our time!*"

Heloise shook her head, and the image faded. She stared at the three-part branch then lifted her gaze to meet Hélène's. "But it's not true," she said, her voice thick with mingled fear and hope. The Final

Water lapped at her feet, and she felt the amazing wetness of it, felt it with more clarity of sensation than she could have known in her mortal body. "I didn't succeed! I tried to dance Le Sacre, just as Evette's picture told me. But I died!"

"Not according to the mortal magic," said Hélène. "The mortal magic, which the Queen of Night even now manipulates for her own purposes, keeps Alala alive. That which sustains Alala's life in the tapestries of generations sustains your life as well."

She laughed then, and if Heloise had not been convinced before that it was her sister who held her hand, she would have known then for certain. For though the face before her was not that of five-year-old Hélène, her laugh was exactly the same.

"What a clever sister we have, Heloise! She has saved you!"

"But—but—" Heloise stammered around the words, afraid to speak them out loud. "You said I'm dead."

"You are," said Hélène. "At least, you are compared to me. But your mortal life is not at an end. I was sent from beyond the Farthestshore to meet you here. My quest was to find you and to send you back to finish that which you have started."

Three branches. Three sisters. Three quests.

They stood together, still holding hands, and the three-part branch gleamed in the light of the lantern sitting on the ground at their feet. The Final Water was vast before them, but not so vast as it had been. Heloise looked out beyond the white-robed boatman and thought she glimpsed a light and possibly a hint of mountains beyond the Boundless.

"Will you return to the Farthestshore?" she asked, suddenly too shy to meet her sister's eyes.

"Yes," said Hélène. "And I will see you again when you come there."

"Meme misses you," said Heloise. "She misses you every day."

Hélène nodded once. There was an entire world of understanding in that one simple gesture. But when she answered, she said only, "When you meet the Mother of Night again, think of Meme and understand."

She took Heloise in her two scrawny arms and embraced her. For a timeless moment they were two small children, just five years of age, holding each other as they faced the big world together. The childish, lisping voice of young Hélène whispered in Heloise's ear, "Mortals were meant to die to themselves so that they might truly live. Don't be afraid, valiant sister! Dance the sacrifice. Dance to the truth you know. Dance to the song of life, the gift of the Song Giver."

A branch of silver, a branch of gold. A branch of diamond adamant.

"Now go," said Hélène. "Go save our sister."

The Family of Night stood in the hall. They stood when they should have been dancing, and Le Sacre played on around them. They stood in ringing circles around the mangled form of the mortal girl lying in hopeless sacrifice.

So, Son thought from his vantage on the dais beside Mother's throne, *another one gives her life. For nothing. How frail these mortals are!*

His heart sank in his breast even as he turned a grim smile down upon Mother's face. She sat as she always did, still as a stone, her eyes closed.

"It's done, Mother," he said. "The cursebreaker is dead. Our law remains unbroken, and—"

Someone screamed. Son turned, his long braids flying, and sprang down from the dais. Even as the scream was taken up and spread in rippling waves through the crowd, he pushed through the thronging members of his family, making his way to that center circle.

There he saw—even as the shawm sang in counterpoint to the ceterone—even as the drum roared its pronouncements of doom and death—the mortal girl lying prone and broken. Only . . . only . . .

She wasn't dead.

The dark Faerie figures fled from the center and disappeared into the shadows along the edges of the hall, there to hide and stare out in wonder at that which transpired. But Son stood where he was, staring down at that little creature.

She raised her head and shook it, her hair tossing like a lion's mane. For a moment he thought she was a lion indeed.

The twelve maidens stood around her now, around him, the captured mortal girls—the tithe that could never fully satisfy the demands of the curse set upon their family. They alone remained on the dance floor, and though Le Sacre bade them obey, they did not dance. They stood as still as Mother herself, watching with the Lion-Prince.

The mortal girl sat upright, the bones of her body re-knit as though they had never been shattered. She held something in her fist, something Son could not see, and she glanced down at it, her face full of wonder.

The shawm shrieked, singing the pain of blood loss and grief. The ceterone bellowed the fear of coming death. The bandora cried out in the agony of sickness, of age. Beneath their voices, the drums roared, *Doom! Doom-doom!*

But the mortal girl stood up. She looked at her limbs as though uncertain they were hers. She frowned as she turned them over, looking for breaks and bruises that should be but weren't. Then she tilted her head as though catching a strain of music. She did not hear the music of the Night that played, more feral, more frantic than ever. Le Sacre and its bidding did not touch her ear.

She raised her hands. She lifted her foot. Then with a leap, she began to dance in a pace and rhythm counter to all the voices of Le Sacre. The drum beat its doom, and it did not move her, did not affect her. She danced hesitantly at first, uncertain of the steps, but with every turn, every footfall, her confidence grew. Suddenly she was smiling.

"What is this?" Son cried, and almost backed into one of the twelve maidens. But she sidestepped, moved around him, and approached the mortal girl, the cursebreaker. She seemed at first to study her sister's movements and then to hear the song for herself. Even as Le Sacre urged her to follow its bidding, she began to move in time to the cursebreaker's dance. One by one, the other eleven maidens joined her.

Le Sacre sang in desperation:

> *"Shadows of the Night,*
> *Dance with me,*
> *Dance with your arms entwined.*
> *Shadows of the Night,*
> *Sing with me,*
> *Sing with yours voices combined."*

But as one voice, the twelve maidens and the cursebreaker sang in response:

> *"Beyond the Final Water falling,*
> *The Songs of Spheres recalling,*
> *When all around you is the emptiness of Night,*
> *Won't you dance with me?"*

Heloise felt them surrounding her. She couldn't see them just then, for her eyes were still full of the brilliant glow of the lantern she'd gazed upon in the Netherworld. But she felt them, felt Evette's hand touching hers, felt Ayodele's hair whirling to brush her face. All her sisters of generations past were caught up together in the new dance, in the new song. Hélène was there too, for Hélène was as much a part of this as any of them. The branch of three . . . the branch of three parts will be the key . . .

An inspiration took hold of her, an inspiration so strong, she wondered that she had not felt it before. Heloise, following the new song in her head, raised her unlovely voice and sang as loudly as she could:

> *"Different as they'll ever be*
> *Yet springing from a single tree.*
> *'Tis more than thee, 'tis more than me.*
> *Now set the captives flying FREE!"*

As the last word left her mouth, something broke. For a moment Heloise could not guess what it was. Then it came to her—Le Sacre! Le Sacre itself broke and dissolved, all the dissonant parts of its creation unwinding, undoing, splintering off into Night and nothingness. The drum uttered a last forlorn *doooooooom . . .* Then it was gone.

The maidens uttered a simultaneous gasp. Then each one shouted in a loud voice without words. They turned and they ran from the circle as fast as their feet could carry them. They ran into the shadows where the Family of Night hid, and the Family itself fled before them. But the maidens cared nothing for this. They ran as fast as they could, each for a separate gate which opened up and beckoned to her. Perhaps a gate leading back to her own time, her own place of belonging. Perhaps a gate leading to the Netherworld and the Final Water.

But not all of them ran. Even as the echo of Heloise's voice died away, even as she twirled about on the tips of her bare, dirty feet, she felt her right hand caught and clasped tight. Evette stood beside her, her face alight with her most enormous, most beautiful smile. And just behind Evette was—

"*What have you done?*"

Mother appeared before Heloise and clutched her arm in a grip of bedrock stone. The white fire covering her intensified, darkening to an ugly red, and it ran along Heloise's arm as well, taking her into its blazing depths. Heloise stared up into eyes of black lava, full of heat and passion and . . . and . . .

She knew that emotion.

"Heloise, no!" Evette cried. But it didn't matter.

Before Evette could protest further, Heloise shook free of her sister's grip and reached out to take hold of Mother's hand. They stood together in the blazing red inferno of Mother's fire, there in the center of the Hall of Night. But though the fire raged over the surface of Heloise's skin, it did not touch her. It was as though they existed in two separate realms, Heloise and the Queen of Night, even when they stood hand-in-hand.

"What have you done?" Mother cried again. The sound of her voice broke a piece of the distant, sky-like ceiling above and sent it crumbling and falling in great chunks of heavy darkness that smote the dance floor and broke it in long cracks. "You've turned my own power against me! You have killed her! You have killed my Alala!"

The words sprang to Heloise's mouth without thought. She knew what she must say, though she could never guess how she knew. Perhaps it had to do with the song she had just sung, the song which played on in her head.

"Dance with me, Mother," Heloise said.

Mother towered over her, as tall as an oak and far more ancient. Her eyes were huge and black, but Heloise could catch not even a glimpse of her reflection in them—Mother had taken that away forever. Instead she saw a reflection of something else. Something she knew well.

"Dance with me," Heloise said again. She moved to the song, the gentle song which slowly swelled up in her heart, gaining power as it grew. The song which Mother could not hear.

"You've killed my Alala," the Queen of Night said. "You are a monster! A destroyer! A murderer!"

It's your fault! You took all her strength! She had nothing left! It's your fault!

"Dance with me, Meme," Heloise said. Tears ran freely down her cheeks. She added, "I'm stronger than you think."

With those words, she pulled Mother into the dance with her. The dance which was not Le Sacre. For where Le Sacre took life, this dance gave life. Though her voice was ugly with mortality, Heloise sang to the new rhythm in which she moved:

> *"Beyond the Final Water falling,*
> *The Songs of Spheres recalling,*
> *When the sun descends behind the twilit sky,*
> *Think again of me."*

Mother tried to resist but couldn't. She hadn't the will to oppose the cursebreaker, not anymore. She fell into step with the mortal girl, and together they spun around the broken dance floor of her hall. As they danced, the hands Heloise held began to fade away, to disintegrate into nothing

"*Beyond the Final Water falling,*" Heloise sang.

Mother responded in a voice of liquid darkness and despair, "*The Songs of Spheres recalling.*"

Then Alala was there. Heloise felt the Princess of Night alive and vivid inside her head as she hadn't been since they met face to face in the Tower. She was present again, and Heloise felt suddenly that it was Alala's hands and not her own holding Mother's. It was Alala's feet moving with far more grace than Heloise's ever could.

Mother knew. The look in her eye would have broken the heart of any mortal not blessed with Faerie blood. "Daughter," she sighed. "I've lost you."

Tell her I love her, said Alala. *Always.*

"She loves you," Heloise sang in time to the dance. "She loves you always."

"And I," Mother whispered, "love her. *Always.*"

Her words melted into the night. The fire surrounding the two of them softened from scarlet to white. It was not the same white fire Heloise had witnessed earlier, sprung from the strange coals. It was more like the white flame flickering in the heart of the silver lantern. For a moment it flamed bright and strong.

It went out. In the darkness that followed, Heloise felt the hands she held slip away and vanish. Though she cast about, turning her head this way and that, she could find no trace of her poor, sad enemy. When she turned her head for the third time, she found that she stood, not in the broken Hall of Night, but in Rufus's Hall, upon Rufus's redwood floor.

Someone was calling her name. Her sister. Her sister was calling her name. Her sister was . . .

Heloise turned around so sharply she almost fell over. "Evette!" she cried, but the name died on her lips.

For before her stood, not her lovely young sister, but some strange old woman whom she did not know.

I STAND UPON THE SHORES OF THE FINAL WATER. I STAND WITH THE *silver lantern in my hand and gaze out upon that endless flow where life and time run into eternity and are lost. I cannot see the Farthestshore from here, but it does not matter.*

I am full of joy. And I am full of sorrow. Just now, it is enough to stand here, held close in this brilliant light, and to watch.

A boat approaches. A boatman in a long white robe pushes the craft along, and a maiden sits in the prow, gazing out with eager, searching eyes. She is one of mine, one of my lineage, though I do not know her name. Her face is very like the cursebreaker's.

"We thought we'd wait for you," the girl says as the boat draws near to this shore. "We thought you might be coming soon and perhaps you would like company on the voyage across the Water."

"Yes," I reply, "I would like that very much." The girl extends a hand, but I do not take it at once. I pause first to look back into the darkness of the Netherworld behind me. Will they come? Will they join me?

"Mother!"

Ayodele, her eyes bright with the lantern's light, emerges from the darkness and runs to me, her arms outstretched. My eldest, my beautiful firstborn! We hold each other there on that shore, reunited at long last. "Mother, Mother, I'm so sorry!" Ayodele whispers. "They made me help, they made me hold you, and I could not fight them."

"Hush, my darling," I say, stroking her hair, cradling her as though she is a child. Here, perhaps, she is a child again, a little one I might carry in my arms. "There is no need for sorrow or regrets, no need to ask forgiveness. All has been restored! We will journey together to find your father, your brother, and your two sisters."

Even then we wait. Others join us, one by one, following the light of the lantern. My daughters of all those long generations, each more lovely than the last, each bearing a mingling of my blood and Rufus's. They follow the lantern light, and they greet us with glad cries.

"Come now," says the girl in the boat, and she beckons to us. "Come, we must sail away. The Farthestshore awaits, and your Beginning is at hand!"

One by one, my daughters climb into the boat, assisted by the boatman and the girl. I wait until last of all, turning my gaze back into *the darkness for a last time. "Are there no more?" I ask.*

"Some have unfinished business to end before they pursue this journey," says the girl in the boat. "They will be along soon enough. You will see!"

Before there can be a beginning, there must first be an end. So let the cursebreaker live out her end with courage and with hope ever shining in her heart! Thank you, child, for your sacrifice. Thank you, sisters three, for your three-fold bond of love, hope, and strength.

Thank you, Song Giver, for the new song we sing.

So I climb into the boat and sit with the girl in the prow. I will see my Rufus soon, upon the Farthestshore.

FORTY

IN THE LAST SEVERAL DAYS HELOISE HAD EXPERIENCED HER SHARE OF terrible moments. Each of those moments flashed across her heart in a single, painful beat: the moment she first saw her reflection move on its own, the moment she heard the shadow sing at her back, the moment she saw the phantoms close in upon the Le Sacre circle, the moment she knew she would have to face the Night Hunt. These memories and many more crowded into her head, culminating in that most terrible moment when, at the final beat of the Faerie drum, she felt her body betray her, felt it break and crumble.

Yes, life had been full of terrible moments in recent days. But not one of them, no matter how strange, frightening, or painful, could compare to that moment—that heartbeat—when she turned to find her sister and looked instead upon the haggard, age-uglied face of the old woman.

There was no time for thought. So, with a sickening plunge of her stomach, she felt rather than thought: *It's all been for nothing. They've taken her youth. They've left her like this. They've spoiled all her—*

Then two arms caught her from behind and pulled her into a hug. The young, fresh voice she knew so well cried out, "Heloise! Dearest!"

There had been terrible moments without number, moments which would come back to haunt her in the small, secret hours of the night for years to come, perhaps for the rest of her life. But not one of them compared to the sudden, glorious, fountaining joy of her sister's voice, her sister's embrace. Then Heloise pulled out of the hug, turned around, and beheld her sister's face. Plain and pretty, tired and rundown, yet glowing with a smile that might burst in its efforts to express the surpassing joy of that moment.

And Heloise discovered she still hated to be called "dearest." The moment was perfect.

It couldn't last, of course; no perfect moment can. Even as Heloise drew breath to exclaim, to speak Evette's name, a tremendous gust of wind blew down upon them from the rafters above and knocked both girls from their feet so that they fell in a tumble on the floor; and the old woman standing near threw up both hands and cried out, "Lights Above, save us!"

Insane laughter surrounded Heloise, and breezy hands plucked at her ragged skirts and tangled hair. "Mortal girl! Mortal girl!" the sylph exclaimed. "You survived! You survived the Nivien curse! You killed Mother, and you survived! Oh, great and powerful and wonderful and beautiful mortal who deals *death* even unto Faeries!"

"What? No!" Heloise exclaimed, scrambling upright and trying to slap the sylph away with both hands. It caught her hands and pulled her around the floor so swiftly that she had to jump and skip to keep from falling. "Let me go!" she cried irritably. "I didn't kill anyone."

Then she thought, *Alala.*

"*You have killed her. You have killed my Alala.*"

But Alala had already died, hadn't she? She had been a ghost trapped in the Tower and the world of Mother's invention. Surely, no matter what the Family of Night claimed, Heloise could not justly be called a killer, a murderer . . .

The wind-spirit, still singing, dropped its hold on Heloise and whirled about first Evette and then the old lady, both of whom gasped in surprise but no fear. After what they had seen and experienced in the realms beyond, they hadn't much fear left over for a being like the sylph. Looking at them, Heloise realized suddenly that she knew who the old woman was. "Cateline!" she exclaimed.

The old woman raised her head and spoke in a quavering voice, more aged even than Grandmem's: "Yes. Yes, I am. I haven't heard that name in—in—well, it seems now, in a long time." She stopped and, lifting her wrinkled, blue-veined hands, studied the age that had come upon her since she'd stepped into the Faerie realm. There was sadness in her faded eyes but no surprise. "Yes," she said, addressing her hands more than Heloise just then, "I am Cateline."

Heloise thought, *I killed the other ten. My sisters of ages past. Ayodele and the rest. They were too old. They couldn't come back. So when I broke the curse, they all . . .*

It was a not a thought she wished to complete. Not then. Perhaps not ever.

Evette approached, her hair loose and whipping in the sylph's wind. She took Heloise by the hand and gazed into her eyes. She was Evette. She was truly Evette. Not aged more than a week, though fear and captivity had added a certain graveness to the soft skin of her cheek and brow. Her fingers, Heloise noticed (with that unconscious sort of noticing one doesn't recognize until hours later), were callused along each fingertip with the excessive use of needle and thread, and the thumb of her left hand was swollen from frequent, accidental stabbings.

"They knew," Evette whispered, squeezing Heloise's hand. "They knew they were old, though they did not look it. They knew time had moved on without them in the mortal realms, that their loved ones were dead and gone. I could not speak to them when in—when in that place. But I could see it in their eyes when we danced each night. They longed for release."

She didn't try to say, "It wasn't your fault."

She didn't try to say, "There was nothing else you could do."

And, because she was Evette, she wouldn't lie and say, "You didn't kill them."

She said, "No one who enters the Faerie realms expects to return unchanged."

Heloise looked from her sister to Cateline, and she saw no accusation in the old woman's face. Sorrow, yes, but also a melancholy sort of gladness.

Moving with great hesitancy on limbs not as strong as those she had recently used for dancing, Cateline approached Heloise and Evette. "I have to ask," she said in her brittle voice, "if my sister is still—"

But Heloise did not hear the rest. A thrill of fear ran through her veins, sprouting from the soles of her feet and racing up to burst in her brain with a sudden clarity of thought. Something was missing. Something was not right, something that had been plucking at the corners of her brain for some moments now.

Forgetting Cateline, forgetting even Evette in that terrible instant, Heloise whirled about and addressed herself to the invisible wind wafting dust in clouds across the floor. "Where is Master Benedict?" she cried. "Sylph, where is the other mortal?"

"What other mortal?" said the sylph, still chuckling to itself. "There are many mortals here! So many, many mortals!"

"The one who was with me," Heloise persisted. "The guards came, and the doctor, and they . . . what did they do to him? Did you not help him?"

The sylph twirled about her skirts, catching the ragged hem in its many fingers. "Mortals are not my business," it said with no malice but with great cheer. "Only you, for the Dame asked me to help you. I helped you, didn't I?"

Heloise stared at the movement of her skirts. Her stomach dropped in a cold lump. Evette, seeing her sister's dreadful pallor, took her hand. "Dearest, what's wrong?" she asked.

Heloise met her sister's confused gaze but found she hadn't the words to answer. So she turned away and told the sylph, who was plucking at Cateline's thin hair, "You've got to help me again. We've got to save him!"

"The shrivening rites are now complete," said Doctor Dupont, standing with his back to Benedict, gazing out the window. The light of the rising sun cast his tall form into silhouette; not even daylight could soften his ghoulishness but rather emphasized it. "When Lumé's light shines its brightest, we will begin."

Benedict looked around the room from his vantage lying spread-eagle on his bed. The three guardsmen each stood at a bedpost, and his manservant, Hugo, stood at the fourth. Hugo's face was grimly determined, but a few of the guardsmen at least had the grace to look uncomfortable. The youngest in particular—a fellow by the name of

Briant with the most impressive Adam's apple known to man—kept casting uneasy glances at the doctor's tools that lay in gruesome display on the bedside table. He looked as if he would faint at any moment, and his Adam's apple bobbed up and down, and up and down again, as he struggled to swallow back his horror.

Horror. That was a good word for it. That's what he should be feeling for himself, Benedict thought. But he couldn't. He was too numb just then, numb with exhaustion, numb with whatever strange sedative Dupont had fed him during the night's "shrivening rites." Even his hands and feet were numb, for the bindings securing him to the posts of his bed were too tight and cut off his circulation.

Or perhaps the horror he felt was simply so big that it had burst out the other side, leaving only a hollow shell of numbness in its wake.

Either way, Benedict lay upon his bed, his gaze moving from Doctor Dupont at the window to the men surrounding him. Never to the tools on the table. Never there. Numbness was better than horror, and he was pretty sure the numbness would vanish instantly if he allowed himself to look there.

"I am sorry it has come to this," said Doctor Dupont. He stood with his hands behind his back, very tall, very straight. "I had hoped to put off this task for many months yet. But you would defy me. You would resist me. And defiance and resistance are the very food upon which devils feed."

The doctor turned then, his face lost in shadows, so bright was the light through the window behind him. His voice, the last word in sepulchral, rumbled up from the cavern of his throat. "Your lordly father entrusted me with your care and keeping. His one desire is to see his legal heir someday ascend to his own high place in the courts of Bellevu. He said to me, 'Good doctor, by whatever means necessary, save my son.'" The doctor sighed and shook his head slowly, the peak of his black cap turning like the point of an upside-down wooden top. "That is a task bordering on the impossible. But—" Here he raised a long finger, and his teeth flashed in something that might have been a smile. "But my order is in the business of working miracles! So perhaps a miracle we will work this day."

He approached the bed. Though they wore stout leather armor and were all them both younger and broader than Dupont, the three guards drew back from him, some more quickly than others. Young Briant practically leaped like a grasshopper to remove himself from the doctor's path, and Hugo made a sorry effort to hide himself behind the bedpost.

Benedict, however, was too numb to react. Somehow he couldn't make himself believe that what was about to happen was truly about to happen. It couldn't. Or if it did, it would happen to someone else. He must *be* someone else, some stranger lying here tied to his bed.

Doctor Dupont's hand trailed across his assortment of tools. "The nightshade should be taking effect," he said. "I cut it with no other herbs, and the full power of its potency must even now be upon you. It will help with the pain, of which I fear there will be much. But in pain alone can the spirit of fire be extracted from your head . . ."

Benedict tried to speak. But the extra dose of nightshade had numbed his tongue along with the rest of his body, and he found he could not remember how to make it work. But his eyes were wide as he watched Doctor Dupont select the first of his tools, watched the bright point of that metal instrument flash in the morning sunlight as it was upraised above his head—

The door burst open.

"*Wheeeeeeeeeeeeeeeeeeeeeeeeeeeeee!*" cried the sylph.

The three guardsmen screamed and raised their weapons ineffectually against the uproarious wind that plucked the lances from their hands and, with another mad laugh, plucked the instrument from Doctor Dupont's hand as well. The guards went on screaming as they ducked their heads and flung up their arms to ward off stray blows from their own weapons, which careened around the room in the invisible grasp of the sylph's many hands. Hugo dove to the floor and tried to stuff himself under the bed.

"The evil spirit!" cried Doctor Dupont, and took up another of his tools. "It has grown in strength and malicious intent!" His voice was almost lost in the roar of the sylph, but Benedict heard every word. "I must work swiftly if there is to be any chance of your salvation!"

With a mad gnashing of his teeth, Dupont leaned over the bed, his new device of choice poised for its lunatic work.

But a new voice—a girl's voice—bellowed into the chamber, rising even above the laughter of the sylph. "He's got another one! *Stop him!*"

The sylph dropped its collected weaponry with dangerous clatters across the floor, darted across the room, caught up Doctor Dupont, and dragged him to the far side of the room, plucking the cap from his head in the process and displaying the doctor's bald, mole-spotted scalp to all.

"Heloise?" The name came thick and bloated from Benedict's swollen tongue. He turned and twisted in his bindings, trying to sit up. He saw her step into the room, short, barefoot, ragged, and alive! More than alive; she was completely, quakingly furious.

Even as the doctor fought and wrestled with his unseen enemy, Heloise pointed at the guards crouched in various positions of dread upon the floor. "What do you think you're doing?" she cried. "Are you really going to let him cut into the head of the marquis's only son?"

"Who are you?" the captain of the guard cried even as he scrambled to his feet, losing his helmet in the process.

"A witch! A witch!" the doctor cried. His robes were pulled away from his body on all sides, making him look like a big black sheet hung out to dry in a high gale. But he pointed at Heloise, a blaze of hatred in his eyes. "It is the witch we saw last night! The mirror witch who escaped through the glass! It is she who has—"

"Don't be stupid," Heloise growled, crossing her arms. She addressed herself then, not to the captain, but to Briant. "You know who I am, Briant Pigman," she said. "You've known me all your life, and you know I'm no witch!"

"Heloise, I—" Young Briant stopped. He stared beyond her to the doorway of the chapel-chamber, where Evette had suddenly appeared. His Adam's apple bobbed up then down in an enormous gulp. Heloise watched as an overwhelming wave of emotion washed over him.

She watched as, quite suddenly, *he remembered her.*

"Miss Evette!"

"Hullo, Briant," said Evette in her sweetest, most patient voice. "It's nice to see you. Strange doings about these days, yes?"

"What—what are you—? Where did you—?"

Evette stepped into the chamber alongside Heloise and looped her arm through her sister's. Heloise could have laughed and shouted with joy at the familiar gestures. Instead she fixed a glare all the more furious upon the captain, who was searching for his lance. Catching that glare, the captain froze, uncertain what to do under these extraordinary circumstances. Doctor Dupont, now wrapped up like a sausage in his own robes, screamed all manner of curses, but no one paid him any attention.

"My sister has something to say," Evette declared. Her voice was so reasonable that it was impossible to ignore or even to think about contradicting. She gave Heloise a nudge. "Tell them, dearest. Tell the good captain what you know."

There was Evette for you. Always in charge. Always in control both of herself and of the situation. It was enough to make Heloise want to scream . . . and to weep with relief at the same time.

Instead of doing either, she addressed herself to the captain, saying, "Doctor Dupont is a thief."

"What?" said the captain, casting an uneasy look the doctor's way. Dupont was now several feet off the ground and gyrating slowly as he hurled curses to the four corners of the room.

"He's a thief!" Heloise repeated. "Master Benedict and I, we saw him steal from the marquis."

"Steal what?" There was perhaps a note of hope in the captain's voice as he asked this question. He knew what to do with thieves and their like. Invisible winds, no. Bizarre doctors and their practices, no. But thieves, absolutely. Canneberges had a strict and ancient policy when it came to thieves.

Heloise slipped free of her sister's arm and hurried to Benedict's bedside. Her eyes widened in redoubled fury at the sight of him bound there, and she plucked hopelessly at one of the knots. "Oh, Master Benedict!" she gasped.

He blinked blearily up at her. "You're alive . . ." The words were almost articulate.

"Master Benedict." The captain rose and approached the bed from the other side, casting wary glances at the cursing doctor all the while. "Sir, does this . . . this peasant girl speak the truth? Has the doctor stolen from your father?"

Benedict nodded. Or tried to anyway. He wasn't altogether certain his head was doing what he wanted it too. "Yes," he said in a thick voice.

"Yes, it's true. South—South—Southlands wine. Check the apomo—apophol—apithle—"

"The what?"

"The apothecary," Heloise translated. "We saw the doctor take a bottle of wine from the dining hall. He might have it in the apothecary."

"Briant!" barked the captain.

The young guard, who had been earnestly speaking to Evette, startled in his skin. "Captain?"

"Go to the apothecary at once and look for a bottle of Monseigneur's fine Southlands vintage collection."

Briant saluted then rushed from the room in what could only be described as a long-limbed scuttle. Doctor Dupont hurled abuse after him and, when that proved useless, hurled even more abuse at the captain. But the captain had reached his limit where Dupont was concerned, and he turned a deaf ear both to the good doctor and to the sylph's continued laughter (which he didn't want to believe was real in any case). He folded his arms and glared at nothing, waiting like a statue for his man to report back.

Heloise, meanwhile, fetched one of the fallen lances. "Help me!" she ordered the other guard, and he didn't think to disobey her, ragged urchin though she was. With the guard's help, Heloise used the lance's blade to cut partway through the first of Benedict's restraints. The rest unraveled when she pulled on it; that done, she moved on to the next one. Benedict gasped in pain as blood rushed back into his hand.

"He gave you more nightshade, didn't he?" Heloise growled. When Benedict nodded, she paused in her labors to free him, her brow furrowed in a scowl of thought. Then she kicked the legs of Hugo, who was still halfway under the bed. He scooted out and stared wide-eyed at her, convinced he gazed upon the face of a real live witch.

"You," Heloise barked. "Do you know what false unicorn looks like?"

"Aye," Hugo gasped. "It's an herb what will—"

"There's a bunch of it growing round the moat. Fetch some at once!"

The manservant got to his feet, looking as though he might protest. After all, he was part of the Centrecœur household, and, witch or not, this girl was nothing more than a peasant. But then he glanced at Benedict's sick and sallow face, and Heloise saw understanding gleam in his eye. He offered a quick nod of acquiescence and darted from the room just as Briant returned.

The young guard carried two wine bottles, one in each hand. Strange *things* floated in dark brews inside them. At first glance Heloise thought one bottle might contain . . . eyeballs. But that couldn't possibly be. So she shook her head and turned to the captain, gesturing with one arm. "See? Didn't I tell you?"

"They're definitely from the Southlands," young Briant said. "I helped Mistress Leblanc store them myself when the shipment arrived."

"And when was that?" the captain asked. After all, it was possible these were discarded empties which the doctor had collected for personal use.

But Briant, guessing his captain's thoughts, smiled grimly. "Two months ago, captain. And his lordship ain't been home in a six-month."

All eyes turned upon Doctor Dupont. He was silent now, his face as thin as a fireside ghoul's and twice as pale. The sylph held him fast and continued to giggle, though it didn't understand a word of what took place around it.

"Well, good doctor," said the captain. "What have you to say for yourself?"

Dupont swallowed almost as impressively as Briant himself. In a cold, clear voice that could not quite disguise a tremor, he said, "Monseigneur gave me authority to—"

"Monsieur the Marquis," said the captain, "would give no man authority to steal from his prized Southlands collection." He took a mottled glass bottle from Briant's hand, turned it over (making the things inside bob weirdly), and checked the carefully painted date on the bottom. He snorted. "Certainly not last year's vintage!" He handed the bottle back to Briant and approached Dupont, who still floated several inches above the floor. "It seems to me, good doctor," the captain said, his brow dark but his eye gleaming, "that you have two options before you. We have a certain method of dealing with thieves here in Canneberges. Do you know what it is?"

He did. Heloise could see the shadow of the gibbet chain flash in

Dupont's hollow eyes. Everyone knew how thieves were treated in Canneberges.

"But I am a merciful man," the captain proceeded, "and you were sent by the marquis to tend his son, which you have done most faithfully."

Benedict, who was now restrained by only one ankle, snorted at this.

"So I put it to you, good doctor," the captain said. "You may leave this room, leave this house, leave this estate at once, stopping to gather nothing, wearing only the clothes on your back. Or you may continue to enjoy our hospitality, albeit under guard in your own chambers, until I've had time to write to Monseigneur and . . . learn his will in this matter."

This time Heloise could almost hear the gibbet chain creak. She shuddered. She had no liking for Doctor Dupont, but no one deserved such a fate as that!

The doctor apparently thought so as well. He stared at the captain for several moments. Then at last he blinked and said, "I will go."

"Put him down now, sylph," Heloise commanded.

"Yes, mortal girl!" the sylph replied, causing every man in that room, Benedict included, to utter a small yelp. Then it obediently dropped Doctor Dupont so that he landed first on his feet and then on his knees.

The good doctor was up like an archer's bolt, and in a flurry of dark robes, leaving his cap behind on the floor, he fled the room, nearly crashing into the returning Hugo as he did so. Hugo ducked out of the way just in time, clutching bunches of false unicorn in both fists. Baffled, he watched the doctor run on past then entered the room. "Um. I've got this?" he said uncertainly.

"Give it to me!" Heloise cried, and plucked the stalks of horn-shaped green flowers from the guard's hands. She returned to Benedict's bedside and hopped up onto the mattress beside him.

"Heloise!" Evette exclaimed, very much herself and very much scandalized at her sister's behavior. It was wonderful! It was perfectly wonderful! Soon everything would return to normal: Evette would always do the right thing, and Heloise would always do the wrong thing, and life would be what it was supposed to be! But Heloise had no time for her sister's proprieties just then.

She mashed one of the green flowers between her hands, rolling it into a moist, bruised pellet. "Open your mouth," she told Benedict. He obeyed without question, and she popped the pellet on his tongue. "Chew," she commanded. Then she added, "This is going to make you really sick. Do you have something you might—"

It was too late. With a groan, Benedict rolled over onto his side, hung his head and half his body over the edge of the bed, and emptied all the contents of his stomach onto the floor. The captain, with a cry of "Dragon's raging teeth!" leapt back only just in time.

"Sorry!" Benedict gasped because he was Benedict. He felt Heloise patting the back of his head even as he shuddered and was sick again.

"There, there," she said. "That'll get all the nightshade out of you.

How do you feel now?"

Benedict couldn't answer for some moments. He simply hung there, breathing. Then he wiped his mouth with his sleeve and sat up. A faint color flushed his cheeks. "Actually," he said, "I must say, I feel a little . . . better!"

FORTY-ONE

"EVETTE!" WHISPERED GRANDMEM.

She sat on her doorstep in the glow of the setting sun to soak in all possible warmth from its rays before the cold night fell. Her hand clutching the shawl around her shoulders relaxed its grip, and she tilted her head to one side as though trying to shake a thought into place. Where did she know that name from? Evette . . . Evette . . .

Then she said out loud, "My granddaughter."

It came over her in a rush so enormous, she might have drowned in it. Her granddaughter! Evette! The one she had forgotten! Only she wasn't forgotten anymore, she was present in the confines of that old, tired memory, clear as a bell!

"She's done it," Grandmem said. For a moment she thought her heart would break, and she could not have said whether it broke with joy or with sorrow. The emotions she felt were too great to be understood, and her body was tired, unable to feel as much as it had back when she was young. It was all she could do to sit there on her doorstep and hold herself together rather than fall into a million tiny pieces.

Then she stood. This took much effort, much groaning, but she could not sit a moment longer. She got herself up and started down the path at the swiftest hobble she could manage. Evette. She remembered Evette. Which meant the curse must be lifted! Which meant . . . which meant . . .

Someone approached along the path that wound between the dark waters of the cranberry bogs. It wasn't the graceful form of Evette or the galumphing figure of Heloise. It was an old woman very like herself, older even. She hobbled along with no stick for support, and she wore the rags of what might once have been a Canneberges-red garment, now faded to gray.

Grandmem didn't know that form. She didn't know that wrinkled, withered face. But then she hardly knew her own face and form these days. Since when did age overtake her so completely?

"Cateline?" she called out in a thin quaver.

"Cerise?" the old woman called back.

A blurring moment or series of moments—a sudden surge of energy in the limbs and a pounding of bare feet on turf—then the two were in each other's arms. Weak, wrinkled, thin old arms made suddenly strong as they held each other close.

568

"Cateline! Cateline, I tried!" Grandmem wept. "I tried so hard!" She was again a young girl struggling with a burden far too great for her limited strength. And her older sister was just that—her older sister. Wiser, stronger, always the comforter.

"I know you tried, Cerise," she said. "I saw you in the forest and I knew. You are brave, and you endured so long! I did not know if you would still be here when I returned. Yet here you are! My brave, brave sister!"

They said no more but simply stood together as the sun set, weeping for sorrow at the loss of their youth, weeping for joy at the life of their love. They would have stood this way for hours more, perhaps, but were interrupted just as dusk fell by a voice speaking from behind them.

"Excuse me."

It was a man's voice. An old man's voice, rough with long years of sorrow, tainted by decades of bitterness, tinged with a sudden, painful hope. Grandmem and her sister turned. In the twilit gloom they saw a bent little figure with a thick growth of beard on his face and a wide-brimmed hat that he twirled in his hands.

"Excuse me," he said, addressing himself to Cateline. "It came over me suddenly a few hours ago, and I wondered if I'd find you here. I knew your sister had moved this way, and I thought perhaps . . . I don't know if you remember me?"

Grandmem heard her sister draw a sharp breath. When Cateline could speak again, her voice was soft and gentle and might almost have belonged to a maid of eighteen. "Indeed, Marcel Millerman. I do remember you. I have thought of you every day."

"And I," said the old miller, his whole heart and nearly forgotten youth catching in his constricting throat, "remember you."

FORTY-TWO

HELOISE AND EVETTE SPOKE VERY LITTLE ON THE LONG WALK HOME from Centrecœur. Only after they parted ways from Cateline—casting glances over their shoulders as the old woman tottered up the path to Grandmem's shack—did Heloise dare to ask, "What was it like? Where they kept you? Where they made you sew that tapestry?"

Evette smiled gently but shook her head. Her cap was gone, her hair as loose as a child's and unbraided. Her skirt and underskirt were torn in long rends, some of which went all the way up to her knee. Wherever she had been, it had been nothing like the pocket world where Alala was kept. "I'll not speak of it now," she said softly, turning her smile upon Heloise, though Heloise could see what a thin mask it was. "I'll tell all . . . later."

Heloise doubted this. The look in Evette's eye conveyed secrets never to be spoken. Perhaps it would be best not to speak of the Faerie world, to let such memories fade and even be forgotten. This wasn't too much to hope for, was it? Forgetfulness?

But, Heloise realized, she didn't want to forget even a single terrifying moment. She also knew, even as the thought came to her, that she never would. Evette might someday slip back into her normal ways and walk of life. Heloise, however . . .

It didn't bear thinking on. Not just now, not when all had been so newly restored. So she took her sister's hand and, in unspoken delight, they made their way home.

When they reached the gate and stepped into the Flaxman cottage yard, they were met by Meme in the front doorway. She frowned, shading her eyes against the setting sun. "Where have you been?" she demanded.

Though she had tried hard not to, knowing the pain such imaginings could cause, Heloise had envisioned any number of triumphal returns should her quest succeed. She had imagined her entire family pouring into the cottage yard from all corners of the estate. She had pictured her brothers hoisting her up onto their shoulders as everyone cheered. Her mother would enfold Evette in her arms, weeping . . . and then put out an arm for Heloise as well, press her close, and whisper into her hair, "Thank you! Oh, thank you, dear child!"

She wouldn't say "I forgive you," because she would no longer think there was anything to forgive. All would be made new. There would be explanations and questions and laughter and tears . . .

It had been a lovely vision. It was nothing like reality.

"Where have you been?" Meme demanded, addressing Heloise rather than Evette. "Did you think you could run away and I'd forget what you did? A whole bushel of flax left in the dirt to ruin! It's a coward you are, child, to run like that. Why did you not come to me at once if the bushels were too heavy? I would have sent Clovis to help. And to disappear three days? To leave me half-mad with worry?"

She didn't look half-mad or particularly worried, truth be told. She looked faintly confused. Her scolding held a tone of business-like necessity as she spoke to Heloise, but she kept glancing Evette's way as though trying to remember something just on the edge of memory.

With a shake of her head, Meme ushered both girls inside and switched her scolding of Heloise to exclamations over the state of Evette's torn gown. Papa, Claude, and Clement returned from the flax fields. Clovis and Clotaire sat by the hearth and weaved flax twine. Baby Clive cooed in his wicker-woven crib. Evette changed into an older gown, took her place by the hearth, and set to work mending the rents in her garments.

Heloise took a seat on the floor rushes near to her sister's knees. In a stolen moment during which everyone else was distracted with their various businesses, Heloise tapped Evette's arm to draw her eye. "Will you tell them?" she asked in a whisper.

Evette smiled. Then she shook her head. "Not yet," she replied. But

Heloise heard instead, "Not ever."

Then it was night.

Heloise lay in her straw pile, wrapped up in her woolen blanket, and listened to the rats scurry about in the thatch overhead. Big rats, most likely, making nests, fighting wars, birthing young ratlings. They lived in a side world of ratdom parallel to the world of humans, sometimes interlinking, never truly blending.

"A pocket world," Heloise whispered. She listened to Evette's peaceful breathing, as peaceful as though she had not just been rescued from Faerie enslavers and bizarre other worlds. So everything was restored. Everything would return to normal.

"Dragon's teeth!" Heloise hissed, and sat upright. She hugged her knees in the darkness and listened to her sister, listened to the rats, listened to all the familiar sounds of her life around her. She reached into her pocket and drew out the three-part branch.

The silver, gold, and diamond gleamed in her hands. As she gazed upon it, she saw a forest of silver, a forest of gold, a forest of shining diamond. She saw monsters and visions, and she felt ideas she had never before known. She heard Le Sacre play, and the greater, majestic Song of the Spheres to which she had danced. She heard the roar of the Final

Water, the splash of the boatman's pole as he guided his craft, and she saw Hélène standing in its prow.

She saw Benedict seated in his chair by the fire, giving orders to his guardsmen and looking much improved. Looking like a lord's son. Looking like a young man who would have no time in his life for peasant girls and peasant concerns . . .

"Dragon's teeth," she said again, more softly this time. Then she tossed aside her blanket, stood up, brushed straw from her hair and skirt, and slid swiftly down the loft ladder. Still clutching the branch in one hand, she stepped soundlessly around her brothers on their sleeping pallets near the fire and hastened out into the yard.

The moon was bright, the sky was clear. The night was cold, but with the cold of new spring, not the cold of lingering winter. Her breath made no clouds in the air before her face. She moved like a phantom across the yard, splashed across the stream, and ran for the hillside dotted over with little half-rotted wooden markers.

The wind moved through the trees, through the grass. Then it laughed, and Heloise knew it wasn't a wind at all. The laughter was catching, and before Heloise reached the top of the hill, she was laughing as well. When she reached the summit, the sylph was with her, darting through her hair, whirling around her in a breezy dance, and she laughed with it at the moonlight, at the starlight, at the mortality all around them.

"Mortal child, are you happy?" the sylph asked amid its giggles.

Heloise did not answer, for though she laughed, she did not know the answer. So, still smiling, she moved through the markers to the smallest one over the small mound. She knelt in the moonlight upon Hélène's grave.

"Perhaps I'll tell her," she said, and she couldn't say if she spoke to herself, to the sylph, or to Hélène. "Perhaps someday I'll tell Meme what I saw. But not yet. Not now."

She bowed down, placed her face close to the grass-grown turf, and whispered, "I love you. Always." Using her hands and the end of the three-part branch, she dug up a shallow layer of dirt, careful not to break the grass roots. Then she placed the three-part branch inside and very carefully buried it. Let it rest with Hélène. Let it be kept safe and close.

This task complete, she stood and flung wide her arms, and the sylph wrapped itself around her like a rich, whirling, invisible gown.

"Would you like to see?" the sylph asked. "Would you like to see the princess?"

"Yes," said Heloise. "Show me the princess."

The sylph held her tight, and she felt the centuries fly past her with incredible speed. She saw the shifting of the landscape, of forests, of buildings, of fields.

Then she saw Centrecœur, and it was not a house but a fortified castle with many tall towers and high, stern walls. Out through the castle gates rode a horseman on a tall red charger, almost as red as himself. At his side galloped a black steed bearing a tall, tall woman whose masses of hair billowed behind her like a banner. They raced each other, neck and neck, laughing with mingled madness and gladness.

In their wake Heloise saw four other horsemen riding. A young girl, on the brink of womanhood and so beautiful it would stop the heart to look at her. Then a boy and another girl, and behind them their sister, the youngest child, another dark-skinned maid riding an eager pony and shouting to the others that she would catch them all.

"Rufus," Heloise said. "Alala. Ayodele. Adanna . . ."

They were happy. In that moment of mortal time, they were together and they were happy, truly happy. Heloise, as she stood on that hill, wondered if in that moment she had glimpsed the truth of the unseen Farthestshore.

She whispered:

"Beyond the Final Water Falling
The Songs of Spheres recalling
When the sun descends beyond the twilit sky
I will remember you."

The sylph held her tight in its arms. It seemed to listen to her song and was, for a sylph at least, solemn. When she finished singing the final note in her rough, unlovely mortal voice, the sylph sighed as though it had just heard the most beautiful of arias.

Carefully it bore her back across the years and set her down on the hilltop beside Hélène's small grave. "Thank you," Heloise said, then bowed her head and let two tears run down her face. "Thank you for everything."

"You are welcome, mortal child," said the sylph. With an extra twirl and gust, it darted away across the moonlit grounds, muttering, moaning, and singing to itself. Heloise, as she watched the movement in the grass and trees that marked its passing, thought it made its way up to the Oakwood, perhaps back to its own world. Perhaps never to return.

Why, when everything was restored to what it should be, did she feel so heavy-hearted?

With a sigh she turned and gazed down upon the silver-lined cottage and cottage yard. The pig pen where Gutrund snored and dreamed piggish dreams. The chicken coop where Rufus the rooster and his wives roosted comfortably. The spinning shed where tomorrow she would help her mother cut and prepare the retted flax—

"There are few indeed who would allow a sylph to carry them back and forth through time as you have just done," said a strange voice from the shadows right beside her. "Indeed, you must have more power than I thought to direct such a wild being so easily."

Heloise didn't scream. She didn't move until she was ready. She held perfectly still and counted breaths up to ten. Then, with absolute control, she turned her head to one side and addressed herself to the darkness. "Who are you?" she asked.

The shadows parted as though they had been a cloak. Light shone from a gleaming flower like a star, and this light illuminated a lovely face, the face of a young woman with old, old eyes. She wore the starflower in her hair, which was long and black and straight. At her waist she wore a knife in a sheath, but her hands made no move to draw it, for in one hand she held a quill pen and in the other a parchment scroll.

"I am the Dame of the Haven, Imraldera by name," said she, "though some still call me Starflower. I have come to find you, even as I promised."

For a breathless moment Heloise did not speak. Then in a rush she exclaimed, "*You're* the one who sent me the message! Starflower! You're the one who told me . . . who told me . . ."

"That you are stronger than you think?" the Dame finished for her then nodded in assent. "And that remains true. You are stronger than you think and, I suspect, stronger than I think as well. Now that I see you in person, I believe there is more of Nivien in your veins than I first guessed."

At this, Heloise shook her head. "Whatever Faerie powers I had are gone," she said. "Mother took them. She stole away my mirror magic."

At this the Dame nearly laughed, and her eyes were bright in the light of the flower she wore. "The Queen of Night took your mirror magic, yes. But you are possessed of far more power than that! She could not take it all even had she thought her law would permit her to do so."

Heloise stared at her. A whole host of new thoughts and ideas pushed around inside her head, and for the moment she couldn't find a way to fit them all, couldn't even think them. So she stood and stared, her mouth hanging open, and looked for all the world like a simple peasant urchin without a brain in her head.

The Dame frowned and *tsked* but without malice. "Your powers have only just begun to manifest," she said. "Do you think any but one born of Faerie graces could command a sylph? Could be carried to and fro in time and not be lost? The sylph itself cares nothing for time, and were you not able, even unconsciously, to direct it, it would have misplaced you along the way and never realized its error."

"I—I didn't know," Heloise whispered.

The Dame narrowed her eyes, considering the girl before her. "I see you have much to learn. And small wonder! This is a remote corner of the mortal world, and you have seen little enough, even with your recent adventures. Perhaps I was wrong to come here. But I rather doubt . . ." Her voice trailed off. She had a look about her face as though she listened to some inner voice which Heloise could not hear. Or perhaps not an inner voice; perhaps a far, far, far outer voice, so distant that only one with carefully trained ears could hope to discern it.

However it was, the Dame paused as though to listen for some time. Then, coming to a decision, she nodded. "I have an offer for you, mortal child."

"Heloise. My name is Heloise."

The Dame nodded. "Yes, that may well be. But don't be giving your name away too freely! Names have power in the Faerie world, and you don't want yours to fall into the wrong hands."

"You gave me your name," Heloise pointed out. "I didn't ask for it."

"Yes," said the Dame. "But I have the knowing of names. Rarely do I meet a soul whose name I cannot discern. So long as I hold the names of my friends and my enemies, they cannot hold mine against me. It is the way of Faerie. The balance, the dance. It is a good, if dangerous, dance. I will teach it to you."

Heloise felt her heart begin to leap in awkward, painful jumps, like a fawn suddenly aware that it has long legs, that it might indeed run if it wished. "You . . . will teach me?" she repeated, scarcely daring to hope for that which followed.

"Indeed," said the Dame. "You have a gift, and your land has a need. Though the curse of the Family of Night is indeed broken, there are yet many gates opened into this part of your world. Beings from the Far may creep into the Near, and the mortals of this realm need someone to protect them. A gate-guarder, if you will. Someone with the ability to understand both mortal and immortal plights. Someone, in short, like you.

"I want to take you away with me. For a short while. I propose that you join me at the Haven of my Lord, which is deep in the Wood Between the Worlds. There I will teach you of Faerie—the writing, the language, the history, and the many, many peoples. There you will learn to harness your Faerie blood, to control it, to discover what powers remain to you beyond the mirror magic you have lost. I suspect they are plentiful and varied—as plentiful and varied as those of any among the

Nivien. I will teach you until you are well prepared then return you here. And you will protect your people, your land, your nation even, from all that might try to pass through the gates."

Her words filled Heloise's head and heart. At first she thought she might smother under the weight of them; the next moment she thought she might fly upon the freedom they offered. She was terrified and enraptured all at once. To leave Canneberges! To leave her family! To leave her peasant life, the world she knew, and learn of worlds beyond! She could not say whether these ideas pleased or frightened or sickened her, for she felt all of these emotions and then some at the same time.

"One thing you must understand," the Dame continued, "is that your time is limited. In the Between, days, hours, and years will pass differently than they do here in your own world. But when you return, you will have but a few years remaining to you before you must make a choice."

"What choice?" Heloise asked.

"The powers of your blood are not powers you may keep forever and still retain your mortality," said the Dame. "Upon the dawning of your eighteenth birthday, you will have to decide either to keep your Faerie gifts and become immortal . . . or to give up those gifts and remain among your own kind. To remain mortal."

To consider such a weighty choice just then was impossible. To consider it would be to fear it, and Heloise wasn't prepared for that. She felt the importance and the dread plucking at the edges of her heart, but she shoved them both back and said only, "I am just fourteen. I have time to decide."

"Four years." The Dame's mouth turned up in a wry smile. "Not so much time as you think." She reached out and took hold of Heloise's right hand. "Heloise, tell me, will you pledge me your service? Will you train with me? Will you learn to harness these incredible powers with which you have been both blessed and cursed, learn how to channel them into the protection of those you love?"

Heloise's heart thrilled with terror and with, if she was honest with herself, joy. Her fear was great, but greater still was the fear of staying here. The fear that this strange woman would leave and Heloise would face the new day knowing she had denied her one great chance. Her chance to be what she was supposed to be.

"Yes," said Heloise, her voice a choking whisper. She coughed and repeated the word with more confidence. "Yes. I will train with you. I will go with you to the Wood Between."

Afterward she wondered if she should have dithered and considered and dragged her feet, out of pure principle if nothing else. But she knew she could make no other decision. She had seen too much. She had done too much.

She would never go back to the life she'd known before.

FORTY-THREE

THE NEXT MORNING, JUST AS THE FLAXMAN FAMILY FINISHED OFF their bowls of pottage, and Papa took up his wide-brimmed hat, ready for a day in the fields, Grandmem appeared at the door and announced without preamble: "My sister, Cateline, needs a wedding gown. May she borrow yours, Berthe? It should fit her right enough."

Thus Meme's prediction of a wedding in the family before the end of spring proved true after all, though certainly not in the way anyone might have expected. Less than a week later Heloise and Evette helped their great-aunt into Meme's soft white gown. Evette braided wildflowers into Cateline's grey hair and wrapped it in a crown of braids on top of her head. Heloise loaned her own hairpins for the task—no one wanted to bother with Heloise's tangle of curls on such a day in any case.

Before the sun was high in the sky, a lot of people gathered at the

Flaxman cottage, a number of old folks in particular who, strangely enough, all knew and remembered Cateline from long ago. No one bothered to ask her where she'd been. No one required explanations or excuses. Heloise had wondered how her great-aunt's reappearance would play out, but it was much like Evette's own return; if anyone suspected anything strange, no one wanted to acknowledge it. So nothing was asked, nothing was said, and everyone smiled.

Marcel Millerman, proud in a new red linen vest over his brown work shirt, his beard and hair combed, drew his bent body almost straight in the center of the yard as Cateline joined him. They stood in the middle of a small circle made up of maidens, including Heloise and Evette (and that wretched Alphonsine Millerman, who as Marcel's granddaughter was obliged to be present, much to Heloise's disgust). The maidens danced the dance-of-joining around the couple. Once this dance ended, others joined the circle, expanded it, and added more circles until Cateline and her reclaimed love were in the very center of an enormous, turning wheel of dance.

Heloise caught glimpses of the couple as the dance progressed. She wondered if perhaps her Faerie sight played tricks on her, for it seemed to her that at every second glimpse she saw them not as the old, gray couple they were but as a young man and a young woman holding hands and beaming with the joy of new love. Perhaps that's what they were at heart. Perhaps this was part of mortal magic and had nothing to do with Faerie blood or Faerie sight.

Grandmem did not join the dance. She was too tired, so she sat on a stool provided for her and smiled and clutched her ragged shawl about her. Heloise, seeing her, recognized a certain sorrow on her grandmother's face. But she also saw a certain contentment that had never been there as long as Heloise had known her.

After all, had the girl Grandmem once was not turned away from the Night Hunt when she did . . . well, Cateline might not have found true love to come back to, even late in their lives as it was. Yes, there was failure in Grandmem's past, but there was triumph as well. Now there could be peace.

When this dance was complete, Marcel and Cateline were declared married. Then the real celebration began, including what passed for a feast among the peasants of Canneberges and, of course, more dancing.

This is how such stories should end, Heloise decided as she caught the hands of her brother Claude and whirled round and round with him. He was so tall, he could swing her right off her feet and make her scream with pretend fear. *Stories like this one—with Faeries and kidnappings and daring escapes—should always end with a wedding.*

At one point she thought she glimpsed Evette talking with Briant, the young guard from the Great House. Another dance later and Evette slipped to Heloise's side. "I've been offered a position," she whispered. "Briant says Madame Leblanc has invited me to join the girls at Centrecœur, to train as a housemaid."

"Is that what you want to do?" Heloise asked.

She and Evette had scarcely spoken in the last several days. Not in words. They had exchanged glances now and then, and each of them glimpsed strange sights in the other's eyes, strange sights and strange memories. But though Evette saw restlessness in Heloise's gaze, Heloise saw, as she always saw, Evette's quiet contentment, which may have been the same as resignation or may have been the same as peace. It was hard to say. Evette was not an easy one to understand.

"I think I would like it," Evette said. "It's an excellent opportunity. If I do well, I may one day be able to travel to other great houses, to see more of our kingdom."

She didn't say, "After all, I cannot journey with you into the worlds beyond." But it was there in her eyes.

Evette was the only person Heloise had told of her impending departure. Everyone else . . . well, she didn't see much point. They wouldn't understand, wouldn't *want* to understand. They would learn soon enough, and Evette would smooth things over as only Evette could. After all, it wouldn't be for very long. Heloise would return in two years, no more.

So she smiled at Evette and said, "I hope you'll take the job then. I hope you'll enjoy working at the Great House . . . even if you have to share a room with Alphonsine."

"Lights Above us!" Evette gasped, and her eyes sparkled momentarily with mischief. "Do you realize we're probably *related* to Alphonsine now? Our great-aunt just married her grandfather, so that makes us—"

"I don't want to know!" Heloise declared, throwing up her hands. Then she darted away and grabbed Clovis for a dance. After him she found Clement and then Clotaire. Last of all she took baby Clive from Meme's arms and swung him about on her skinny hip while he giggled and shrieked with delight and Meme called out warnings for her to take more care.

This dance complete, she deposited Clive back in her mother's arms, paused . . . then, on impulse, bent and kissed her mother's cheek. Meme blinked, startled. But after a brief hesitation she smiled and patted Heloise's head. "Madcap girl," she said, and there may have even been a trace of fondness in her voice.

Before she could disgrace herself with tears, Heloise laughed as wildly as a sylph and darted away. She passed through the dancers, quite close to Cateline and her new husband, who held each other close and didn't try to dance the wild paces of the young folk around them. She passed near her Papa and right by Evette, who had graciously agreed to give Gy Pigman a dance.

Evette caught Heloise's eye. Just for an instant. She didn't say anything. She didn't nod or smile. She simply looked. That was all the goodbye they would have.

For that's what this day was, Heloise thought as she left the cottage yard and forded the stream. While the wedding music played brightly behind her, she climbed the hill to the little graveyard and, from that vantage, paused to look back. Today was a day of goodbyes. Nothing public. Nothing spoken and nothing drawn out. She couldn't bear it and feared that if she tried, she would never actually leave.

At Hélène's grave she knelt and placed her hand on the spot where the three-part branch was buried. This was as close to an embrace as she could come. Then she stood and descended the hill on the far side and entered the field beyond. She stepped through the rows of newly planted flax and saw signs of its growth. She progressed on through the bogs and took the road, the familiar road that would lead her up to the Oakwood. Only this time she carried no basket or peeling knife. She carried nothing at all. Her feet were bare, her hair was loose, and she would enter the Between as poor and shabby as ever a mortal could be. She hoped it would be enough.

The sound of pounding hooves caught her ear. Heloise smiled even before she looked around, a silly, small, foolish smile.

The lord of the estate's son would not attend a peasant's wedding. But he would have received an invitation in the form of some shuffling farm boy's verbal message delivered at the scullery door and conveyed to him by the housekeeper or bailiff if they deemed it important enough.

Heloise had wondered if Benedict would receive his invitation. She turned and shaded her eyes to watch the horseman approach. She saw the feathers and the one broken feather-stump in his cap. He spotted her and lifted a hand to wave.

The horse slowed and tossed its head as Benedict reined it in. He dismounted, almost losing his hat in the process, and stood rather awkwardly before her. "I—I'm sorry I didn't come to the wedding," he said. "I would have, you know, but I didn't think it would, well . . ."

"It's all right," Heloise said, scowling to disguise her smile. "They managed to get married without you, not to fear."

"Oh, well, it's not like I thought . . ." His voice trailed off, and he scratched at his ear uncomfortably. "I haven't seen you since that day. How . . . how are you?"

"Well enough," said Heloise. "How are your innards?"

"Much better!" Benedict smiled ruefully. "You were right, of course. I think I've made steady improvement these last few days of *not* taking Doctor Dupont's medicine. A more solid diet has helped as well, I should think. I feel I might even be, as it were, on the mend."

It wasn't entirely true, and he knew it; Heloise saw it in his eyes. The Winter Fever still held him, deep inside. It wasn't gone entirely, and one day it would return in full strength. But one day might be many years down the road. Who could say what would happen in the meanwhile?

"I'm going away," Heloise said suddenly, surprising herself. Until she said it, she hadn't known she was going to tell Benedict about her departure.

"Away?" he repeated. "Away where?"

So she told him about the Dame of the Haven. She told him about her Faerie powers and about the gates that remained open to this world all around the estate. "I'll return soon enough, and then I'll guard the gates," she said. "I'll make certain we're not plagued with Faerie beasts and the like, and . . . and I'll protect Canneberges. And the kingdom."

"When are you leaving?" Benedict asked.

"Right now." Heloise nodded her head in the direction of the Oakwood. "I'm to meet the Dame up there by sundown. She will lead me to the Haven. She says it will be a long journey but that time will not matter. And she says my training will take a long while but that I'll be back here in no more than two years as mortals count." She ducked her chin but looked up at Benedict from beneath her snarl of curls. "Two years isn't so long as all that."

Benedict nodded. His face was very pale under his pale hair. "May I escort you to the wood?" he asked.

"Um. Yes?"

So Benedict, leading his horse, fell in alongside Heloise, and they walked together up the road, taking their time and saying little. At one point he told her that he planned to return to university in the fall, so long as his health continued to improve. At another point Heloise asked him what the guardsmen had done following the events with the sylph and Doctor Dupont. At this Benedict laughed.

"I think they've decided the wind-spirit never happened. I don't know whether they discussed it among themselves or if each came to the same conclusion on his own. One way or the other, no one is talking about it! As far as the folk of Canneberges are concerned, Faeries and other worlds can remain in stories, at least for the time being."

"For the time being," Heloise murmured, thinking about what the Dame had said of the open gates and the various beings of the Far World eager to find access to the mortal realms. She wondered how long "the time being" could last.

They came to the edge of the Oakwood. Though she did not ask him to, Benedict stopped. He would not follow her inside. This was to be her adventure and hers alone.

"Well," said Heloise and wondered what to do with her hands and elbows. This was why she'd avoided goodbyes with her family. It was just too . . . awkward. And a little bit unbearable. "I wish you all the best, Master Benedict."

He looked at her. That is, he didn't merely look at her—he *looked* at her. Rather boldly, she thought afterwards, particularly coming from him. His eyes were full of things he wanted to say. Things she hoped he wouldn't say, things she didn't think she was ready to hear or ready to understand.

But then he smiled and took the peacock-feathered hat from his head. To her surprise, he swept her a low and very elegant bow. "May the Lights shine bright upon your path," he said.

She didn't wait for anything more, nor did she try to speak. She turned on heel and darted into the welcoming, familiar shadows of the Oakwood, leaving him and his horse and his hat behind. If there were tears in her eyes, she ignored them, so they might as well never have been.

It was strange, walking these familiar paths. She knew the Oakwood so well, had come here so many times alone or with her brothers. If anything, she felt this might be the most painful goodbye. "But it's just two years," she said aloud. "It's just two years, and then I'll be back. And I'll take care of . . ."

A shiver ran through the forest, touching her skin and shuddering down her spine. She felt a presence. A huge, dark, angry presence. Very near, in the shadows. Heloise kept walking, following the path into the deeper reaches of the Oakwood. Still the presence pursued, close and watching her. She knew who it was, but she didn't like to acknowledge this. Acknowledging him would be to acknowledge fear. This was a concession she could not make, not now, not after everything she'd been through.

So she drew long breaths and let them out slowly as she walked, and she pretended she didn't wish for her peeling knife.

At last she came to a place where the path faded away and only thick, untamed forest stood before her. She had come here many times in her life, always to turn back, to return home. Now she would wait for the Dame, and she would continue out of this wood and into another, much greater Wood.

The lurking presence was near. No breath, no warmth, nothing to give him away. But he was near all the same.

"Prince of Night," Heloise said, "why are you still in Canneberges?"

The sound of footsteps, soft but pronounced, filled her ears. The Lion-

Prince, wearing his man's form, stepped out from among the trees before her where only shadows had loomed a moment ago. He wore fine garments of a strange cut and design, more elegant than anything Heloise had ever seen from her own world, even Benedict's jackets and embroidered cloaks. But his hair was loose, not tied back in the usual elegant queue. It fell in long braids over his shoulders, past his waist. His sky-colored eyes gleamed at her from the night blackness of his face.

"Cursebreaker," he said, approaching her. Through Heloise's mind flashed the knowledge that with the curse broken and the law satisfied, he no longer had any reason *not* to kill her. She could not help herself; she cast about, searching for a branch she might take up in her hands, some sort of weapon. She saw nothing, nothing that would serve against so formidable an opponent. So instead she drew herself up as tall as she dared, squared her shoulders, and looked him in the eye.

The Lion-Prince stopped. He stood but three long strides away from her, and she could see every detail of his face, so clear, so real. More real than all the reality around them, and far more beautiful. Though she looked for it, she saw no death in his expression, not even her own.

"Cursebreaker," he said again, "you are stronger than we thought."

She found her voice with difficulty, and still it creaked as it came up through her throat. "So I've been told."

"You have liberated Sister," he said. "You freed her according to her long sought-after wish."

Heloise nodded. Her heart rammed like madness itself in her throat.

She hoped he could not see the pulse of it from where he stood. He probably sensed it though, like a cat senses the mouse's fear.

But her heartbeat sped even faster when, to her tremendous surprise, the Lion-Prince suddenly swept her a bow. It was completely different from Benedict's bow. This was a wild movement like a wildcat crouching in respectful submission before the pride master. His hair brushed the ground, and the cloak he wore swept back like a bird's great wings. It was the most graceful, the most elegant gesture Heloise had ever before witnessed, and it completely took her aback.

"I loved Sister," the prince said even as he straightened. "It pained me to see her in pain. So, cursebreaker, for the sake of Princess Imoo-Alala, I thank you for your deeds."

Heloise could not speak. She was fairly certain that if she tried she would probably croak or giggle or do something absolutely appalling for which she would never forgive herself. It was all she could do to stand there large-eyed and silent.

"As a token of gratitude," the Lion-Prince continued, his rich voice filling all that space around them, "I wish to give you a gift: my name. I entrust it to you along with my respect. I am the Prince of Night, Son of Nivien, firstborn of Mother and Father. I am Imoo-Tau."

A sacred gift. Heloise, ignorant though she was of the doings beyond her world, knew at once that she could not allow such a moment to pass without returning some gesture of her own. She rather doubted the Dame of the Haven would approve of her giving her name so readily, but what else could she do? Before she could talk herself out of it, she said, "I am Heloise. Heloise Oakwoman."

She blinked, startled at herself; startled at the ease with which *Oakwoman* slipped out in place of *Flaxman*. But here, standing among her own oak trees in her own beloved Oakwood, how could she give him any other name? After all, he had entrusted her with his. She must give him the truth, for he would recognize a lie.

"Heloise Oakwoman." The prince spoke the name slowly. It was as strange to him as Imoo-Tau was to her. "Heloise Oakwoman, I thank you for your gift. Now I must tell you that I will never forget the crime you have committed. I swear upon the lost life of my mother that I will hunt you down. I will find you again one day, and I will make you suffer for what you have done."

"What?" Heloise drew back, her eyes flashing. "What do you mean? I thought—I thought you wanted your sister saved! You—didn't you—I mean—"

The Lion-Prince growled. The sound was completely animal, full of power, full of the promised doom he had spoken. He took a step toward her, covering that already small distance. "You have broken Mother's curse," he said, and he was more lion now than man, and equally magnificent. "In so doing, you have destroyed the second of her three lives. For this I can never forgive you. For this you must pay the price. Not today. Perhaps tomorrow. Someday, for certain, *Heloise Oakwoman*. Someday, sooner than you think, you will find me at your door. And then we will see just how strong you are."

He leaped. For a terrifying heartbeat, Heloise thought he sprang at her. Instead, transforming mid-air into his leonine form, Prince Imoo-Tau passed over her head and darted away, his massive bulk disappearing into the thick-grown foliage without a sound, as though he were made of no more than smoke or shadow. The last she heard of him was the echo of his growl, which rang in her ears for some minutes and haunted her memory for many nights.

Heloise stood beneath her oaks at the end of the path and stared in the direction he had gone. His final words rang clear in her memory, terrible words full of terrible accusation.

She whispered softly, as though speaking a confession, "I killed Mother."

The world was silent around her. In her chest she felt her heart beat a steady rhythm. It was like the beat of the Le Sacre drum.

She was a murderer, a cold-blooded killer, and yet here she stood. What did she hope for? Some absolution? Some softly spoken promise that she'd had no other choice, that she hadn't known what it was she did when she did it?

But nothing would change the truth. Nothing ever could.

"She has three lives," Heloise whispered, remembering what Princess Alala had told her in the pocket world. "She will return one day."

Did that, even for a moment, clear Heloise's name of the charge laid at her door?

Heloise drew herself up. She felt the enormity of her actions like a burden on her shoulders, but she was strong. She knew she was strong. So she drew herself up as tall as possible, supporting that burden and setting her jaw. "I will never kill again," she said. "I vow upon the blood of Nivien in my veins. I vow upon the life of Mother, which I took, the life of Alala, which I freed. I vow on the sisters of my line who died by my deed—I will never kill again."

The Wood heard her. She felt its listening ears pricked. More than that, she felt her own blood and spirit respond to the vow even as it fell from her lips. She wondered suddenly what the Dame would say to such rash declarations. She wondered what repercussions vowing on Faerie blood might entail.

None of this mattered. Heloise faced her actions, faced her response, and she knew she could do nothing less. She had dealt enough death in her short life, and she would deal no more.

It seemed a long while that she waited for sundown, waited for the Dame to arrive. But this may have been only an impression, not the truth. At last, even as the sun set on Canneberges . . .

. . . even as the dancers at the wedding grew tired and the celebrants departed . . .

. . . even as Cateline and her miller slowly made their way to their new life, their new home . . .

. . . even as Meme asked Evette where Heloise had gone off to, and Evette drew a long breath and said, "Well . . ."

. . . even as Master Benedict de Cœur pulled off his riding boots, sat down at his desk, and drew forth a sheet of paper full of Corrilondian verbs . . .

. . . the Dame of the Haven appeared in the Oakwood. She stepped from a path Heloise had not seen, a path full of sunlight, though Heloise stood in the gloom of deepening twilight and forest shadows.

"Are you ready to begin?" the Dame asked.

"Yes," said Heloise. "I am ready."

ABOUT THE AUTHOR

Anne Elisabeth Stengl makes her home in North Carolina, where she lives with her husband, Rohan, a kindle of kitties, and one long-suffering dog. When she's not writing, she enjoys Shakespeare, opera, and tea, and practices piano, painting, and pastry baking. Her novel *Starflower* was awarded the 2013 Clive Staples Award, and her novels *Heartless*, *Veiled Rose*, and *Dragonwitch* have each been honored with a Christy Award.

CPSIA information can be obtained at www.ICGtesting.com
Printed in the USA
LVOW08s1938080616

491761LV00003B/681/P